The Third Day

by David Epperson

ISBN 978-0-9838411-2-8 (paperback)

Please visit the author web site at http://www.davidepperson.com.

Grateful acknowledgement is made for permission to reprint the following – all rights reserved; used by permission:

Version 2011.08.10

<u>Dedication</u>

To my parents, Marcus and Ann Epperson, who instilled in me a love of books at an early age and for whom I can never be thankful enough.

Acknowledgements

I would like to extend my profound gratitude to readers of my early drafts who offered such helpful insights along with the vital encouragement that pushed me to see this novel through to completion.

In addition to my wonderful sisters-in-law Mary and Susan Epperson, I would like to convey my most heartfelt appreciation to:

Cherie Gary, David Wilkie, Elizabeth Dame, Kent Roberts, Gwynn Gorsuch, Dr. Richard and Jackie Hirshberg, Martha Sonnier, Dr. Kim Martin, Marc Thompson, Geoff Lawson, Ron and JoLynne Carlo, Leon Gary, Jr., Candace Gary, Elizabeth and Larry Jones, Joe B. Fortson, Pat Akroyd, and Dr. Kimberly Aaron.

I could not have done this without you.

I would also like to thank David Gary for IT/Web support, Dr. Sharon Skeans for editorial and proofing review, and Biblical scholar Allen Houk for first-century fact-checking. Any mistakes that remain are entirely my own.

JERUSALEM THROUGH THE AGES

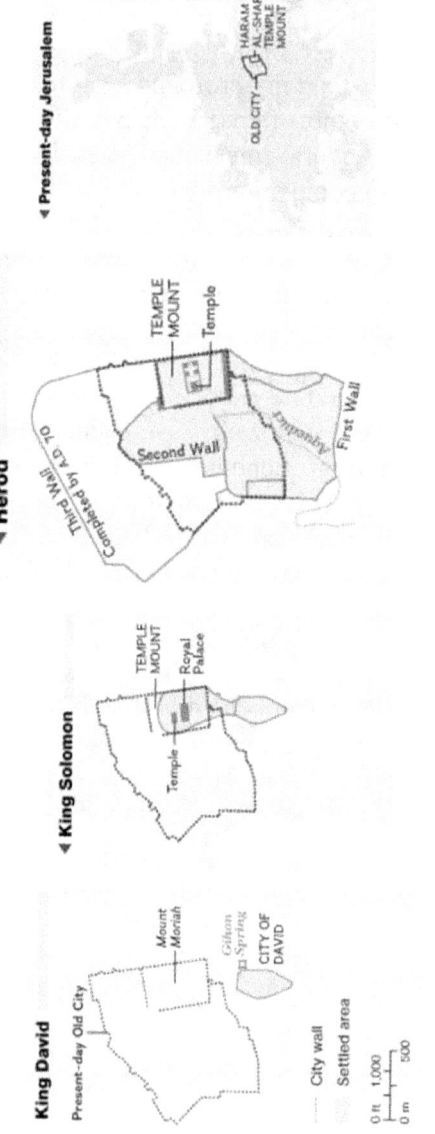

King David
- Present-day Old City
- Mount Moriah
- Gihon Spring
- CITY OF DAVID

City wall
Settled area

0 ft 1,000
0 m 500

◀ King Solomon
- TEMPLE MOUNT
- Royal Palace
- Temple

◀ Herod
- Third Wall Completed by A.D. 70
- TEMPLE MOUNT
- Temple
- Second Wall
- First Wall

◀ Present-day Jerusalem
- OLD CITY
- HARAM AL-SHARIF / TEMPLE MOUNT

Fernando Batista/National Geographic Stock, used by permission of the National Geographic Society

Chapter 1

The line between brilliance and insanity is often quite blurred.

I had always known this – after all, the artist Van Gogh sliced off his own ear – yet as I looked back on the past few weeks, I could only hope that I would never again see this principle demonstrated so convincingly; or at such grave risk to my own life and limb.

My unusual journey began with a simple request, as such things so often do. I had retired from the military a few years earlier but wasn't yet ready for the rocking chair.

Since one of my postings had been in Intelligence, an old friend suggested that I hang out my shingle as a private investigator. She even referred me to my first client, a "widow" whose husband had faked his own death in an attempt to avoid going to prison for embezzlement.

Success with that case led to others, and before long, I had grown more prosperous than I deserved, sifting through the detritus of human folly.

Thus, it came as no surprise that one fine spring morning, I found myself in Greenwich, Connecticut, seated in the office of Jonah Markowitz – the manager of one of the city's innumerable hedge funds – listening to his suspicions about a physicist he had hired three years earlier.

He held up his cell phone.

"I haven't been able to reach him in over a month," he complained. "We used to chat at least once a week. I try not to micromanage, but it is *my money* they're spending."

I had worked with Markowitz before and knew he had a paranoid streak – reinforced by years on Wall Street – so my first instinct was to discount his grumbling. Nobel Prize winning physicists didn't just vanish into the ether.

"What about Juliet?" I asked. "What does she say?"

Henry's wife, Dr. Juliet Bryson, had shared in his Nobel Prize.

"She told me he had been burning the midnight oil and needed a break. First, it was an offshore fishing charter; now, he's supposedly spelunking in New Hampshire somewhere."

I considered this for a moment. "Places with conveniently limited cell phone reception?"

"It's hard to stay out of touch that long unless you're really trying."

I glanced down at the phone I had laid on Markowitz's desk and sighed. Fewer than ten minutes had passed, and the counter already displayed eleven unopened emails.

"We all have reasons to try, Jonah," I said.

Markowitz had no hard evidence that the good professor had done anything other than take a well-deserved break from his labors.

But if I had learned anything during my years of investigative work, it was that happy clients pay better than unhappy ones – and faster, too. Since my firm had conducted the initial background check, I agreed to run the traps to find out what was going on, just to be sure.

***

I sent my assistant a quick message to retrieve the Brysons' file while I spent the next half hour fighting traffic on the way back to my office and pondering what might be happening.

The notion of physicists working in the investment world was no longer out of the mainstream. For the past two decades, leading Wall Street houses had raided university physics and mathematics departments in an ever escalating arms race to develop the algorithms that would give them the slightest edge over their competitors.

In the intense, aggressive world of high finance, the burgeoning hedge funds soon joined the fun – much to the joy of the scientists themselves, who had undoubtedly grown weary of scraping by on university salaries while their colleagues in the computer and biotech fields struck it rich.

Markowitz, a man whose net worth *Forbes* had recently pegged at $3 billion, had snatched the Brysons away from MIT with a mandate to develop a state-of-the-art trading algorithm and to build the quantum computer on which to run it. He told me at the time that he had envisioned spending up to $200 million on the venture – though he'd recoup the money in weeks if all went according to plan.

I had the average layman's comprehension of quantum mechanics, which is to say I knew slightly more about the subject than did a house plant. Quite frankly, the concepts – electron spins and simultaneous states of matter, being both here and there at the same time – made my head hurt.

Still, my time in Army Intelligence had given me enough exposure to the topic to make me aware of the enormous advantages that would accrue to whoever managed to develop a working prototype of a quantum device.

***

I pulled into the parking garage and made my way up the stairs to my desk. What I found in the Brysons' file confirmed my recollections. Other than being the two smartest people I had ever met, I couldn't remember anything particularly unusual about either one.

The couple lived in a quaint brownstone a few blocks from campus, which they had decorated with tasteful but not overly expensive furniture. They drove ordinary middle-class cars. By all appearances, Henry and Juliet Bryson lived the quiet, modest lives of career academics.

They met their teaching requirements in a tag-team fashion which proved highly popular with MIT's undergraduates. The only complaint I could recall was that the couple were not known for being liberal with partial credit – though neither was the world; something these students would learn soon enough.

The Brysons had few hobbies, which came as no surprise. Their only real interests outside of work consisted of Henry's fanatical devotion to the Boston Red Sox and the couple's odd fascination with creation stories across the globe – though I suppose that was only natural for scientists whose research explored what had happened during the most infinitesimal fraction of a second after the Big Bang.

I couldn't blame them for wanting to cash in, either, since the proposition carried such little risk.

If their venture with Markowitz blew up, they could always return to what they had been doing before. In fact, MIT, unwilling to admit their stars had moved elsewhere, persisted in calling their departure a leave of absence.

***

Still, people changed; and in my experience, usually not for the better. People disappeared all the time, too. The FBI's database listed over 51,000 missing adults in the US alone, though I doubted any of them had picked up prizes in Stockholm.

I called in one of my newer associates, a CPA I had lured away from one of the big firm sweatshops, and assigned her the task of updating the Bryson's financial records. I thought about driving to Boston to ask Juliet directly, but Markowitz had instructed me not to provoke a confrontation until we had better information.

Chapter 2

Susan, the CPA, greeted me a couple of days later with a worried look on her face; the kind that told me she knew something was wrong without being able to explain why.

That was a feeling I knew all too well. The solution, in my experience, was just to lay everything out on the table and let the chips fall where they may, though as soon as she did so, I wished that she hadn't.

I stared at the figures and turned pale.

"762 *million* dollars?"

This, according to the statements, was the happy couple's present net worth.

Susan nodded. "Their contract with Markowitz allowed me to call the bank to confirm the numbers. By the way, they've parked it all in 180 day T-Bills, set to roll over automatically."

I leaned back in my chair, closed my eyes and took a deep breath; though at that moment, I'll have to admit I was less concerned about the specifics of what my accountant had found than in how I could explain an oversight of this magnitude to my client and keep even a shred of my professional reputation.

"How in the world did they make it?" I finally asked.

"Let's just say that Warren Buffett is a rank amateur by comparison."

I motioned for her to hand me her notes. As it turned out, the Brysons had bought $10,000 worth of Wal-Mart stock in December 1973, which had grown to $2.5 million by the time they finally sold in June 1990.

"That's a good start," I said. "What did they do next?"

Susan laughed.

"Not being content with winning the lottery, our brilliant physicists went out and plunked it all on a single number on the IPO roulette wheel."

"What did they buy, Microsoft?"

"Even better: Cisco. Our intrepid investors took their Wal-Mart profits and bought 80,000 shares of Cisco in August of 1990 – not long after the IPO. Between then and the new millennium, the stock split almost every year. They ended up with roughly 11.5 million shares, which they sold in February 2000 – right at the top, mind you – for an average of $120 per share. You do the math."

I did. Even after capital gains taxes, the Brysons were billionaires.

"But their house is still mortgaged!" I said.

She nodded. "They took out a standard 30 year fixed at 5 1/4 percent when they bought the place ten years ago. I had a lawyer run by the courthouse yesterday to look at the documents. It's all standard stuff. They even took advantage of the down payment assistance program the university offers so promising faculty can afford to live near campus."

"Did they refinance?"

"No."

"And their cars?"

"State registration data still list the same ones they owned when you conducted the first background check – an Explorer and a Camry."

Markowitz would at least get a laugh out of that. Bonus time in Greenwich kept Lamborghini dealers in fine fettle. Any of his traders driving a Camry would have been either laughed out of the building or dismissed as a hopeless eccentric.

"A billion dollars, huh?"

"Afraid so. If it's any consolation, you weren't the only one to miss it. A billion got you on the *Forbes 400* in those years."

At the moment, that was small comfort.

"What about their taxes? Could you get hold of their returns?"

She smiled as she opened her briefcase and extracted the documents. She slid them across the desk.

"Paid in full," she said.

I made a note to speak to my contact at the IRS, whose reliability suddenly fell into serious doubt.

"Are they amended returns?"

"No, as best I can tell, these are originals."

I thanked her and then poured myself a fresh cup of coffee, though I was sorely tempted to go for something stronger.

I supposed it was possible. Despite the popular images on celebrity TV, the truly wealthy people of my personal acquaintance took pains to avoid ostentatious display. Even Sam Walton, with all his billions, drove an old pickup truck – though I suspected that after a while, this became part of a carefully crafted PR campaign.

And the question remained: why? Why would a couple of billionaires seek investor money when they could have just as easily set up shop on their own?

***

What the television dramas don't show – for obvious reasons – is the unbearable monotony that constitutes much of an investigator's lot.

The Brysons' contract obligated them to send quarterly financial statements to their benefactor, along with copies of the invoices for all major equipment purchases. Sorting through these was the clear first step.

My staff and I spent the next week examining purchase orders, matching the requisitions with legitimate vendors, and confirming shipments with FedEx and UPS – mind-numbing tedium, to be sure, but it had to be done.

We even visited suppliers to verify that the prices the Brysons had paid reflected economic reality and didn't involve hidden kickbacks between the lab and their confederates at the equipment dealers – an all too common scam.

The net result of our endless hours of toil: if the Brysons had been cheating their patron, we didn't have the slightest idea how.

***

What was even more bizarre was our realization, as we waded through spreadsheets and sifted through endless piles of paper, that the intrepid physicists had poured millions of their own stock market winnings into the project.

When we added it all up, their own contributions had matched, or even slightly exceeded, what Markowitz himself had invested, and all of this had occurred within the previous nine months.

I gave my office a few well-earned days off as I considered what to do. We had found no other trading accounts, so it didn't appear that the Brysons had set up their own hedge fund – though my client would surely point out that we hadn't found their billion dollars the first time around, either.

One more issue nagged me as well. I flipped open the folder and re-read their bios. *Henry Bryson, born Buffalo, New York, October 12, 1958. Juliet McGovern Bryson, born Sweetwater, Texas, August 4, 1963.*

So, when they bought their first Wal-Mart shares, he was chasing girls at the local burger stand, while she was a happy fifth grader playing hopscotch in a small town 1,500 miles away. Compounding the mystery, we had found no family fortunes on either side. Henry's father worked as an electrician; hers ran a drug store. Both mothers stayed home.

None of this made any sense.

I put off calling Markowitz as long as I could, but eventually I had no choice but to pick up the phone.

Over the course of my years in the Army, I had learned that I was usually better off just admitting that I didn't know something rather than trying to BS my way through, so I just laid out the facts as we had found them.

Markowitz appreciated the candor. Though he still suspected that we had botched the initial background investigation, he admitted that he found the lack of overt fraud as puzzling as I did.

We concluded that our logical next step was to go to Boston and confront Juliet directly – though he added a catch.

"I'm sending Ray with you," he said.

I had met his son once. The boy – actually a young man in his late twenties – seemed bright enough, and unlike so many of his wealthy peers, his vices didn't extend to the white powder and club-hopping. Instead, the kid spent his family's fortune on his obsession with adventure sports.

"I'm not sure what he could do," I said. "What does he know about any of this?"

Markowitz, to his credit, restrained himself from snide comment; and I had the sense to realize that this was a battle I couldn't win. He wanted another set of eyes – completely reliable eyes – and I was in no position to refuse.

Chapter 3

Ray met me in my office the next morning, and we drove up to Boston together. Alicia, the receptionist, greeted us with a friendly smile, though I could detect a faint whiff of irritation that our presence had forced her away from her primary duties – split between the latest fashion magazine and a half-finished game of solitaire.

She pressed a button and announced that Markowitz and yours truly, Bill Culloden, were waiting at the front entrance. A minute or so later, a set of double doors opened.

"Welcome," Juliet said as she shook our hands.

Apparently, she had known we were coming.

I was pleased to see that she had remained the trim, attractive woman I remembered from three years before. The only visible changes were that her hair now carried the thinnest shocks of gray, and that she had replaced her gold rimmed glasses – the ones that reminded me of my junior high math teacher – with something more fashionable.

She walked over to a set of double doors. "Would you gentlemen please follow me?"

We entered a cavernous room that resembled one of the big warehouse stores, though instead of merchandise, the shelves were stacked floor to ceiling with black electronic boxes, each flashing lights of various colors.

Markowitz and I glanced at each other in curiosity.

"*This* is the quantum computer?" he asked.

Juliet smiled. "Not at all."

She kept going toward the rear of the building, though she finally turned around when she realized we had not followed.

"I assume that as part of your audit, you examined our electric bills? The power consumption of this facility is enormous."

"It did cross our minds," I said.

Indeed, one of the ironies of the information age was that supposedly the greenest of all industries gobbled up massive quantities of coal fired electricity, a fact the young activists rarely considered as they updated their social networking pages.

"Nothing here has the slightest relevance to our research," she said, "but it provides a reasonable cover story. Do you remember your visit a couple of years ago, Mr. Markowitz?"

He nodded.

"A month or two later, we had what passes for a heat wave in this region, and the power company called to ask if we could cut back our usage temporarily. After that, we decided that we needed a way to explain what we were doing in case some authority showed up and demanded a better look."

"I get that, but why the racks full of servers?" replied Markowitz.

"To a casual observer, we could explain that we were either storing vast quantities of data or conducting an exercise in massive parallel processing. Either way, they would see what they expected to see: the bustle of industry and lots of flashing lights."

I couldn't help but laugh. "You sound like you've read those management books: 'Bias for action' and all that nonsense."

She smiled. "Feverish activity is the essence of progress, is it not? At least in the minds of the unthinking."

***

Juliet flipped a switch and the racks of machines went dark.

"We only turn them on for the occasional visitor," she said. "After all, they do consume power we could otherwise devote to more constructive purposes."

"Yes," I replied. "If you don't mind, we'd like to ask you about those purposes."

"You *have* built a quantum computer?" said Markowitz.

"Of course."

Juliet led us to a small box and pressed a security code. After a brief second's delay, the door opened to a small room containing a bank of lockers.

"This way, gentlemen, if you please."

The door closed quickly behind us and we immediately noticed that the temperature had dropped at least twenty degrees.

Juliet opened one of the lockers, took out a thick yellow jacket, and then handed us two larger ones – both colored in the most fashionable safety orange.

"These appear to be your size," she said.

Markowitz and I glanced at each other, then donned the coats and followed her to another door at the opposite end of the room. She punched the codes once more, and after a brief delay, this door opened automatically as well.

This passage led into a storage closet, filled with file cabinets. However, when Bryson removed a key from her pocket and turned the lock closest to our left, the center cabinet swiveled around, exposing an elevator sized opening.

"Go ahead," she said. "It's just what you think it is. Just be sure to step over the red line."

She stepped in behind us and pressed a button. The doors closed and we could feel ourselves descend. About half a minute later, the doors opened again to reveal a large rectangular chamber, with banks of computers and instrumentation lining each of the four walls from floor to ceiling.

Markowitz shivered and pulled his coat tight. He glanced up at a thermometer atop the nearby console: minus 20 °C, or minus 4 °F.

"How far down are we?" he asked.

"Thirty meters," she replied. "About a hundred feet."

I glanced around. "Do the building inspectors know about this?"

"Partially," she replied. "This was originally an old mine dating back to the Colonial era, From what I've been told, it played out before the Civil War. Over the intervening years, developers attempted a variety of schemes to make the property commercially viable, without success. The last one went broke in the 1970s."

"How did you acquire it?"

"We cut a deal. As you would expect, the previous owners had left a mess, so we agreed to clean up the site to modern environmental standards."

"And in return, the city agreed not to ask too many questions," I said.

"Something like that. Of course, they had to approve our structural plans. They didn't want responsibility for a cave-in."

"How did you explain what you were doing?"

"Cryogenic research for the Defense Department," she replied. "All top secret."

"They bought that?" asked Markowitz.

"Why not? It's perfectly plausible."

"Why here? Why not out in the country somewhere, where you wouldn't have to deal with inspectors at all?"

"What do they call it – hiding in plain sight? In the country, nosy neighbors would watch every delivery made to our site and compare notes. Here, we're just another pair of MIT researchers – two out of hundreds."

Markowitz pulled his coat tighter and shivered. "Don't tell me you spend all day working in this cold?"

She smiled and shook her head. "Personally I prefer the beach. However, extreme cold was crucial to achieving the quantum effects that we sought."

Bryson stepped through an opening in the bank of instruments at the center of the back wall and led us to a Plexiglas enclosed chamber the size of a tennis court. Inside that chamber rested a glass cube about two meters across, and inside that sat a black box roughly the size of a household air conditioner compressor.

"This, gentlemen, is the heart of the quantum computer."

Both of us stared forward, trying to comprehend what we were seeing. Five narrow tubes, connected to a web of multicolored wiring, pointed toward the center of the black box.

"There's a sixth tube under the floor," she said. "One for each face of the cube. It is a coordinated laser array, which is the final step."

"The final step of what?" asked Markowitz.

"You'll be pleased to know that even pointy-headed academics can conduct a cost-benefit analysis. We cool the surrounding air – this room we're in now – using standard meat-locker technology.

"This allows us to save money when we lower the temperature of the outer chamber to minus 196 °C using liquid nitrogen, which, as you know, is relatively inexpensive. For the cube in the center, we use liquid helium, which gets us almost where we need to be."

"Where is that?" I asked.

"Absolute zero," she replied.

"The lasers get you there?" asked Markowitz.

"This represents our real breakthrough. Three of our colleagues at MIT succeeded in cooling materials within a few micro-Kelvins of absolute zero using a similar process, but so far they've managed it only for an object the size of a coin. Our lasers are the first to accomplish the same feat with something of this magnitude."

"When did you first achieve this success?"

"With what you see here, about four months ago," she replied.

"You should have called us. My father would have rested easier knowing his money had not been wasted."

"I can assure you, Mr. Markowitz, that the funds he allocated to construct the quantum computer went into our device. I will be happy to go over the accountant's statements with you, if you'd like. They are correct to the penny."

He considered this for a moment.

"That won't be necessary," he finally said. "However, I would like to know about the second half of your charge. How close are you to accomplishing that task?"

She hesitated for a brief instant before replying. "You're referring to the quantum trading algorithm?"

Markowitz nodded. "You weren't only to build a computer. My father also intended it to accomplish a specific purpose."

An uncomfortable silence ensued. Finally, after a couple of minutes, I spoke in a quiet voice.

"I believe you have something to tell us."

Bryson stared ahead for a few moments and then wheeled around and marched to the chamber's entrance. "Let's get out of the cold. Now that you've seen the device, we can discuss it in the comfort of my office."

Chapter 4

We went back up the elevator, hung our coats in the locker, and walked through three additional doors before we reached Juliet's spacious but windowless office.

Its appearance was just what I had expected of a busy academic. A 36-inch computer monitor dominated half of Bryson's desk. The remainder was covered in stacks of technical papers, as was the credenza behind her chair. A 5x7 photo of herself and Henry – scuba diving, by the look of it – rested to one side.

Whiteboards hung from two of the four walls, each covered with incomprehensible scribbles and diagrams. The only things that seemed out of place were the four Aeron chairs, though Juliet explained that she had picked them up on the cheap from a bankrupt dot.com.

Whatever the case, the elder Markowitz could rest assured that the recipients of his largesse hadn't wasted his money on frills.

Ray walked over to the coffee pot in the corner and picked out one of the motley collection of mugs. He poured each of us a cup, and the warm liquid felt good after our time in below-zero cold.

We took our seats. After some brief chit-chat, she spun the monitor around and scrolled through a few PowerPoint slides detailing their progress over the last three years. I couldn't help but be impressed.

Markowitz, though, hadn't lost sight of his father's original purpose.

"Your achievements to date are remarkable," he said, "but what of the trading algorithm? How have you progressed with that?"

She leaned back and sighed.

"I might as well admit it," she finally said. "We haven't done a thing. In fact, such a construct is not possible. We've known all along that the entire premise is flawed."

"But other Wall Street firms – "

"In our view, our colleagues have either taken their backers' money knowing their project will fail, or they have somehow deluded themselves into thinking that a complex system involving millions of widely dispersed human beings could ever be calculated with precision. The idea is preposterous on its face."

"Even with a more powerful quantum computer?"

She pointed to the coffee cup in Markowitz's hand. "Let's leave the global markets alone for a moment and focus on one person, one simple decision – that is whether you would pour yourself a cup of coffee when you came into this office a few minutes ago."

"It seems quite simple to me, either I do or I don't."

"That would be the random choice," she said, "just like flipping a coin. However, if you had a large sum of money contingent on the outcome, you'd want to determine the odds with greater precision, would you not?"

"Certainly."

"Once you started working it all out, you would find that in the real world, a calculation of even this seemingly simple option would require an almost infinite number of variables. You may not drink coffee at all, for health or religious reasons, or you may drink it for precisely those concerns.

"You may be exceptionally tired today and want more, or be so buzzed with your 18th cup that even the sight of the stuff makes you ill. You might even pick up the pot but decide from the aroma that you don't like that particular brand. The possibilities are endless."

"But – "

"To achieve the required level of precision for just this one simple choice, I may need to know, for instance, that in the afternoon of the Thursday following the second full moon after the autumnal equinox in a leap year not ending in zero, you drink four cups of coffee instead of three, provided the brand is something other than Starbucks.

"I could model that, if I knew the relevant variables. But suppose I needed to work out the possibilities for ten people, or a hundred, or a thousand."

"Faster computers could accommodate those calculations," said Markowitz. "For instance, weather forecasting is far more accurate than it was even a decade ago."

"For natural phenomena, perhaps; but don't forget that with the markets, we're dealing with people. Human beings do inexplicable things. Not only do they not always seek – how do the economists put it – *maximum utility*, but they can, and often do, act in a manner directly contrary to their own self interests, or even their own self preservation.

"Young people demonstrate this every day on those silly video web sites. As a private investigator, Mr. Culloden, surely you would concur."

"Unfortunately that is true."

"But you still took the money, knowing what he asked you to do was impossible," said Markowitz.

"We did, and I'll apologize for perhaps misleading you. That being said, under our contract, your father owns the lion's share of patent rights to our work, which should be sufficient for him to recover his investment, and earn a decent return to boot."

While I could see the wheels of his mind turning, Markowitz made no immediate reply.

I waited a few moments and then spoke softly. "We'd like to ask you about that return, if it's not too much trouble."

She stared down at the floor and did not respond.

"I believe you left something out of the account of your progress here."

Again, she did not speak.

"A little over a billion somethings, if my math is correct."

Finally, she glanced back up. "You mean our stock in Wal-Mart and Cisco?"

"You presented yourselves as modestly prosperous academics," I replied, "something we checked thoroughly before Jonah Markowitz hired you and provided the funding for this venture. It turns out you were multimillionaires all along. I believe you owe us an explanation."

She hesitated for a few moments as she turned the screen back around to its regular position.

"When you found the basis of our wealth, I assume you checked the purchase dates?"

I nodded. "That was a puzzle. You were ten. He was fifteen."

"How did you explain that? Rich uncles? Hidden trust funds? Ed McMahon showing up at our doorstep?"

"We couldn't find anything."

"No, you couldn't, could you?"

"Then how did you do it?"

She smiled. "It was actually quite straightforward. We sent our orders back in time."

Markowitz nodded as if that were the most logical thing in the world – for the few seconds it took his mind to fully register what she had just said.

Then his jaw fell. "You did *what*?"

"We sent our purchase and sell orders back to the particular moments that would provide us with the highest possible returns, since we had the advantage of knowing how the investments would turn out."

Markowitz considered this for a moment, then shook his head. "You'll have to excuse me, but I find this a bit hard to swallow."

"That's understandable, but nevertheless what I said is true."

She turned once more to me. "Like you said, your first investigation of us was quite thorough. In your latest audits, you undoubtedly wondered how you could have overlooked something of this magnitude."

"I've had my staff running in circles for days," I replied.

"I'm sorry to have caused them so much trouble," she answered.

"Three years ago, we had an idea but no funds to pursue it. MIT, as you know, is as open to backing new scientific concepts as any of our institutions, but we knew that we could never get anything like this through the grant review committees. Normal university channels were therefore closed to us."

"So you went looking for suckers," said Markowitz.

"I wouldn't refer to your father in those terms, Mr. Markowitz. He wasn't the only person on Wall Street to fall for that particular delusion."

"Call me Ray."

"OK, Ray. What happened was this: with his initial investment, we developed the technology to the point where the central processing unit was the size of a typical laptop. We found that we could use this to transmit a two dimensional object, such as a letter or a fax."

"How did you know it worked?" I asked. "Surely you would have wanted to test it before you wired money."

"We had some fun with Alicia up front. We'd send a seemingly urgent fax back to the previous hour, and then we'd ask why she hadn't informed us immediately of its arrival. The poor girl became quite befuddled."

Markowitz finally laughed. "So once you proved it up, you sent the order back for Wal-Mart?"

She nodded. "At that point, our biggest challenge was finding a bank that had stayed both solvent and in one location for the past 35 years. That took a couple of months."

"How did you send back the initial investment?" I asked. "You started with $10,000 as I recall."

"Henry remembered that his father had a savings account that he left untouched for years, so we sort of borrowed it for a while. We had a lawyer draw up all the documents; then we printed them on a font commonly used in the 1970s and sent them to the bank's trust department. The documents contained specific instructions for the disposition of our account, as well as the return of his money, with interest and a substantial return for his trouble."

"When did you know it worked?"

"Last fall, Henry sent the papers while I logged in to our account. A few seconds later, our bank's web site showed the totals change. It was quite thrilling."

Incredible.

"So you finished the rest of the project with your own money?" Markowitz asked.

"We didn't feel like we could go back to your father for more funds without disclosing what we had achieved. Once we confirmed our initial hypothesis, it was merely a matter of expanding on our previous work."

I laughed. "Merely?"

She smiled. "It may have been a bit more complicated than that. After a few more months of work, we eventually succeeded in transporting a three dimensional object, using the mechanism you saw below."

"Nothing living could survive that level of cold," said Markowitz.

"No. The transport facility is immediately above the quantum processor. I'll show it to you later, when everyone has gone home. Only one other member of our staff knows that it exists."

Markowitz closed his eyes as he stretched his hands over his head; then he turned to me. "I'm still not sure I believe this."

I wasn't sure what to believe, either. All I could muster in reply was that her explanation seemed to square with the facts as we knew them.

I did have a question, though. "You keep using the word 'we.' Can you tell us where your other half is now?"

Juliet didn't answer. Instead, she flipped open her phone and tapped a quick text message before turning to a side door that I had not noticed earlier.

"Excuse me, gentlemen. I need to check on something in the lab. I'll be right back.

Chapter 5

Juliet returned a few minutes later and beckoned us to follow her into the facility's conference room. She had furnished it, like her office, with good quality second hand stuff, but that wasn't what drew my attention.

I had thought the lab kept itself out of the public eye, but seated at one end of the long table were two other visitors. The man was dressed in jeans, old boots and a work shirt that would have fit in on any of the city's burgeoning construction sites. Though not rugged, he clearly spent a fair amount of time outside.

I pegged his companion to be in her late 30s; a natural blonde who, a decade earlier, probably caused traffic accidents. Her face still retained its youthful luster, and from her fit, toned arms, I surmised that she didn't sit on the couch all day gorging on potato chips and watching talk shows.

Juliet introduced the four of us. Our new acquaintances were Sharon Bergfeld and Dr. Robert Lavon – what type of doctor, she didn't say.

Markowitz hadn't expected company, either. Though polite, he was clearly unhappy.

"Dr. Bryson, I've always assumed that the work of this facility would remain confidential. Our contract specifies – "

"I'm aware of the contract, Ray, but I also understood that you were interested in the whereabouts of my husband."

"We are," he replied.

"My guests found him. They arrived a couple of days ago. Since I knew you were coming, I asked them to stay."

This was a surprising turn of events.

"OK," I said. "Where is he?"

"Israel," said Lavon. "I'm afraid Dr. Bryson is dead."

I glanced over to Juliet, but I couldn't think of anything to say except that I was very sorry. I found the news so unexpected that I failed to notice that her demeanor didn't exactly match that of a woman suddenly bereaved.

Lavon unfolded a map of Israel and turned it so that Markowitz and I could read it easily. He had drawn an X where they had located the body – just off the freeway bisecting Jerusalem's outer western suburbs.

"We found him at this site, about three weeks ago," he said.

"What on earth was he doing *there*?" asked Markowitz.

I could think of a number of reasons. Veterans of the Israeli army had turned the country into one of the world's burgeoning tech centers. Perhaps someone had offered him a better deal.

I glanced again toward Juliet, but she didn't volunteer an answer.

"Have the police released their initial report?" I asked. "If not, one of their investigators owes me a favor. I'd be happy to make a few calls to speed things along."

"Thank you," she replied, "but I doubt that would help."

"Why not?" I asked.

In my dealings with them, the Israeli police had exhibited the highest levels of competence and professionalism.

"Because, um."

She gave Lavon a fleeting look. *Go ahead.*

"The police wouldn't be interested because the tests we ran on his skeleton indicated that Dr. Bryson died approximately two thousand years ago," he said.

Markowitz nodded, just as he had when Juliet explained the source of their great wealth. A few seconds later, though, Lavon's words registered.

"Two thousand *what*?" he blurted. "Did you say two thousand *years*?"

Lavon handed him a computer printout. The younger man quickly scanned it before tossing it back.

"Radiometric Labs, Tel Aviv. What are you people trying to pull? What kind of doctor are you, anyway?"

"My Ph.D is in archaeology – University of Michigan, with honors. Go check if you'd like."

I made a note to do that, but he didn't seem like the type of person who would lie about something so easily verified.

He held up another printout.

"We found the initial results to be as incongruous as you do now, so we headed back home to retest our findings with two independent labs here in the States. None of the three facilities had access to the work of the others."

"I assume they reached the same conclusion?" I asked.

"They did," said the woman. "We also found some fragments of cloth near the bones. These dated to the same period as the skeleton."

She spoke with that soft Texas twang that drove my Army buddies crazy.

Markowitz paid no attention to that. He stared at them, making no effort to conceal his skepticism.

"That would be expected, wouldn't it?"

"Yes," she replied, "except the fabric was sewn by a machine, the thread had a polyester core, and fiber analysis revealed that the cotton surrounding the core –

fiber dating to the *first century* – was itself spun from a genetically modified strain, originally native to the Americas."

They passed the reports to me – all on official looking letterhead that either could be authentic or the creation of a halfway decent graphic designer with a laser printer. It was so hard to tell these days.

"Tell me, Doctor," I said, "how did you determine that the bones belonged to Henry Bryson? I don't think they wore dog tags or carried driver's licenses two thousand years ago."

Lavon reached into a gym bag and pulled out a clear plastic cylinder, resembling the ones used by banks at their drive-in windows. He tossed it over to me. Inside, fixed in place with bubble wrap, were the distinct bones of a human finger, held together by a metal pin.

"We traced the serial number on the pin to the hospital, which connected us to a surgeon's office, which ultimately linked us with Juliet here."

"He enjoyed woodworking and accidentally sliced his finger off with a band saw several years before you first met him," she said. "Some fine surgeons over at Mass General sewed it back on and eventually he made a full recovery. He didn't even notice it after a while. It was almost as if the accident never happened."

I reached into my jacket pocket and took out my reading glasses, better to focus on the pin. As a veteran of the Army special forces, I was all too familiar with bone fractures and this particular medical technology.

"You dated the specific bone, around the pin?"

"You have the printouts right there," said Lavon. "We'll make a copy for you, if you wish, for later study. Take all the time you need."

"DNA?"

"None recoverable from this specimen."

I rolled it around a couple of times. "This pin wasn't simply drilled in later?"

"That was our first thought, too," he replied: "somebody was playing a trick on us. It happens all the time in our line of work. That's why we confirmed the results with completely independent labs. I hand carried each of the specimens as well, to ensure the integrity of the chain of custody."

I glanced back down at the cylinder.

Now I've heard some whoppers in my day, and in my business, I had to deal all too often with people who were, as Twain famously put it, "economical with the truth."

On the other hand, Juliet Bryson had not tossed them out straightaway, which is what I would have done to anyone spinning such a tale, unless …

"Dr. Lavon, you mentioned bones, plural. I presume you recovered the rest of the skeleton."

He nodded. "This fragment and our small test samples were the only portions the Israeli authorities would allow us to take out of the country."

"Where are the other bones now?"

"At the lab, in Tel Aviv. I can show you, if you'd like to see them."

***

I assessed both visitors closely once more. Truly pathological liars often have the innate ability to inspire confidence, which is why certain types of investment swindles remain so consistent over time.

But if the Brysons' work, and fortune, had in fact remained unpublicized, I couldn't figure out what these two could have hoped to gain from their story.

"Yes," I replied, "I would like to see the bones. Actually, I'd like to go through the entire sequence of events that led you here, starting from the very top."

"Certainly," he said.

I held up the tube. "I can't exactly go back to my client and present this as definitive proof of Dr. Bryson's whereabouts."

Chapter 6

That was how I found myself on the next El Al flight out of New York. Markowitz couldn't go; he had a social commitment he couldn't avoid without the gossip columnists taking note, but he did agree to give his father only a basic outline of our findings until we had a chance to make further inquiry.

Sharon, too, chose to stay behind, for reasons she didn't elaborate.

While we waited for our flight to board, Lavon explained that her father, a Dallas real estate developer, had provided the lion's share of their excavation's funding for the past several years.

He wasn't just any developer, either. According to the *Wall Street Journal,* Edward Bergfeld, Jr. owned the second largest collection of Class A office buildings in the United States, and it came as no surprise to hear that he also ranked among the top contributors to conservative religious and political causes.

"Do you have a sense of Sharon's own views?" I asked.

Lavon paused to consider the question.

"Somewhat like her father's, from what I can tell," he replied, "but I've learned not to probe. In our business, we take funding where we can find it. The old man seems satisfied with our current arrangement and I don't want to jeopardize our work by getting into unnecessary theological disputes."

I nodded. This made perfect sense.

"How much time has she spent at the site?" I asked.

"She visited for the first time earlier this year."

"Does she have any archaeological training?"

"No. She just happened to be there when we uncovered the skeleton; but I'll give credit where it's due: She was the one who initially noticed the polyester core in the thread. The brand is called D-Core; it's quite common today."

Since others waiting at the departure gate could overhear our conversation, we agreed not to discuss further specifics until we reached our destination, though I couldn't resist making a final pass through online databases before having to shut the system down for takeoff.

***

Considering that I had made my last trip to Israel in the back of a noisy, windowless C-130, I couldn't complain too much about having to fly coach. We landed about six the next morning, cleared immigration and customs, and were comfortably ensconced in our rental car by eight, crawling slowly forward in Tel Aviv's rush-hour traffic.

Half an hour later, we pulled into the parking lot of Radiometric Labs and greeted the friendly receptionist. She escorted us to the back, where two technicians had laid out the skeleton on a metal table in the center of the room.

"I called ahead," said Lavon.

We introduced ourselves. Radiometric's manager, Jonathan Dichter, had studied with Lavon at Michigan before returning to his native country.

The lab was arranged in a typical fashion. A long bench ran the entire length of one side, covered with an array of beakers and reagents, an autoclave and couple of laptop PCs – though I suppose I should qualify the term "typical." Old movie posters of Godzilla breathing fire upon Japanese cities festooned the walls.

"Two thousand years from now, confused scientists might attribute the destruction of our present world to such a cause," Dichter explained.

I shrugged. To each his own.

We chatted a few more minutes and then got down to business.

"When did you first realize you had a problem?" I asked.

"Let me start by explaining our normal procedures," Dichter replied.

"When a skeleton comes in from an excavation site, we lay it out on the table and count the bones, to determine whether it is completely intact and to resolve the question of whether two or more sets of bones may have been mixed together."

"Fair enough," I said.

"Then we take preliminary measurements of the long bones and x-ray everything."

"That would have picked up the pin, wouldn't it?"

"That's correct, if our equipment had been working. Our machine broke down a few days earlier, but the local hospital had priority access to the parts we needed. Getting it repaired took over a week."

"That's when you found the pin?"

"Yes, but by then that was only one of many anomalies," said Lavon.

Dichter continued, "From the femur length, we estimated the man's height at 185 centimeters. That's six foot one to you Americans; tall for the era, but not Goliath."

From my recollection of Henry Bryson, that sounded about right.

"Once we did that," Dichter said, "we took random samples of the bones and calculated a preliminary age using a standard radiocarbon process. In this case, the results dated consistently to the first century, with a margin of error plus or minus a decade or two."

"This all seems rather straightforward," I said. "When did you first suspect that you were dealing with something out of the ordinary?"

Dichter reached up to grab a bright circular lamp, similar to the type found in a dentist's office. He turned the skull toward me and focused the light.

"Let's see if you can do any better than I did," said Lavon. "Tell me if you notice anything unusual."

I studied the skull for a couple of minutes, but nothing looked terribly out of place. "I can't see anything," I finally said.

"Count the teeth," Lavon instructed.

I did so. "23."

"The normal adult human has 32," said Dichter.

"Right, but didn't everybody lose teeth two thousand years ago?" I asked.

Dichter and his assistant both laughed. "Robert said the exact same thing."

I examined the skull again. The odd thing was, I saw no gaps between the teeth that remained.

"Ah," said Dichter. "Now we're getting somewhere."

"That's what we first noticed," said Lavon. "Plus the loss of teeth is symmetrical. The bicuspids are missing, top and bottom, as are the wisdom teeth."

"The left side of the upper jaw is missing one more," I said.

"The second molar," replied Dichter. "We extracted that one ourselves to run a separate test, using the Electron Spin Resonance method as opposed to radiocarbon. ESR is ideally suited to dating tooth enamel, but it requires input in powdered form."

"We had to grind it up," said Lavon.

"And?" I asked.

"First century, more or less. ESR is not as accurate as radiocarbon, but the tooth was definitely not modern."

***

None of us spoke for a while as I considered this.

"Now you know what we're up against," Dichter finally said. "Until a few years ago, orthodontists regularly pulled teeth before installing kid's braces, but I've never heard of such a thing in the ancient world."

"I'm not sure I'd want to," Lavon joked.

I certainly didn't.

"Could someone have grafted the teeth in later, like, um …"

"Piltdown Man?" said Lavon.

Both archaeologists laughed. "Discovered" by an English professor in 1912 and heralded for years as the missing link between ape and human, Piltdown Man remained one of archaeology's most well-known frauds. Later examination revealed the specimen to be an orangutan's jaw with chimpanzee teeth, attached to a medieval skull.

"I don't think so," said Dichter. "This jaw showed no signs of tampering at all. Although it took scientists forty years to prove Piltdown a hoax, we'd spot the same thing in minutes today."

"That just means the fraudsters have to be smarter," I said.

Lavon and Dichter laughed again. "They are."

The trade had become a never-ending game of cat-and-mouse. A renewed interest in ancient history, compounded by rising affluence across the globe, had created a growing pool of new and relatively unsophisticated buyers.

"In our world, demand begets supply," said Dichter. "Do you remember the *James Ossuary* from a few years ago?"

I vaguely recalled the story: something about a box of bones that supposedly belonged to Christ's brother.

"It got so much publicity because if authentic, it would have been the first physical reference to Jesus directly traceable to the first century," said Dichter.

"But not long afterward, the IAA – the Israel Antiquities Authority – raided a warehouse owned by the ossuary's discoverer. Inside, they found dozens of so-called artifacts, along with the tools the man and his associates had used to create them. Later investigations revealed that this gang had been running a forgery ring for twenty years."

"That crew was in it for the money, but sometimes, people conduct hoaxes for more personal reasons," Lavon added.

"When we start out in this business, we all dream of excavating spectacular ruins and recounting our finds to rapt audiences of society's movers and shakers at the Met. But not everyone's career turns out the way they expected it to in graduate school. It can be awfully tempting to cross that line, even if it's just to make somebody you don't like look like a total fool."

I sighed. "Like now, for instance."

"Yes," said Dichter, "though I can't imagine who could be behind this. None of us have publicized our findings, and the only artifacts found at the site, other than the skeleton and what's left of the clothing, were a handful of Roman coins."

I glanced at Lavon, who walked over to one of the laptops and tapped a few keys before turning the screen toward me.

"An authentic Roman *denarius*," he said. "Ten bucks on eBay."

"They're nothing special," said Dichter.

This was news to me, though it would explain how Bryson had obtained them – if these bones truly were his.

"You mentioned other anomalies?" I asked.

"I'm not sure I'd call them that," said Dichter. "It's just that whoever this man was, he was remarkably healthy for someone in the first century. Obviously he was a member of the upper class, but even for this type of person, I've never seen a skeleton so free of any signs of infectious disease."

"You can tell that from the bones?"

Both Lavon and Dichter nodded.

"Amazing," I said.

And it truly was. I had no idea the science had advanced that far.

"Just out of curiosity, how old was this man when he died?"

"I'd say late forties, early fifties, thereabouts." Dichter replied.

He directed my attention back to the skull.

"These zig-zag patterns are called 'sutures.' The skull of a newborn is flexible, to make birth easier, and the sutures join up and fuse as the person grows older."

The assistant adjusted the light so I could see them better.

"The frontal suture, this one, closes when a child is quite young. Others begin to close between the ages of twenty and thirty, and the last ones, back here, don't fuse completely until the person reaches seventy."

Once again, this was in the ballpark.

I racked my brain trying to come up with alternative explanations for what I was seeing, but this proved to be a futile exercise. I simply couldn't think of any.

Chapter 7

We tossed ideas around for a little while longer and then I bought Jonathan and his crew lunch, to thank them for their trouble. Afterwards, Lavon and I hopped in the car and headed for Jerusalem, less than forty miles away.

I didn't expect to learn anything new at their dig site, but I needed to be able to say I had crossed every "t" and dotted every "i" before writing my final report to Markowitz, assuming I decided to write one after all.

We didn't say much to each other along the way, but eventually, Lavon couldn't resist asking me what I really thought of it all.

I can't believe I'm quoting a fictional detective," I said, "but I think Sherlock Holmes may have pegged it pretty close."

"What did he say?"

"Eliminate the impossible and whatever remains, however improbable, must be the truth."

"The question is," I continued, "have we eliminated the impossible?"

"You said the Brysons' money is real enough," he answered. "You couldn't think of any other way they could have acquired so much."

I had, and I still couldn't.

"Let me ask you another thing," I said. "How did Juliet react when you first showed up at her door with that story? Did she show any sign of doubt that what you were telling her was true?"

"That's what surprised me. It was almost like she had expected the news – or perhaps she just felt a sense of relief, finally knowing what had happened to him."

"A sense of closure, then?"

"Yes."

***

By then, we had reached the outskirts of Jerusalem and took the exit to the road leading to Lavon's dig.

From the highway, about a hundred meters away, the site resembled any one of the dozen nearby building projects. A chain link fence topped with a strand of razor wire surrounded the three-acre property, while a faded yellow Caterpillar backhoe and other well-worn earth moving equipment rested in the corner of a gravel parking lot.

We got out of the car and made our way to excavation headquarters, a secondhand construction trailer donated by a local builder. Lavon spoke briefly to the graduate student he had left in charge during his absence and then gave me a quick tour of the dig itself.

Their efforts focused on a half-acre plot at the northeastern corner of the site, with the work organized along the lines of a Wheeler box grid, a common archaeological technique that enabled a small professional staff to supervise a high number of eager but untrained volunteers.

"Imagine a chess board," Lavon said, "with each square two meters by two meters. We leave the red squares alone, while we excavate the black ones. That way, we can measure both vertical and horizontal dimensions with precision."

"Where did you find Bryson?" I asked.

He pointed to the far southwest corner, about 150 meters away from the primary excavation area, and we walked over to have a look.

"A couple of engineering students took our ground penetrating radar to the inactive areas of our site, just for practice. They found the collapsed cave and on an off-day, we decided to take a look."

"And the skeleton?"

"We knew it was old, but without testing, we couldn't say more, so we bundled it off to Radiometric. You know the rest."

***

I did, and I also realized that I had asked where they had found Dr. Bryson without using a qualifier to indicate that I had some doubt as to the veracity of the story.

"Robert, let me ask you something: assuming for the moment that we're not falling for some elaborate practical joke, what do you think he was doing in this location, in the first century?"

It didn't take long for both of us to reach the obvious conclusion: *Anno Domini* – the Year of our Lord – the reason the first century is the *first* century, and not the fourth, or the eighteenth, or the 223rd.

Before I could say anything else, Lavon jumped up and ran back to the main excavation site, where he rushed into the trailer with a couple of graduate students in tow. A few minutes later, he emerged with a thick green binder and began to flip rapidly through the pages as he headed back toward me.

The file contained a thumbnail photograph and a brief description of every item – ancient or modern – that any worker had uncovered at the site, from the first day of the excavation until that very moment.

For the sake of scientific precision, and to fend off allegations of potential site contamination, the documents even recorded the details of a volunteer's lost car keys that a doctoral candidate had found in one of the grids the following day.

I waited until he was out of earshot of the students to ask my question aloud.

"Has anyone located a missing video camera – one with some slight wear and tear, perhaps?"

My attempt at humor escaped him and he continued to flip through the printouts, but eventually he concluded no one had found such a device – at least not yet.

Finally, he closed the binder and just stared at the sky.

"Would a DVD or flash memory survive two millennia under the sand?" I asked.

Neither of us knew; nor did we have any way to determine whether Henry Bryson had met his end coming or going. Any recording device the diggers unearthed could just as easily be blank.

Chapter 8

We returned to the Brysons' lab, both still jet-lagged from our whirlwind trip. Juliet led us into the conference room, where we were surprised to see that Markowitz and Bergfeld had not left Boston after all.

"I had to hear the rest of the story," he said. "How was your trip?"

As Lavon and I explained what we had found in Israel, each of us struggled to come up with an alternative that fit the facts as we knew them. No one succeeded.

We could see, too, that Juliet had something else on her mind. Her face reflected a strange sense of peace, serenity almost, that didn't square with her husband's demise. I made the mistake of commenting on this.

"I've thought of little else since you left," she said. "I came up with a plan, one that should require only a simple adjustment to the transport apparatus."

"What kind of plan?" I asked.

"We can still save Henry, Mr. Culloden. Now that we have the precise coordinates of his whereabouts, a rescue should be straightforward."

"But that means someone else will have to – " Lavon cut himself short.

"Yes, Robert, and I am thankful that we have a person in this room so uniquely qualified for the task."

I would have expected Lavon to jump at the chance, but to my surprise, his first impulse ran against the idea.

"He could have died somewhere else," he protested. "There's no guarantee anyone would find him alive in that cave."

"No," she replied, "but do you think a perfect stranger would have carried his body very far, in that climate?"

Lavon shook his head.

"And you told me yourself that his bones showed no signs of gross physical abuse. Did you mean that, or were you just trying to avoid causing me any more sorrow?"

"No, I meant it. The lab in Tel Aviv analyzed the skeleton with great care, given the discrepancies we found. I think it's safe to assume he wasn't executed, nor was he torn to pieces by a mob, or by wild animals."

"Well, then, it should still be possible to save him."

"Or leave *two* skeletons in that cave instead of one," Lavon grumbled. "Your husband could have died from dozens of other causes that would have left no impact on his bone structure."

The rest of us watched without saying a word.

"Robert, I implore you: you're the only one who really understands that world. You're the only one who speaks the language."

"I *read* ancient Greek," he said. "There's a difference. Plus, not everyone in that area spoke Greek. If I encountered the wrong people, I'd be more likely to get a knife in my gut than directions to Jerusalem. In fact, that may have been what happened to your husband."

"But you know he wasn't robbed," she replied. "You found a bag of Roman coins by his bones, did you not?"

Lavon nodded. The cache amounted to three months pay for a typical unskilled laborer. No brigand would have left that behind.

"I'm not too proud to get down on my knees and beg if I must."

Lavon sat in silence for another minute or so. Finally, he sighed. "There's no need to beg," he said.

"Just think of the knowledge you'll gain from just a short visit."

"I said I'd do it," he snapped.

***

The rest of us heard the words, but like so much of what we had seen over the last few days, their meaning failed to register immediately.

"You're serious about this?" Markowitz finally asked. "Someone else can really go back?"

"Yes," said Bryson. "It will involve an element of danger, but the odds of success are high enough to justify the risk."

Markowitz pondered this for another moment; then his face lit up.

"*Fantastic!*" he said. "I want to go, too."

Lavon shook his head, as did Bryson. This was a bad idea.

"Ray, I've never heard you express any interest in the Biblical era," I said.

"No," he admitted. "But what an adventure this could be."

"This will be incredibly hazardous," said Lavon. "I don't think you have the slightest comprehension of the dangers we're likely to encounter."

"I can handle it," said Markowitz. "Climbing K2, *that* was hazardous. Diving the *Andrea Doria* – people die doing that every year, too. We have to have confidence in ourselves. If we listened to the naysayers, we'd be afraid to walk out the front door."

"Ray, that may be true," I said, "but this enterprise has already lost one man. You've seen the photos of the skeleton. You saw Dr. Bryson's finger sitting right here on this table, in a jar."

"Yes, I did. And we're going to get him. Actually, we have a golden opportunity not only to save Dr. Bryson, but also to complete his original plan. While you were gone, Juliet told us why he was there; the question he sought to answer."

I was afraid of that.

"No, *we* are not going anywhere," said Lavon. *I* am going to retrieve Dr. Bryson and come straight back. The risk is too high to attempt anything else."

"You exaggerate," said Markowitz. "I'm sure he just ran into a freak infection or something. Don't those stories about the Black Death all say that the victims died within the hour?"

Lavon sighed.

"Ray, tell me: would you go to Iraq today, as a tourist? It would be a fascinating trip. Some of the greatest archaeological treasures on the planet are there: Babylon, Nineveh, the seats of ancient empires, most never completely explored."

"No," said Markowitz. "I'd probably get blown up."

"And why is that?"

"Religious fanatics – nut-jobs who think killing an American is God's will."

"I'm going to give it to you straight," replied Lavon. "By the time of Christ, ancient Judea had suffered through nearly two centuries of very similar religious and political strife. *Two hundred years* of constant low level guerilla violence – not to mention the regular depredations of ordinary thieves and highway robbers."

Markowitz paused for a moment, but then his expression grew firm. "It's not like we're planning to stay long. Whatever happens, we'll deal with it.

He glanced over to Juliet. "My family's money made your initial work possible. I don't mean to be obstinate, but either I go or I'll shut this place down."

Bryson didn't speak, but she finally nodded her assent. After all, he had the ability to do just that.

"Then I'm going, too," said Sharon. "I've studied the Bible my entire life. There's simply no way I can pass up the opportunity to see what it describes for real."

"No!" said Lavon.

Though his forcefulness surprised me, I agreed with Lavon's thinking. However intelligent and capable she might be, Sharon didn't strike me as a person who had ever experienced anything going completely and horribly wrong.

I could imagine many things happening to such a woman in the first century – none of them good.

"You can't tell me what to do," she said. "My family has provided ninety percent of your funding for the last three years."

"I'm not saying you *can't* go," said Lavon. "I'm saying you *shouldn't*. It's simply too dangerous."

Like my client's son, though, logic could not dissuade her.

They bickered for several minutes before the archaeologist shook his head and let out an exasperated sigh.

He glanced over to me, looking for support, but this time he found none. I'll admit it; while the others argued, I caught the bug, too. Markowitz was right: Whatever happened, we'd figure out a way to deal with it.

Finally, Lavon recognized the inevitable and admitted defeat.

"All right," he said. "I need to round up some provisions. We'll meet back here in a few days after you've all had a chance to get your affairs in order."

Like Markowitz and Bergfeld, I neglected to consider the usual meaning of that phrase.

Chapter 9

Three days later, Lavon wheeled in four large boxes and stacked them in an unoccupied corner of the conference room. One of his old colleagues had recently left an Israeli dig to open a Biblical study center in rural Georgia, where he had meticulously recreated a first century Palestinian village. Lavon had gone there to borrow clothing and replica artifacts.

He could see that none of us had changed our minds, though he did have an unanswered question.

"Juliet, you never explained how can we signal this, um, *device* to return?"

She didn't immediately respond, which we all found disconcerting.

"We *can* signal it to come back, can't we?" he asked.

"Yes," she finally said, "you should be able to initiate a transfer on your end."

She reached into her pocket and pulled out four thin plastic wafers that resembled the flash memory cards in digital cameras.

"The system is programmed to return you to the present time automatically after a pre-set interval, but if you run into a more urgent situation, squeeze this for ten seconds, and you'll bring back all mammalian life forms within a two meter radius."

Unless we got tangled up with rabid dogs, that sounded easy enough; too easy, in fact.

"What's the catch?" I asked.

"The *catch* is that the transport process requires a tremendous electrical surge. If we schedule your arrival in advance, we can have the capacitors charged ahead of time. But we can keep them in that state for only one hour. After that, we must shift to a stand-by function."

"How long does it take to go from standby to fully operational?" asked Markowitz.

"We've narrowed the time required to thirty minutes."

"I see. So if we end up running for our lives?"

"You'll have to keep running for half an hour. I'm sorry. It's the best we've been able to do."

***

The others grew quiet as they considered this, but in the end, they didn't lose any of their determination to proceed. Still, one more issue nagged at me.

"Juliet, given that all new technology goes through a gestation period, so to speak, where the kinks are worked out, I assume you tested this before Henry ventured back?"

She nodded.

"Once we developed the capability to transmit three dimensional objects, we conducted a number of experiments using dogs. The automatic recall apparatus proved successful, and more importantly, we could detect no ill effects on the animals' biological systems, either at the time or several weeks later."

Bryson opened a cabinet under the credenza to her right, pulled out a remote control, and pressed a button to lower a screen from the conference room's ceiling.

"For the first human trial, Henry simply went back to the previous hour. Once we confirmed that success, we decided to run a second experiment, to a place and time where he could easily survive and earn a living in case he could not, for some unexpected reason, return to the present."

"Makes sense," nodded Markowitz. "Where did he go?"

"Dallas; November 1963. Had he been trapped there, his scientific talents would have proven useful. I doubt he would have had trouble finding employment, and as you're already aware, he would know exactly where to invest any money he happened to earn."

Markowitz chuckled. "Don't tell me he was a conspiracy theorist!"

She shook her head. "Not at all. He considered them unbalanced souls with overly active imaginations and too much time on their hands."

"So why that particular moment?"

She smiled. "If we were going to perform a test anyway, why not clear up some other mystery while we were at it?"

She opened a cabinet and removed a DVD. Then, she dimmed the lights, dropped the disk into the machine and pressed 'play.' For a brief moment, the screen remained blue, with only the date and time stamp showing at the bottom right-hand corner. *1963 11 22 12:27:31.*

"Two minutes," she said.

The image that came to light was that of a long, narrow grass-covered slope about thirty yards long and bounded at the top by a low wooden stockade-style fence and a concrete pergola.

A few people walked quickly by, heading toward the east where the President's motorcade was turning onto Houston Street, but the others – I counted nine – seemed content to remain where they were. One even had a movie camera.

"OK. Here we go."

Five seconds later, three shots rang out – audible, though not obvious in the midst of the crowd noise. Then came the screams. Still, the camera did not move, but remained focused on the fence and the trees marking the edge of the slope.

Despite the chaos nearby, the camera recorded nothing of consequence.

"The Grassy Knoll?" asked Bergfeld.

"Nothing but grass," said Bryson. "No hidden gunmen at all. I'm sorry to disappoint you."

She didn't reply. Like most natives of Dallas, Sharon felt the faster that memories of Kennedy's assassination faded, the better – something that was easy for her anyway, since she had been born over a decade after the event.

"So who did it?" asked Markowitz.

"How would I know?" Bryson replied. "You've read the books; you've seen the web sites. There are dozens of those nutty theories. This only disproved one of them."

"Why didn't he try to stop it?" asked Sharon. "He could have called the police."

Juliet shook her head.

"Suppose he had made that call. Suppose he found a pay phone earlier that morning: *There's someone on the sixth floor of the Texas School Book Depository waiting with a rifle to shoot the President.* Let's suppose he had said that. Then what?"

"Someone would have checked," replied Sharon.

"Yes," said Juliet, "with information that specific, someone certainly would have investigated. But as you know, Oswald was quite willing to kill police officers; he did, in fact, murder one after shooting Kennedy."

"So," she continued, "it's likely that he would have killed at least one policeman or Secret Service agent as they tried to apprehend him. Afterward, as with any police shooting, the rest of the force would have been very angry. One of their own had gone down."

"They'd look for others," said Lavon; "other conspirators."

"Beginning *exactly* with the person who made that call," said Bryson. "They could easily trace the pay phone as well as the precise time the call was placed. Other witnesses could identify the person on the phone. Ask yourself, as the Secret Service surely would have, who else would have known the gunman was hiding in the building besides a co-conspirator who had gotten cold feet?"

"That's how a lot of conspiracies come to light," I added. "Somebody chickens out at the last minute."

"He could have explained," said Sharon.

"How?" asked Bryson. *"I'm from the future and I'm here to help?"*

"No," she said, shaking her head, "he could have done nothing without risking a long stretch in either prison or the lunatic asylum. Besides, if Kennedy had not died in Dallas, someone else may have gotten him at his next stop. The what-if games are endless."

"He could have changed history," said Markowitz.

Juliet's expression grew solemn. "Yes; and you will all have to be careful that you do not. It's time I explained some ground rules."

Chapter 10

The Brysons had debated the subject endlessly among themselves: could a single event or individual really change the future in a meaningful way?

Juliet had leaned toward the perspective that one could. In her view, people tended to look at the broad sweep of human affairs without imagining how close some of the most important turning points really were.

What if, she had argued, the wind had shifted direction on that fateful August day in 1776, allowing the British fleet to sail up the East River and trap George Washington on Long Island, snuffing out the American Revolution before it could truly be born?

What if a young Hitler had lingered a minute longer in a bunker on the Western Front instead of departing, as he did, just before an Allied shell struck, killing everyone?

The possibilities were endless.

Her husband had started with the opposite view. Humans for the most part went about their business and then died; and the next generation did the same. Even the seemingly grand events were inevitable in their own way.

Had Grant been in command in 1863 instead of the more cautious Meade, Union forces might have trapped Lee's Confederates after Gettysburg, thus shortening the American Civil War. But whether the conflict had ended then, or as it actually did two years later, the North still would have won.

Henry considered this principle even more self-evident in scientific endeavors. Alexander Graham Bell had beaten his rival Elisha Gray to the patent office by only a few days – and though little known today, the controversy over who invented the telephone had dragged on for years, complete with sordid tales of the bribery of an alcoholic patent clerk.

Had the Wright Brothers never been born, he argued, someone else surely would have invented the airplane, an assertion bolstered by the fact that the Wrights themselves spent much of the decade after their initial success in the courtroom, fighting infringement litigation against other aircraft manufacturers.

"How did you resolve the issue?" Sharon asked.

"We agreed to disagree," said Bryson, "though in the end, I could tell that he was coming around to my point of view."

Sharon smiled, and the two women exchanged surreptitious glances, as if to say that even the most dim-witted men eventually did the same.

"Practically speaking, what did you end up doing?" I asked.

"Since we couldn't answer the question with certainty, we decided that except for the camera, Henry would take no other modern implements back with him: no weapons, no explosives, not even a flashlight."

We all agreed with the logic, although Juliet must have sensed my discomfort with the notion of having no real means of self-defense.

She looked me squarely in the eye.

"Henry agreed to follow this protocol," she said, "and I'm going to insist you do likewise, even under our current circumstances. Do you still want to go?"

After a moment's reflection, I gave a half-hearted grunt, in the affirmative.

"We're not going to pick fights," Markowitz added. "We've got nothing against any of those people."

This prompted Lavon to repeat his earlier warning.

"Just because we don't have anything against anyone two thousand years ago doesn't mean that the reverse will be true," he said. "I still don't think any of you grasp what we might be getting ourselves into."

The others, though, had ceased paying attention.

"We've been over that – time and again. I'm going, and that's final," said Markowitz.

"Me, too," said Bergfeld. "Don't try to stop us."

***

Lavon did, however, make one last attempt.

"What about the time paradox?" he asked, "the notion that we could accidentally kill one of our ancestors, and thus never be born."

"We debated that for a while," Juliet replied, "but we never came up with a good answer. Given that both of our families originated in northern Europe, we decided that the possibility of Henry encountering one of our ancestors in ancient Judea was so remote that we shouldn't worry about it."

Lavon gestured towards Markowitz.

"What about him?" he said. "His ancestors –"

Markowitz cut him off.

"By the first century, Jews lived all across the Mediterranean world," he snapped. "The odds are extremely remote that I could do myself any harm in that regard."

Whatever the outcome, the paradox struck me as something easy to test.

"Couldn't we take a handful of newly hatched chicks back a few days with their mother, kill the hen, and watch whether the chicks disappear?" I asked.

The others, though, greeted my contribution to scientific progress with stony silence. Either they considered the idea cruel, or most likely, they realized that such an experiment would only delay our departure.

Finally, Juliet shrugged.

"I can't tell you what to do," she said. "But I'd think about it – at least one more night."

Chapter 11

Of course, no one reconsidered, so at five o'clock the next morning, we followed Juliet – coffee in hand – down narrow corridors whose eerie green-glow reminded me of a movie set's haunted house.

We had gone about a hundred meters when she finally stopped and opened an electrical box that looked old enough to have been installed by Thomas Edison himself.

A gleaming metallic panel popped up. Juliet punched a code and placed her right eye on the scanner. A second later, the panel light turned green, and we heard a whoosh as a section of the floor in front of us dropped, exposing a ladder leading to a chamber below.

"We need to keep the prep room away from prying eyes," she said by way of explanation. "Our staffers are very bright; curiosity is part of their job description."

Fluorescent lights came on automatically as we descended into a room about twenty-five feet square. The ubiquitous industrial tiles made up the ceiling, while several wooden benches had been bolted to the floor. Apart from a few spots of exposed cinder block, a variety of lockers and storage cabinets covered the walls.

I helped Lavon lower the boxes he had brought from Georgia. Once we had climbed down and closed the entrance above, Lavon opened the nearest box and removed three thigh-length brown tunics. He kept the darkest one for himself, then handed the others to Markowitz.

"Take your pick."

"Does it matter?"

"No."

Markowitz selected the tan one, and after he had put it on, Lavon opened a second box and extracted a long brown-striped robe. Markowitz donned it, shook a couple of times to adjust the fit, and then stood in front of the mirror, quite pleased with himself.

"We'll fit right in," he said.

Lavon warned us that he couldn't entirely be sure. Even with years of training and field experience, he had to admit that much of what he "knew" about the ancient world was more informed conjecture than a true comprehension of the facts.

So few articles of clothing from the first century had survived that he couldn't help but wonder whether we could suffer the fate of the occasional tourist in Miami or Los Angeles who got murdered because he unwittingly wandered into the wrong part of town wearing the colors of a rival gang.

"Hey, what about underwear?" asked Markowitz. "All I have are my Fruit of the Looms."

"That should be fine," Lavon mumbled as his eyes dropped to the floor.

"One more unknowable," he said to me, out of the earshot of the others.

I glanced over to Sharon, who had laid out five different robes and head coverings, and sat in deep contemplation trying to pick the one she liked best.

"What about her?" I asked.

The modern notion of an independent single woman was inconceivable in the time of Christ. A woman *belonged* to someone – to a father, a husband, or to some other male relative. As for those who didn't, who were truly alone in the world, they didn't call it the oldest profession for nothing.

"I'm working on it," he said. "For her own protection, she needs to be noble."

"Makes sense."

"The trouble is, — "

"Hey, what about this one?" Markowitz interrupted in a loud voice.

We looked up to see that he had opened another box and taken out a gleaming white robe, bordered with a deep purple stripe.

Lavon shook his head. "No, Ray, leave that one here."

"Why?" he asked as he held it up to the mirror. "It makes me look dignified."

"We're not trying to look dignified. We're trying to blend in, as best we can. We don't want to draw attention to ourselves if we can help it."

***

While Lavon checked on the others, I waited until Juliet's back was turned and then stuffed a few items — well, maybe more than a few — from my gym bag into my travel pouch, just in case we had to stay longer than we had planned.

I also took a more careful look at my traveling companions. For obvious reasons, we'd have to defer to Lavon's judgment; and I took comfort in the fact that over the past few days, he had struck me as competent and efficient.

Still, I couldn't be sure who would fall apart if our venture didn't proceed according to expectation – if, for instance, the others had to witness a man being eviscerated in front of their own eyes, as I once had.

Our modern world is so incongruous in this regard.

On one hand, our televisions beam a constant barrage of twenty-first century atrocities into our living rooms, ranging from mass rape as an instrument of policy in parts of Africa, to youthful militias routinely hacking off the limbs of members of rival tribes, to women, even to this day, being stoned.

Yet the viewers watching these horrors buy their meat from grocery stores in shrink-wrapped plastic, and inhabit a society where leading animal training schools have to ensure that incoming students won't be traumatized by having to kill *rats* of all things, in order to feed the snakes and birds of prey at their zoos.

***

The more I considered our party, the more I realized that it was my client's son who worried me most. Though sober and level-headed in comparison to many of his peers, Markowitz had never quite shaken the attitude common to men born into great wealth – a superficial acknowledgement of authority that only partially concealed a central belief that the rules did not apply to them.

I walked over and pulled him away from the others.

"Ray, you do understand the seriousness of what we're about to undertake?"

"Sure."

My stern gaze did not change.

"Relax, Bill. It'll be just like Everest. A man could get killed there, too, if he wasn't careful."

The mention of Everest was not altogether reassuring. Back in my Army days, I had trained with a New Zealander whose brother had spent years as a Himalayan guide.

The bars of Kathmandu resounded with complaints about would-be adventurers who believed that payment of their $60,000 fee entitled them to an ironclad guarantee that they would reach the summit, regardless of poor weather or their own limited mountaineering abilities.

"I mean it, Ray. This isn't a joke."

"Bill, on Everest, when the guides talked, I listened. It was the same when I learned to fly helicopters, and I'll do the same here. Trust me."

As Markowitz stepped away, I glanced over to see Lavon slide next to Sharon.

"I hate to ask this, but it could be important," he said. "Are you close to, um, your time of the month?"

She smiled, though more at his hesitation than from the nature of the question.

"Happened last week," she said.

I just sat there and shook my head. A woman's monthly cycle; such a simple thing, yet I had not thought of that.

Chapter 12

We didn't have any more time to reflect, though. Bryson knocked on the back door of the chamber. A few seconds later, a geeky kid in coke-bottle glasses opened it from the other side.

"Allow me to introduce my assistant," she said. "This is Scott Ellison. He's one semester away from completing his Ph.D. I'm serving as his informal dissertation advisor."

"What is your specialty?" asked Markowitz.

The young man's eyes lit up. "I'm writing about Non-Abelian Anyons and Topological Quantum Computation."

He waved his hands excitedly as he launched into a description of his work. "It is inevitable that the next generation of quantum devices will depend on the existence of topological states of matter whose quasiparticle excitations are – believe it or not – *neither bosons nor fermions*, but instead are particles known as non-Abelian anyons, meaning that they obey non-Abelian braiding statistics."

I nodded as though I understood more than a single word he had just spoken.

"I'd expect that to be obvious," I chuckled.

"You lost me at 'is'," said Lavon.

The young man laughed, though a bit uneasily, since he seemed unsure what the rest of us found so humorous.

"How old are you, if you don't mind me asking?" I said.

"I turn 23 next week."

"I brought Scott here to explain some of the transit procedures," Juliet said; "to give you an idea what to expect."

"I hoped *you* knew that," said Lavon.

"Yes, I do," she said, "but much of Scott's work is out of the mainstream. To progress in this field, he will need to become more comfortable making presentations to skeptical audiences, so this seemed like a good opportunity for him to get some practice speaking to total strangers in at least a partially scientific context."

Ellison coughed and led us over to another thick plexiglass window. Looking through it, we saw an adjoining room about the size of an average bedroom, though the walls had been polished perfectly smooth and the corners were rounded. At the center, we could see a cube delineated by what appeared to be thin yellow twine.

"The walls are coated with a specialized ceramic," said Ellison. "They are essentially frictionless, for reasons it would take me hours to elaborate."

"We don't have hours," I said, hoping to avoid a long, incomprehensible lecture. "What's all that string at the center?"

"I believe that Dr. Bryson has already described to you the limits of the transport apparatus. That marks the departure point."

I considered this for a moment. "So we have to go back one at a time?"

"That's correct. You sit on the floor within those string markers."

Lavon turned to face Bryson. "You told us the return key would bring back all mammalian life forms within a two meter radius."

"Our calculations point to that conclusion. That's why the transit room itself is larger."

"But you've never really tested it?"

"Only Henry went back. How else would we have had the opportunity to do so with more than one person?"

I glanced at the kid. He seemed competent enough; but I had enough experience with human nature to realize that under the right circumstances, this young man would be perfectly capable of stranding his benefactors in the past and seizing their invention as his own. Bryson's real reason for sending only one person back wasn't hard to figure out.

"So we're the guinea pigs," Markowitz said to Bryson.

"We believe our device is completely safe. You can always elect not to go," she said.

Markowitz shook his head and chose not to argue.

"How do we know *exactly* where we'll end up," asked Lavon.

She and Ellison walked to the other side of the room, where the Brysons had hung a topographical relief map of ancient Jerusalem and the surrounding area.

The kid pointed to a hilly spot about ten miles west of the city walls.

"Dr. Bryson selected this location because he thought the hills meant that fewer people would be likely to spot him when he first entered the world."

I studied it carefully. It was not far from where Lavon and his crew had discovered the skeleton.

"I would have started out ten miles *east* of the city," I said, "in the desert where the likelihood of someone spotting me would be next to zero – and where any strange sights could be attributed to a mirage."

"He considered that, but he worried about the flux variation," Ellison replied. "He didn't want to be stranded in such a desolate area without water."

No one spoke for a brief time. Finally, Markowitz voiced our thoughts: "are you saying error bands on this thing are that wide?"

"It is a precisely tuned scientific instrument," said the young man.

Bryson raised her hand. "What Scott is trying to point out is that probability functions are a foundation of quantum mechanics. Heisenberg demonstrated this nearly a century ago, when he concluded that an observer could not simultaneously know both the position and the momentum of an electron."

"I can't speak for the others," said Lavon, "but I'd like the *probability* of arriving in one piece to be one hundred percent."

"Your anatomical structure will not change," said Bryson. "I can assure you of that. What we are referring to as probabilities only apply to the temporal and spatial dimensions of your arrival in the past world."

Lavon stared into her eyes, trying to determine if she was telling the full truth.

Juliet continued, "Given the time to be crossed and the distance to be traveled, our calculations based on our latest modifications of the device indicate that the spatial standard deviation will be 12.3 meters. This means that you have a 95% chance of ending up within a 25 meter radius of our target, which is just outside the entrance to that cave."

Lavon thought of the buried skeleton. "What if it puts us inside the cave, say wedged between a couple of rocks or something?"

"The transit system is designed to require at least a two meters of clear space in all directions," said Ellison. "If you don't have it, you'll automatically return here, to the present. Don't worry; we won't bury you in a ditch or anything like that."

"And the time parameter?" asked Markowitz. "How accurate is that?"

"Henry set the coordinates to arrive mid-morning of the Tuesday before Passover. He chose this point because it would give him most of the day to get oriented, with a lesser possibility of surprising anyone in the darker early morning hours."

"Makes sense. What kind of temporal variation can we expect?" I asked.

Ellison answered, "For some reason, the temporal aspect is more of a Poisson distribution. However, our calculations based on Dr. Bryson's trip to Dallas indicate that the arrival time should not deviate from expectations by more than one hour. In fact, we believe such a deviation to be a mathematical impossibility."

"That's what they said about all those subprime derivatives," said Markowitz. "The probability of default was eight or nine standard deviations from the mean – something that would happen about the time the next asteroid hit the earth."

"We're quite confident that our calc – "

Bryson stepped forward. "We're talking about physical phenomena here, Ray, not the behavior of people. Protons and electrons by themselves are incapable of such stupidity."

"What's the weather going to be like?" asked Sharon.

"The normal low in Jerusalem for this time of year is 47, with a high of 66. It should be quite pleasant," said Bryson.

"What if that day's not normal? As I recall, the Gospels tell of people huddled around a fire in the courtyard, trying to stay warm."

"I don't know about you," replied Juliet, "but I find 47 degrees rather chilly. It's a dry climate, so it will warm up quickly once the sun comes out. You can take an outer robe of wool, though, if you'd like, just in case."

That sounded like a good idea, so we all grabbed one. Finally, Sharon asked one last question.

"What does it *feel* like?"

"Henry described it as waking up from a nap. You know, how you need to shake the cobwebs loose for a few seconds after you wake up."

"Do you feel any sensations on the trip itself?"

"No. He said it was like falling asleep. Only you wake up somewhere else."

No one spoke. Bryson waited a few more seconds and then said, "If you are all ready, then I suggest we get going."

Chapter 13

Juliet pressed a button near the plexiglass window as the kid returned to the transit control room. A sliding door dropped down through the floor leaving an opening about five feet tall.

No one said anything as they checked their clothing and travel bags; then re-checked them, and then re-checked them again for good measure.

I laughed quietly to myself. My traveling companions were behaving like raw recruits before their first parachute jump, trying to mask their anxiety with a burst of activity.

After a couple of minutes, the system powered through a final test cycle and all was in order. Bryson glanced at Lavon and pointed to the opening.

"Robert, I believe you're first."

The archaeologist slid his staff and cloth travel pouch through the door, then took a deep breath and crept through the entrance. We heard a soft whoosh of air as the door closed, and then watched through the plexiglass as he sat on the floor between the string lines.

After closing his eyes and taking another deep breath, he looked to the control window and flashed a thumbs-up. The spindly kid pressed a button; seconds later, Lavon vanished.

"That's it?" said Markowitz. "No flash of light or puff of smoke?"

Juliet smiled. "Our first tests produced an intense burst, but we have refined the apparatus since then. I'm sorry to disappoint you," she said.

I wasn't disappointed at all. I for one would have found *smoke* quite worrying.

She turned to me. "Your turn, Mr. Culloden."

I grabbed my bag and eased over to the transit room door, hoping they couldn't see that I was as nervous as they were. After situating myself in the correct spot, I signaled to Ellison. *Time to go.*

An instant later, I found myself lying on the ground, shivering suddenly in the cold. I also saw that someone in Boston had miscalculated. Instead of it being late morning, a faint strip of orange had just emerged from the horizon to the east.

Despite the timing error, all of my body parts seemed to be intact. I was still shaking the cobwebs loose when I heard a quick 'psst' and looked over to see Lavon, lying flat on the ground about thirty feet away.

When he saw me, he signaled toward a small slit in the rock, barely visible about a hundred yards in the distance. We both crept toward it without speaking.

We had only gone a short distance when we saw a bright flash. A man in a robe jumped to his feet and started frantically casting about.

Markowitz.

"Robert? Bill? Where are you?" he called out.

Lavon rushed forward and tackled him. "For God's sake shut up."

We sat there for about a minute, listening and hoping no one had heard us, before we crept closer to the cave. I hesitated at the entrance, though Lavon reminded us that the state of the Professor's bones meant that whatever had happened to him, a wild animal lurking inside had not torn him apart.

Silly me.

Once we had gone in, I could tell that the cave broadened considerably, though without a portable source of light, it was impossible to tell how deep into the hills it went.

I had just begun running through my own mental checklist when we saw another flash about twenty-five feet in front of the cave entrance.

"They're getting more accurate," whispered Lavon, who chirped a quiet 'psst' and helped Sharon into the cave.

Her eyes bulged with disbelief. I asked her, as a joke, how things were back in Boston, but she was too stunned to speak.

We didn't have long to gather our wits, though. As she eased herself into a comfortable spot, Lavon continued to stare out the narrow slit with an expression of total concentration.

Something was out there.

All I could see in the early dawn light were rocky, scrub-covered hills that ran on for some distance. But Lavon's senses proved correct: not long afterward, we heard bleating and watched a shepherd drive a small flock of about two dozen animals into a narrow ravine a quarter mile away.

He was in a hurry, too. Just behind him, two other people moved quickly to catch up; one of them a small child whose legs struggled valiantly to maintain the pace.

I would have laughed at the little munchkin – he was trying so hard – but moments later, we heard a distinctive clanging sound, one that even I, with my Army damaged ears, could hear plainly. It was the sound of equipment, and armor.

Soldiers, I mouthed to Lavon, who nodded.

Sharon started to peer outside, but he pulled her back – just in time, too – for a few seconds later, a primeval shout broke the morning's quiet, followed immediately by the impact of stones against shields.

I muttered a silent expletive. This was an unpleasant turn of events.

We couldn't do much but lie flat on the ground and listen as the clashing of swords accompanied the screams of men as they were hit. Making matters worse, the first casualties started trickling past.

Sharon blanched at the sight of a man hobbling by, though she had the presence of mind not to make a sound. It couldn't have been easy: the man's left arm had been nearly sliced off at the elbow and his knee length tunic was soaked in blood.

By some miracle, he didn't seek shelter in our cave. Either he didn't know of it, or, more likely, he suffered from the tunnel vision so common to wounded men in headlong flight.

As time went on, the images outside failed to improve. Two bearded men passed by next; one helping the other, who held his hands over his belly, struggling with only limited success to keep his own entrails from falling to the ground.

That one wouldn't make it very far, I knew. Whatever these people had planned, it had gone badly wrong.

A stream of men followed, all dressed in similar beige tunics, scrambling down the hill as fast as they could. A few still held onto their swords, but most had either lost their weapons or thrown them aside in their haste to get away.

I heard a splat as another wounded man fell flat on his face only about ten yards from our position. It was then that we got our first glance at their enemies. Seconds later, a Roman soldier ran the injured man through with his sword.

Though Sharon and Markowitz had turned their faces away, I didn't think either of them would forget the hideous gurgling as the Roman kicked his victim to free his weapon from the man's ribs.

I was concerned that the soldier would spot us, but after dispatching his adversary, he charged forward, looking for others. Moments later, two more squads of Romans ran past. Like the first man's, their weapons glowed red; and it wasn't long before we heard additional screams coming from down the hill to our left.

After that, no one passed by for several minutes, so I began to relax. However, my relief was premature. I heard Lavon swear quietly and glanced up in horror as a lone man, about fifty yards away, ran straight toward the cave at full speed.

The runner had reached a point only about twenty feet from the opening when a brilliant light flashed directly in front of him. We heard the collision before our eyes could adjust. When they did, we saw both parties sprawled on the ground, momentarily stunned by the blow.

Unfortunately, the Romans saw it, too. One drew back his spear.

At the sight of the soldiers, the two staggered to their feet. The first man took off running in the opposite direction, and I could only watch as a legionnaire, as if by instinct, tossed his long *pilum*.

I couldn't see exactly what happened, but the sound of a thud, followed by a sharp cry of pain, told me enough. That runner wouldn't be going home tonight.

The other man staggered into the cave and collapsed, groaning and holding his bleeding nose. Though he had grown a short beard, Henry Bryson hadn't otherwise changed in the last three years.

I dragged him back into the darkness and cautioned him to be silent.

He was, for a few moments at least. As he recovered his wits, though, his curiosity got the better of him. He knew he had seen me before; he just couldn't figure out where.

"Who are you?" he finally asked.

"People trying not to get killed," I replied. "Not that you've helped much."

"How did you get here?"

"Your wife sent us."

"My wife? Juliet? Why would she do that?"

My eyes, however, had turned to the Romans approaching the cave's entrance.

"Be quiet," I said. "Your new friends are coming to visit."

Chapter 14

Now I've been in some hellish scrapes during my fifty-plus years on this planet, but in spite of all that followed, I can't think of a time when I felt as much absolute raw terror as I did that morning in the cave.

Lavon, too, had turned pale, as well he might. That the others hadn't was only due to their blessed ignorance of the typical fate of Roman prisoners.

About twenty feet away, three soldiers stepped cautiously toward the entrance with their swords drawn and their shields held high. The rising sun shone straight into their eyes and I could tell they were hesitant to go charging into the darkness, not knowing what dangers might lurk inside.

That was the only thing keeping our merry little band alive, but it wouldn't last long. We had to figure something out, and fast.

It's strange, the thoughts that come to mind in times of mortal peril. I recalled a BBC interview I had seen many years before, featuring a survivor of the *Piper Alpha* oil rig disaster in the North Sea. The man had jumped over a hundred feet into freezing water. When asked why, he said the choice was simple: the rig was on fire; certain death lay behind; only probable death lay ahead; so he jumped.

I glanced back toward the interior of the cave. I couldn't see how far it ran, but it surely came to an end. If the Romans came in after us, they would kill everyone and sort it out later. We had no real options.

I leaned over to Lavon and whispered, "Can you tell them we're travelers, that we're not their enemies?"

He had reached the same conclusion. He cupped his hands to his mouth and shouted in Greek.

The soldiers stopped, though they did not lower their swords. One, however, called out and moments later, a senior man appeared. The red transverse crest of a centurion topped his helmet.

"Come out," the officer ordered.

As Lavon translated, I took stock of our odds. Both he and Markowitz were clean shaven, while the Romans' enemies that morning all had beards – Jewish Zealots, I guessed. We had a plausible chance.

"Tell him not to kill us," I said. "Tell him we're not Jews."

Markowitz spoke for the first time. "I'm Jewish."

"That's not something I would advertise right now," I grunted.

Lavon spoke once more in halting Greek. Nothing happened for a second or two, but then the soldiers lowered their swords. Though the Romans continued to hold their shields high, this was at least a step in the right direction.

We had one last card to play. I tapped Sharon on the shoulder and instructed her to say, in loud English, "We're a peaceful people. Don't hurt us please."

She protested. "They won't understand a word."

"Just do it," I said. "Let them hear a woman's voice."

This had the intended effect. The soldiers finally lowered their shields, even though their wary expressions did not entirely disappear.

I turned to Lavon again. "We're going to have to go out. Tell them we have no weapons."

He did so; then he lifted Sharon to her feet and pulled back her shawl to expose her blonde hair. After a quick instruction not to resist in any way, I gently nudged her toward the cave's mouth.

At the sight of her, the centurion visibly relaxed and ordered his men to take a few steps back.

That was progress, I thought. We might live to see the end of this day after all.

She walked slowly toward the Roman with her hands held shoulder-high. As she got close, the centurion pointed to a spot of flat ground off to his right and motioned for her to sit.

Sharon followed these instructions and sat upright, with her arms around her knees. A junior soldier hovered over her, but he made no overtly hostile move.

After watching for a few more seconds, Lavon glanced back and took a deep breath. "Well, here goes nothing."

He stepped out of the cave with his hands in the air and received the same instruction. This time a Roman pushed him to the ground, though Lavon quickly collected himself and crawled to Bergfeld's right, where he sat upright in a similar fashion, with his hands easily visible.

The rest of us followed, and after being frisked – none too gently, I might add – we found ourselves seated on the ground, facing the cave's mouth.

A couple of the soldiers began to rummage through our bags, but found no weapons other than my small folding knife. One of them opened and closed the knife with great curiosity, but the centurion soon ordered him back to his duties.

A second soldier pulled a sack of coins from Markowitz's bag. The centurion once again shook his head, so the legionnaire replaced the money and joined his comrades – reluctantly, I could tell, since I don't think their morning's exertions had brought them much in the way of loot.

I could see right away that our centurion was an old pro. A few minutes later, he called for a torch and sent two men into the cave, just to be sure. They emerged after a short time, shaking their heads, and at that point, the immediate tension abated. Whoever we were, he could see that we were not Zealots.

The soldiers had not yet completed their tasks, though. The officer glanced up the hill and signaled to a legionnaire standing next to their supply wagon. Then he turned and motioned for us to stand up and follow him.

As we trudged up the slope, a handful of nearby Romans searched through the scrub for wounded enemies hiding in the brush. Those they found, they either finished off with swords or crushed their skulls with their heavy shields.

At each splat, Markowitz and Bergfeld gasped, without understanding the kind hand fate had dealt these men. That may seem an odd type of kindness to the uninitiated, but everything's relative, as we all would see shortly.

Chapter 15

When we got up to the road, a soldier directed us to sit off to one side, across from their supply wagon. The centurion and Lavon got into a conversation, and I watched him point to a short stick about five feet to his right and gesture to the Roman in supplication.

The centurion nodded. Lavon picked up the stick and scratched something in the dirt that looked like a map, as several other legionnaires watched with great interest. For his finishing touch, he drew three large triangles near the bottom right-hand corner of his diagram.

The Roman officer stared at the ground for a minute; then he burst out laughing and directed Lavon back over to join us.

I couldn't tell what the man found so humorous, but I thought it best to remain silent for the moment. Aside from a few leering glances toward Sharon, the soldiers paid little attention to the strangers in their midst. I wanted to keep it that way.

I looked around and counted about eighty in all. Two legionnaires stood as lookouts at the top of the tallest nearby hill, about a hundred feet away, while twenty or so others gathered equipment that had been scattered in the fight and brought it back to the wagon.

To our west, a group of about a dozen – either men new to the unit or soldiers on punishment detail, I guessed – had the unenviable task of collecting disemboweled Zealot bodies, which they stacked haphazardly by the side of the road.

I counted thirty-eight dead Zealots, and the soldiers gathering the enemy corpses didn't appear close to finishing their work. Against this, only six Roman casualties had come hobbling back; all but two under their own power.

"Efficient, aren't they?" I muttered to Lavon.

He nodded slowly but didn't reply.

I glanced over toward the map he had scratched in the sand. "I assume that centurion wanted to know where we came from?"

"Yeah; I told him we were from a place called Norvia. If the Romans ever make it to Finland, it might end up with a new name."

That made everyone chuckle quietly.

"What are those shapes you drew?" I said.

"He asked me what we were doing *here*. I told him we were travelers heading to Egypt. We wanted to see the Pyramids."

I laughed out loud. "Think he bought it?"

"We're still alive, aren't we?"

"So far."

***

The centurion wasn't the only person seeking answers that morning. I reached under my tunic and pulled out my chip, which I held up to Bryson.

"Dr. Bryson," I said, "I think I can speak for all of us when I ask if you have any idea why this thing is not working."

"Your wife said the capacitors only needed half an hour to charge," added Markowitz. "We first saw these soldiers over an hour ago."

Bryson looked genuinely nonplussed. He shook his head. "At the moment, I have no idea what could possibly be going wrong."

"Then I suggest you think harder, Professor," said Lavon. "We are by no means out of the woods."

Bryson stared at him curiously. "Pardon me, but I don't think we've met."

"Forgive me for not introducing our travel companions," I replied. "You know Ray, of course – Jonah's son."

Bryson nodded.

"And this is Dr. Robert Lavon, a leading archaeologist, and to his left is the lovely Sharon Bergfeld, who made a key contribution to unraveling an odd mystery at their Israeli dig."

Bryson nodded in their direction, but made no move to shake their hands. He rubbed his aching forehead, where his bruise had begun to swell into a nasty dark purple splotch. He eyed them for a couple of minutes as his mind absorbed what he had been told.

Finally, he turned to me. "How did you all get here?"

"Like I told you in the cave, your wife sent us."

"Juliet sent you all?"

"Not exactly," admitted Markowitz. "Her plan was for Dr. Lavon to come alone, but after hearing the story, the rest of us decided to tag along."

He glanced up at a passing Roman. "Perhaps that was a mistake."

Bryson turned to Lavon. "Why would she send *you*? I know most of her friends. I don't recall ever meeting you."

"I specialize in reconstructing the history of this region."

"So?"

Lavon looked him straight in the eye. "It's actually quite straightforward, Dr. Bryson. You died. Sharon and I are the ones who dug up and identified your bones."

Bryson shook his aching head again, wondering if perhaps he might even have a mild concussion. He listened as Lavon explained how their paths had crossed, from the first oddity noted by the Israeli lab to the surgical pin they had traced back to the hospital in Boston.

For what seemed like an age, Bryson just stared down the hill. Finally he turned to Lavon. "You really uncovered my skeleton, in that cave?"

Lavon nodded. "It seems an odd thing to say, but indeed we did. Tell us, Professor, why were you running so fast?"

"Bad luck, I suppose. I landed near the road just as these poor bastards launched their attack. I ducked down behind some rocks, but my curiosity got the better of me. I stood up to video the battle, and two Romans spotted me before I realized my error. They came straight at me. I saw that opening and realized it was my only chance."

"Not much of one, as it turned out," said Lavon. "They must have come in there after you."

Bryson grew pale as the realization sank in. He stared down the hill for several more minutes before finally turning to the archaeologist. "You have my gratitude, Doctor."

Lavon glanced at two Romans tossing yet another Zealot body onto the pile. "We'll see. How does that saying go – out of the frying pan?"

I was about to ask the Professor if he still had his camera when two soldiers dragged the remains of a young man past them and dropped their burden at the feet of the centurion. An animated discussion broke out between the three Romans.

Bryson stared at the corpse, whose face was caked with dried blood and whose white robe was now drenched bright red.

"My God!" he said. "It's Scott. What was he doing here?"

I scratched my head for a moment as I tried to place the face; and then it struck me: the lab geek from the control room.

So that's why our return ticket hasn't worked.

Bryson, though, wasn't thinking of home, and none of us managed to jump up fast enough to hold him back. He ran over and knelt beside the kid's body.

"Oh, my God. Oh, my God," he kept repeating.

The centurion watched for a few moments with a puzzled expression before he finally signaled for Lavon.

I couldn't understand him, but there was no mistaking his tone. Whatever had just happened, he didn't like it, and our chances appeared to have taken a noticeable turn for the worse.

I could see Lavon trying to explain, but the Roman didn't appear to be going for it. A minute later, he sent Lavon and Bryson over to us. Then he barked an order; and two soldiers grabbed the corpse by the ankles and dragged it back down towards the cave.

Chapter 16

"That brainless imbecile," Lavon muttered as he took a seat on the ground between Sharon and myself.

She looked at him as if he were the most callous brute on the planet. "You can't say that! The poor boy is dead."

"He may yet take us with him," Lavon replied.

I asked for an explanation, and the archaeologist, to his credit, paused briefly and took a deep breath to settle himself down. It wouldn't do for the Romans to see us arguing among ourselves, something he had the good sense to recognize.

"Did you see the purple stripe bordering his white robe?" he asked.

"The robe you told me not to take?" asked Markowitz.

Lavon nodded. "That stripe marks the wearer as a Roman citizen, entitled to special privileges and protection. Pretending to be one when you're not is a serious offense."

"That shouldn't matter now. No one can question him," said Markowitz.

"No, it's worse," said Lavon.

"A Roman citizen killed by a Roman spear," I interjected.

"That's right. That centurion probably sees his career going down the toilet just a few years before he can retire."

"It obviously happened during the heat of battle," said Markowitz.

Lavon shook his head. "Roman soldiers took pride in their discipline. That white robe stands out; and the kid doesn't bear the slightest resemblance to these Zealots. At best, the centurion will have some explaining to do, and it stands to reason that whoever threw that spear won't be our friend."

Markowitz's eyes followed the men lugging the body down the hill. "I don't know. It looks to me like they've decided to cover it up."

I still wasn't sure what the fuss was about, either. The Romans could always say the Zealots had done it. And it wasn't as if the kid's family would come looking for him here.

"I'm sure they will," said Lavon, "but the story could still get out. What bugged the centurion, though, is how he became associated with us. Unlike that kid, we're all wearing common garments. Why were we together?"

"Who said we were together at all?" asked Bryson.

Lavon stared at him hard. "It's obvious that you knew him."

"How did you explain it?" I asked.

"Not very well, I'm afraid. Though I read it fine, I'm still struggling with the spoken Greek. I didn't have enough time to make up a proper story."

"So what did you say?" asked Bergfeld.

"I told the centurion that we met the man in Caesarea. We agreed to travel with him for a few days because he insisted that we see Jerusalem before going to Egypt."

"That's plausible," said Bryson.

"It would have been, except for your carrying on. From Caesarea to this spot is only a two-day walk. He quite naturally wondered why you would mourn so ardently over a man you had known for such a short time."

"What did you tell him?" I asked.

"I made up some story about your grandfather owing his a great debt, but I don't think he was convinced."

That was plain enough.

"What do you think he'll do?" I asked.

Lavon shook his head. "His own men are under control. If he's going to keep this quiet, he only has a small group of other problems."

I struggled not to cringe. Having a hardened killer – and that's what a Roman centurion really was – view me as an inconvenient witness was not something to keep my stomach settled.

The others were a bit slower on the uptake, but I could tell by their collective shudders that they finally figured it out.

And there wasn't a thing we could do.

I turned to Bryson and smiled. "I wouldn't worry about it, Professor. I doubt they'll kill us. They'll probably just cut your tongue out."

***

We stewed for another half hour as the Romans finished mopping up. The Zealots had gotten us into this fearful mess, and as it turned out, a Zealot saved us, though I'd expect that our health and good fortune were the last things on his mind.

The centurion started toward us with a gesture that could only be interpreted as unpleasant when we heard a piercing cry near the base of the hill. A wounded Zealot, barely clinging to life, had summoned his last reserves of strength and had lashed out at his tormentors with a knife.

This final act of defiance found its mark, and two stretcher bearers leaped off the supply wagon and ran to attend the injured soldier. I watched them rush back to the road, where a Roman medic struggled in vain to staunch the bleeding from the man's thigh.

If, as I suspected, the blow had nicked the femoral artery, the soldier wouldn't last long. The centurion had apparently reached the same conclusion. He spat on the ground and shook his head in helpless frustration.

I reached into my bag and pulled out a packet about four inches square and then I turned to Lavon.

"Ask him if I can help."

Lavon did so, but the Roman only snapped, "What can you do?"

I held up the packet and pointed to the leg. The centurion stared at his medic for a brief instant – the man was obviously losing this battle – and then ordered him to back away.

It was the chance I needed, and I didn't let it go to waste. I immediately knelt down beside the wounded Roman, ripped open the wrapping, and pressed the bandage into the gash. Thankfully, it worked as advertised. Within a couple of seconds, the bleeding came to a complete stop.

I then pressed the two sides of the wound together which had the effect of folding the back sides of the bandage onto themselves, where they quickly bonded together. I held everything in place for a few minutes and then took a strip of gauze tape out of my bag and wrapped the man's leg several times.

Satisfied that the wound would not rip apart, I stood up and took a step back.

"Tell him that this soldier should live," I instructed Lavon.

He did so, but the centurion didn't move. He kept staring at the leg – waiting for the vessel to burst open again, I suppose. Finally, he seemed convinced that his man would be all right.

He turned back toward us and gestured in my direction. "Tell this man he has my gratitude," he said to Lavon.

I nodded in acknowledgement. Then he spoke to Lavon again. Not surprisingly, this time his tone was friendly.

"I am Publius," he said.

Lavon stated his own name, but the centurion struggled with the pronunciation when he tried to repeat it. Lavon introduced the rest of us, too, but our names were apparently even more incomprehensible. The officer shook his head, muttered a few words along with something like "Lavonius," and headed toward the front of the assembling Roman column.

Lavon started laughing.

"Well, what did he say?" asked Markowitz.

"He said we had strange names."

"That's it?"

"No; the best part is that he insists that we accompany them to Jerusalem."

"Why is that so funny?" asked Bryson.

Lavon chuckled again. "He said it's not *safe* for us to stay here."

Chapter 17

After the morning's misadventures, I needed no convincing to move on. An army escort to the city would at least raise the odds that we would arrive in Jerusalem in one piece, though unless Bryson's wife got that machine working again, I couldn't say I had the greatest confidence that we would depart in the same condition.

A Roman medic helped Sharon into the wagon where she took her place on a side rail next to three of the wounded who were unable to make the journey under their own power.

Being men, it was assumed that rest of us would tag along on foot, despite the fact that Bryson only managed to squeeze in minimal cardio work while Bergfeld had run two triathlons in the past year.

To his credit, the Professor didn't complain, and Sharon was prescient enough to take her luck where she could find it.

Publius by now had trotted up to the front of the column, leaving his second in command, who introduced himself as Decius, to supervise the rear. An *optio*, Lavon called him, just below a centurion in rank.

Decius struck me as a pleasant enough fellow – one who would remain so as long as we stayed out of his way and didn't cause any trouble. He had the gruff but competent demeanor of a seasoned NCO, the soldiers who are the backbone of any army worthy of the name.

We stood aside as the *optio* made a few final checks and then signaled to Publius that the column was ready to proceed. Moments later, a trumpet sounded and we started forward.

As I expected, we had barely gone a quarter mile when the questions started. Lavon was quick-witted enough to mumble something to the soldiers about his Greek not being good enough for medical terminology, but this excuse wouldn't work for our own party.

I explained that I had utilized the Army's latest high tech bandage. A powder on one side became part of the clotting matrix, while an antibiotic-impregnated glue on the other held the sides of the wound together as securely as if they had been sutured.

It was, truly, a miracle of modern chemistry. US field hospitals are first-rate, but wounded soldiers still had to live long enough to get there. Bleeding out was one of the main reasons they didn't.

"How do you remove it once the wound has healed?" asked Bryson.

"You don't," I replied. "That's the best part. In a couple of weeks, the body's own enzymes begin to dissolve the material. A few days later, it disappears entirely."

Lavon glanced over to the injured Roman. "What are his chances, realistically?"

Fortunately for us, they were pretty good. Profuse bleeding often carries out the dirt, so the odds were at least reasonable that his wound would not get infected.

"He's lost a lot of fluid, though," I said. "I'd put in an IV drip, if I had one. A tetanus shot wouldn't be a bad idea either."

They all laughed, except Bryson, who had swung around to Juliet's thinking on the issue and chided me for possibly changing history.

"I brought no weapons, Professor, but I sure as hell wasn't coming back to a primitive world without a decent first aid kit."

"That man would have died. Now he will live."

For all his academic brilliance, Dr. Bryson didn't have the best sense of priorities. "At the moment, I'm more concerned about *us* living," I replied.

He frowned.

"Tell me how they could reverse engineer this sort of thing?" I said. "The wrapping is biodegradable, too. In a week or so, it will vanish completely. It's especially designed to decay in this type of climate."

"I didn't realize the Army had gone green."

"I'm not pretending we have, Professor, but our enemies over the last fifty years have proven resourceful at using our throwaways against us. You undoubtedly know that the Viet Cong made booby traps out of old ration tins and shell casings. The Afghans did the same thing to the Russians, and are doing it again to us, from what I hear. The less we leave behind, the better."

It was then that I thought of the camera.

"Speaking of left behind, Professor, do you have your video camera?"

He didn't, of course, so Lavon asked Decius if we could go back and retrieve it, explaining that the good Doctor had dropped his money bag in his haste to flee the Zealots.

Decius agreed, and we went trotting back down the hill. We started at the cave's mouth and headed west, intending to retrace his steps. As I suspected, Bryson couldn't track his own backside, so it fell to me to find his trail, which I did after a short search.

As in all dry climates, the morning had warmed quickly. Though I was more comfortable, this left one downside: the air reeked of hacked off limbs, rotting intestines, and other detritus of the earlier battle.

I glanced over to Bryson and grinned. I'm not exactly fond of such things, but I got a bit of undeserved enjoyment from his queasiness. So far, his return chips had failed; and our lives hung in the balance.

"I assume your wife can operate the control room by herself, without that young fool's assistance?" I said.

"His name was Scott," replied Bryson. "He was my most promising student."

"What do you think he did?" I asked. "Sneak in on his own, or did he blackmail her by threatening to go to the media, or to the police to report your disappearance?"

"Blackmail?" he replied. "Is that all your twisted mind can think of?"

"It's why *we're* here, Professor."

Bryson turned and stared. "What?"

"Like we told you earlier, Juliet wanted to send only Dr. Lavon. He was the logical choice, since he's studied this region for years and is the only one among us able to communicate properly with the locals. This, by the way, was Lavon's choice, too. He wasn't very excited to have company."

"So why *are* the rest of you here?"

"Ray decided he wanted to go, too. Once he accepted the idea that you had actually managed to pull this off, no one could stop him."

"Surely Juliet tried?"

"She did, but Ray brought up the contract you had with his father. If he couldn't go, he threatened to shut your whole operation down, which, of course, would have left you – "

"Lying in that cave."

"Yes."

"What about the woman? Why is she here?"

"Lavon leads a university archaeological team. Conducting a dig according to the most rigorous scientific principles can be an expensive proposition. Sharon's family has provided the majority of their funding for the past three years."

"So she threatened to close his project down, too."

"Something like that."

"That doesn't explain why you're here. What is it you want?"

"Well, if we're discussing blackmail, I wanted to speak with you about how to split up that billion dollars you made."

Bryson jaw dropped and he stared at me with wild eyes.

I laughed. "Just kidding, Professor." *Sort of.*

He wasn't quite sure how to respond, so he just followed along as I traced his path. It wasn't pretty. His trail crossed the tracks of the fleeing Zealots. Dried blood covered part of a footprint, and carrion-eaters had not yet carried off the chunks of human entrails lying next to a rock a few feet away.

I pointed to the remains and grew serious. "You asked me what I wanted, Professor? Actually, I'd like nothing more than to get the five of us together, press this button, and go back to Boston while we still can."

But he never responded. Just then, his trail became so obvious that even he could trace it. He charged forward.

"Here it is," he shouted, holding the video camera high in triumph.

"You, um, might not want anyone else to see that," I said.

He dropped his arm quickly, with a sheepish grin on his face. "Of course."

***

In a less dangerous moment, I would have found Bryson's transformation fascinating. Less than an hour earlier, he had wailed over his dead lab assistant like a long lost son. Now that he had his camera, he didn't give the kid another thought, so single-minded he had become.

I asked him about it, and he explained that we could return and retrieve Scott the same way we had come back for him.

Assuming we survived, I thought, but I decided not to argue.

We went back to the cave to recover the kid's chip – having no value to the soldiers, they had left it dangling on the string around his neck – but otherwise, prudence dictated that we not linger. The Roman column had disappeared around a bend, and nearby, I spotted a hacked-off forearm lying beside a small scrub bush. Something, vultures probably, had already taken a nibble.

"I suggest we get back. These people might have friends, and I don't think we want to be around if they show up."

***

I asked Bryson to hand me the camera in exchange for my money bag, just in case Decius asked the Professor to demonstrate what he had found, but my concerns were unfounded. The Roman said nothing to us when we returned. Instead, he and the wounded men in the wagon appeared to be telling each other jokes.

My first platoon sergeant had done the same thing, and for the same reason, I guessed: to lift their spirits and thus enhance their odds of survival.

The rest of our party was in surprisingly good humor as well, despite the fact that by modern Western standards, they had seen more than a lifetime's worth of violent death. Once we pulled away from the scene itself, Bryson, Lavon and Sharon began to relate to each other their impressions of what they had witnessed.

Only Markowitz stayed out of the conversation. He just stared back in silence at the birds circling over the battle site.

After a little while, I grew concerned. "You OK there, buddy?" I asked.

He didn't reply.

Without acknowledging me at all, he stepped over to Lavon and tugged on his shoulder. "Robert, can you ask this centurion what will happen to those bodies?"

Lavon did so, but the Roman officer just looked at him blankly and shrugged, as if unable to comprehend why anyone would care.

Quite frankly, I wondered the same thing.

Decius turned and said something to the men in the wagon. It must have been another joke, for the injured soldiers began laughing uproariously.

Lavon told me later what they had said.

"The dogs and vultures must eat, too," replied one of the legionnaires. "Would the gods approve of us depriving them of their sustenance?"

As the soldiers burst out in laughter again, Lavon chuckled along with them. As for me, I put the issue out of my mind.

I shouldn't have.

Chapter 18

We marched for close to an hour before Publius brought our column to a halt just outside a small village. As soon as we stopped, the Romans launched into a well-drilled routine. Two lookouts scrambled up the nearest hill, about twenty yards away, where they stood with their backs to each other, each scanning a semicircle for potential threats.

Two unlucky squads – the Roman term was *contuburnia*, Lavon explained – remained on guard while the others dropped their heavy burdens and quickly found shade underneath nearby olive trees, though an additional group of soldiers did not begin their break until they had erected an improvised cover to shield the wounded men in the wagon from the sun.

As the soldiers rested, four servants who had accompanied them carried jugs of water and ladled refreshment out to each man before scurrying back to the center of the village to fill their containers from a crudely dug well.

Like the soldiers, Bryson and Markowitz headed for some large rocks underneath a shade tree. By contrast, Lavon and Bergfeld ran straight up a small hill to the edge of a three-foot stone wall that enclosed a flat, hard-packed surface about twenty-five feet in diameter. I decided to join them.

Sharon trained her sight on what looked like a sled leaning against the opposite side. Pieces of it were flaking away at the edges, and compounding its bedraggled appearance, dozens of rock fragments were embedded into the wood on one side. To me, it belonged either in a landfill or as décor in a cheap, all-you-can-eat steak house.

"Wow, check that out!" she said.

Lavon seemed equally excited. I followed them around the wall's perimeter but finally had to ask.

"What's so interesting about that piece of junk?"

The subject of their enthusiasm turned out to be a threshing floor, and what I took for a sled was actually the threshing machine. Local farmers would pile their sheaves of grain on the hard surface and hook up the sled behind a donkey or an ox, fragment side down.

Then, they'd pile stones on top of the sled for extra weight, and the animal would drag the thing back and forth, shredding the sheaves and separating the grain from the straw. The whole process sounded terribly inefficient.

"I thought they just threw it up in the air and let the wind blow away the chaff," I said.

"That was the next step," Bergfeld replied.

I was right about the inefficiency, though. Lavon explained that anyone who could afford to mounted iron blades on the underside of the sled. This thing was better than nothing, but just barely.

"These people are really poor," he said.

I glanced around at the surrounding structures and could not argue. Only in the loosest definition of the term could they be called buildings. The best of them consisted of rough, unfinished stone, held together by an altogether inadequate amount of mortar. Most didn't even have roofs. Instead, they were covered by a thick black fabric.

"It's goat hair," said Lavon. "It works better than you'd think. The hair expands as it gets wet, so it does a reasonably good job of keeping out the rain; and when it dries, the small open spaces allow for some air circulation."

I mumbled something about preferring shingles, but they paid me no mind and went charging ahead. I followed along and stood behind them as they poked their noses into the next house. Inside this one, a crude, unfinished table rested in the center, while two equally rudimentary benches sat to either side. One had toppled backwards.

The occupants had mounted a rough-hewn wooden shelf on the back wall, but it held nothing; and the only other object in sight was a broken pot on the floor.

"Someone left in a hurry," I said.

"I think they all did," said Lavon. "They probably heard the soldiers coming and decided not to stick around. I'm sure word of the skirmish this morning has already gone ahead."

That jolted me into glancing back toward the road. Given the side we had chosen – or rather had chosen for us – I didn't want to be too far from the Romans if any of the village's residents decided to come back early.

My companions, though, had other things on their minds. By the time I caught up to them at the top of the next hill, they were chattering excitedly; this time over a house on the other side – built atop what looked like a cave.

"It's nice to know modern archaeology got something right," said Lavon. "This is exactly what I've always pictured a first century Judean house looking like."

"The family stays upstairs," said Bergfeld. "When the weather is nice, as it often is around here, they'll sleep under the stars on the flat roof."

"Who lives on the lower level? Livestock?"

"Yes," said Lavon, "along with household servants, if they have any. It's quite a clever setup. They take full advantage of the terrain in an environment where construction lumber is prohibitively expensive."

I glanced back around. "Clever" wasn't the first word that occurred to me.

Taken as a whole, the ramshackle village reminded me of a more primitive version of a third world shantytown, though I suppose as in those places, these people did the best with what they had, which wasn't much.

"Jesus would have been born in something like this," said Lavon.

"This?" I asked.

"Not this particular town, of course, but it was this kind of house, we think. The upstairs part was full, so Mary and Joseph had to go to the lower level. It wasn't quite as bad as the modern English version of the Christmas story makes it out to be. The mean old innkeeper wasn't exiling them to the barn."

"Childbirth without anesthetics – that would have been the bad part," said Bergfeld.

I had never thought of it that way, nor had most men I was sure.

"How many people would you estimate live here?" I asked.

Lavon studied the village for a moment. "I'd guess about a hundred, more or less," he said. "Bethlehem was probably about the same size," he added.

"It's an area the church's critics get wrong," said Bergfeld. "Some of them say that Herod's slaughter of the infants never took place, since no source outside the Bible mentions it."

"What they don't understand," said Lavon, "is that in the scheme of things in the ancient world, such an event – though tragic to the families involved – would have barely registered a blip."

This day was turning out to be full of surprises, and we had barely begun. I had always pictured Bethlehem as a small but thriving town. Growing up, the priests had made Herod's actions sound like the massacre of a large American grade school. I told them so.

This was not unusual.

"I grew up with the same impression," said Lavon. "But a town of this size wouldn't have held more than a handful of boys of the requisite age. Plus, they were peasants. No one else really cared."

I was about to ask another question when we heard a trumpet blow, so we turned to head back. We walked toward the east, making a circle along the back side of the village.

As we neared the road, we encountered the only local residents who had remained behind. One miserable old woman kneaded dough, while her equally wretched companion placed it onto hot rocks, which she then covered with a flat clay pan.

A thin, faded tan-colored shawl covered each of their heads, while the rest of their clothing consisted of little more than rags. Neither woman even bothered to look up.

"They're so pitiful," said Bergfeld. "I wonder why they didn't run like the others?"

I guessed it was because they had nothing left to lose.

Finally, one of them glanced at us, and Lavon reached under his tunic and pulled out two *denarii* – Roman coins worth about a day's wage for an unskilled laborer. He tossed one to each woman.

Feeling a bit ashamed, I reached into my money pouch and did the same.

The trumpet blew again before we had time to do more, so we hustled back to the wagon. Decius watched us approach and greeted Lavon with a broad smile.

"Ah, Lavonius, you're back," he said. "You can tell your companions that they will no longer need to see Egypt. After such a wonder as this, they will undoubtedly find the Alexandria Lighthouse disappointing."

The nearby Romans burst out laughing, as did we after Lavon translated. We all stood there for a minute or two while the soldiers talked amongst themselves; then Sharon interrupted with a question.

"Do you know the name of this village?"

None of them did, so Decius dispatched an Aramaic-speaking legionnaire to ask the two women. Moments later, the young man came trotting back.

"Emmaus," he said.

Bergfeld and Lavon stared at each other for a brief instant before quickly turning away and staring at the ground.

"I'll be damned," I heard him mutter.

Decius eyed them curiously, as did I. I had heard the name before, but couldn't for the life of me think of where. But that wasn't my real concern. I could see the obvious question running through the Roman's mind: how would travelers from the edge of the world have heard of such a pathetic little place?

I went back to the wagon to check on the wounded soldier I had treated and told Sharon to follow with some water. I made sure Decius saw it, too, better to reinforce the notion that we were useful people, worth keeping alive.

Jerusalem During the Time of Christ

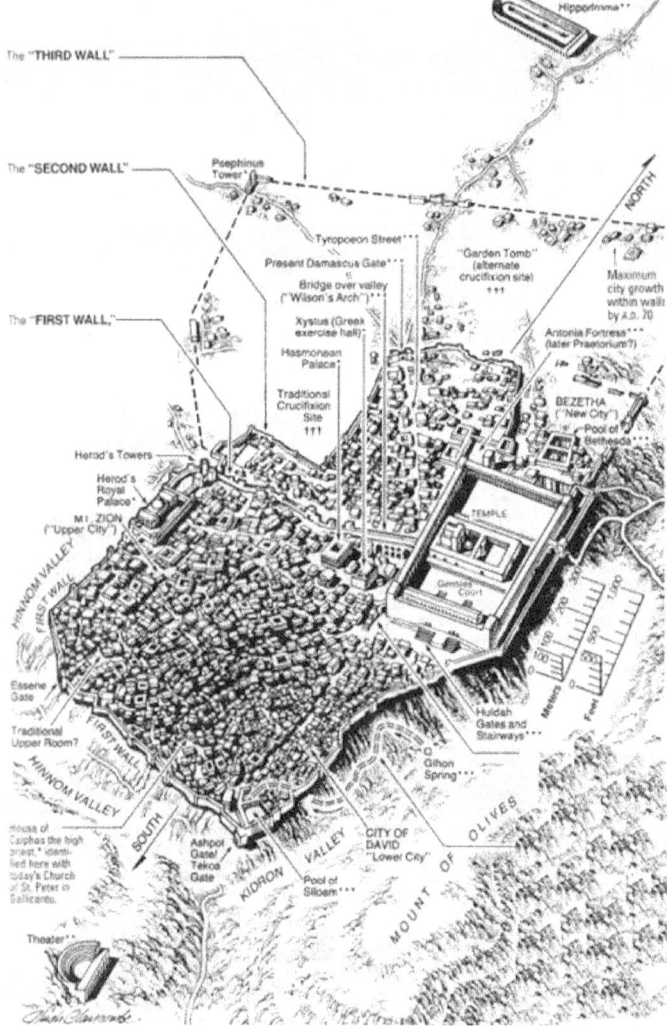

Hippodrome

The "THIRD WALL"

The "SECOND WALL"

Psephinus Tower

Tyropoeon Street

Present Damascus Gate

Bridge over valley ("Wilson's Arch")

Xystus (Greek exercise hall)

Hasmonean Palace

The "FIRST WALL,"

Traditional Crucifixion Site

Herod's Towers

Herod's Royal Palace

Mt. ZION ("Upper City")

HINNOM VALLEY

FIRST WALL

Essene Gate

Traditional Upper Room?

HINNOM VALLEY

House of Caiphas the high priest," identified here with today's Church of St. Peter in Gallicanto.

Theater

FIRST WALL

SOUTH

Ashpot Gate/ Tekoa Gate

KIDRON VALLEY

Pool of Siloam

CITY OF DAVID "Lower City"

Gihon Spring

Huldah Gates and Stairways

TEMPLE

Gentiles Court

BEZETHA ("New City")

Pool of Bethesda

Antonia Fortress (later Praetorium?)

"Garden Tomb" (alternate crucifixion site)

Maximum city growth within walls by A.D. 70

NORTH

MOUNT OF OLIVES

Vista Bible Royalty, copyright © used by permission of Zondervan

Chapter 19

The soldiers re-packed and formed a marching column with their customary efficiency. Seeing that all was in order, Publius gave the command and we trundled forward once more to the east. As before, Sharon rode in the wagon and did her best to tend to the injured Romans, while the rest of us kept pace on foot.

Once we had settled into a rhythm, I pulled Lavon aside.

"Decius noticed that you recognized the name of that village," I said.

"I know," he admitted. "It took me by surprise."

"Why was it so important?"

"Luke's Gospel records that after the Resurrection, Jesus met two of his followers walking down the road from Jerusalem to Emmaus. They didn't recognize him, and he had a little fun with them. He pretended to be a stranger who knew nothing of what had happened in Jerusalem over the previous few days."

I was still confused. "OK, but that doesn't explain the significance of the place."

He considered this for a moment.

"It's not the location," he finally replied. "It's the name itself. In our time, *Road to Emmaus* is the name of a well-known Christian retreat, along with Christian schools, an Orthodox journal, and all sorts of other things related to the church. I always thought of the town as more significant for that reason."

"Is it mentioned anywhere else in the Bible?" I asked.

He shook his head. "I don't think so."

"I'm starting to think I should have paid more attention in Sunday school," I said.

It was not the last time I would find myself echoing that sentiment over the next few days.

Both of us pondered this for a few minutes; then Lavon glanced over toward Bergfeld.

"We might have another problem as well," he said. "Decius asked about her. Who was she? How was she related to the rest of us?"

"And?"

"I told him she was the second daughter of her father, our king."

I gave Lavon an odd look. That wasn't the story we had cooked up in Boston.

"I know," he sighed. "It sounds really stupid. But we need to protect her, and I thought that if she were a princess, the soldiers would be less likely to molest her. In the first century, the daughter of a merchant, even a rich one, was often just another trading commodity."

"Did he buy it?"

Lavon shrugged. "Maybe. He commented that her clothing did not match her station. I answered that by telling him we concealed her status because we were a small party, unable to defend ourselves against robbers. We didn't want to make ourselves any more of a target than we already were."

"That sounds reasonable enough," I replied.

"Yes, but now we're safe from attack. He seems genuinely puzzled as to why she is still helping his soldiers instead of sitting back and expecting everyone to wait on her hand and foot. I think that has been his usual experience with the royal families around here."

"How did you explain that?"

"I said our king required all women of high rank to spend time serving others, to keep them from becoming mean-spirited."

He struggled not to laugh. Obviously Decius knew nothing about the ferocious social competition of the Dallas charity ball circuit. From Lavon's description, it was even more intense than that of his native Atlanta.

"So what do we do now?" he finally asked. "What should I say if he brings up the subject again?"

I advised him to let it rest for the moment. "We'll have to pretend to give Sharon some deference, though," I added.

As soon as I did, I wished I hadn't. Lavon glanced backward and waited for her to notice him. Then he bowed obsequiously, leaving her wondering just what on God's green earth that was about.

Decius saw it, too, and though he chose not to comment, I had a suspicion that he would make inquiry at some point. I could see the wheels of his mind turning, trying to resolve a puzzle with a more than a few pieces still out of place.

***

For the moment, though, there was nothing to do but march on, and that's what we did. We proceeded uneventfully for another hour as the road weaved its way through low, rocky, scrub-covered hills.

At first, we didn't see many other travelers, although we could hear the bleating of sheep being driven on parallel tracks about a hundred yards to either side.

Perhaps the Romans had laws against flocks of animals soiling their roads. With everything that transpired later, I never found the opportunity to ask.

A short while later, Publius called for another break and the Romans went through the same well-drilled procedure – though with different squads stuck on guard duty.

Based on the Biblical account of the journey to Emmaus and the time we had traveled, Lavon guessed that we were about four miles from the city center. He and Bergfeld both stared up at two big hills to our right, trying to identify vaguely familiar landmarks.

"I think the modern freeway passes just over there," she said. "We're getting close."

Lavon concurred. As for me, I could only shake my head at the incongruity of it all.

Sharon's assessment of the geography turned out to be correct, and once we started up again, it wasn't long before the city itself hove into view for the first time.

We all stopped in our tracks at the sight. Although it's a bit embarrassing to recount, I'll have to admit that I stood and gaped along with the rest of them, like backwoods hillbillies seeing tall buildings for the first time.

I had not expected to be impressed. I had done the tourist circuits across the globe and had become jaded to old ruins. After a while, one pile of ancient bricks was the same as another.

But *this* Jerusalem was not a museum piece.

The city itself stretched for about a mile from end to end. An outer wall, varying between forty and sixty feet high, ringed the perimeter, which was interspersed with taller battlements spaced about a hundred feet apart.

Situated, as it was, at the top of a hill, the picture was even more imposing. One didn't have to be an old soldier like myself to shudder at the hazards of attacking this place.

Lavon explained that the fortifications were constructed mostly of tan crystalline limestone, known in modern times as *meleke*. These glowed in the mid-afternoon sun, only adding to the splendor.

"Match what you expected?" I said to Lavon.

"Honestly, I don't know yet," he replied.

As it turns out, much of what modern researchers know of Roman-era Jerusalem derives from a single source, the writings of the slippery Josephus, whose actions in the Great Revolt suggest that scholars employ at least a modicum of caution when interpreting his works.

Lavon directed my attention to three tall towers at the city's mid-section which rose to a height of about twice that of the nearby walls. "How tall would you say those are?" he asked.

My eyes went back and forth from the towers to the people passing by on the road running just underneath the walls. Given the distance, I found it a bit hard to judge.

"Eighty or ninety feet," I guessed.

"According to what I've read, the tallest one was 130 feet."

I shrugged. "Maybe they added on to it later?"

"Perhaps," said Lavon, though he remarked upon one other bit of modern conjecture that was clearly incorrect. A popular scale model of the ancient city in the Israel Museum depicted the center tower, the Phasael Tower, as square while the other two were rounded at the top, with a columnar base.

But we could see that only the southernmost tower bore that design, and the tower to the northeast, the Hippicus Tower, had no exterior columns at all.

I didn't say anything else. I had a feeling that a lot of what we thought we knew would turn out to be wrong – a sensation which proved to be accurate, and concerned matters of far greater importance than the height of a tower.

***

Despite our fascination, we couldn't linger. The Roman column had gone on about two hundred yards ahead when we heard a sharp command from Decius urging us to keep up.

It didn't take long to see why.

As we got closer to the city, a growing tide of humanity began to travel in our wake. Though the pilgrims prudently gave our column wide berth, the more I studied their faces, the more their increasing numbers began to make me uneasy.

One glance at Decius told me that I was not alone in my apprehension.

To say that the locals were not overjoyed with our presence would be an understatement. Some, mostly young women, clasped their shawls tight and kept their heads down in an effort to avoid eye contact. The majority, though, stood to the side of the road and stared straight ahead as we passed, their expressions sullen and resentful.

"I don't exactly feel the love," I said to Lavon.

He shook his head.

"Those people hate us," said Bergfeld. Her face could not conceal the fact that she found this deeply unsettling.

Making matters worse, a handful of young men glared at our procession with such undisguised odium that even the most hardened Romans grew nervous. I watched several of the legionnaires grip their weapons tighter, and the casual banter so common among soldiers on the march had ceased.

"Foreign occupation by godless degenerates," Lavon explained. "And the Romans return the favor. They view the people in Jerusalem as uncultivated savages, longing for the imagined glory days of David and Solomon a thousand years earlier."

As always, the real story was a bit more complicated, but that was the heart of the matter. At least, thank God, they didn't have IEDs.

"I wouldn't want to meet any of those fellows in the dark of night," I said.

Lavon glanced back and forth at them as well, but was careful not to let his gaze linger. Neither of us was sure what it would take to set them off, and a person didn't have to know much about counterinsurgency tactics to realize that the second these people thought they could get away with it, we'd have one hell of a fight on our hands.

Few of the pilgrims wanted to force a conflict, I was sure, but the atmosphere was so tense that it might just take one hothead –

I looked over to the supply wagon, glanced at Sharon, and then turned my attention to the spare swords and spears at the bottom. Fortunately, my true thoughts managed to escape notice, though Lavon did perceive my interest in the weapons.

"You ever use one of those things?" he asked.

I laughed. At one point in my career, I had spent six months in England, assigned to a squad whose commander led an enthusiastic Roman-era reenactment crew – fighting Caesar's landing every other weekend.

"Only enough to be a danger to myself and innocent bystanders," I replied. "What about you?"

He shook his head. "It wasn't part of the curriculum at Parris Island."

This surprised me; I never took him for a Marine.

"Lance Corporal Robert Lavon – retired," he said. "In return for a few years with Uncle Sam's Misguided Children, the GI Bill paid for most of my college education."

"See any action?"

He chuckled. "The closest I got was as an embassy guard in Beijing. I had orders to check everyone and everything going into the building; and you know how these politicians on fact-finding junkets can be when they forget their ID."

I laughed, imagining Senator Blowhard turning red in the face with the *do-you-know-who-I-am* routine. Half of his own constituents probably wouldn't recognize him. Why should some Jarhead on the other side of the world?

"And you?" he asked.

"Oh, a little bit; here and there," I replied.

Chapter 20

Before he could inquire further, we crested another low hill and for the first time, we could see over the outer wall and into the grand panorama of the Temple complex. Once again, we gave our best impressions of gawking hicks from the back of beyond, and once again, Decius had to call out for us to catch up.

We had arrived at just the right time of day. The tan *meleke* glowed almost white in the early afternoon sun, a spectacle enhanced by the rays sparkling from the gold trim along the top.

"Wow," said Bergfeld. "It's magnificent."

The others responded in the same way.

Markowitz, though, said nothing. He just stood there, mumbling something I didn't understand, over and over.

Decius called out again, and I had to gently prod Ray forward, and even then, his eyes never strayed from the building. Roman engineers had paved this part of the road, too, so I had the additional task of keeping him from tripping over the curb.

"Just think," said Bryson, "you're the first Jew to see this in two thousand years."

Markowitz didn't reply. He just continued to stare at the Temple and kept on with his mumbling. Finally, he took a couple of steps over to Lavon and tapped him on the shoulder.

"Robert, where is the Western Wall? Can you show me what part of the Temple survived?"

The Jerusalem of Christ's time consisted of two elevated areas separated by valley running along a north-south line through the center of town. Herod's palace, including the three tall towers, dominated the western portion, which was known as the Upper City and served as the home of Jerusalem's wealthy elite.

A long stone bridge, barely visible from where we walked, spanned the valley from the Upper City to the Temple Mount. Lavon pointed to it.

"In modern times, we call what's left of that bridge Wilson's Arch," he said. "Now, look off to its right, to the southwestern corner of the Temple compound."

Markowitz turned his eyes towards the top of the section Lavon had pointed out. "I can see it," he said.

Lavon shook his head. "No, the upper part was torn down. The only thing that survived was the retaining wall underneath. That's the Wailing Wall. The Romans destroyed everything else."

Markowitz didn't reply. He stared at the soldiers for a few minutes as he considered this, occasionally glancing back to the Temple.

"These Romans." he finally said.

"*These* Romans are keeping us alive," I reminded him.

"That's right," said Lavon. "Besides, by the time the revolt started, most of these guys were already dead, and those who weren't were hobbling around with canes and looking for their teeth – or whatever old people did back then."

We all laughed, and Markowitz smiled. I could see it was forced, but he didn't want to raise a stink. None of us did, really.

That included the Romans.

I looked ahead and saw Publius whisper quietly to the standard bearer at his side. The soldier, sporting a wolf's head over his helmet, walked back double-time to the wagon with the *signum* – the unit's standard that displayed its numerous commendations for distinguished service. He took the standard off its pole and carefully, almost reverently, wrapped it in a thick red velvet blanket.

Afterward, the *signifer* removed his wolf skin and wrapped it with equal care in another red blanket. Then he squeezed himself into the wagon and squatted next to his parcels. One of his wounded colleagues moved over to give him room.

"What's he doing?" asked Markowitz.

"Something smart," said Lavon. "Publius knows it's provocative, so he sent his standard bearer back to cover it up. As you know, the Second of the Ten Commandments forbids "graven images," which the more traditional-minded segments of the population interpreted as *any* representation of a man or an animal."

The two sides' mutual incomprehension on this subject proved to be a fertile source of conflict from the beginning of the Roman occupation until the crushing of the final revolt. The possibility of miscalculation was enormous, even in the best of times.

Just to be sure of his interpretation, Lavon questioned Decius, and the Roman confirmed what he had suspected.

He didn't seem to like it very much.

Chapter 21

When we reached a point about a quarter mile from the gate, a soldier on the tallest battlement blew a trumpet, and our trumpeter blew his acknowledgment in return.

Lavon, though, paid this activity little attention. His eyes remained riveted on the gate itself – a straightforward, practical structure conveying a sense of solidity and strength.

Massive stone blocks overlaid an arch resembling an upside down U. Two battlements, twice the height of the surrounding wall, flanked the gate itself. Both were well equipped with slits for archers and gaps through which defenders could rain heavy stones or boiling oil down upon their attackers from any direction.

"You seem surprised," I said.

"It's not quite what I expected," he replied. "The Damascus gate still exists – in our world. I took a tour group through it only a month ago."

"It looks like this?"

"Not at all. It's smaller, and the stonework is much more elaborate."

He paused for a moment and looked around.

"Of course, this one does serve a real defensive purpose. The Ottomans built the modern gate in 1542, long after gunpowder weapons had rendered stone fortifications obsolete. They could afford to be decorative."

That made sense.

"You have one problem, though," I said. "When we get back, how are you going to convince anyone that your version is correct as opposed to all of those artist's conceptions floating around?"

It was a question he couldn't answer, and we both knew it.

"I haven't quite worked that out yet."

We never made any more progress resolving that issue, for at that moment, Sharon let out a horrified gasp.

Each of us turned in her direction, where we were confronted by the most gruesome spectacle I have ever had the misfortune to witness.

The nightmares still occasionally return.

Just off the side of the road, at the junction between the road we were on and the path running along the city wall to the southwest, stood what had once been the trunks of a dozen olive trees.

Horizontal beams were lashed to two of them, and hanging from those beams, suspended by nails, were objects that first appeared only as dark, reddened gelatinous masses. Shreds of flesh dangled downward from each, and both were covered almost entirely by hideous swarms of black flies.

Psychologists tell us that our minds have their own internal tricks to avert recognition of true horror, and it took us a few seconds to internalize that these ghastly objects were in fact men, still alive, with their faces contorted in agony and desperation.

Markowitz took one glance and immediately ran to the other side of the road, where he knelt and heaved his insides out. Bergfeld held her head down with her hands over her eyes, while Bryson stood motionless, transfixed by the dreadfulness of it all.

The next few minutes passed in a blur. I struggled to focus my attention forward and put the spectacle out of my head, but after we had gone about fifty more yards, Decius glanced back and saw that Markowitz and Bryson had not moved. Markowitz, in fact, remained on his knees, with his head down and his eyes staring blankly into the pool of vomit.

Decius said something to Lavon, but the archaeologist had turned pale as well and didn't respond. Since I could gather the gist of what the *optio* was trying to say, I went back to retrieve the others.

I saw no guard around the victims, so I reached into my first aid kit and ripped open two white packets. I removed the small cylinders, pulled off the lids, and jabbed one into the foot of each man.

I got lucky. Both had visible veins.

I turned and pushed Bryson in the back toward the general direction of the city; then I lifted Markowitz up by his robe.

"Hurry up," I said. "Let's get out of here."

I gave them both another shove, and we pressed forward in silence, with Markowitz still wiping the spittle from his mouth. It wasn't until we had almost reached the tail end of our column that Bryson finally spoke.

"What did you give them, cyanide?"

"Sufentanil," I replied. "It's a synthetic opioid; like morphine, only much stronger."

Bryson glanced back, as did I. Both victims' heads had dropped.

"Are they dead?" he asked.

I shrugged. The dosage I had given them would keep them unconscious for the next three to four hours. I could only hope nature would take its course by then.

At least I had tried.

When we got back to the wagon, our party remained visibly shaken. Those of us who hadn't grown up Catholic had all, at one point or another, made the tourist circuits through the cathedrals of Europe. The crucifix looked nothing at all like what we had just seen.

Lavon closed his eyes, hoping to banish the image from his memory, though I knew he would never completely succeed. He mumbled something to Sharon about the hymn-writer having it wrong – that there was nothing *wondrous* about any of this – but she only gave a weak half nod and grunted in reply.

His words struck me as a restatement of the obvious, though I wasn't quite sure what he was talking about and decided not to press the issue.

Lavon finally explained that that the cross had not become the outward, visible symbol of Christianity until the latter half of the fourth century – after at least a generation had passed who had been unfortunate enough to see one for real.

The logic of that was not difficult to comprehend. Nor would any of us find it hard to refute the idea, still bandied about by fringe conspiracy theorists, that Jesus had somehow survived his execution.

For one thing, I doubt he would have wanted to.

Hospitals would run out of sutures before the wounds from that type of flogging could be sewn up, and without a massive infusion of antibiotics, infection would have killed him within a month anyway – a month in which he would have known nothing but the most intense and terrible pain.

Lavon spoke quietly. "Now we know what Paul meant by the stumbling block."

Sharon just stared ahead. "I never really understood until now."

"You couldn't have, could you?"

She shook her head. "No."

"Understand what?" asked Markowitz.

"In his letter to the church in Corinth, Paul wrote about people not accepting Christ's message because of the stumbling block of the cross," she replied.

"In other words," said Lavon, "how could a Lord, the Son of God, die in such a horrible and degrading manner?"

I couldn't argue with that.

For the next few minutes, we walked forward in silence. In fact, none of us even noticed that we had passed through the Damascus Gate and into the city itself.

"Who do you think those men were?" Bryson finally asked. "I glanced up at the sign above their heads, but I couldn't read it."

I had seen it, too. A wooden placard described their crimes in three languages, none of which I could understand.

"The Greek word is *lestes*, answered Lavon. "Literally, it means 'bandit,' but in our world, we'd pick a different term – 'terrorist,' probably. Not just an ordinary brigand, but one acting from a political or religious motive."

"Zealots, then?" asked Markowitz. "Jews fighting the Romans, like the ones we saw earlier today?"

Lavon nodded. "Probably."

Chapter 22

A few minutes later, we got another reminder of the seething cauldron into which we had inserted ourselves.

Our column passed through a narrow alleyway that ran between a continuous row of three story stone buildings. A small boy – he couldn't have been older than five or six – stood in a third floor window. Sharon looked up at him and waved.

The kid giggled and waved in return for a brief moment before we saw a hand reach out and jerk him back into the apartment. We heard shouting, and though we could not understand the words, the scolding tone was not hard to interpret.

The boy protested, and moments later we cringed as we heard the impact of a slap. The child bawled for a few seconds before a second slap brought about a pitiful whimper.

We looked back to see a weather-beaten old woman step up to the window and make a rude gesture, before spitting in a truculent display of loathing and disgust.

Bergfeld turned to Lavon, her expression uncomprehending.

"All I did was wave."

Lavon just shook his head, as did I.

For all we knew, that woman's son was one of the poor unfortunates writhing in agony outside the city gate. Perhaps her husband, or father, or brothers had lost their lives fighting the Romans.

Or maybe her family had been driven off the land by the crushing burden of taxation; or worse, her inability to pay the ruthless and corrupt tax farmers may have forced her to sell a daughter into a life of degradation and slavery.

The possibilities were endless as they were terrible.

***

We didn't have long to reflect, though. A minute later, we turned another corner and entered a broad plaza. A ten-story crenellated wall on the opposite side dominated the square. Archers stood at the top, guarding their colleagues' entry.

"It's called the Antonia," said Lavon. "The first Herod built this fortress about 75 years ago and named it after his patron Mark Antony."

That seemed odd.

"I thought Antony lost," I said.

"He did," Lavon replied, "but Herod had a unique ability to curry favor with whoever held power in Rome. Unlike his contemporaries, he never sidestepped the fact he had chosen the wrong side. Instead, he told Augustus that he had had served Antony proudly, but would now serve his new master with equal devotion."

"Obviously it worked," said Bryson.

"Yeah," he replied, "though I'm not sure Augustus had any other good candidates for the job. Despite his nasty personal reputation, Herod had demonstrated that he could keep order in a troublesome part of their world, which is what the Romans really cared about at the time."

"Our son of a bitch," I muttered.

Markowitz and Bergfeld eyed me strangely, but I didn't reply. President Eisenhower had made that crack about a brutal Central American dictator who had proven adept at fighting the Communists. It was an era they were too young to recall.

"I thought a Roman governor ran Jerusalem," said Bryson.

Lavon nodded. "One does now, though when Herod died, his kingdom was divided among three of his sons. The trouble was, the one who got Jerusalem inherited all of his father's cruel bloody-mindedness without a speck of his administrative ability. After a few years, the Romans got rid of him and installed their own man."

***

The soldiers we traveled with, however, couldn't have cared less about governors. When they saw the fortress, the men spontaneously surged forward, like horses returning to the barn after a long, tiring ride.

The gate opened from the inside, and we pressed on until we halted near the center of an open courtyard about the size of a football field. I glanced up and counted eight rings of windows lining the walls, along with stone-lined passages into the interior.

"It's bigger than it looked in those drawings," said Bergfeld.

Lavon also seemed surprised by the scale of the place.

"The artists' renditions don't do it justice," he said.

He steered our attention to the battlements. "At least this part is as Josephus described it. A few modern scholars have argued that the fort contained only one main battlement, but here, you can see that there are four; one at each corner."

This made sense to me. I guessed that each one stood about forty feet above the rest of the fortress. Unfortunately, our circumstances were unlikely to afford us the opportunity to take more exact measurements.

As soon as we stopped, Publius called the men to attention and gave a brief speech, which, from his troops' demeanor, sounded like congratulations for a job well done.

Their day wasn't over, though. After being dismissed, the soldiers first stacked their shields on a rack along the front wall, where specialists inspected each one for damage and made chalk marks on the ones needing repair.

As they did this, I helped Sharon off the wagon; then Lavon and I carried stretchers bearing the wounded Romans to a shady spot. Attendants took them from us at that point and toted them inside – presumably to what passed for a hospital. I wasn't sure what I could do, so I made no effort to follow them.

After a short break for water and a bite to eat, the soldiers set to work preparing their armor and weapons for whatever lay next, turning the courtyard into a veritable hive of industry.

Slaves brought wire brushes and joined the soldiers in scrubbing off the gore and the bits of rust that had accumulated earlier that day. Once they had finished this, others polished the armor with cloths until they could see their own reflections.

Additional servants turned grindstones as the soldiers re-sharpened their own swords, with each man stepping back occasionally to test his weapon for a razor-sharp edge; while still others applied oil to leather straps and repaired torn cloth.

I glanced over to Lavon. "Brings back memories, doesn't it?"

As lowly recruits, both of us had spent hours after long training marches cleaning our rifles and equipment before we were allowed any rest.

***

Publius didn't stick around to watch. His men knew what to do, and he had other tasks to complete. Just after he dismissed the soldiers, an older man in a white tunic stepped out from the shadows.

The centurion saluted him and then followed him back into the fortress – no doubt to give a brief summary of the day's activities before spending the remainder of his evening producing a report, in triplicate.

"Do you think that's the governor?" asked Bryson.

Lavon shrugged. He had no idea what Pilate would have looked like. No one from the modern world did.

We all pondered this for a moment before Sharon noticed an object at the far end of the courtyard. A cylinder, about eight feet tall and roughly the diameter of a telephone pole, had been planted in the stone floor. Two short chains hung from the top, with a metal shackle at each end.

"What's that?" she asked.

"A place none of us want to go," I said.

"Flogging post," said Lavon.

She stared at it a bit longer and then turned back to face us.

"Was this the place?" she asked.

"I don't know," said the archaeologist. "Some scholars say Jesus was scourged here; others say it happened in Herod's palace. The truth is nobody knows for sure."

"I guess we'll find out soon enough," replied Bryson.

HEROD'S TEMPLE

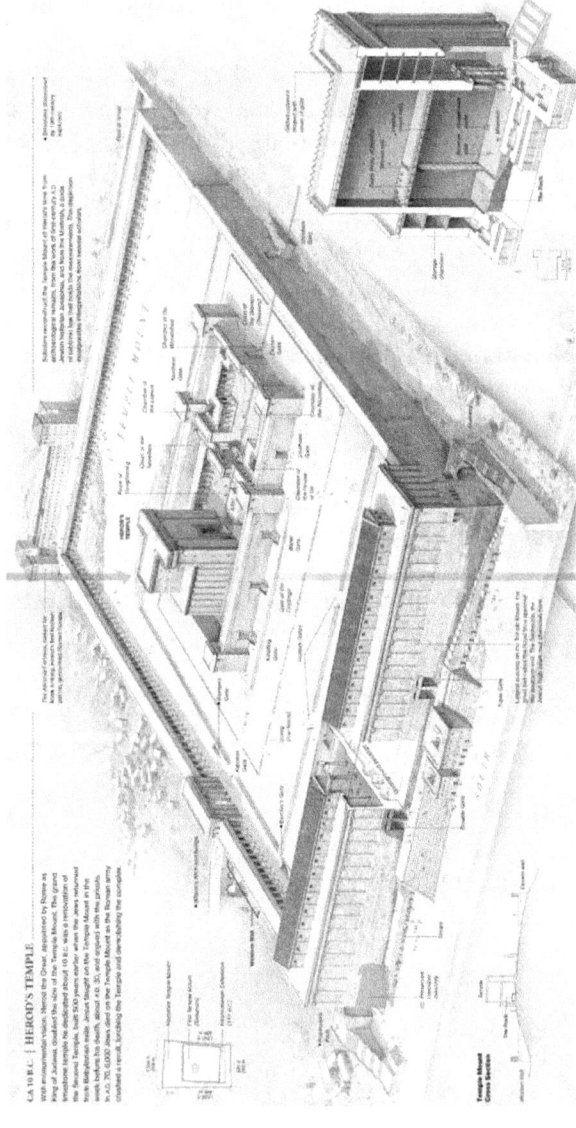

Fernando Batista/National Geographic Stock, used by permission of the National Geographic Society

Chapter 23

We watched the soldiers work for another half hour before a young man wearing sandals and a plain brown tunic approached and beckoned for us to follow. He led us to the southeast corner of the fortress and started up a flight of stairs, taking the steps two at a time all the way to the top.

Except for Bryson, we all made it with a minimum of huffing and puffing. It had to be a test, though of what I wasn't sure; nor could I know whether or not we had passed.

The kid waited patiently at the top landing for the Professor to catch up before leading us down a short corridor and inserting a key into a thick wooden door.

He gestured for us to go inside.

The room was larger than I had expected – about fifteen by thirty feet. The walls were built of the same *meleke* limestone as the rest of the fortress, with thick cedar beams running across the ceiling. Four windows, each about three feet wide, faced the Temple courtyard to the south, while two narrower windows opened to the west, giving the room a red glow from the late afternoon sun.

The furniture was sparse, but functional, as I would have expected in a military establishment. A large bed, wider than king-sized by half, sat in the northeast corner of the room, away from the windows. A wooden table, surrounded by six crude-looking chairs rested in the center.

"What's that?" Sharon asked, referring to a bucket on the floor in the far corner, opposite the bed.

I couldn't help but laugh. "Piss pot," I replied.

She blushed. "Oh."

"Go, if you have to. We'll all turn the other way."

She was about to speak when the young man said something to Lavon.

It must have been about food, because after hearing the archaeologist's response, the man shouted down the stairs. A few minutes later, two slaves appeared carrying warm bread and a jug of wine, followed by two more servants holding five metal goblets and a stack of blankets. The men deposited their cargo without speaking and immediately turned for the door.

After the kid left, I motioned for everyone to gather around the table for a de-brief but quickly realized that it was hopeless. Each of the others raced for a window, where they stood mesmerized by the activity in the Temple courtyard below.

From our vantage point near the top of the southeastern battlement, we could see white-robed priests – drawn by lottery earlier that day – as they completed the evening offering and prepared the Temple for the night.

Each man was dressed identically in a white linen tunic, with a red belt and white linen, turban-like headgear. To our surprise, the priests went about their tasks barefoot.

Bryson edged himself out and around the sill of the far left window in an effort to get a better view.

"Fascinating," he muttered to himself. "Utterly fascinating."

It most assuredly was.

The Temple itself faced to the east and was situated slightly south of center on the broad rectangular Temple Mount, whose flat white surface covered about thirty five acres. From our position, only a few feet below the Temple roof, the setting sun highlighted the gold edging in a spectacularly beautiful way.

Lavon peered straight down and broke out in quiet mirth.

One of his old college professors had published a paper asserting that the Antonia was an integral part of the Temple complex, while a colleague had just as emphatically maintained that the fortress was situated about six hundred feet to the north, connected to the Temple only via breezeways.

In the manner of so many obscure academic quarrels, their dispute had become so bitter that despite having offices in the same building, neither man spoke to the other for more than two years.

Both of them were wrong.

Herod's engineers had been clever, we could see. They had located the south wall of the Antonia about thirty feet from the Temple Mount's perimeter. A system of gates and bridgeways permitted the easy flow of soldiers and materiel from the fortress to the Temple, but would present an almost insurmountable obstacle to anyone trying to get through the other way.

"They appear to know what they're doing," I said – and not for the last time.

Lavon nodded; then he looked up and saw that Bryson had eased himself dangerously close to the window's edge. To make matters worse, we could see the bright red LED on his camera.

Lavon coughed. "Ahem; Professor, you might not want anyone to see you with that thing."

To his credit, Bryson quickly realized his mistake and eased himself back inside.

"By the way," I asked. "How much battery life do you have left?"

Bryson squinted at the small screen. "Three hours; that should be enough."

Lavon wasn't so sure. The Gospels recorded only that the body was gone by the time the women arrived around dawn on Sunday morning. None of them set forth a precise chronology as to when the actual event had occurred.

"Did you bring any spares?" I asked.

"Two."

"Do you still have them?"

Bryson smiled as he felt for the small pouch he had tucked into his tunic. His expression, though, quickly changed to one of worry and embarrassment.

"I must have lost my pouch as I was running this morning," he finally said.

I figured as much. I turned to Lavon. "That will make for an interesting find, will it not? A two thousand year old battery from a Handycam."

Lavon shook his head as he thought back to the odd discovery that had led him to his current situation.

"No one will be able to date it," he finally said.

***

As the western sky faded to dusk, a servant brought in an oil lamp and placed it in the center of the table. After the man departed, I took the wine jar and filled five goblets.

After handing one to Sharon – the others could fend for themselves – I took the seat facing the door and held up my chip.

"Speaking of lost pieces of plastic, does everyone still have theirs?"

The others reached into their pouches and said yes. Bryson, too, pulled his out and laid it on the table, though this one looked a bit different. Instead of being composed of a single uniform wafer, like ours, the center of his glowed red.

"It's a low power LED," he explained. You all have earlier prototypes. Given the unknowns involved in this venture, we realized that it might become essential for me to have some warning that my return could be delayed, so that I could have at least a minimal opportunity to take evasive action."

I couldn't argue with that, though it hadn't done us much good so far.

Bryson continued to stare at the chip. Finally, he just shook his head. "I just don't know what *possibly* could be wrong?"

"Well, *something* is not right," said Markowitz.

The others joined in and I let them vent for a few minutes. Finally, though, I held up my hand. We needed solutions, not arguments.

"The way I see it," I said, "we need to work out hypotheses as to what the problem might be, though our key concern for the moment is how long we'll have to stay in the good graces of the Roman army."

Bryson held up his wine goblet. "You seem to have done a decent job of that so far. Obviously, we're not prisoners."

"No."

"Then why do you think – "

Lavon rose, walked over to a window and once again looked down. The drop was over one hundred feet.

"We're not prisoners, but we can't exactly leave," he said. "I don't think they know *what* to do with us. With all the crowds coming in for the Passover, they're rather busy, so my guess is they're going to keep us here until the festival is over and sort everything out then."

"Keep us here, in this room?" asked Markowitz.

"Yes, as *guests* – unless something changes their mind."

"Do you think they believe our story?" Sharon asked.

"It's plausible," Lavon replied. "Rome took control of Egypt around 30 BC, or about sixty years before Christ's ministry. The army brought enormous quantities of loot back to the capital, and wealthy Romans went nuts over the stuff. Owning Egyptian artifacts became the 'in' thing for the high society of the time."

"I saw Egyptian obelisks in modern Rome," she said.

"That's right," replied Lavon. "There's even one at the center of St. Peter's Square. Medieval popes restored many of the ones that had fallen after the Empire crumbled."

"OK, then," I said. "'Plausible' should be good enough, at least for the moment."

"Saving that soldier got us some Brownie points, too," said Markowitz.

"Yes, but that's also part of our problem," replied Lavon. "Word of something so obviously useful …"

"They'll want more," I said.

"I'm certain of it. How many more of those things do you have?"

"Three."

"I'd be prepared to hand them over, though the more difficult question will be where you got them in the first place. To the Romans, the Germans are uncultured barbarians, and anyone from lands beyond Germany is probably even worse.

"Let's face it," Lavon continued, "Two thousand years ago – or right about now, as strange as it is to say – our ancestors were crawling around the forests of northern Europe wrapped in animal skins. The Industrial Revolution is a long way off."

"Mine weren't," said Markowitz.

I gave him an odd glance, but let his comment pass.

"Couldn't we have picked up some technology along the way?" asked Bryson.

"Sure, but where? I had to tell Publius that we came to Judea around the eastern part of the Black Sea. The Romans already occupied the western side – modern Romania and Bulgaria – and I couldn't run the risk of saying we had traveled though some place this guy might have actually seen in person."

"Why is that a problem?"

"To the east you either have steppes, home to nomadic horsemen, or the Caucasus, the domain of wild mountain tribes. We're unlikely to have picked up any advanced science from either group."

"What about China?" asked Bergfeld. "They had advanced technology for the era, and the Silk Road went – "

I had to interrupt. Complex webs of lies eventually spun out of control, a phenomenon that had allowed me to make a nice living over the past few years. The closer we stuck to the truth, the less risk we would run.

Bryson, though, was no longer paying attention. He stared down at his chip, which still glowed bright red.

"I think I've figured out what happened: Scott must have reprogrammed the machine. I configured the chips with an automated recall feature. We had to have that anyway for the first live animal tests, and Juliet insisted that she retain some way to retrieve me later on, even though we had proven that the technology operated precisely according to its design parameters."

"OK, but how does that impact our situation now?" I asked.

"You were right in your suspicions earlier today, Mr. Culloden: there's no way Juliet would have voluntarily permitted him to come back here. Since he undoubtedly knew that, he would have altered the recall feature to keep her from bringing him straight back to Boston as soon as he arrived in this world."

"I would imagine he'd want to go back at some point," said Lavon.

"True; but he would have wanted to stay through Sunday. The young man was quite a fan of Dawkins, especially his latest work."

Several years earlier, Richard Dawkins, an English biologist, had written a book entitled *The God Delusion*. At last count, it had sold over a million copies.

"He would have seen this as a golden opportunity," said Bryson.

"To do what?" said Sharon, "to show that we Christians are all fools?"

Bryson nodded. "I cautioned him that a true scientist must keep his mind open to the objective evidence, whichever way it falls, and not try to *demonstrate* anything, one way or the other."

"That's what all scientists are supposed to do, isn't it?" asked Markowitz.

Bryson laughed. "It's a nice theory," he replied. "But I believe it was Planck who said that no one is ever converted to a new idea in science. It is only after the generation who clung to the old idea eventually dies off that the concept finds broad acceptance."

"He spoke of religion?"

"No," said Bryson, "quantum mechanics; which was, as my wife undoubtedly explained, a most outrageous notion at the time."

He paused for a moment; then peered into Bergfeld's eyes.

"As I said, I cautioned Scott to keep both his eyes and his mind open. I must ask you the same question: are you, Sharon, prepared to act in accordance with the evidence we encounter?"

She didn't reply.

"If we see – if *you* see – the disciples carting the body out of the tomb, are you prepared to face what follows?"

"That there is no God?"

"No, we'd still have no proof of that either way; but we would see that the Jesus of your childhood wasn't the deity you sang to in Sunday school."

Sharon stared down at the table. She didn't say anything, but in her heart, she had to have recognized his point.

Though I consider myself a pretty rational person, most of the time at least, I had to consider the same thing. Perhaps some things *were* better off not known.

Chapter 24

While the others continued to debate, I poured myself a second cup of wine and then reached into my bag to extract a small rubberized bud, which I managed to slip into my ear just before two men strode into our room as if they owned the place.

That was because they did.

It took me a second to recognize the centurion Publius, since he had stripped off his armor and donned a clean white tunic.

The other man, a Roman named Volusus, had served as the fort's commander for past two years. A slave followed in their wake with another jug of wine and two additional goblets, though as soon as he filled them, he scurried out of the room.

Lavon and I both stood and beckoned the two Romans to take our seats, but they chose to remain standing.

Publius got straight to the point. "I have explained what your companion did for my man," he said to Lavon.

I spoke through Robert to ask Publius how the soldier was doing, and whether his wound had remained free of infection.

Fortunately for my image as a miracle worker, it had.

"He is doing remarkably well for a wound of that severity," replied Publius. "In fact, I have seen no others who have survived such an injury."

"We must have more of those bandages," said Volusus.

Lavon's warning had been prescient. I had no choice but to reach into my bag and pull out two. I offered them both to the commander.

"Tell him these are all we have. I am keeping only the last one for ourselves in case we encounter an emergency."

Volusus looked puzzled. "Can you not make more?"

"Unfortunately, I cannot. I brought these from our country, where we buy them from skilled artisans. I have seen no others since we left, months ago."

The two Romans exchanged odd glances. We learned later that both men had served in Germany. As Lavon feared, at no time had they ever heard of advanced civilizations in the unknown territory beyond.

Hoping to divert their attention, I held up the remaining bandage. "Tell them that they must save these for the most severe cases. And they must never open the package until they are ready to use it."

"Why not?" Publius asked.

"It reacts with the moisture in the wound, or in the air," I explained. "If it is exposed too early, it will not function properly. Also, tell him that only the white side may have direct contact with the injured body part; *only* the white side."

Publius considered this; then asked me if I was a doctor.

I thought about saying yes, but decided not to press my luck.

"No," I replied. "I received basic training only. Other men worked as physicians, as in your unit."

"You are a soldier, then?"

"Was," I said; "Many years ago."

"How many men did you command?"

I paused as if having difficulty understanding the translation. An American colonel in the line commanded anywhere from three to five thousand men – nearly a legion's worth. If they believed my answer, hearing of an army that size would alarm them. Later, as an intelligence officer, I had led a small team of five. The Romans would consider this a joke.

"Tell him about eighty," I said.

Lavon did so.

Publius smiled; then glanced over toward Volusus. "I told you he had the look of a centurion."

***

A loud crash interrupted our conversation as a pile of stacked rubble fell to the ground outside. All of us, including the two Romans, hurried over to the windows, where we observed a torch-lit procession of laborers – men we had not seen earlier – hard at work, carrying a mountain of rubbish out the complex's eastern gate.

Volusus directed our attention toward a team of workers attacking a similar mound of debris at the other end of the courtyard.

"As I mentioned earlier," he said to Publius, "we, too, have had some challenging days."

"Did you take casualties?"

"None so far, thank the gods."

"What happened?"

Volusus shook his head and spat. "Another one of their damned prophets."

Publius rolled his eyes. "Again?"

Volusus pointed to our left. "Late in the afternoon, two days ago, this man came riding into the courtyard on the back of a donkey through the Shushan Gate, right over there. A large crowd followed him, waving palm fronds and shouting all sorts of nonsense."

"Where did he come from?"

"My informants tell me that he started in one of those little villages to the east, though no one could give me a definitive answer. What is undisputed, though, is that a horde of this rabble ran ahead of him the whole way here, scattering their branches along the road – 'preparing a path' they said."

"For what?"

"I'm still trying to get a straight answer to that. We've heard so many conflicting stories."

"What happened next?"

"Strangely enough, nothing. He stayed only a few minutes before turning around and going back out the same way."

"That doesn't sound like much of a disturbance," said Publius.

I glanced over to Lavon. *Prophet; palm fronds.* I could see that he, too, was struggling to keep an expressionless face.

"No; but he came back. Yesterday, this same man popped up in the market area with a whip. He overturned the merchants' tables, opened the bird cages, and drove away the animals – shouting at them the whole time."

Volusus paused to let the image sink in.

"You should have seen it; you know how excitable these people are. Everything just fed on itself – men crawling about on the ground, fighting each other for loose coins; panicked animals running every which way, with their owners trying to chase them down through the swarms of pilgrims coming in through the south gates. You can't imagine the chaos."

I watched Publius struggle to keep a straight face. In another set of circumstances, the scene would be almost comical – at least from a safe distance when their own careers didn't hang in the balance.

Volusus spat again before he continued. "The whole thing took us by surprise. At least an hour passed before the Temple police could get the crowd back under control. By then the market area was a complete wreck. As you see, they're still working to haul the debris away."

Both men stared at the laborers for a few moments.

"Did this prophet say why he did this?" asked Publius.

"Supposedly, he was upset with how much money they're making. 'Den of thieves' was his exact term, or so I hear."

"It sounds like he's called that one right. Our good Roman money is conveniently unclean; the people's own livestock are blemished and unacceptable for an offering. It's quite a racket they have, if you ask me."

"That may be," snapped the commander, "but we can't afford this kind of disorder – not this week."

"If this man caused a disturbance at such a sensitive time, why didn't you arrest him?"

"On the Temple Mount? All that marching in the hot sun today must have melted your brains. If those people saw a Roman uniform on their holy spot in the middle of their festival, we could have a full scale insurrection on our hands. You know that."

"The prefect would be most upset," said Publius.

"The *prefect* would be the least of our worries. Even with your entire century, we'd not have one chance in ten of getting back here alive. That mob would tear us to pieces."

"Why didn't their Temple police arrest him, then?"

Volusus sighed. "He has sympathizers in their high council. I can scarcely believe it, but he came back to the Temple, once more, this morning – yet they did nothing."

"Have you seen this man yourself?"

The commander shook his head. "No. My informants mostly just repeat the rumors they've heard. A miracle worker, some call him; heals the sick; turns water into wine."

Publius lifted his empty cup. "A handy person to keep around, I'd say."

The other man laughed, possibly for the first time that week.

"It gets better. A story is circulating that a few days ago, he raised one of his childhood friends from the dead."

"Even handier," said Publius. "I'm beginning to like this fellow."

Volusus laughed again and visibly relaxed.

"Just get us through this week without a riot," he implored. "Then these people will all go home, where they belong, and we can return to civilization in Caesarea."

"Until next year."

"Next year, this will be your problem. I am retiring and will recommend to the prefect that you take my place. After the festival is over, you can come visit me on my farm."

Chapter 25

"Are you going to tell us what they were talking about?" said Markowitz after the two Romans had left.

Lavon shook his head. "I'm having trouble believing it – not what they said, but that we're here to see it."

"What *did* they say?" asked Markowitz.

"They were complaining," said Lavon, "griping about the crowds and a new prophet who has appeared on the scene."

"Prophet?"

The archaeologist pointed to the southern end of the Temple complex.

"Right over there; that's where the merchants sit. Yesterday morning, this prophet came charging in and drove them all out."

"The moneychangers?" said Sharon.

"The same," said Lavon. "The commander is worried that he'll come back. The crowds are so volatile; anything could happen."

Bryson looked at him skeptically. "It can't be that bad," he said.

Lavon didn't speak for a few moments. Finally he directed our attention out the window toward the west.

"Look down at that wall," he said, "the one extending from below our room to the battlement on the other side of the fort. A few years from now, a Roman soldier stationed there will turn his backside to the crowd on the Temple Mount and break wind in a very loud and deliberate way. According to Josephus, more than twenty thousand people died in the ensuing riot."

"But Robert," replied Bryson, "you've said it yourself: These ancient writers were prone to exaggerate."

"Yes; Lavon replied, "the casualties may have been half that number, or a tenth, but that still means two thousand dead. The ancients didn't have tear gas or water cannons. Once a crowd got going, the only way to stop it was to march through the streets, killing everyone who got in the way. That's why the Romans pounced so hard on the slightest whiff of trouble. It didn't take much for a situation to get completely out of hand."

"That was an intentional insult," said Markowitz. "The soldier should not have done that."

"I'm sure he was punished, but it goes to show how unstable things really were. You saw it coming in – the looks on peoples' faces."

They mumbled assent.

"And on the flip side," Lavon continued, "Roman officials didn't have to worry about videos of dead children showing up on the internet. The whole setup was a recipe for abuse."

I didn't doubt that, either.

Inflaming the situation still more, most of the "Roman" soldiers were in fact auxiliaries, recruited from a pool of the Jews' traditional enemies.

For a while, we all continued to stare down at the activity below. The Temple area had finally gone quiet. The workers had departed and only the Temple watchmen remained. We could see two of them making their rounds, while a third priest fed the fire that burned perpetually on the altar.

"So where does this leave us?" asked Bryson. "Assuming this prophet they're talking about really is Jesus Christ, will he come back to the Temple again? Could we even get a recording of him teaching from our vantage point here?"

Lavon glanced over to Sharon. "If I remember correctly, the Gospels don't record anything Jesus did between some teaching on Tuesday and the Last Supper, which is Thursday night."

"So you don't know where he will be until then?" asked Bryson.

"We don't really know even then," said Lavon. "We can only speculate where the Last Supper was held. We know he was arrested later that night, but we don't know where they took him afterward.

"Was he brought before the full Sanhedrin here in the Temple complex, or to a smaller gathering at Caiaphas's house? We don't even know whether Pilate sat in judgment here in the Antonia or at Herod's palace, on the other side of town."

"How can we find out?" asked Bryson.

"For starters," Lavon replied, "we'd have to go outside and have a look, but I'm not sure that's such a good idea."

"Well, we need to do something," said Markowitz. "We can't just sit here until Sunday."

That's *exactly* what we should do, I thought, though I didn't expect the others to see it the same way.

"Let's do this," I finally said. "We've had a long day. Let's get a good night's sleep and work out our plan with a clear head, in the morning."

Chapter 26

Our next day got off to an abrupt start just before dawn. Several men ran shouting into the room, but I couldn't understand a word. Lavon stared at them with equal incomprehension; whatever they were speaking, it wasn't Greek.

Moments later, Publius strode in, carrying a torch and laughing uproariously. He waved his hand and the others scrambled away.

"Decius has lost his bet," said the centurion. "I told him there was no chance you were Parthian spies."

"*Spies*?" said Lavon. "That's what this was all about?"

Publius nodded. "The best test is always a surprise. Each of these men spoke different languages, telling you that the fortress was on fire, and that you should run quickly to save your lives – Parthian, Aramaic, Egyptian. It is obvious you know none of them."

"I could have told you that and saved them the trouble," said Lavon.

"What's going on?" asked Markowitz.

Lavon motioned him to be quiet. "Why would Decius think we were spies?"

"He thought it was odd that you, a traveler from so far away, seemed to have known the name of that little village we passed through yesterday."

Lavon thought quickly. "It resembles the name of my ancestral town, in Norvia."

"You also displayed great interest in the construction, pitiful as it was."

He turned toward Bergfeld. "Her father has an interest in how other countries house their poor. He left us specific instructions to investigate this."

Lavon wasn't sure the centurion believed any of this, but Publius merely stared at him for a few more seconds. He then barked orders for the servant outside to bring us food and water and left without saying another word.

Lavon gave us all a few minutes to settle down. He broke a piece of bread off the large loaf and passed it to Bryson, who had taken a seat to his left.

"I'm as guilty as anyone," he said as he briefly explained what had just happened, "but we'll have to all take better care to pretend we don't know some of the things we do."

"Parthian spies?" asked Bryson. "Who the hell are the Parthians?"

"Persians," Lavon replied. "At its height, their empire was probably as large as Rome's."

"I've never heard of it."

"Few Americans have, but the Romans and the Parthians fought over this part of the world for several centuries. They don't care much for each other."

That much I knew. At the Army War College, we learned about Crassus, a Roman general who had blundered his way into the desert and gotten most of his men killed. As the story went, his reputation as the richest man in Rome had preceded him; the Parthians executed him by pouring molten gold down his throat.

"Why does this matter to us?" asked Bryson.

"The route we would have followed from Norvia would have taken us through Parthian lands. I'm sure the Romans are curious how we managed to get through."

***

Before he could say anything else, Markowitz called us over to the windows. In the dim light, we could barely make out two priests stacking a pile of wood on the altar. Another man, near the center of the inner courtyard, appeared to be hauling away ashes from the day before.

The sun slowly edged over the horizon, sending luminous rays glistening off the gold trim that bordered the Temple's roof. Shortly thereafter, more white-clad priests appeared – to assist with the morning sacrifices, we supposed.

Markowitz stared at priests intently; then turned to Lavon.

"Robert, what do we in the modern world really *know* about the Temple rituals? I mean no disrespect, but whenever you've described things to us so far, you keep using terms like 'guess' and 'suppose.'"

Lavon sighed. He had heard the same complaint from modern-day tour groups. Unfortunately, the short answer was "not very much."

"In forty years," he said, "everything you see here will be a smoldering ruin. Once the siege finally ended, the Romans systematically leveled much of what was left. Josephus wrote afterward that no one visiting the spot would believe that it had once been inhabited."

"Surely he exaggerated," said Bryson.

"Yes, probably; but that was only the starting point. Sixty years after the Temple's destruction, or roughly a hundred years from now, the emperor will decide to scrape what remained of old Jerusalem and build a new city along Roman lines. That triggered another revolt, leading to another round of complete devastation."

"OK, I get the point," said Bryson.

"I'm not sure you do. No city on earth has been destroyed and rebuilt as many times as this one. In the 600s, after the Western Empire collapsed, Jerusalem passed back and forth between the Byzantines and the

Persians – sacked, of course, each time. I think you've seen enough already to understand what that means."

We all nodded.

"In 1099, European Crusaders conquered the city. They lost it about eighty years later to Saladin and the Mamluks from Egypt. After that came the Ottoman Turks, the British and finally the modern Israelis.

"We try, Ray, but think about reconstructing your own house after it burned down and a tornado ripped away the slab. Then consider how well someone could do it a hundred years later, with only a letter from their great-grandmother to go on. Archaeology is an inexact science. We do the best we can."

Markowitz thought quietly for a moment; then his face grew bright.

"That's why we *must* go inside," he said. "We have to see it for ourselves, while we have the opportunity."

***

I started to argue, but at that moment, we heard a knock on the door. A slave entered and beckoned us to follow.

"Where are we going?" asked Lavon.

"My instructions are to lead you to the baths."

We glanced at each other, as if to say *why not*, and then ambled toward the door. As the others stepped outside, I walked back over to the corner to retrieve my bag. I suggested the others do likewise.

"No," said the servant. "We will provide everything you need."

I ignored him and hefted my kit into a comfortable position.

"If he doesn't like it," I said to Lavon, "tell him to bring it up with Publius."

Just as I expected, the man backed down. Slaves, after all, did not complain to centurions.

"As you wish," he said.

The servant led us down the stairs, then across the courtyard toward the opposite side of the fort. We could see about fifty Romans huddled near the north gate, checking equipment and preparing to go out on patrol. A few of the soldiers glanced up, but the rest of the men paid our group no mind.

We entered a stone passageway underneath the northeast battlement and went down two levels before turning into a narrow room about twenty feet long, which was illuminated with two oil lamps.

I counted fifteen U-shaped stone seats lining one of the walls. Behind each seat rested a stick with what appeared to be a sponge fastened to one end.

"Toilets," said Lavon. "Those sponges are for washing your back side. They change them out after each use, so you don't have to worry about having a clean one."

"Wow," said Bryson.

"Where's the flush handle?' joked Markowitz.

"Don't laugh," said Lavon. "I'm serious."

He spoke briefly to the slave; then turned to the others.

"It's an ingenious system. The aqueduct brings water into a cistern at ground level. We're two floors below that, and our, um, material drops one level more. Every so often, they open a sluice gate and gravity pushes the stored water through at a high speed, washing the whole mess into the sewer. From there, it flows into the Kidron Ravine, which has been a garbage dump since the time of Solomon.

"Even if they don't understand bacteria, they seem to have basic sanitation figured out," said Bryson.

"As far as personal hygiene goes," said Lavon, "the average soldier in this building probably lived better than the court at Versailles."

"Where is the women's restroom?" asked Bergfeld.

Lavon questioned the servant, but the man only stared back blankly. There wasn't one.

"I know this is an army post," she said, "but surely women visit from time to time?"

The archaeologist scanned the room again. "This fits with what some of my colleagues have worked out from digs in Britain and Italy. Their theory is that men and women rarely had separate facilities in the Roman world."

"Oh."

Lavon spoke to the servant again, who nodded and then gave Sharon an unctuous smile.

"I told him that our customs are different. He will give you a few minutes of privacy, if you'd like."

"Thank you," she said, as the rest of us turned toward the door.

A few minutes later, she came out and thanked the servant again. He bowed his head, as if unaccustomed to such niceties, and turned toward a set of steps at the other end of the corridor.

"Now we will go to the baths."

He led us up one level, toward another corridor that opened into a chamber about the size of a modern tennis court. Two windows in the ceiling, covered with metal grates, provided illumination.

"You begin your bath here," he said.

We saw no water. Instead, to our great surprise, rows of dumbbells lined both sides of the room, with two racks of heavy barbells mounted on the opposite wall. A dozen Romans, stripped down to loincloths, puffed away at the weights, while in the far corner, other soldiers took turns punching a heavy leather bag.

"I wonder if they sell monthly memberships?" Markowitz joked.

Bergfeld picked up a nearby dumbbell without thinking. She raised it over her head and did two quick sets of tricep extensions, one for each arm. It was only as she replaced the weight on its rack that she noticed the room had gone silent. Every man stared at her; a few gaped in open astonishment.

"It's the Amazon," one finally said, as his compatriots burst out in laughter.

She blushed as Lavon translated and quickly ducked behind the rest of us.

Not one to miss a workout, I stepped forward to grab a few quick sets with the dumbbells, and the others followed. A few minutes later, Sharon got over her embarrassment and came back to join the fun.

After we finished, we stepped back into the corridor and followed the servant down the hall, wondering what other surprises were in store.

"It's called the *Palaestra*," Lavon explained. "The Romans believed that it was best to work up a sweat before bathing."

"Fascinating," said Bryson.

"Did they really call me an Amazon?" asked Sharon.

"*The* Amazon, if I heard him right," said the archaeologist.

"Did such women really exist?"

"Supposedly their lands were to the north of the Black Sea – today's Ukraine," answered Lavon, "but it's hard to say how much credence the Greeks or the Romans gave to the tales. Some of the stories were pretty bizarre."

"Isn't that where you told them we came through on the way here?" I asked.

He frowned. "I never considered the link," he admitted.

"Link to what?" said Bergfeld.

"Since the Amazons didn't allow men to live in their country, the legend was that they'd venture out once or twice a year to have sex, in order to keep their line going.

In that case, it's plausible that a few of them might journey this far, for variety's sake, I suppose."

Considering the other myths about the Amazons, that sounded reasonable enough.

***

The servant stepped through another passage and directed us into the *apodyterium*, or changing room. Numbered shelves lined the walls, though most were empty at this time of the morning.

"Here's the drill," said Lavon. You can leave your clothes here. Once you've done that, you have a couple of choices. The Romans didn't use soap like we do. Instead, bathers would cover their bodies with oil to loosen the dirt. Then, servants would take a curved metal tool and scrape it all off."

"What's the other choice?" I asked. The first option sounded distinctly unappealing.

"You can go straight to the *caldarium*, which is a hot water bath. It's heated by a fire directly under the pool. The tiles are pretty hot, too, so, they'll give you wooden clogs to keep from burning your feet."

"I think I'll go with Plan B," I said.

The others laughed.

"I figured you would," Lavon replied. "After you've spent however long you want in the hot water, you go to the next room and dunk yourself in the cold water pool, to close your pores. That'll wake you up, I can assure you."

"And after that?"

"In places like Pompeii, they'd have food and wine, and probably some musicians or other entertainment. There, the baths were a social occasion, and Roman writers often complained about people who stayed too long and became drunk and obnoxious."

"But this is an army base," said Bryson.

"Right," said Lavon. "I'd expect it to be rather functional, without the decorative touches we've found in the resort towns. Once you're out of the cold water, come back to the changing room and retrieve your clothes, and you'll be done."

"What about me?" Sharon asked.

He quizzed the servant again. Once again, the man flashed a sycophantic smile before beckoning her to sit. The rest of us would go first; she could follow once we had finished.

That made sense, though something at the back of my mind didn't feel right. Although he was a servant and thus accustomed to deferring to others, his demeanor seemed just a bit *too* obsequious – like a sleazy stockbroker trying to convince his intended victims of his honest nature.

"I'll stay with her," I decided.

"But you must – "

I rose. "Tell him I'll stay here. Someone needs to watch over our stuff, anyway. I will bathe later."

The servant shrugged and then led the other three toward the warm water.

Chapter 27

An hour later, a beaming Lavon strode back into the changing room.

"Incredible," he said. "The chow is good, too: baskets of fresh bread, fruit, and dates are set up on the sides of both pools. Eat all you want."

"I'm hungry," Sharon chirped. "Let's go."

I was, too, but something wasn't right. I peered behind Lavon into the corridor leading to the *apodyterium*.

"Where are the others?"

Lavon hesitated.

"They have a change of clothes waiting for us after we get out of the cold water pool," he finally said. "The servants will wash the ones we left here and bring them up to our room later this afternoon after they've dried."

"That's not what I asked."

Lavon shook his head. "I can't stop them, Bill. You know that. They're likely to need someone to translate."

I was afraid of something like this.

"Where are they now?"

Lavon reached up to a shelf and grabbed his bag, along with the two others'.

"They're waiting for me by the fort's eastern gate. The road from there continues on to the northeast, to the Mount of Olives. We'll circle around there, come back in through the City of David and work our way up to the Temple. You have to enter the Temple complex from the south, anyway. Going this way should help us avoid the worst of the crowds."

"I thought only Jews could enter the Temple."

"Foreigners were allowed in the outer courtyard, just not the Temple building itself."

"You've seen how Ray has been acting," I replied. "He'll try to get in somehow. Bryson will too, with that camera. God help them if they're caught."

"Ray *is* Jewish," said Lavon.

"I know that, but he doesn't look like any of the locals I've seen around here."

"That won't matter. The Babylonians destroyed Solomon's Temple roughly six hundred years before Christ and deported Judah's upper classes to Babylon and beyond. By Roman times, Jews had scattered all over the world. The Passover was *the* big festival; they could be coming from anywhere."

I cast him a dubious glance.

"I'm serious. Some of the exiles even wandered as far as China. Over time, they began to assimilate with the local populations. After several centuries, their physical appearances would have begun to vary."

"If they don't buy it, you're screwed."

"No, it's plausible," Lavon insisted. "And don't forget, the Assyrians wiped out the northern Kingdom of Israel even earlier – about 150 years before the destruction of Solomon's Temple. They followed the same policy: transport the people of a conquered region somewhere else, so they'd have no homeland of their own to defend, no reason to rebel. By the first century, those people could have gone anywhere. If worst comes to worst, I'll tell them he's from one of the Lost Tribes, coming home."

I sighed, but made no further move stop him. Lavon was the expert, after all.

"Just don't get yourself killed, OK. We still need someone who can actually talk to these people."

"Don't worry, Bill," he replied. "Besides, it will be helpful to scout the ground outside this fort, wouldn't you say?"

***

I couldn't *not* worry, but there was no use arguing. For a brief instant, I followed Lavon up the steps into the courtyard, where I saw Markowitz and Bryson pacing back and forth on the other side of the open gate.

On the ramparts above, a Roman sentry watched them curiously but made no move to impede their progress. Apparently, we could come and go as we pleased.

As Lavon joined the others, I just waved and then walked back down to the baths.

"This is a bad idea," I said to Sharon.

"Did they take the camera?"

I nodded.

"Well," she smiled. "That's one less thing we have to worry about here. No one can steal it while we're bathing."

"I suppose not."

"What are we going to do while they're gone, after our baths?" she asked.

I stared down at the floor and shook my head. "Perhaps we can go upstairs and watch the riot that starts when those three try to get into the Temple. That should be entertaining."

"I'm serious."

So was I.

I decided not to complain, though. There was nothing I could do.

"I'd be interested in learning how the soldiers train," I finally replied. "Unfortunately, I can't talk to them, and even if I could, they'd have questions for me, too. What could I tell them that they could possibly believe?"

"What did you do in the Army before you retired?"

"My last assignment was to improve the coordination between our covert field operatives and their linkages to satellite reconnaissance and drone aircraft."

Sharon laughed. "Yeah, I see how that might be hard to explain. What did you do when you first enlisted?"

"Chased Viet Cong through the jungle and tried not to be the last man killed."

The truth was the other way around – except for the trying not to get killed part – but I saw no reason to complicate matters.

She eyed me strangely. "How old were you?"

"Seventeen. I had stolen a car. The draft had ended but the Army still needed recruits. The judge told me I could either enlist or go to jail. It wasn't really a hard choice."

"I suppose not."

"As it turned out, I was pretty good at it – soldiering, that is. After I came back stateside, they gave me an intelligence test, and the next year, I was off to OCS. After that, one thing led to another."

"And here you are."

I glanced around the room. Though the evidence was overwhelming, my mind still struggled to accept the fact that I was indeed sitting in the bath facility of a first century Roman fort.

"Yeah, here I am."

The fawning servant interrupted and beckoned once more for us to follow. Sharon decided it would be best if she went ahead, though before she did, I waved the man away, reached into my bag and pulled out an object resembling a common ear bud, which hung from a Kevlar thread, like a pendant.

I draped it around her neck. "Before you go, take this."

She looked confused – as if unsure whether I was giving her something she would need in the next few minutes or trying to convince her to let me join her for some rub-a-dub-tub.

"It's a transmitter," I explained. "Actually, it's more than that. If you put the bud in your ear, it will also make translations."

"You're kidding!"

I was not. The latest wars found American soldiers toiling in ever more remote parts of the world, and needing to communicate with people who spoke languages few Americans knew. DARPA scientists had labored over the technology for years, though they had only recently managed to construct viable prototypes.

"What it won't do," I said, "is translate your speech back to them. I've disabled that feature, since I'm not sure how a first century Roman would react to a little talking disk."

I didn't think they'd burn us as witches, but saw no need to take the chance.

"As a safety precaution, it senses body heat; so if it's not seated in your ear, it won't make a sound."

"How well does it work? The last computer translation program I had was a joke."

"It's not perfect," I admitted. "I got the gist of what Publius and the other man were saying last night, though."

"Wow."

"The Greek should be functional. I programmed it with modern Greek during those few days we were getting ready to go."

"But the Greek spoken here is different."

"Yeah, Robert told me that it's the equivalent of a modern American reading Chaucer in the original. Still, the eggheads at DARPA say that the software is adaptive. Although Chaucer isn't easy to read, it's still a lot easier for us than it would be for someone who didn't know English at all."

"You couldn't program the Aramaic?"

"I had no access to modern speakers on such short notice. Besides, we'd have the same language drift problem – worse, probably."

Do the others have one?

"I could only get my hands on three. I was going to give one to Lavon, but I didn't expect the other two to take off like they did, which is a shame, since it can also serve as a two way radio."

Moments later, the servant returned. He was more insistent this time; we must have been holding up the line.

"Go ahead," I said. "It's waterproof. If you keep it around your neck, you won't be able to hear me, but I should be able to hear you."

She stepped behind the drapery and hung her clothes on a rack. Then she walked down a narrow corridor until she reached the entrance to the *caldarium*, where she slipped on the wooden clogs that the attendant had laid at the threshold.

As I was to see a few minutes later, the pool itself was surprisingly large – about seventy-five feet long and roughly half as wide. We could hear the fires from the furnace underneath – a *hypocaust*, Lavon had called it. Hot air mixed with steam rose from hollowed out bricks along the edges of the room, producing a sauna-like effect.

I could hear her kick off the clogs and ease herself into the water. It sounded like she swam a couple of easy laps before gliding over to the steps and leaning back.

"It's about the temperature of a Jacuzzi," she said. "The only things lacking are the bubbles."

I smiled. We had, perhaps, enough mechanical knowledge between the five of us to invent some sort of pump out of available materials, though I for one didn't want to hang around long enough to find out.

Sharon stayed in the water and helped herself to the refreshments beside the pool. A little while later, we both heard a bell ring, which was the signal to move on.

I gave her a few minutes before I, too, deposited my clothes on the shelf. I walked into the *caldarium* and set my bag next to the edge of the pool. I also swam a couple of slow laps and then just rested on the warm steps, sampling the food. Lavon was right: it was delicious.

Between the warmth and the chow, I lost track of time. A little while later, though, the bell rang again, so I got out of the water, picked up my bag, and headed to the next station.

This room, the *frigidarium*, Lavon had called it, was only a quarter of the size of the one I had just left. People were less likely to linger here, and this made sense.

I suppose some creatures – polar bears, perhaps – might have described the water as 'invigorating.' To me, it was just plain cold, although it did shake the cobwebs loose.

A stack of towels sat on a nearby table, so I jumped out and dried myself off. I tossed the first towel into a wicker basket, wrapped another around my waist, and placed my ear bud back into position.

"What do you want?" I heard her say – and not to me.

"Sharon?" I called out.

I stepped out of the *frigidarium* but instead of walking into one corridor, I found myself at the intersection of three.

"Sharon?"

I listened intently, but heard only a soft murmur.

Then I heard a shuffling sound: the toadying slave appeared in the right hand corridor and signaled for me to follow him.

I glared at him. "Where is she?"

He couldn't understand my words, but I suspected he knew their meaning.

The worm motioned me forward again. This time, his manner reminded me of the pimps I had once seen all over the Far East – obnoxious pests who followed me everywhere touting 'I have deal for you my friend.'

Right.

Since he was rushing me to go in one direction, I obviously wanted to go in another. But which one?

I pretended to stumble and reached down to grab my ankle. When he stepped closer to assist me, I grabbed my folding knife from my bag, whipped it open and held it to his throat.

"*Where. Is. She?*" I said.

The words weren't important. He knew exactly what I wanted.

He pointed down the center corridor, and somewhat foolishly, I backed toward it, intending to turn around and push him through in reverse.

I never made it. A second later, I felt a thump and my world went completely black.

Chapter 28

The next thing I remembered, a man was shaking me awake. I instinctively recoiled and reached for my knife, then felt several sets of arms holding me down as I flailed about.

It took me a few more seconds to fully come to. As I did, I could see three men, bald, clean shaven and dressed in identical white tunics, standing around me.

One of them spoke. I couldn't understand a word he was saying, though as my vision improved, I noted the look of concern in his eyes – all of their eyes, for that matter. Whoever these people were, they weren't part of the crew in the baths.

Once I was completely conscious, the three of them took a step back and watched as I reached behind my pounding head to feel for blood.

Fortunately, I found none, and after minute or so, two of them reached down and helped me stagger to my feet.

I gestured my thanks as best I could and then glanced past them to take in my surroundings. The tallest man pointed to a spot just outside the city wall and gestured that he had found me there. He had then recruited his colleagues to carry me to my current location, a shady spot beneath an olive tree about a quarter mile to the northeast of the Antonia.

Why, I couldn't tell. Maybe they were Good Samaritans – perhaps even the original ones.

I could see from the position of the sun that it was only mid-morning, so I hadn't been out all that long. I also noticed, for the first time, that a boisterous crowd had gathered around a colonnaded structure a hundred yards to the north.

There, several groups of men, each carrying stretchers, attempted to push their way through the southernmost entrance. However, those already inside closed ranks to block their passage.

My benefactors watched the burgeoning drama with a sense of concern. One of them, evidently the leader, ordered the other two to deal with the situation.

As they hustled away, their boss gestured for me to follow him, but I just held my hands up, silently asking to remain in place a little longer.

He stared into my eyes for a few seconds and then shrugged, as if to indicate that I was no longer his responsibility; then he ambled up the path to join his colleagues.

I still couldn't figure out what was happening. The stretcher-bearers continued to jostle for position without success, until a couple of them finally set their loads down and turned on the crowd blocking their way. I watched half a dozen men fall to the ground, where they grappled and threw wild punches as bystanders cheered them on.

My rescuers did nothing for several minutes. Finally, they shoved the crowd back, and after another brief interval to let the brawlers tire even further, they pulled the combatants apart, like modern policemen breaking up a bar fight.

Knowing the Roman tendency to pounce on the first inkling of trouble, I glanced back to the Antonia, half expecting a squad of soldiers to come charging up the road. Neither sentry, however, paid the commotion any mind. Apparently, this sort of thing wasn't unusual, at least not here.

After they broke up the altercation, the man in charge glanced back in my direction and once again signaled me to follow.

I hesitated briefly. My first inclination was to return to the Antonia, and if I could have been certain that Publius was there, I would have. He'd sort it all out, I was sure, probably first by seizing that slave and flogging him to within an inch of his life.

But the more I considered it, the less reasonable this plan sounded. For one, I couldn't communicate properly. Making matters worse, my attackers had dressed me in a tunic so old and worn out that the sentries would perceive me as just another member of the swarm of disheveled beggars mobbing the city gates. They would surely turn me away.

Whatever this place was, it was my best bet at the moment. For some reason, these people seemed inclined to help me, and if nothing else, they might at least let me wash my clothes.

I was pleasantly surprised to see my bag lying on the ground next to where my rescuers had placed me. My knife, of course, was gone, as was the sack of coins that Bryson and Lavon had so painstakingly assembled in Boston; but the rest of my kit appeared to be intact.

If only the thieves knew.

**

It was only then, as I felt for the pendant hanging from my neck, that I realized with a horrible sinking feeling that my attackers probably hadn't been thieves.

I stuck my earpiece in.

"Sharon," I called out. "Sharon, can you hear me?"

Nothing.

"Sharon, come in."

I heard a whooshing sound, then an unintelligible voice.

"Sharon?"

"Bill?"

I sighed with relief. "Sharon, can you hear me?"

"Yes, where are you?" Her reply was louder this time; her tone anxious.

"I'm still trying to figure that out. All I know for sure is that I'm northeast of town, outside the city walls. I got walloped on the head and just came to a minute ago. Where are you?"

"I don't know. I'm in a litter. They're taking me somewhere."

"A litter?"

"Yes, just like those old movies. It's like a queen sized bed mounted on poles. Four guys on each side are carrying it. There's the curtain; the whole works."

Litters had always puzzled me – surely the most impractical mode of transportation ever devised, suitable only for a culture with vast pools of expendable labor and little desire to go anywhere in a hurry.

Still, this was encouraging. Someone intent on hurting her wouldn't be transporting her in that manner.

"I heard another voice. Is anyone with you?"

A pause.

"They can't understand you," I said. "Just look up at the sky like you're praying or something. At worst, they'll think you're half crazy."

Another pause.

"There's only one man. He's dressed pretty nicely, compared to the others we've seen. The material looks like silk. Do you know if they had silk in the first century?"

I wasn't sure. I only learned later, from Lavon, that the Roman upper classes had such a voracious appetite for the stuff that a succession of emperors had attempted to ban the trade in order to keep the empire's gold reserves from flowing to China.

They should have sent Treasury paper instead. No wonder their empire collapsed.

"I don't know. Probably, I'd guess. Is he Roman?"

"I don't think so," she replied. "He's darker than the guys in the fort, with curly black hair and a short beard."

I muttered a curse at Lavon for running off as I tried to work out what was going on.

"Can you ask him his name?" I said.

"We've been through that already. We can't understand each other, but we did get that far."

This was doubly encouraging. Someone intent on causing her serious harm wouldn't have cared to know her name.

Neither one of us spoke for a moment. Then I heard her say that the litter's curtain was open. Under the right circumstances, she might have a chance to make a run for it.

She had finished her latest Olympic distance triathlon in well under three hours, so I didn't doubt her ability to evade her pursuers – at least on open ground. But the crowded city probably wouldn't give her the space she needed; and the real issue was where to run *to*.

"I'd stay put for the moment," I replied. "I'm sure that worm in the baths had something to do with this, but I doubt he acted alone. We've got to figure out who is behind this."

"Publius wouldn't do this to me, would he?"

I didn't think so, but then again, my aching head couldn't be sure of anything at the moment.

"Can you ask him where you're going?"

"I don't know any Aramaic or Greek," she said, "so I tried Spanish. Supposedly, that's the language closest to Latin."

I smiled. This girl did have her wits about her.

"And?"

"A blank stare."

I racked my brain trying to recall the Latin that the Jesuits at my high school had tried so hard to pound into my thick head. Then, for some reason, the name of an old movie popped into my mind.

"I've got it. There was a film way back in the Fifties – one of those old Christians thrown to the lions flicks. You may have seen it, too: *Quo Vadis* – it means 'where are you going.'"

"*Quo Vadis*?"

"Yes, look him in the eye and ask him that."

She did so, and I heard the answer: *noster rex*.

"The king," I said.

"Herod?" she replied.

Azariah, the other fellow in the litter, must have heard her, too.

"*Noster Rex Herod Antipas*," he said. *Our king, Herod Antipas.*

At least part of the picture started to fall together. Word of a blonde-headed Amazon must have spread and reached the ears of the king – a monarch who had once been so enamored with a dancing girl that he had a man's head cut off to please her.

I suppose I should have considered myself lucky for just being knocked cold.

Sharon must have realized the implications of where they were heading, too, because she didn't say anything for a minute. When she finally spoke, she did so in a subdued voice.

"When I was in junior high Sunday school, I remember reading a passage in the Book of Acts that described how Herod had been 'eaten by worms' and died. I recall that today only because it sounded so gross at the time, and the boys in the row in front made such a big deal out of it."

She didn't say more, but it wasn't hard to guess what she was thinking. What did the Bible really mean by 'worms?' Was it contagious, or worse, some nasty sexually transmitted disease?

I doubted that the society matrons of the First Baptist Church had dwelled much on that subject.

"Do you know if this is the same Herod?" I asked. "As I recall, several kings went by that name."

"I know it wasn't the one who killed the babies," she said, "but I'm not sure about the others. I had no reason at the time to keep them all straight."

"And they say history is bunk."

I heard her laugh; not loud, but enough to know that she retained a sense of humor. This was important.

"We've stopped," she said. "They're setting the litter down."

"Have you reached the palace?"

"No, we're still inside the city."

Another pause.

"It's all right; it looks like they're just giving the porters a break. They're switching sides, too, so they can use their other arms."

I considered this for a moment. "It sounds like it will take a while for you to get there, so here's what we'll do: I'm going to find the others, and then we can sort out what happened."

"OK."

She didn't say anything else. I told her that we'd both try to keep our ear pieces in if we could do so without drawing too much attention to ourselves; but if not, we could at least leave the transmitters on, just in case. I also implied that I had more than a few bandages and a radio in my bag of tricks.

"I'm going to sign off now," I said. "Hang in there."

"Be careful," she said.

Chapter 29

My benefactor gestured to me once more, so I started up the trail and tried to conceal my sense of foreboding.

Despite what I had led Sharon to believe, I had no bag of tricks. How long it would take her to figure that out, I couldn't be sure; nor did I know whether Herod would set to work on her immediately after she arrived at his palace.

I could only hope not, and "hope" was never a very effective plan. I had to find the others – and soon.

As I got closer to the main structure, I struggled without success to make sense of the chaos. The two assistants had pushed their way without difficulty through a mob of invalids struggling to get inside. Others, though, weren't so lucky.

One particular unfortunate, a skeletal figure draped in rags and hobbling on makeshift crutches, pressed his way into the crowd. He disappeared for a moment, but shortly thereafter, I watched as he was hurled back and left sprawling in the dirt.

The man gestured and shouted as he struggled to sit up, and I didn't need translation software to understand that his words would be unprintable in a family publication.

Observing this, my rescuer motioned for me to sidestep around to the eastern side of the complex and then follow him to the north. I complied, though to reach my destination, I had to push my way past a gauntlet of aggressive beggars who lined the stone pathway holding a variety of chipped and dented cups.

What they thought they could get from me, in my deplorable condition, I had no way to know; but I suppose all distress is relative.

One wretch gave my tunic a hard tug and even I struggled not to gag as I looked down and saw the blackened tumor, roughly the size of a golf ball, that marred the left side of the miserable creature's face.

***

With all the invalids lying about, I guessed that the place was some type of sanatorium – a presumption that turned out to be at least partially correct.

As I got closer, I could see that the complex consisted of two buildings, both square in shape. The southernmost structure, where the action was concentrated, measured about a hundred feet from end to end; roughly twice the size of its northern counterpart.

Their builders had constructed the two story walls with the familiar *meleke* limestone. Colonnades ringed the perimeters and provided a covered walkway between the structures as well.

I followed the priest around to the back where guards admitted us into what turned out to be the administrative center for the site. We passed through an uncovered patio surrounding a small circular pool about ten feet across. There, the man instructed me to shed my filthy tunic.

I dipped my toe into the water first – I'll admit to being a wimp when it comes to the cold – and then plunged in. I splashed around for a minute, and then climbed back out, where a servant waited with a towel as well as a clean tunic.

I now felt like a human being again for the first time since coming to. I pointed to the crowds thronging into the other building with a questioning look. He answered, but either he didn't speak Greek or the translation software wasn't working quite right, so I only caught a few random words.

Then I experienced something even more bizarre. Another assistant, bald and dressed exactly like his counterparts, emerged from a back closet grasping a handful of docile brown snakes. He lifted them up to his boss, who appeared to *bless* them.

As soon as the old man had finished, the kid bowed and headed toward the main building.

This I had to see.

I gestured my request and the priest nodded his approval, signaling me to follow. Surprisingly, given what I had observed earlier, the mob let us pass through with only a minimum of pushing and shoving.

But as soon as I got inside, I wished they hadn't.

An indescribable stench assaulted my senses. Surrounding an irregularly shaped pool at the courtyard's center was a veritable sea of human misery. Hundreds of men – they were almost all men – with twisted and broken limbs lay packed, sardine-like, on woven pallets.

Others, who had been shunted off to one side, bore a ghastly array of tumors, pustules, and open wounds. Most of them simply stared up at the sky, alone in their thoughts, while friends or relatives attended to a fortunate few.

My companion, though, paid none of this any heed. Instead, he deposited his serpentine burden at various places near the pool and then scooted out the opposite door, with no more emotion than a package delivery service.

The reptiles slithered out of sight almost immediately, though to my surprise, none of the assembled wretches showed any consternation at their presence.

This seemed to be normal, or whatever passed for normal in this strange place.

And that wasn't the half of it. A short time thereafter, the air began to buzz in a cacophony of languages as the more vigorous of the sick and injured jostled for position at the edge of the water, pushing and shoving in search of a favorable spot.

I could sense the energy of the crowd. They were waiting for something with eager anticipation, though I didn't know what.

I gestured to a priest, but he just kept his eyes on the water and shrugged.

A few minutes later, I felt a low rumble, and the crowd suddenly stilled, with every eye riveted on the pool.

Seconds afterward, a bubble broke the surface.

As if a starter's gun had fired, the entire mass of humanity surged forward as best they could in a pell-mell scramble, leaving dozens of the front ranks to flail about wildly in the churning water.

This went on for some time, until the thrashing finally started to slow. At that point, a priest gave a signal, and a group of younger men – apprentices, maybe – began to shove the crowds back with wooden batons.

Once they had cleared sufficient space to work, a second crew began to fish the soggy unfortunates out of the pool and carry them back toward the walls as the poor creatures squawked in futile protest.

As the laborers were about to leave, though, one of their number pointed down into the water and signaled to an older priest. He sauntered down with a long wooden hook that reminded me of the ones used by theater impresarios in Saturday morning cartoons to yank dreadful performers off the stage.

Only this time, I didn't laugh. After two tries, the man snagged his quarry and pulled the drowned body to the surface.

Except for that priest, not another soul in the building cared.

Chapter 30

I pushed my way toward the south entrance, dodging the dispirited packs of invalids as best I could until I finally made it outside. From there, I kept going for another fifty yards as I strained to recall the details of the map Lavon had shown us before we departed Bryson's lab.

I stopped for a moment to get my bearings, savoring the fresh air. To my east, a narrow path ran between a disheveled pile of construction materials at the edge of a steep cliff. According to Lavon, this was most likely the initial segment of what would become a third wall surrounding Jerusalem's growing northern suburbs.

I didn't see any laborers, though, and this also fit with what the archaeologist had told us earlier: the Third Wall had been a haphazard enterprise for decades until the Revolt finally lent urgency to its completion.

Not that the effort did the Jews much good. When push came to shove, Roman siege engineers broke through it in a matter of days.

But that was forty years into the future. If I wanted to last forty more hours, I needed to find the others.

Looking down, I could see a narrow trail snaking its way down into the valley below before turning back up to the other side. There, a long ridge ran parallel to the city's eastern walls: the Mount of Olives.

I didn't see any other man-made path, so I surmised that travelers wanting to go south from where I was would cross over to the Mount and then follow a parallel track along the back side.

If that was where the others had gone, I still had a chance.

I trekked along the path until I reached the base of the Kidron Ravine, where I turned right and headed down my improvised shortcut at a steady jog. Fortunately, the vegetation had not grown too thick, so I made good progress.

The place smelled – I recalled Lavon's comment about the ravine being the city's garbage dump – but after what I had experienced already, I couldn't complain.

I could also see, as I looked up at the city's imposing eastern walls, why no invader had ever attacked Jerusalem from this direction. From where I stood, the top of the fortifications must have risen over two hundred feet, straight up.

The scrub trees got thicker, and thornier, as I reached the halfway point. The cheap sandals that my friendly snake-charmers had lent me protected my feet, but it didn't take long for my arms and calves to look like I had wrestled in barbed wire.

I pressed on, though, and after a few more minutes, I spotted a large crowd of people and animals gathering at Jerusalem's southern gate.

To my relief, I also saw that the main road swung far to the south of the Mount of Olives before turning back north toward the city. As long as the others had traveled at a normal pace, the odds were good that I had managed to reach the gate ahead of them.

I slowed my pace to a fast walk and decided to check in with Sharon.

I inserted my earpiece, but didn't even have a chance to call out.

"Oh my God," she said.

I heard some shouting in the background, too, but it didn't translate.

"Sharon, what is it? Are you OK?"

She didn't reply for a moment. When she did, I could tell she had seen something horrific.

She struggled to find the right words. "We just stopped again; this man is holding up a cup; he wants me to give him something."

"What kind of man?" I asked.

"I … I, uh, I'm not sure."

She finally collected herself enough to give me a rough description.

Hardened spherical nodules, several larger than a quarter, covered his face and neck. Live insects crawled through the remnants of a gray, scraggly beard. Compounding the dreadfulness of his appearance, a strip of cloth fell away as the man edged closer, revealing a huge open red sore.

Except for the insects, I had seen this once, years ago, in central Africa.

I had hoped never to see it again.

"Look at his hands," I said.

She did so, and gasped.

As I suspected, the fingers had degenerated into stumps, the flesh eaten away.

"It's leprosy, Sharon; an advanced case. Try not to touch him."

I needn't have worried. Sharon's captor didn't want him around either. He called out to one of the litter bearers, who stepped up and kicked the man square in the chest. The rest of their crew laughed as the beggar scrambled away, crawling on all fours.

She didn't say anything else for a moment. Leprosy was not an ailment that twenty-first century Americans thought much about. Like togas and spears, the disease belonged to a long-vanished age.

If only.

"A boyfriend in college once told me that the armadillo could be a carrier and that I should avoid handling them for that reason. I didn't believe him, though. He was always telling these ridiculous stories."

"He was right about that one," I replied, "although from what I've read, modern research has found that it's not quite as contagious as people once thought."

"Is it curable?"

"Antibiotics are effective if you catch it early enough."

She went quiet for a moment.

"What if we're …?"

"Stuck here past Sunday?" I replied.

"Yeah. Could we get it? I mean, an advanced case, like that one?"

"I don't think it spreads that fast."

Still, it was to our advantage to avoid the disease, if we could.

A pause.

"I, uh … you know, kicking that man …"

"Don't worry about it," I said.

"The laughing … the cruelty … that was *wrong*."

"Yes," I replied.

She didn't respond.

"Look, it's OK," I said.

I knew it wasn't, but at the moment, we'd gain nothing by dwelling on the subject.

Lavon told me earlier that Sharon had spent the last five Thanksgiving holidays dishing out meals at a homeless shelter. Now, this kind spirit had to confront, first-hand, why people of the ancient world held the disease in such abject terror, and admit that they had a legitimate reason for responding the way they did.

She would just have to work through it in her own mind.

"Do you have any idea where you are?" I asked, as much to take her thoughts off that particular struggle as to obtain a geographical coordinate.

She hesitated for a moment while she poked her head through the curtain once more. "We're outside the city," she said. "I think we passed through the Damascus Gate a minute ago. Now we're heading south, toward the palace."

"OK."

"Azariah is eyeing at me kind of strangely, too. He has to be wondering why I keep talking to myself. I think he's worried I'll bolt."

"Hang in there. I'll call you again when I find the others."

Chapter 31

I removed the earpiece and slipped it under my tunic; then I climbed up toward the city until I got within about a hundred feet of the main road.

Once there, I sat down on a rock next to one of the ubiquitous olive trees and watched. I figured if anyone questioned what I was doing, I'd do my best to pretend that I was a slave waiting for his master, as ordered, by the gate.

I needn't have worried. In an era without reliable timekeeping, slaves occasionally had to wait for days. Lavon explained later that this was common practice.

By the look of it, the Romans had outsourced security in this section of town to the local constabulary. Black helmeted sentries, in uniforms resembling those I had seen on the Temple police, paced the walls, while a half dozen or so of their colleagues manned their stations at ground level.

Occasionally, they pulled travelers aside and inspected their cargo, but otherwise they made little effort to stop the flow of people and animals into the city. Given the nature of the crowd, I'm not sure they could have, even if they had wanted to.

About one in every five itinerants either rode a donkey or led one laden with provisions, and I was reminded of what the world must have smelled like before the widespread adoption of the internal combustion engine.

Not every donkey was as eager as its owner to go inside, either. I watched one heavily burdened animal sit down on a flat stretch of road and simply refuse to take another step. Its owner cursed and swore, flogging the poor creature with a thin piece of cane.

It never so much as budged.

The passers-by just laughed. One of them must have made a snide comment, for suddenly the owner launched into an even greater frenzy, until the unfortunate beast rolled over as best it could under its load. Whether it had died or was just resting, I never got close enough to tell.

**

I had waited for about half an hour, soaking in the scene, when I finally spotted Lavon.

That wasn't as hard as I had initially feared. As it turned out, the average man in first century Judea measured less than five foot six, so each of my fellow travelers stood head and shoulders above the rest.

All three appeared to be going strong. Their eyes, though, were so focused on the city walls and the crowd at the gate that none of them saw me slip into the file of travelers behind them.

"Does anyone have spare change for a poor mendicant beggar?" I said.

They all turned, but it took a moment for the English words to register, and a moment longer for them to realize the person behind them was me.

"What are you doing here?" said Markowitz.

We stepped off to the side of the main road and they appraised me from top to bottom.

"You look like hell," said Bryson.

I didn't think it was that bad, especially since my rescuers at the sanatorium had let me take a dip in their pool, but my throbbing head must have diverted my mind from other damage.

Markowitz noted a darkening welt growing at the side of my left eye, and I explained what had happened as best I could. Lavon burst out laughing when I got to the part about the snakes.

"You saw that, too?" I asked.

"We were so close that I couldn't bear to walk past without having a peek inside. That building is an *asclepion* – a healing center dedicated to Asclepius, the Greek god of medicine. Once again, my thesis advisor was wrong. He didn't think the site served that purpose until the second century."

"Why the snakes?"

"Snakes were sacred to Asclepius."

I cast him a dubious glance.

"You should pay more attention the next time you go to the doctor," he chided. "The snake wrapped around the pole, the symbol of modern medicine, that's where it comes from."

Of course. I knew that.

"What about the mob scene at the pool?" I described the raw pandemonium I had witnessed.

"You saw that?" he asked, incredulous. Apparently, nothing remotely similar had happened during their visit.

"Why was it so important?" I asked.

"Rise, take up your mat and walk," he replied.

I stared at him blankly.

"Evidently, some sort of geological phenomenon causes the underlying spring to bubble up every now and then. The people here, in the first century, believe that it's an angel stirring the waters. Whenever that happens, the first one in gets cured of what ails him."

That explained the mad rush, though not the rest of the story.

"What did you mean with the bit about the mat?" I asked.

"John's gospel records it as one of Christ's first miracles. An invalid had been lying there beside the pool for 38 years when Jesus walked up and asked him if he wanted to get well. Rather than say yes, the man launched into a litany of excuses about how someone always beat him into the water. Christ healed him and told him to go home."

"Does this spring still exist, in our time?"

"Not really. The Church of St. Anne rests over the site now, but that's a twelfth century Crusader structure, renovated in the late 1800s. We think the current building replaced a Byzantine church, but before that, who knows. Like I keep saying, Jerusalem has been scraped and rebuilt many times. Exactly where things were is a matter of conjecture."

"Why allow a Greek temple there?" asked Markowitz.

"I'm not really sure," admitted Lavon. "My guess is that the Jewish priests didn't have any better answers to medical problems. I suppose it gave people hope."

"Or provided a good place to shuffle off grandpa," said Bryson. "You could dump a sick relative there and not feel bad about it."

***

I encouraged the others to continue this line of discussion, but despite my best efforts, I couldn't evade the inevitable question.

"Where's Sharon?" asked Lavon.

I explained what little I knew.

Once I had done so, Bryson and Markowitz immediately began arguing about the best way to rescue her. Their schemes, though, struck me only as efficient ways to commit suicide. None would have done Sharon any good at all.

Lavon didn't seem to think so, either, but he stepped away from us for a moment, lost in thought.

"I think she'll be OK," he finally said,

"We can't just abandon her!" said Markowitz. "You know what they're going to do."

He nodded. "Yes, but we have a little while to work out a plan. Ancient documents describe a regimen of baths and beauty treatments to be completed before a girl was deemed fit for the king. This will take time."

"How much time?" I asked.

"At least a day," said Lavon. "Possibly two or three."

"Today's Wednesday, right?" I asked.

They nodded.

"Then we have until tomorrow night at least," I said, "Friday if we're lucky."

I didn't have to add that we hadn't exactly had the best of luck so far.

"This is my fault," said Lavon. "Kings sent retainers to round up pretty girls all the time. I just thought we'd be safe in the Antonia, in addition to the story of her being royalty."

"Obviously they didn't believe that," said Bryson.

"That was my fault, too. We all slept in the same bed last night. If she had been a real princess, she would have had the bed to herself and the rest of us would have spent the night on the floor. I just got carried away watching everything else; it slipped my mind."

"What do you think they really take us for?" asked Bryson.

"Our hands, even yours Bill, are not the rough hands of manual laborers, and our clothes are too well made to be peasant garments. I'm guessing they see us as prosperous merchants."

"Exactly what we started out pretending to be," said Bryson.

Lavon nodded. "Ironically, whoever did this might even think they're doing us a favor. If she pleases the king, she could open up profitable trading opportunities."

"I can't imagine her feeling very good about that," said Bryson.

"No," said Lavon, "but this is the first century; she is a woman. Her feelings are of no consideration at all."

Chapter 32

At that point, the only sensible thing to do was to head straight back to the Antonia the way we came. That would allow us to avoid the worst of the crowds, and with Lavon able to speak for us, I was certain that we could eventually persuade a soldier to fetch Publius.

I suggested this, but my comment had the opposite effect. Markowitz and Bryson strode forward toward the city, while Lavon just rolled his eyes and followed.

In truth, he wanted to see the Temple as badly as the others did; he just wouldn't admit it.

We pushed our way back into the line of travelers and passed through the gate without incident; and once we got inside the walls, we could not have turned back even if we had wanted to. The stream of itinerants had become a river, flowing in only one direction, to the north.

We passed a spring where a gaggle of angry women stood in line with buckets, and I realized then that if the area surrounding Herod's palace was Jerusalem's high-rent district, we had now crossed over to the wrong side of the tracks.

The main path leading north from the Tekoa Gate followed along the western edge of the ridge bisecting the city all the way past the Temple Mount. West of our path, the ground sloped down into a deep valley, filled with densely packed structures that reminded Bryson of a colleague's research facility at MIT.

From what I could see, the lab rats probably had it better. At least they didn't have to live under a pall of acrid smoke.

Bryson coughed and struggled not to gag. "What is that smell?"

"Firewood is expensive," said Lavon. "They use dried animal dung as fuel."

I had seen this before, in India, but never on this scale.

Off to our right, Lavon pointed to a collection of shabby stone buildings, noting that this area constituted the original Jerusalem, the City of David.

"Who could have figured it?" he said.

We each had to acknowledge the peculiarity of it all. David's Jerusalem extended only a few hundred yards in each direction, covering ten acres at most. At its peak, it probably housed fewer than a thousand inhabitants.

Yet such a place, the headquarters of a man who was in reality more of a tribal chieftain than a king, became the focal point of three global religions with billions of adherents.

***

I was still reflecting on this oddity a few minutes later when I heard a loud yell. I ducked out of the way just as a boy, about ten years old and sporting a ragged tunic at least one size too small, ran past us with two angry men in hot pursuit.

The kid probably would have made his getaway but for a loose paving stone that protruded up about half an inch.

Seconds later, he tripped over the block and went sprawling face-first onto the ground. He attempted to rise, but the men were on top of him in an instant, pounding his body with wooden staves.

The boy cried out but soon fell silent under the weight of the blows. One of his pursuers reached down and grasped a cloth pouch. He displayed a brief expression of triumph; then both men trotted back down the street without giving the child a second thought.

Bryson stood aghast. "We've got to help him."

The crowd, however, continued to push us forward, and no one else expressed the slightest concern over the boy's fate. A street urchin, they had most likely concluded; and good riddance.

Lavon tugged Bryson's robe. "Come on; there's nothing we can do."

***

After we passed the City of David, our pace slowed even more as side streets fed additional pilgrims onto the primary thoroughfare. Given that we had a little time, I finally had a chance to ask Bryson a question that had been bothering me since the beginning of our excursion.

"Professor," I asked. "How did you know where to find the tomb?"

He hesitated briefly.

"Its location is well-accepted, is it not? Ironically, we can thank Hadrian. The emperor was so fervently anti-Christian that he razed the impromptu shrine the early believers had built on the site and erected a pagan temple in its place, inadvertently marking the spot for all time.

"When Constantine legalized Christianity two centuries later, all the followers of Christ had to do was tear down Hadrian's monstrosity and build their own church."

That sounded plausible enough, though I could read the skepticism on Lavon's face. He told me later that this theory was probably correct, with an emphasis on *probably*. An alternative site, the Garden Tomb, lay to the north of town. Modern archaeologists continue to debate the matter.

But that wasn't the most pressing issue.

"How do you plan to find it today?" I asked.

"I just told you."

"No," said Lavon. "You told us how a twenty-first, or a fourth, or even a second century man would locate it; but there's nothing there now. According to the Gospels, it's Joseph of Arimathea's family plot. Did you plan on walking into a meeting of the Sanhedrin and asking him to show you where it is?"

"I've taken satellite photos and overlapped the Holy Sepulcher with known archaeological coordinates from this era. We can triangulate between the Damascus Gate and the Phasael Tower. Both of those structures survived into modern times."

"Triangulate how?" I asked. "Did you bring a compass?"

Even if he had, the reading wouldn't necessarily be accurate. The earth's magnetic field had shifted considerably over the intervening two thousand years.

"You've got another problem, too," said Lavon. "Only the foundation of the Phasael Tower remains in our world. This covers a fairly broad area, not the pinpoint location you'd need to triangulate something as small as the tomb."

Bryson didn't reply. Instead, he muttered something about getting close as he stared off to the west.

I couldn't figure it. He seemed too much the careful scientist to go off half-cocked. Either he knew something he wasn't telling us or I had completely misread the man. The truth, as it turned out, was a little bit of both.

Chapter 33

At that moment, the logjam in front of us – caused by another recalcitrant donkey, we finally saw – cleared away, and the crowd surged forward, sweeping us along for the ride.

As we came closer to the Temple Mount, we felt an electric energy surge through our fellow travelers, a sensation I found akin to fans going into a rock concert or a championship football game.

"Stay together," Lavon ordered.

I didn't argue. Religious gatherings have no exemption from the forces of crowd dynamics. Hundreds of modern pilgrims die almost every year in stampedes at the Hajj in Mecca; and worshipers are trampled so regularly during Hindu festivals that the Indian media have invented a distinctive term for such events: "temple crushes."

I didn't need an overly active imagination to picture the same thing happening here. Lavon must have thought so, too; for the first chance he saw, he ducked into a narrow side alley and led us along a circuitous path that ended at the southeast corner of a broad plaza.

There, we all stopped and stared upward, gawking the way we had when we had first spotted the city from a distance.

From our perspective at the base of the retaining wall, the red-tinted roof of the Temple's royal colonnade must have risen at least two hundred feet above our heads – the height of a twenty-story building. I, for one, stood in awe, which was, as I realized later, the whole point.

"Incredible," said Markowitz.

Then he charged forward.

We had to sprint to catch up, which we did just as he pushed his way into a stream of pilgrims heading up the broad stairway to the Temple entrance.

At this point, we had no option but to fall in with a line of men inching toward the eastern set of double doors. Once inside, additional passages opened into a broad network of shallow pools, known as *mikvas*, where worshipers performed the ritual purification ceremony required to enter the Temple itself.

Markowitz disappeared for a moment before Lavon managed to spot him going into the closest body of water. He reached out and pulled him back.

"Not yet," he said. "Let's stay together and get the lay of the land first."

Markowitz complied, though not for long. Once more, the incoming throng surged behind us and pushed us apart.

The next time I spotted him, he had already traveled a fair distance and was making a beeline up the steps toward the open plaza of the Temple Mount, with the Professor and Lavon trailing close behind.

***

By then, I couldn't do much else than go along with the general flow of the crowd, and after a few minutes of being jostled about, I found myself in the animal market.

The moneychangers had returned to business with a vengeance, and this morning they were taking no chances.

Guards of the Temple police, conspicuous in their black helmets and armed with spears and cudgels, stood roughly ten feet apart behind each row of tables. Disturbances today would prove remarkably unhealthy, something I was to observe all too clearly later on.

I made one more quick search for the others before turning my attention back to the marketplace itself. Though appearing chaotic at first glance, I could see, upon closer inspection, that the Temple authorities possessed a firm grasp of operational logistics.

Servants traveled in a one-way path through specially designated corridors, carrying fresh sacrificial inventory to the vendors from the lower levels and then removing the empty cages to a holding area, where other attendants gathered them and returned them to stocking pens below.

I found the overall layout quite clever as well. Worshipers emerging from the *mikvas* entered immediately into a one way labyrinth of tables and cages before pouring out into the Temple courtyard.

Taken as a whole, the place bore an uncanny resemblance to the departure terminals of modern international airports, whose designers shamelessly funnel passengers through a maze of duty free stores before allowing them to reach their destination gates.

In truth, the only real difference was the smell.

I had stepped aside to avoid two boys wrestling with a recalcitrant lamb when I heard shouting in the direction of the Temple itself.

Instinctively, I turned my head to see what the commotion was about – and could only grit my teeth and swear.

Next to the *soreg*, a meter high barricade that delineated the boundary between the Temple Mount's common area and the part reserved exclusively for Jews, an angry mob had surrounded Markowitz and the Professor. Lavon struggled to push his way through, and he reached them only with great difficulty.

A young priest standing nearby appeared to be the only thing holding the agitated crowd back from a violent response. The trouble was, the kid looked as nervous as I felt. I wasn't sure he could restrain them for long.

I gave quiet thanks that I had managed to slip my remaining transmitter into Lavon's hands only a few moments before we all got separated, and I managed to get my earpiece seated just in time to hear Markowitz try once more to explain what he wanted.

"Tell these people I'm Jewish," he said. "I want to see the Temple."

Lavon glanced around, looking for a way out, though it didn't take long for him to realize that attempting to back away would only prove their evil intentions in the minds of the crowd.

Seeing that he could only take one action, and live, he stood tall and spoke with the most authoritative voice he could muster.

"This man is Jewish," he shouted.

Upon hearing this, the crowd grew quieter. The agitated murmuring did not entirely disappear, but at least a few of them seemed to understand, thank God.

The young priest did not, though to my great relief he signaled for a colleague to come over and help. As far as I could tell, the new man's clothing carried no insignia of rank, but I could see immediately that his colleagues deferred to him. More importantly, his age and demeanor had a calming effect on the mob.

"How may I assist you?" he asked.

His voice rose barely above the level of a whisper, which forced the crowd to become even quieter in order to hear. I let out a sigh of relief. Whoever he was, this priest clearly understood human nature.

Lavon pointed to Markowitz. "This is a man of Israel."

The old man stared at them for what seemed like an eternity before asking where they were from.

"Norvia," Lavon replied. "A land far to the north, beyond Germania."

The priest nodded as if this was a sufficient explanation for their white skins and light hair, but I could see he wasn't entirely convinced.

He studied the three of them with genuine curiosity. "Tell me, how did sons of Abraham find their way to such a place?"

Lavon spun him the same tale he had told me earlier; about exiles and Lost Tribes and Babylonians long ago.

To my surprise, the man seemed to go along with the story.

I learned later that the Babylonians who destroyed Solomon's Temple made a practice of incorporating talented young men from captive nations into their administrative structure, and that some of the Jewish exiles – notably Daniel of the celebrated lion's den – had risen to high positions in both the Babylonian government and the Persian empire that followed.

Lavon had been right. Many of the exiles never went back.

Go figure.

The old priest then focused his gaze on Markowitz. "What have you been taught regarding the ways of God?' he asked.

"What are they saying?" asked Markowitz.

"He wants to know what you've learned of the Jewish faith," said Lavon.

Markowitz's face brightened as he explained his Bar Mitzvah; as if the traditions of twentieth century Manhattan would be the same as those of two thousand years before.

"He says that he learned the ten commandments of Moses," Lavon replied. "Nothing more."

"He acts like he wants to tell us more," said the priest.

"He is an emotional fellow," said Lavon. "He is reciting each of the commandments. He rarely has the opportunity. So few in Norvia show any interest in the ways of his God."

"What God do you worship in Norvia?" asked the old man.

Lavon hesitated. I suppose he hadn't expected this question, at least not under these circumstances. Finally, he said, "we worship the God who created our forests and the seas."

It seemed a safe enough answer.

The priest pondered this information for a moment; then he turned to his colleague, gesturing toward Markowitz's tunic.

The young man began to lift it, but Markowitz pushed him back.

"Be still," said Lavon as he realized what they were doing. "They need to check."

"Check what?"

"That you're circumcised. That's one thing all Jews would have done, even in exile."

I held my breath as priest took a quick peek.

I needn't have worried. The man let go of Markowitz's tunic and the elder stretched out his arms.

"Welcome brother," he said.

At that point, the murmurings of the crowd ceased and most of them drifted away. Lavon breathed a visible sigh of relief. I did, too, for that matter.

Moments later, the young priest turned to the archaeologist, intending to repeat the inquiry.

"No," said Lavon. "I am here only because no one else knows this man's language. I came to assist my friend in finding his way home."

"For that, we thank you," said the senior priest.

Then he directed his attention to Bryson, who up to that point had remained silent. "What about him?"

"He is with me," said Lavon. "He is also not a son of Abraham, but he traveled with us, in order to protect our friend on his journey."

The elder repeated his thanks; then turned back to Markowitz. "What is his name?"

Lavon asked Markowitz what his middle name was, hoping it was a good Old Testament one, I suppose.

It was.

"Benjamin," said Markowitz.

"I am Nicodemus."

I watched Lavon stare for a brief instant with open astonishment, though he quickly caught himself. If the old man had noticed, he chose not to comment.

"Can I go in now?" asked Markowitz.

Lavon translated.

"Have you washed?" asked Nicodemus.

Markowitz shook his head.

"Then that is your first step. After you have purified yourself, purchase your sacrificial offering – a lamb, if you can afford one; a dove if you cannot."

Nicodemus paused. I could see him assessing our party's clean and well sewn clothing.

"It appears that God has favored you with prosperity. I would suggest a lamb," he said.

"Of course," said Lavon. "Then what?"

"Return here with his offering, and I will show him what he must do. He will be several hours inside."

"What about us?"

Nicodemus directed their attention to an opening in the *soreg* at the southwest corner of the Temple. "You may wait there for his return."

Lavon bowed to the old man. "We thank you for your kindness. I will return shortly with the lamb."

"He should select it himself;" said Nicodemus. "It is his sacrifice after all."

Chapter 34

I ran forward to catch up as they headed back to the vendors' booths and guided them into a relatively isolated corner.

Lavon's face had turned pale, in the manner typical of a near miss survivor whose mind has finally begun to soak in a full understanding of how close they had all come to total disaster.

Before I could say anything, he grabbed Markowitz by the lapel of his robe and threw him against a stack of empty cages, holding the fabric up to his neck as if to choke him.

"Are you *trying* to get us all killed?"

I glanced around at the surge of worshippers and moved to separate them. Personally, I wanted to throttle the impulsive fool as well, but I could see that others were beginning to take notice. The last thing we needed was to create another scene.

"Where is the harm?" he protested. "That priest welcomed me as a brother. And don't forget: I *am* one!"

Lavon threw the handful of cloth back at him in disgust, took a couple of deep breaths, and then lit into Markowitz a second time. I let him vent for a moment; then suggested that we all slip away and head back to the Antonia, while we still could.

The archaeologist shook his head. "It won't work. Too many people heard Nicodemus tell him to buy a lamb and come back. Some of them are undoubtedly still watching. We can't take that chance."

"What about me?" I asked.

Lavon studied my torn tunic and thorn-shredded arms and calves.

"You never got close to the *soreg*, so they can't accuse you of trying to get inside. If anyone asks, I'll tell them you're my servant, and that I'm sending you away. I think you'll be OK."

He walked over to a merchant's table and tossed out a couple of coins. I watched him take a small scrap of what looked like parchment and write. When he came back, he handed it to me.

I studied the precise Greek lettering.

"It's a request for the sentries to let you in to see Publius," he said.

"I can't read it."

"That shouldn't matter. Most slaves were illiterate. You have your orders, though I'd do my best not to show the note to anyone on the Temple Mount. Some fanatic might think you're a spy."

Wonderful. I couldn't tell whether he was serious or not.

"What will you and Henry do?" I asked.

"Exactly what Nicodemus told us to do: sit there at the corner and wait for Ray to finish his sacrifice."

He paused for a moment.

"*Nicodemus.* I can't believe that's who we were talking to."

"What is so important about him?" asked Bryson.

"John 3:16," replied Lavon, as if that explained everything.

It didn't, of course. Not having grown up with the church, the Professor and Markowitz associated the verse only with rainbow headed freaks holding up signs behind the goal posts at football games.

"It's one of the most well known passages in the New Testament," said Lavon. "'For God so loved the world that he gave his only begotten Son, that whosoever believeth in Him shall not perish, but have everlasting life.' That's who Jesus was talking to when he spoke those words – Nicodemus. He's a respected elder, a member of the Sanhedrin."

He turned to Markowitz. "And a man who saved your butt."

***

Considering that I also wanted to save mine, I didn't waste any time making my way back to the fortress. I stuck the receiver in my ear as I walked out the eastern gate toward the ravine, and I could only laugh as Lavon helped Markowitz purchase his lamb and lead the animal back to the Temple itself.

It bleated softly.

"A cute little critter," I heard Markowitz say.

"Don't get too attached to it," Lavon replied. "In less than an hour, you're going to be cutting its throat."

"Me?"

This was a surprise. I had thought the priests handled that end of the business.

I couldn't help but chuckle at the picture forming in my mind. For all his enthusiasm for adventure sports, I doubted Markowitz had ever killed a large animal except by hitting one with his car. Hopefully he wouldn't make too big a mess of it.

As I turned back toward the north, I tapped on my ear bud to shift frequencies and check in with Sharon.

To my relief, not much had changed on her end. After passing through the Damascus Gate, her litter had made its way south along the city wall.

She sounded subdued, though, and after she told me the story, it wasn't hard to understand why.

Their procession had stopped two more times to rest the porters. Each time, guards had kept the swarm of mendicants following them at bay. On the last stop, though, one beggar, seeing a soldier's attention diverted, had rushed up to the litter and thrust a cup through the curtain.

Though this man wasn't a leper, Azariah called out to another guard, and Sharon could only watch helplessly as the soldier cudgeled the poor fellow with a strong blow to the back of the head, leaving his skull cracked open and his motionless body bleeding in the dust.

"He walked on as if he had stepped on a bug," she said.

From his perspective, he probably had.

She explained, too, just what a close call our Temple excursion had been.

Roughly thirty years later, on what could have been the same exact spot, excitable self-appointed busybodies – the curse of every religion – had accused the apostle Paul of bringing "Greeks" into the Temple and defiling it. He barely escaped the subsequent riot in one piece and never took another step as a free man – eventually going to his death in Rome, in chains.

No wonder the archaeologist had turned so pale.

Otherwise, Sharon seemed OK, so I tapped my ear to switch back to Lavon's frequency. Although he didn't respond to my inquiries, I could hear him speaking calmly and concluded that Markowitz must have made it into the Temple without further incident.

Bryson, though, was a different matter. As I threaded my way back though the trash and thorn bushes of the Kidron Ravine, I listened to him speak of his latest brainstorm.

"Would he know Joseph of Arimathea?" he asked.

"What?"

"Nicodemus: would he know Joseph?"

"Certainly," said Lavon.

"Then that may be our answer. Culloden's right. I'm not sure I'll be able to find the exact site of the tomb the way I had planned. Triangulating with sufficient accuracy will be harder than I thought."

Lavon didn't reply. By now he could guess what was coming next.

"If you go back there and ask him, perhaps he can introduce us to Joseph."

This was lunacy.

Obviously, Lavon thought so, too.

"Let me ask you something. Say some stranger walked into your MIT lab and asked where your family's cemetery plot was. What would you do?"

"I'd ask why they wanted to know."

"Yes, just before you called campus security to come with a straitjacket. What answer could we possibly give? *In a few years, you'll have the most famous tomb on the planet?*"

Bryson didn't say anything for a moment.

"I suppose you're right," he finally replied. "Still, we should find some way to inquire of these people while we have the chance. Maybe we could report a workman got injured or something."

Chapter 35

I couldn't listen to any more of this nonsense. Besides my ear was starting to itch, so I popped the device out as I climbed up the steep incline toward the Reptile Garden. Though I had learned the facility's true purpose, I couldn't help calling it that.

Once there, I located my benefactor and dropped the handful of the coins Lavon had given me onto a table. I'm good for my debts as a matter of principle, and given the way things had transpired so far, I didn't think it would hurt to have a few more friends, just in case.

The priest gestured as if he wanted me to stay, but I showed him Lavon's missive and motioned that I needed to be moving on.

I had only a short jog to the Antonia. Lavon's note worked as expected, and a few minutes later, I found myself escorted into the presence of Publius, who was conducting a final equipment inspection before he sent two squads out on patrol.

He eyeballed my bedraggled appearance with a look of surprise. Since my earpiece wasn't in, I couldn't understand a word he was saying, though the gist wasn't too hard to figure out.

"*Lestes*," I replied. It was the only Greek word I knew.

I suppose a story that I had been attacked by bandits was plausible enough. Fortunately he didn't press the issue, since the last thing I wanted to mention was Markowitz's venture into the Temple.

Instead, he directed my attention to a cluster of soldiers standing around a small canopy about twenty yards away.

I strode over to the group without looking back, dodging a pile of armor as I went. One of the soldiers glanced at Publius and then instructed the others to move out of my way. As they did so, it wasn't hard to see why.

I wasn't the only one having a really bad day.

Medics attended to two seriously wounded Romans lying on stretchers in the shade. I could see immediately that the man on the left wouldn't last long. Blunt force trauma, from a club, probably, had caved in the side of his skull just behind his left eye. I was no expert, but even in a modern hospital, I would have rated his odds of survival no better than one in five.

I turned to Publius and shook my head before addressing the second case.

This man also faced grave peril. As the medics removed his blood-soaked tunic, I spotted a deep gash in his abdomen, and a closer inspection confirmed the worst: a small tear in the peritoneal sac surrounding his intestines.

I called for water as I considered what to do. The primary danger with this type of injury is infection, usually resulting from fragments of dirty clothing or intestinal material itself seeping into the abdominal cavity.

Army field protocol for such wounds calls for a soldier to press sterile gauze into the opening and then wrap the wound snugly, followed by a quick evacuation of the patient to a field hospital where physicians can clean out any foreign matter and administer the required antibiotics.

Today, though, I was on my own. I could only try and hope for the best.

As a servant placed a large bowl of water on the ground beside me, I reached into my bag and removed a small package of powdered iodine, which I dumped into the bowl and stirred until the solution was an even light brown.

The other soldiers watched curiously as I washed my hands in the iodine and then made a closer inspection of the wound. I used tweezers to pull several small fragments of the man's tunic away from the opening before thoroughly cleaning the surrounding area with a patch of iodine soaked gauze.

Afterward, I clamped the opening with a couple of butterfly bandages and covered the area with an antibiotic laced compress. It was all I could do. He might not live, but he'd at least have a fighting chance.

To the extent that I could pantomime, I instructed the others to give the man only boiled water to drink and nothing to eat for at least a day, though I wasn't sure how well I got my instructions across.

***

I had to wait for the soldiers' attention to be diverted before I could slip my ear bud in once more. I tried first to reach Lavon, but for some reason, he didn't respond.

A moment later, however, Sharon's voice came through loud and clear.

"You wouldn't believe this place," she said.

She sounded as if she had entered a different world — which in fact, she had.

She explained that her litter had entered the palace about half an hour earlier and she had been unloaded, so to speak, in a verdant, sun-lit courtyard roughly the size of three football fields.

Deep channels crisscrossed lush, grassy lawns, carrying water to a remarkable assortment of shade trees and a stunning variety of flowering plants. An "oasis of serenity" she called it. Topping things off, hundreds of white doves flew back and forth between the trees.

I couldn't help but laugh. "You sound like you're writing ad copy for Donald Trump."

"His resorts are a pigsty compared to this," she said.

She didn't add that Herod probably hadn't filed for bankruptcy as many times, either.

"Who else is there with you now?" I asked.

In the background, I could hear what sounded like a dozen women frolicking in the water – teenage girls, by the pitch of their voices.

"Azariah sent me to join the others by the pool area," she said.

"What about guards?"

She spotted a few pacing back and forth atop the fifty foot crenellated wall that ringed the palace complex to keep the riff-raff in their place, but otherwise, she couldn't see any.

As I thought about it, this made sense. Based on her description so far, the palace didn't sound like a place many people tried to escape.

Besides, an army of servants tended the grounds, and punishment of slaves in the Roman world was both brutal and collective. Everyone had an incentive to watch everyone else. If she tried to slip away, she wouldn't get far.

I heard her sigh – a pleasurable sigh, from the sound of it. Part of me wanted to let her rest and enjoy the afternoon in the sun, but she could not afford to let her guard down. Herod's palace might top even the most modern luxury resorts, but so did the price of admission.

Not that she had forgotten.

I explained to her what Lavon had told me about the bath treatments and that gave her an idea.

"Just be careful," I said. "I'll keep checking in when I can."

Chapter 36

I tried once more to contact Lavon but had no better luck than before. I couldn't help but worry. Though I couldn't see what was happening, the cascade of wounded Romans streaming back into the fort told me that all was not sweetness and bliss outside.

Compounding my anxiety, I found myself going through my first aid supplies at an alarming rate. Once I ran out, my only real trump card would be gone.

I gestured to a nearby officer in an attempt to back away.

He ignored me, for at that moment, a squad of about a dozen Romans passed through the north gate, dragging five men linked together with heavy chains around their ankles, wrists and necks. For good measure, two more soldiers followed behind, prodding the captives forward with the occasional lash.

Everyone in the courtyard, even the medics, dropped what they were doing and edged over to have their first real look at their adversaries.

Two of these bruised and battered unfortunates were relatively young men, including one who looked as if he'd barely qualify to drive back home.

Whatever great adventure they had embarked on earlier in the day had gone horribly awry, and from their terrified expressions, they were only now beginning to realize how horribly indeed.

Two others appeared to be in their mid-twenties, but as if by instinct, I glanced past them to the captive at the head of the queue. This man, older by a decade and evidently their leader, displayed what I can only describe as sheer animal hatred.

No 'hearts and minds' for that one, I knew.

I looked to my left and spotted a servant leading an older man toward the now kneeling file of prisoners. The squad's leader saluted Volusus and briefly explained what had happened, while I re-seated my ear bud as discreetly as I could manage.

Volusus spoke to the prisoners through an interpreter. Whether he didn't understand Aramaic or simply wanted to use the delay in translation to formulate his next question, I couldn't tell.

The Roman commander stepped closer to the leader and asked his name, but the prisoner didn't even acknowledge the question. Instead, he continued to stare straight ahead, his eyes aflame with raw intensity.

Volusus repeated his question; slowly, and in an even tone.

"I will ask you again: what is your name?"

Once more, the man did not respond.

Volusus stared at the captive for a few seconds and then nodded to the closest officer. The *optio* drew a dagger from his scabbard; then two soldiers pressed the prisoner to the ground while the officer sliced a finger off the man's right hand.

He didn't utter a peep. Despite the trauma, his eyes continued to blaze defiance.

The soldiers lifted the prisoner to his knees, and Volusus repeated his inquiry a third time. Hearing no answer, he nodded again to the *optio*, but before the Roman could act, another prisoner cried out.

It was the youngster, who had turned a ghostly pale; and that wasn't the only sign of the kid's terror. His knees rested in a widening pool of his own urine.

"Hold to the strength of your father, Abbas!" he babbled.

"Your name is Abbas, then?" said Volusus.

This had a deflating effect on the man. He cast an irritated glance at the boy and then turned to the Roman commander.

"No, I am only his undeserving son."

"I see."

"You see nothing. You are blind to the truth, as are those vermin of our race who condemn themselves to eternal punishment by collaborating with your iniquity. They defy the ways of God."

The prisoner then cut loose with a stream of invective. I caught only bits and pieces as the interpreter struggled to keep up, though the parts that did come through – something about pig-eating sons of whores and their rightful place of damnation – made the gist of this fellow's speech quite plain.

The people of the modern Middle East had elevated swearing to an art form. It didn't sound like things had changed very much.

Volusus said nothing. He had heard it all before, I was sure, and perhaps experience had taught him that it was best to ignore their florid insults. Nevertheless, I could see that he was losing patience, and allowing such brazen defiance to go unpunished could give the others courage that they didn't otherwise possess.

He nodded to the *optio* again and the Romans repeated the drill, this time slicing the index finger off the same hand. They weren't quick about it, either.

The leader's grimace grew more evident, though once again, he stifled a cry. How he managed to do it, I couldn't imagine.

Volusus watched in silence. This wasn't getting anywhere.

"Take them below," he finally ordered.

I didn't want to think about what awaited them in the dungeons. I moved off to one side as soldiers dragged the unfortunate creatures away and two slaves rushed over with buckets of water to mop the congealed blood off the stone floor.

A few of the words, though, turned over and over in my mind as I watched: a son who seemed to worry only that he had not killed enough Romans to do his family proud. One Son of Abbas.

"I'll be damned," I muttered to myself. Son of Abbas. *bar* Abbas. *Barabbas*; arrested for – how had the Gospels put it – insurrection and murder.

My thoughts turned to the awful scene at the gate coming in. This Barabbas, if he was truly the one, was unaware of how lucky he would prove to be, and how quickly his fortunes would turn.

Chapter 37

While the guards led Barabbas and his crew to their fates below, I focused my attention back to the Roman wounded.

Suddenly, I heard a loud shout. By instinct, I jerked my head up and glanced around in all directions; though a brief moment later, I realized the sound had come from my earpiece.

I heard the shuffling of feet, followed by what sounded like a pile of lumber crashing to the ground. I called out, but got no response. Instead, I heard Lavon's sharp whisper.

"Lie down on the ground. Don't move."

This couldn't be good.

"Damn it, I said *don't move!*" The voice was still a whisper, but it carried an insistent tone.

I closed my eyes in order to concentrate. I could hear footsteps – running men by the sound of it – but I had no way of knowing what had actually happened.

Then I heard Lavon speak again, just as quietly as before, but with even more urgency.

"You must pretend to be dead, which you will be if you don't do exactly as I say."

And that was all.

I opened my eyes to see a couple of legionnaires looking at me with odd expressions, though the awkward moment passed quickly. Moments later, the *optio* who had dismembered Barabbas's hand called out and ordered them to fall back into formation.

Even I could see that whatever started outside the walls had now escalated into major trouble. A trumpet blew atop one of the battlements as another officer signaled for reinforcements, and I had a feeling that Barabbas wouldn't be the only man dissected today.

I was right about that, too.

For the next hour or so, wounded Romans either stumbled or were carried back in through the north gate.

I treated them to the extent I could and discovered that my reputation had spread through the ranks. Soldiers I had never seen before made a beeline to me with the most serious cases, though for some of them, I, like their colleagues, could do nothing but hope for the best.

Shortly after the last reinforcements had gone out, the returning legionnaires began to drag in coffles of battered prisoners, whose faces and clothing were caked in dried blood.

I had no way to know whether these men had suffered their injuries in the fighting or whether they had been beaten by vengeful soldiers after their capture. Obviously, the Romans issued no *Miranda* warnings, and a phone call to a lawyer was out of the question.

Very few of the captives carried themselves with the firm bearing of hardened combatants, and none displayed the intense fury I had witnessed in Barabbas.

I shook my head at the madness of it all. They probably never had much of a plan. Instead, full of misguided enthusiasm, these young men had gone charging forth on a grand campaign.

It would end as anything but that.

Having my hands full treating the injured Romans, I paid less attention to the prisoners as time went on. As the legionnaires dragged in a later batch, however, I glanced up and noticed one face that stood out, though the sight was so unexpected that it took my mind a few moments to process what my eyes had seen.

I spat and muttered a quiet expletive.

Bound fifth in the string, with his right eye blackened and blood dripping down behind his ear, was Markowitz. His face reflected a mixture of both confusion and raw terror.

Just before the Romans dragged his line through the doorway leading down to the dungeons, he shouted out my name, and Publius's – though he fell silent after a soldier slapped him hard on the face and barked at him to shut up.

I ducked behind a column as I considered what to do next. I called out to Lavon, but received no answer. I closed my eyes in yet another effort to recall a few tiny fragments of Latin, but it was no use. Even if I could remember more than a phrase or two, that was a far cry from being able to communicate properly.

I'd put it off as long as I could, but I knew that at some point, I'd have to make a decision: whether I had a realistic chance to save our reckless friend, or whether, by trying, I would share his fate.

***

I stewed over this for a little while; then to my relief, I heard Sharon's voice. As Lavon had predicted, Herod's servants had taken her to the baths, which were, unsurprisingly, a luxurious contrast to the Spartan, barracks-like facility in the Antonia.

"Can you tell me exactly where you are now?" I asked.

"I'm upstairs on the northwestern side of the compound. It's like a big dorm."

She described the chamber as being situated two floors above another *caldarium*. The room, about the size of a basketball court, had long cedar beams stretching across the ceiling that reminded her of her high school gym. Twin beds, spaced about four feet apart, lined the long walls. She counted sixty in all.

Once again, Herod's engineers had been clever. Heat from the furnace below the baths flowed upward through vents in the chamber's floors. At the far end, mounted to the wall, a two-foot diameter wheel rotated valves that permitted the heated air to flow through the room when the weather turned cold and shunted the excess to the outside on warmer days.

I couldn't help but ask whether the women fought over the thermostat.

She chuckled briefly before turning serious.

"Have the others come back?" she asked.

"Not yet," I replied.

I wasn't about to say more. Though her mental state seemed to be holding up well, I was sure that at the back of her mind, she held to the certainty that once Lavon came back and we could speak to the Roman commander, we'd have her back in the fortress before anything untoward could happen.

How she would react once she realized she'd have to fend for herself, I had no way to know.

***

I returned to my duties and had worked for another hour when the gate opened and forty horsemen charged inside.

After the soldiers came to a halt, grooms rushed forward to claim their mounts and lead them to the stables. Like everyone else involved with the Romans, the stable-hands went about their tasks with a brisk efficiency.

One man stood at the center of attention. After he dismounted, he remained still while attendants removed his armor. It was only when Volusus emerged from a side entrance and saluted that I realized the likely identity of the new arrival.

I nudged a nearby soldier, pointed to the man, and shrugged.

He understood. "The prefect," he replied. "Pilatus."

Though I was too far away to hear what they were saying, from their demeanors, it appeared that the prefect and the fort's commander were on reasonably good terms.

Pilate asked a few questions, but mostly he just listened to the officers' accounts. His face reflected very little emotion, one way or the other.

I tried hard not to stare. My own mental image, derived from both the Gospels and Hollywood, depicted Pilate as a weak, vacillating figure torn between his own conscience and the demands of the howling mob. As with many of my other impressions, I began to suspect that this one, too, was wrong.

After hearing the reports, Pilate walked over to speak to a group of wounded soldiers. He told a few jokes, from the look of it, and then directed his attention to a final group of ragged captives who knelt on the stone floor, awaiting transfer to the dungeons.

"Who are these people?" he asked.

A junior officer responded. "We picked them up in the disturbance today. We're in the process of questioning them."

"Take them below and give them to Titus Labernius," said Pilate. "He will know how to get the truth from them."

A loud, blood-curdling scream wafted through the courtyard from below.

"Two men are there now, excellency," said the officer.

The prefect considered this for a moment before turning his attention to Volusus.

"Very well. I'd like you to prepare a full report concerning everything that has happened over the past few days. We'll discuss it after my bath."

Chapter 38

I could do nothing but wait. I cringed at each scream from the torture below, and relaxed only after I was certain that the victim had not spoken English. After a while, I even found myself hunting for some wine, to steady my nerves.

At long last, just as dusk was beginning to settle over the courtyard, the gate opened and two familiar figures passed through. I breathed a sigh of relief as I whistled and waved them over.

"Thank God you're here," I said.

Lavon looked around the courtyard, his face lined with worry. "Did Ray make it back?"

Both he and Bryson winced as a prisoner let out a loud wail that echoed through the fort.

I dipped my head toward the paving stones at my feet. "He's down there, with the others. Tell me what happened."

Lavon explained as best he could. Shortly after Markowitz entered the Temple, a disturbance had broken out. Unable to see the source of the trouble, Lavon and Bryson had scurried away as unobtrusively as they could and had hidden themselves in the midst of empty animal cages.

That's what I had heard earlier.

They had waited for the chance to go back to the *soreg* and retrieve Markowitz, but the opportunity to do so in reasonable safety never came.

"We figured he'd make his way back, eventually," said Lavon. "I just never imagined that he would get caught up with the rioters."

"Do you have any idea how it happened?" asked Bryson.

"No," I replied. "The Romans dragged in a dozen or so batches of prisoners. Ray was in one of the latter groups. That's all I know."

"Is he OK?" asked Bryson.

"Other than being beaten to a pulp and facing slow torture, I'd say he's fine."

My sarcasm eluded the Professor, though not Lavon.

"Did you try to speak to him?" asked the archaeologist.

I glanced over to a group of wounded soldiers. "Today hasn't been a great day for the Romans, either. I figured I'd be just as likely to join him downstairs if I tried to speak out."

Lavon nodded in understanding.

"By the way, you won't believe who the mob's leader is." I said.

I explained.

"*The* Barabbas?" said Bryson.

Lavon, though, didn't seem surprised.

Just then, we heard another long shriek.

"We've got to get him out," said Bryson. "Where's that centurion friend of yours?"

"In with the governor, I think," I replied.

"Let's go talk to him," said Bryson.

I shook my head. Dozens of his men had been wounded earlier in the day, and at least four had died. At the moment, our fates were the least of his concerns.

"You said 'governor?'" Lavon asked. "Did you mean …"

"Yeah, Pilate."

"What was he like?"

I gave a brief description: height – about five-six, or roughly average for the region; age – late forties to early fifties; physical bearing – not muscular like the legionnaires, but reasonably trim and fit. The governor had limped a bit as he got off his horse, but other than that, I hadn't noticed any obvious health issues.

"What about his demeanor?" asked Lavon.

I considered this for a moment. "Keep in mind that I only saw him for a few minutes."

"And?"

"Businesslike," I replied.

Honestly, I couldn't think of a better term. After all that happened, I still can't.

***

Just then, Lavon spotted Decius and called out to him. The Roman came over to us, but this time, he didn't seem all that friendly.

"What is it you want?" he asked.

I couldn't tell whether his gruff attitude was directed at us specifically, or whether he was simply weary after a long, troublesome day. We could only hope for the latter.

"One of our party was caught in the midst of the disturbance today," Lavon explained. "We need to see him."

"Where is he now?"

"Some of your men took him downstairs, but he does not even know the bandits' language. There must be some mistake."

"How did he get mixed up with them?"

"I don't know. We need to ask him that very question."

Decius hesitated for a moment; then motioned for us to follow. He led us down a dim torch-lit staircase and then along a narrow passageway leading to an iron grate. Upon seeing the *optio*, a sentry saluted, then reached for his keys and opened the lock.

The light inside was even dimmer than on the stairs, though the most overpowering sensation was the stench – urine, feces, and the odor of burned entrails. Bryson turned to the side and threw up. The guard smiled, as did Decius. Neither of them made the slightest move to clean up the mess.

Decius called for a torch and they scanned the faces of the bound prisoners. To the far left, curled into a ball in the corner on some filthy, rotten straw, lay Markowitz.

I called him by name, but the English words didn't register immediately.

"Ray, it's me: Bill."

A barely audible voice replied. "Is that you? Where are Henry, and Robert?"

"We're here, too," they said. "What happened?"

Markowitz sat up, staring into the light as if he couldn't be entirely sure that his visitors weren't mere apparitions.

"I don't really know," he said. "I finished the sacrifice, but when I walked out of the Temple, you were gone. I looked around the courtyard for a few minutes, but I couldn't see anyone.

"I was about to go back inside when a group of these crazies came up and pushed me from behind. Two of them grabbed me and sort of herded me out the gate to the west, where maybe a hundred or so others were already waiting."

"Then what?"

"They were yelling and shouting, though I couldn't understand a word they were saying. They spotted a troop of Romans and all started picking up rocks and throwing them. I didn't want to, but one of them held a knife to my throat and handed me a paving stone. I didn't have much choice."

"Did you hit anyone?" asked Bryson.

"I have no idea. A few minutes later, I got struck by something and must have been knocked out. The next thing I knew, I was tied up with some others and pushed along the road until we got back here."

"So you've managed to make enemies on both sides," I said. "Congratulations."

Markowitz glared, but I took this as a positive sign. Some of his strength was coming back.

He looked down and didn't say anything for a minute or two; then he stared back up at us with pitiful, plaintive eyes.

"You've *got* to get me out of here. Do you know what they're doing?"

"We know," said Lavon.

The archaeologist explained to Decius what Markowitz had told him, emphasizing again that the prisoner did not speak the language of the bandits, and therefore could not have been part of their plotting.

Decius nodded but said nothing.

Lavon then reached over and started to help Markowitz to his feet. "May we take him back to our room?"

"No," said Decius.

"They may torture him if he stays here," said Lavon. "He must be moved to avoid a mistake."

Decius considered this for a moment; then called out to the sentry, who returned a few minutes later with two heavy chains.

"I will keep him apart from the others," the *optio* said, "but I have no authority to release him. Only the commander or the prefect may do that."

Decius barked another command and the sentry untied Markowitz and chained him around the neck and ankles.

"What's happening?" asked Markowitz.

"You're going to solitary until the prefect can hear your case," said Lavon.

He then spoke a few words in Greek to Decius. The officer signaled to another soldier, who returned a few minutes later with a chunk of bread and a jug of water. We then left the squalid pen and walked about thirty feet to a tiny crawl space.

The sentry opened the grate and motioned for Markowitz to go inside. The cell wasn't much bigger than the entrance – about five feet long, three feet wide, and four high, with a cold stone floor. Worse, no light reached the interior.

I shuddered as I considered that the ancients locked people in such spaces for months, if not years. Most – the lucky ones, really – would go mad in short order.

Lavon spoke to the guard, who handed me a torch and explained that I would be allowed a brief time to tend his prisoner's wounds.

Fortunately, Markowitz still had all of his teeth and he didn't appear to have any broken bones. I cleaned his face as best I could, given the circumstances, and then turned to leave. As I did so, Markowitz reached out to grab my arm.

"Your friends will let me go, surely."

"If Decius thought you were a Zealot, you'd still be with the others," I replied.

Markowitz sighed with relief, but his voice still registered concern. "Robert, he'll convince the commander, won't he?"

I pulled away. At the time, I felt like it would serve the kid right to squirm a bit.

"I'm sure he will," I said, "but just so you know, the governor arrived not long ago. You'll be at the tender mercies of Pontius Pilate."

Markowitz didn't respond, and just before the guard closed the door, Lavon reached inside and asked Ray to hand over his robe.

To my surprise, he did so without protest, or even asking why.

Once we returned to the courtyard, Lavon wadded the robe into a ball and threw it into the nearest charcoal brazier.

"Why did you do that?" asked Bryson. "He'll get cold."

"Better cold than dead."

"What?"

"He must have switched robes inside the Temple," said Lavon. "Jewish men wore tassels on the four corners of their garments. That's what I tossed into the fire."

"But Ray is Jewish."

"We're going to have enough trouble as it is. Let's not remind the Romans of that if we can help it."

Chapter 39

We trudged back up the twelve flights of stairs to our room. As we rounded the last corner, a dark-haired young man of about eighteen spotted us and leapt to his feet. He opened the door and motioned for us to enter.

Evidently, the rest of us were still in the good graces of our hosts, for the servant had already lit an oil lamp and supplied us with two loaves of fresh bread and a jug of wine.

Lavon spoke briefly and the kid hustled back downstairs.

"I sent him for dinner. We're going to need more than this."

Both he and Bryson hadn't eaten since the baths earlier in the morning, so they tore into the bread. I, for one, needed more liquid refreshment. I filled my goblet halfway, quickly chugged that, and then poured full cups for us all.

I leaned back in my chair and sighed. "A hell of a day," I said.

The other two did not argue. We just sat there, in silence, for some time.

"What are we going to do?" Bryson finally asked.

Lavon got up and walked over to a window. He stared at the Temple, watching the priests complete their evening rituals, while he attempted to work out a plan.

"Our best bet will be to lay low for a few days," he concluded.

That sounded reasonable to me, as long as the Romans let us. I certainly didn't have any better ideas.

"We can't just leave Ray in that cell," said Bryson.

"He'll live," said Lavon.

"You can't be serious! He doesn't have water. For crying out loud, he doesn't even have a bucket."

"I didn't say he'd be comfortable. I said he'd *live*. If we're lucky, they'll forget about him. We can ask Volusus to let him go after Pilate has gone back to Caesarea."

"How can you be sure that will happen?" Bryson asked.

"The Roman governors all hated this place," Lavon replied. "Caesarea, by contrast, had been built along Roman lines from the beginning, with all the comforts of home. They came to Jerusalem only when they had to, for festivals and such."

"Or when they expected trouble," I said.

Lavon nodded. "That's our second problem, although now it's all starting to make sense."

"What is?" asked Bryson.

"Why Pilate is here, in the Antonia," he answered. "Some of my colleagues believe that Jesus was condemned in Herod's palace instead of the fort, since Pilate, as a visiting Roman prefect, would naturally stay in the city's equivalent of the Presidential Suite. Somebody even filmed a TV show about it a few years ago, supposedly 'proving' why the Via Dolorosa is in the wrong spot."

"Makes sense," I said. "Except that he's obviously staying here."

"Yes. I overheard a couple of soldiers speculating about this, since it's so unusual. According to the rumors, some of the emperor's advisors have questioned whether they appointed the right man to govern Judea. Pilate is taking no chances. He wants to be in a position to stomp on any trouble the instant it develops."

"All the more reason to keep Ray under wraps," I said.

"That's what I'm trying to say. Let's hope they forget about him. Pilate could just as easily decide to kill all of the prisoners and be done with it."

"We might have to stay here beyond Sunday, then?"

Lavon nodded. "Do you recall if Ray still had a chip? I forgot to look."

In all the commotion, I had too.

***

I didn't want Sharon to think we had forgotten about her, so I reinserted my ear bud and called out.

She whispered quietly. "I've been trying to reach you," she chided.

Lavon also inserted his earpiece. "Hello, Sharon," he said. "Where are you?"

"A dressing room, by the looks of it."

That, as it turned out, was a bit of a misnomer, since the women typically departed with considerably less apparel than they had on going in, but we found her description fascinating nonetheless.

The room was about half the size of the dormitory. Along one side, a stone bench jutted out about three feet from the main wall, with a conduit of running water flowing down the middle from one end to the other. From what I could tell, the only things missing were the faucets.

A wheel like the one in the sleeping quarters controlled similar heating vents. Oil lamps provided illumination, and in a far corner, musicians played soothing tunes.

"They brought me here a few minutes ago. There's not room for everyone to dress at the same time, so the others are getting ready in shifts."

"Have you seen where they are going?"

"The banquet hall."

She paused.

"Hold on. Rebekah's coming for me."

Rebekah served as the madam – a former courtesan who ran her part of the operation with Roman-like efficiency and who was entirely devoid of sentiment regarding her charges' assigned tasks.

Rebekah led Sharon toward the banquet hall, following five girls whose clothing consisted of the merest snippets of fabric. Not that any of it stayed on very long.

Sharon described the scene with more than a hint of disgust.

As soon as they arrived, the five began to slink provocatively toward the head table and within a couple of minutes, all were completely naked. One, in fact, had almost immediately begun to have sex with the king's favored guest.

My kind of party, I could tell.

"Do you still have your clothes?" Lavon asked.

"For the moment. I think she's just trying to show me what I'm supposed to do tomorrow."

She paused.

"You've *got* to get me out of here," she said.

"We're working on it," I replied.

"Well, work harder!"

"We are," said Lavon, "but we have another problem."

He briefly explained what had happened to Markowitz.

"We may have to cash in all of our chips to keep Ray in one piece," I said.

I didn't need to explain what that might mean to her.

"Oh."

There wasn't anything else to say. In the lottery between 'bad' and 'worse,' she had drawn 'bad.' For now, she'd just have to live with it.

***

That didn't mean I was happy about it, though. I kicked over my chair and swore; then I cursed again for losing control of myself.

I set my chair back upright, took a deep breath and another swig of wine, and then sat back down.

"Well," I said, "any ideas?"

Lavon shook his head. Even if Ray hadn't been languishing in that hellhole, the Romans were unlikely to assist a woman who wasn't a Roman citizen. To make matters worse, according to the Gospels, Pilate and Herod didn't care much for each other.

"In the twenty-first century, we'd call it a turf battle," he said. "Plus, the domains of local client kings weren't fixed, so these little monarchs were constantly scheming to add to their territories. More land meant more tax revenue. I'm sure Pilate got tired of it after a while."

"What about the worms?" I asked.

Both Lavon and Bryson looked at me blankly.

"Sharon said something about Herod dying after being eaten by worms. Worst case, if she really has to sleep with him, do we need to worry about this?"

Lavon laughed. "No, that was Herod Agrippa, the current king's nephew. In a few years, he'll conspire to have his uncle deposed and sent into exile."

"Serves him right," said Bryson.

"Serves both of them right," said Lavon.

I thought about calling Sharon back to let her know about this, but I didn't think it would be much comfort, at least not now.

Chapter 40

We all wanted to rest, but we agreed to sleep in relays so that one of us would be up at all times. I volunteered for the graveyard shift – a term I hoped wouldn't prove literal – and headed over to the sack, trusting that one of the others would wake me.

Since the moon had risen just after the sun had set, we at least had a reliable clock, and about two in the morning, Lavon shook me awake.

I ran in place for a few minutes to get my blood circulating and then wrapped a blanket around myself to ward off the chill.

Then, I decided to call out on a lark. "Sharon, are you up?"

Surprisingly, she was. For the past several hours, she had stared out her window, mulling over ideas to get away, each one more impractical than the last.

Then she lit upon the craziest scheme of all.

Her dormitory was located on the third floor of a three tiered complex, with her window facing toward the west.

Under the illumination of the full moon, she could see that only a flat grassy lawn separated the central structure from the city's outer wall, about twenty yards away. A set of stone steps lined the wall, which allowed soldiers to ascend to the parapet that ran along the top.

A few hours earlier, she had observed a black-helmeted guard climb up in relief of the man stationed there. Upon reaching the top of the stairs, the new sentry had kicked his predecessor, who had evidently fallen asleep.

The men, however, had exchanged no harsh words. Instead, the other soldier simply got up, grabbed what looked like a wine skin, and came trotting back down.

This surprised her. She had always heard that the Roman penalty for sleeping on guard duty was death.

I explained that this was true, but that these men were not legionnaires – and the more I thought about it, what she had seen made perfect sense. Trouble, if it came, would spring from the crowded city to the east.

No robber bent on survival would try to scale a fifty foot wall when easier pickings lurked all around, and the presence of the legions ensured that no force capable of besieging the city could be found within hundreds of miles.

The sentries on the western wall had nothing to do, and they knew it.

I made the mistake of saying this to Sharon.

"Then it's worth a try," she said.

"Try *what*?" I asked, struggling to conceal my alarm over what might be coming next.

"While the other girls were gone, I found a pile of blankets and tied them together, just in case. I hid them under my bed."

I didn't know what to say.

"The level below my window is only ten feet down. If I hang on to the ledge, the drop will only be about three more feet. I won't get hurt."

"They'll hear you."

"No, I don't think so. Not if I do it right."

"You still won't be on the ground."

"I'll do the same thing, two more times, and once I'm on the ground, I won't make any noise at all crossing the lawn. After I get to the wall, I'm certain I can climb up to the top without being seen."

"But that soldier is still there."

"I've been watching him. As soon as he got up to the platform, he started drinking, too. It's harder to see over there now, but I can still make out a vague shape, sitting down and leaning against the wall. He's either passed out or asleep. As soon as the moon sets completely, I'll loop my blanket rope around one of the crenellations and head down the other side."

"That guard can't be the only one."

"Any others are likely to be as drunk as this one. I'll take my chances. I saw what those other girls had to do."

I could only think of one thing that might stop her. "The sun might rise before the moon completely sets. If that happens, you'll be spotted for sure."

She hesitated, but only for a moment.

"I'll call you when I'm ready to go. You can look to the east and tell me if the sun has started to come up."

***

This was insane; though when she contacted me saying she was heading outside, I couldn't bring myself to lie.

The next hour was one of the longest of my life. Had I been prone to nail-chewing, I would have probably gnawed off my fingertips. As it was, I could only move a chair over by a window and sit facing east, watching for the first sliver of dawn.

It came just as I heard Sharon's voice.

"I made it," she said.

"Thank God; where are you?"

"Just outside the wall. I had a couple of scary instances when I wasn't sure my knots would hold. For a moment, I thought I might end up splattered like Jezebel."

Like so many other names from the Bible, this one rang a bell, though I couldn't place it.

Sharon explained that the woman had been an Old Testament queen whose reign came to a gruesome end when her husband's rivals tossed her onto the street from an upper story window, leaving her body to be devoured by the city's stray dogs.

"Why on earth would you remember that?"

"That's what the preacher called us if we went dancing – Jezebels. I suppose it was nicer than 'whore.'"

I didn't quite see the connection, but it wasn't time to ask.

"Can you see where you're going?" I said.

"Only for a short distance, but the sky is getting brighter."

I had considered her options while she made her escape. I had run through the Kidron Ravine twice and had the scars to show for it. According to the topographical map back in Boston, the valleys to the southwest of town were just as deep, and equally likely to be overgrown with dense vegetation.

"I'd hate for you to get lost in the scrub," I said. "I think your best bet is to skirt around the wall to the north. Once you've done that, make for the Antonia's side gate, the one that Robert and the others went through after their baths. When you get close, we'll go down and see if we can convince the Roman sentry to let you in."

She agreed, and for a few minutes, she eased along in the dim glimmer of dawn.

But her luck did not hold.

"I hear soldiers coming," she said. "Yesterday, I saw some caves off to the west, so I'm going to hide in one of them."

As long as the men were Romans, I thought she could bluff it out and continue around the city wall, but she had already started in the other direction.

She followed a rabbit's warren of trails until she spotted a small opening and went inside.

"I can't see much," she said. "I can feel a rock ledge here in the back, though. So I'm going to sit down for a minute."

I waited for her to give me a status update, but except for soft, steady breathing, that was the last I heard. She had stayed up all night, and the adrenalin rush of her escape had quickly worn off.

"Sharon, wake up!" I called out.

She didn't respond.

Her earpiece had most likely fallen out. There was nothing else I could do.

Chapter 41

The Antonia quickly came to life as the sun's rays broke over the eastern horizon. I woke Lavon and Bryson, but I barely had time to explain what Sharon had done before a servant entered our quarters and summoned me.

"Where are we going?" I asked.

"The prefect has need of your assistance," the man replied after Lavon had translated my question.

I grabbed what remained of my first aid supplies and headed toward the door, with the others in tow.

"No," said the slave, "only you."

I tapped my ear to remind Lavon to stay connected and then followed the man all the way to ground level. From there, he led me through a maze of tunnels until we reached a spacious, if rather Spartan office.

Pilate sat behind a wooden table covered with scraps of papyrus, a few scrolls, and a half eaten chunk of bread sitting beside a bowl of olive oil. Volusus and Publius sat on stools on the other side, while four junior Roman officers stood at ease against the nearby wall.

Two scribes, pens and inkpots in hand, waited at the far end, ready to take dictation.

Pilate looked up from his papers as I entered the room. I nodded my head in kind of a quasi-bow and then stood still, wondering what this was all about.

Though I only learned the details later, the governor had fallen off his horse on his way into the city the day before – something quite easy to do in the era before the invention of the stirrup.

Not wanting to show weakness in front of the soldiers, he had ignored the cut in his left instep; but now it was becoming infected.

Pilate barked an order to a servant who rushed over with a stool. He then plopped his leg up on the support and beckoned me to come over and have a look.

Other than starting to turn septic, the injury was not serious. Had he asked me to clean it yesterday, I could have done so easily. I still could today, though I'd have to scrape off some of the scab that had started to form.

This would sting; and I suddenly realized I was working for a man who had no compunction against killing those who displeased him.

I pantomimed my intentions as best I could, but Pilate just motioned for me to get on with it. I daubed some topical numbing cream and waited as long as I thought prudent before setting to work.

He didn't utter a peep, though I'd like to attribute this to my superior medical skill. In any event, just as I finished wrapping his foot with the last of my sterile gauze, a messenger ran in with a dispatch. Pilate took it, then sat back down and began to read.

As he did so, I backed away and eased myself over toward the wall, hoping they wouldn't think to send me out.

They didn't, for their minds had turned to more weighty matters. Whatever the dispatch said, I could see by Pilate's face that it wasn't good news. He laid the scroll down and then glanced up at the two senior Romans with more than a hint of exasperation.

"Let's get right to the point. I will not tolerate a disturbance like the one yesterday. Tell Caiaphas to crack down hard on any agitators. I mean it: show absolutely no mercy to troublemakers."

"Yes, excellency," said Volusus.

"And one more thing: if Caiaphas can't do it, I'll find someone who will. Make sure he understands that."

The commander nodded again and then turned to one of the secretaries, who scribbled a hasty note and then sped out through the office's main entrance.

This seemed to have a calming effect on the governor. He leaned back in his chair and then called for a slave to bring them more food.

As they ate, he glanced down at his notes. "Of the prisoners you brought in yesterday, how many are still among us?" he asked.

Volusus turned to one of the junior officers along the wall.

"About half, excellency," the man replied.

Pilate chuckled. "I see Titus Labernius has not lost his touch. Did we learn anything we didn't already know before they so tragically expired?"

"Not really," said Publius. "We got the names of their associates who got away, but otherwise, it was the usual stuff – doing God's work by driving the infidel out of the holy city; that sort of thing."

"Did any of their leaders escape?" asked Pilate.

"Two," replied Publius. "We have agents looking for them now. Just so you'll know, one of them is a priest."

"Irrelevant," said Pilate. "Kill them both."

He spoke with all the emotion of a man ordering breakfast.

"Yes, sir." Publius signaled to the officer standing closest to the door, who turned and hustled out.

Pilate shuffled through a few other scraps of papyrus.

"Now, what about this prophet you told me about? Was he involved with these riots?"

"Not to our knowledge, excellency," said Volusus. "We have no reports of him being in the city yesterday."

"So he is not connected with these prisoners?"

"Not really. Two of them confessed that they had followed him for a year, in Galilee. However, they grew disillusioned with his teaching and left his service. Now they consider him a – um, what is the word?"

"Apostate," said Publius. "A backslider; someone who does not devote himself to their God with the necessary resolve."

Pilate looked genuinely puzzled. "Why do they say this?"

"Something about a failure to observe all of their silly rules, I'm told," replied Volusus. "Apparently, he has also preached that they should love their enemies, and not try to kill them. They didn't care much for that."

Pilate considered this for a moment. Then he held up a scroll and waved it at the commander.

"This report says that he destroyed the Temple marketplace three days ago."

Volusus nodded. "Yes."

"An odd form of love, is it not?"

Neither the commander nor Publius could muster a reply.

After a brief moment, one of the officers along the wall spoke for the first time.

"There may be some basis to this, sir. I've heard reports that he instructed the people to pay their taxes without complaint."

Pilate's eyes widened. "A Jewish prophet telling them to pay *us*?"

"That's what they said."

Pilate shook his head. "Impossible. Your agents must have misunderstood. If this prophet said that, any following he had would melt away in an instant. I've been around this accursed country long enough to know that."

No one spoke as Pilate scanned a few more of the loose scraps. Evidently, he was still wrestling for a solution in his mind.

He fished through the reports once more.

"What's this about a kingdom?"

Volusus sighed. "So many wild stories surround this fellow. We've had a hard time sifting through them all to find the truth.

"He hasn't called himself a king, then?"

Publius smiled. "Oh, I think his ambitions run much higher than that. Last night, I heard one of the high priests complain that he declared himself to be God – not *a* god, mind you, but *the* God, their one and only."

They all laughed for a moment; then Volusus turned serious.

"If you want my assessment, I'd call him a mystic – one of these starry-eyed dreamers who pop up every now and then, preaching universal brotherhood, surrounded by fantastical tales of healing and miracles and food falling from the heavens."

"That was another reason the prisoners abandoned him," said Publius. "If he had a kingdom, it was, how did they put it?"

"*Not of this world*," said Volusus.

"If he gets enough of the wrong sort of followers, it will be," grumbled Pilate.

"True enough," acknowledged Volusus, "but we've had our hands full this week fighting the bandits. And if this prophet had any followers on the Temple Mount when he assaulted the merchants, none of them chose to join in. We had to focus on our immediate priorities."

"Yes, of course. But here's what I find so strange: you say in this report that he came back the next day and preached for over an hour. Yet the Temple authorities did nothing."

"We know he has sympathizers in the Sanhedrin," said Publius, "but these are rational, educated men, not ignorant peasants chasing after the latest craze. They have as much to lose as we do from any serious trouble, which was another reason we chose to exercise caution."

Pilate didn't reply. Instead, he stared ahead, lost in thought.

"That may be," he finally said, "but even if he has backers in their council, I find it hard to believe that he could destroy one of their biggest moneymakers and walk out untouched; not to mention coming back the next day and calling them – "

Pilate glanced down at the written report. "– 'hypocrites, robbers of widows,' and here's my favorite – '*whitewashed tombs,* with their shiny exteriors concealing the rot and corruption within.' Even with that provocation, they still failed to act. Why?"

Publius and Volusus glanced at each other but did not respond. They had asked themselves the same question without reaching an answer.

"I'll tell you why," said Pilate. "They're afraid of him. He may be waiting for the right moment to give the signal."

"We considered that," said Publius, "but we have yet to uncover a single shred of evidence pointing to such a thing."

"No, but we have no guarantee that this is *not* his plan, either."

Pilate shuffled through more of his notes.

"I recall a report, about a year ago, that said so many people crowded in to hear him preach that he had to hop on a boat and speak to them from off shore. These sheep can believe the most preposterous stuff, as you well know."

The others nodded as Pilate grew more animated.

"And if he turns them against the high priests, do you think for a moment that they will not rise against us? At best, our careers will be ruined. We may, in fact, be lucky to escape this place with our lives."

"That's true enough," said Volusus.

"What, exactly, do you want us to do?" asked Publius.

"Arrest him."

"Unless he comes back to the Temple, the most difficult part will be finding him," said Volusus. "Once we have his location, perhaps the safest course will be to do away with him quietly, out of the public eye."

Pilate looked down at the scrolls again; then shook his head.

"No; it's too late for that. If we fail to make a proper example of him, the mob will conclude either that we implicitly accept this conduct or that we are too weak to stop it."

"With all of the people in the city at the moment, if he truly is popular, then killing him openly could trigger the very uprising we're trying to prevent," argued Volusus.

Pilate stayed quiet, lost in thought, as the groans of several prisoners came wafting through a corridor.

"No, it won't," he finally said. "We'll think of something."

Chapter 42

I stood against the wall, so mesmerized with what I was hearing that I paid only limited attention to what was going on outside.

A guard, dressed like those we had seen in the dungeon the previous evening, stepped up to the doorway. He signaled to one of the junior officers, but Pilate saw him and beckoned him to come in.

The man saluted and stood at attention.

"You keep the prisoners?" asked Pilate.

"Yes, sir," he replied. "I have one held in isolation, but I had no instructions as to whether he should be fed."

I struggled to keep a straight face, hoping the governor would send the man away with a sharp command not to bother the officers with such petty concerns. But Pilate seemed curious as to why one prisoner had been separated from the rest. Decius was away, and none of the other Romans knew.

"Bring him here."

The governor rose and walked around the table toward the doorway leading to the courtyard. A few minutes later, two soldiers dragged a very confused and frightened Markowitz up from the dungeon and threw him to the ground at Pilate's feet.

The Roman stared at him, as if appraising an insect previously unknown to science.

"What is your name?" he finally asked.

Markowitz looked up, his face completely blank.

"He does not speak Aramaic or Greek," said the guard.

"How do you communicate with him, then?"

"I'm told he has companions."

Publius didn't move to intervene, though I couldn't tell whether the centurion didn't recognize Markowitz in his current state or whether he had simply elected to remain silent.

Either way, I knew it wouldn't be long before all eyes turned to me, so I stepped forward – better to look as if I had nothing to hide.

Markowitz recognized me first. I told him to shut up, as gently as I could and still get the point across. Then I gestured to Publius.

He understood and dispatched a soldier to fetch the others. A few minutes later, Bryson and Lavon walked in. Both of them had the good sense to bow to Pilate and remain silent.

"Which one of you speaks Greek?" he asked.

Lavon raised his hand and took a step forward.

Pilate glanced over to Markowitz. "Who is this man?"

"He got caught in the crowd yesterday, excellency," replied Lavon. "Although he could not get out of the crush of people before your soldiers rounded everyone up, I can assure you that he is no bandit."

That seemed plausible enough, though I could tell the governor hadn't bought it.

Something seemed to jog his memory. Pilate went back to his desk to fetch a piece of papyrus. His attention focused on the writing at the bottom.

"This report mentions an unusual blonde-haired stranger going into the Temple. Is this man that individual?"

Lavon didn't even bother to translate. There was no point lying. "Yes, excellency. He was insatiably curious about what lay inside."

Pilate frowned. "How did he get in? Only Jews may enter their sanctuary, and they are extremely strict on this point. Is he a Jew?"

"We come from a far country, but one in which our babies are sometimes circumcised. He learned the Jews also undertook this practice and sought to find out why, since it is so uncommon elsewhere."

Pilate, though, was having none of it. "You didn't answer my question: Is he a Jew?"

"He is not one of these Jews," said Lavon.

The governor didn't reply, and we could both see that his doubts persisted.

The archaeologist pressed on. "Our grandfathers tell us that our ancestors migrated long ago from a hot land far to the south. An absurd legend, no doubt, but in the middle of winter in the frozen forests, such stories have an obvious appeal."

Pilate chuckled, which was a good sign; though again, he didn't seem entirely convinced.

"Perhaps he mistook ancient fables for the truth," said Lavon. "He is an excitable young man, and not completely right in the head."

"Why take him on such a long journey, then?"

"His father ordered us to. He is rich, and we serve him, in our country."

At that point, I could see Lavon running out of maneuvering room. I stepped forward.

"This man's father charged me with keeping him out of trouble," I said. "If there is any fault, it is mine for not discharging my duty."

Pilate turned to Publius and they spoke briefly, though I couldn't understand what they were saying.

Then he turned back to Lavon. "You're telling me for a fact that this young man was caught up in the midst of the bandits and forced to go along with them, against his will?"

"Yes, excellency. He is only a traveler from a far country."

***

I couldn't tell what Pilate was thinking, but there were obvious holes in our story.

"I will be frank," he finally said. "A respected member of their high council admitted this young man to their sacred Temple, so if he is not a Jew, some important details are being omitted from your account. He was caught with the brigands and by all rights should share in their punishment."

Once again, I'll give Lavon credit. He kept a straight face and didn't say a word.

Pilate continued, "On the other hand, he does not know their language, and your fellow traveler has rendered us valuable assistance."

"Yes, excellency," replied Lavon.

"Since I have no time to investigate the matter further, I will grant him an opportunity to redeem himself, with a simple demonstration of where his true loyalties lie."

Before Lavon could reply, Pilate barked an order that my earpiece didn't quite catch. The dungeon guard scurried away while the Roman officers exchanged glances of approval.

Lavon, though, had turned pale.

"What did he say?" asked Markowitz.

"He's going to let you go," said Lavon.

"Thank God." He reached up as if to unshackle the iron collar around his neck.

"There is, um, a catch." Lavon explained what he was going to have to do.

Markowitz shook his head. "That's cold blooded murder! I won't do it!"

Though he didn't understand the words, Pilate could see Markowitz's obvious reluctance. He didn't like it.

"Is this prisoner going to turn down my generous offer?" he asked.

"With all due respect, excellency," said Lavon, "his error was not intentional. He is merely an impulsive young man who got caught up in a situation beyond his control."

Pilate frowned. "An impulsive young man, you say?"

The governor pointed to the flogging post at the other end of the courtyard.

"Very well; in that case, I will have him scourged. That should bring him to his senses, and teach him to surround himself with a better crowd."

Lavon fought to suppress an upwelling of panic.

"No, excellency," he replied, "this man will not refuse your generosity. His hesitation stems only from the fact that he has never killed before. He is no warrior."

"All northmen are warriors," said Pilate.

"And all have long hair, rotten teeth, and paint their faces blue," said Lavon. "I tell you the truth. This man works as a scribe in his father's house, to learn the merchant trade so he can carry on when the old man is no longer able to pursue it."

"A scribe?"

"Yes, excellency."

"Has he never hunted?"

"Of course," Lavon lied. "But in the forest, the quarry has a sporting chance."

That gave one of the Romans an idea. He stepped forward and whispered into Pilate's ear.

The governor smiled. "An excellent suggestion; the men could use some entertainment. See to it at once."

As the officer marched away, Pilate informed Lavon of his decision. The archaeologist started to remonstrate, but I tugged his arm. We had pressed our limited luck just about as far as it would reach.

"Ask him if he'll give us time for preparation," I said. "Tell him that regardless of what happens, it will make for a more interesting show."

This struck Pilate as reasonable. "You have one hour," he said.

"What are they saying?" asked Markowitz. "Are they going to let me go?"

Before Lavon could reply, a soldier walked up with two wooden training swords and a couple of small shields. He handed them to me.

"What are those for?" asked Markowitz.

I smiled as best I could as the guard unchained him; then I led him to the other side of the courtyard.

"Let's go over here. There are some things you need to learn in a hurry."

Chapter 43

After about a third of our allotted hour had elapsed, I instructed Markowitz to sit down and catch his breath while I went to fetch water for us both. As I did, Lavon walked up to me and spoke quietly.

"How's the lesson going?" he asked.

I just shook my head. Though I had more subject matter expertise than my pupil, I was still a bumbling amateur compared to anyone who had grown up using these weapons.

The archaeologist must have sensed my doubts. "Does he stand a chance?" he asked.

"It depends on who they bring up," I replied, "though his real problem is that he hasn't mentally accepted what he's going to have to do. Do you know if he managed to kill that lamb in the Temple yesterday, or did the priest have to do it?"

"I don't know. I never saw him again until we got back here."

I just stared ahead for a moment, trying to get my head around the insanity of it all. I had always thought that these types of fights were organized ahead of time, though once again, my impressions were wrong. Lavon explained that impromptu exhibitions of this nature were commonplace throughout the ancient world.

"There's even an example in the Old Testament," he said. "Two of King David's commanders got together, and I suppose they were bored. One of them said to the other, 'let's have some of my young men fight your young men.' So they paired up a couple of dozen and went at it."

"What happened?" I asked.

"Each man stabbed his opponent. They all died."

I sighed; then I glanced up at the sun and forgot all about the water. I strode back to Markowitz and slapped him hard across the shoulder with my wooden sword.

"Get up," I said. "Hit me."

He shuffled to his feet and made a halfhearted attempt. I swatted him again, this time hard enough to really sting.

"I said, *hit me!*"

Though better, his next effort still fell well short of the mark.

I popped him again, and again.

He fell back at first, but finally he let out a loud yell and took a wild swing. Although I deflected the blow with ease, this was progress. For the first time, he attacked as though he meant it.

We sparred for a little while and then I tried to show him how to make the killing stroke. He struggled; the motion was not what he had expected.

"You have to forget every sword fight you've ever seen in the movies," said Lavon. "You're holding a Roman *gladius*, not a medieval broadsword. You're trying to stab your enemy, not lop off his head."

Lavon spotted an idle Roman soldier and called him over. They spoke briefly; then the man demonstrated the procedure far more competently than I could have. The legionnaire grinned as Markowitz repeated the drill several times, then patted him on the back and ambled off to rejoin his unit.

"Remember," I said, "go for the gut. If you stab him in the ribs, your sword could get stuck. While you struggle to pull it out, your opponent will be able to kill you before he dies."

He nodded, though this seemed to be more of a reflex action than a sign of genuine understanding.

"Have you ever killed anyone?" he asked.

"Yes."

"How did you deal with it?"

Inwardly, I groaned. We could discuss philosophy afterward, if he lived.

"I dealt with it by thanking God that my enemy was laying there on the ground instead of me," I snapped.

This was accurate enough, though for much of my career, their destruction had taken on an antiseptic quality. On my last posting, I had reviewed the videos of missile strikes from the air conditioned comfort of a headquarters conference room, with a cup of coffee in my hand.

"Don't tell me you enjoyed it!"

"In war, enjoyment is not a factor. It's kill or be killed. Take your pick."

"I don't want that on my conscience," he said.

"Your conscience should be the least of your worries. At least one of you will not walk away from this place. Besides, if you win, the worst thing you'll be guilty of is the desecration of a corpse."

He looked at me in confusion.

Lavon came to the rescue. "Ray, Bill's right. The prisoners here are all dead men. Within a week, not one of them will be alive, regardless of whether you fight or not; whether you win or lose; live or die."

Markowitz stared at him as if he were trying to convince himself of the truth.

"Do you remember that terrible sight coming into the city?" I asked. "Of course you do. You'll never forget that as long as you live. *That*, you must remind yourself, will be your opponent's fate should you fail in your duties here."

"What you do will be an act of mercy," said Lavon.

Finally, his mind started to point in the right direction; and not a moment too soon, either. At the other end of the courtyard, about thirty Romans had begun to form a ring with their shields.

"This gives the Octagon a whole new meaning," I quipped.

Lavon laughed. Markowitz did not.

The archaeologist headed across the fort; I suppose to stall the inevitable as long as he could. Meanwhile, I worked Markowitz through a few blocking moves with the shield and found his progress to be satisfactory enough.

Well, not really *satisfactory*, but he had advanced as far as he could reasonably go without tiring himself out before the fight.

Just then, Lavon came back and beckoned us to follow.

"Showtime," he said.

***

A crowd of off-duty soldiers had gathered in the second floor windows to observe the action, though neither Lavon nor I paid them any attention. Instead, we both watched the passage leading down to the dungeon, eager to learn the identity of Markowitz's opponent.

A few minutes later, I breathed a sigh of relief as two Romans dragged up the youngster they had hauled in with Barabbas. If anything, the kid looked even more frightened and bedraggled than he had the day before.

"Ray might have a chance after all," I said to Lavon.

The ring of shields opened to permit the combatants to enter. Soldiers had deposited a *gladius* and a small Thracian shield at opposite corners of their square. Markowitz picked his up and noticed that it felt much lighter.

"The practice swords are heavier, to build strength and speed," said Lavon.

Ray ran his thumb across the blade and nearly cut himself. I watched his opponent do the same.

"He can't be older than sixteen," said Markowitz.

"Don't think about that," I ordered. "Remember what we told you: he's a dead man whether you do anything or not. Kill him quickly and he won't suffer with the others."

Moments later, Pilate looked down from a second story window and motioned for them to go ahead; but those expecting a good match were disappointed.

Each combatant stood as far away from his opponent as he could, grasping his sword in a most unsoldierlike manner. Neither man showed the slightest inclination to begin.

"Hey Antonius," one of the soldiers upstairs yelled out. "Now we see how scribes fight. Maybe they can throw ink pots at each other."

The others roared laughing, but Markowitz and the kid didn't move.

Finally, Pilate lost patience. He motioned to an officer: *Get on with it.*

Soldiers in each corner pushed the combatants forward. Both took a few half-hearted swings, though these grew more forceful as the full gravity of the situation started to sink in.

"Ray, you idiot," I yelled. "Get a grip on yourself. Run him through now!"

Markowitz's face reddened as he screamed and charged forward. The trouble was, he closed his eyes at the last minute, unwilling to see the result of his strike.

The kid ducked out of the way, though fortunately he wasn't experienced enough to capitalize on the mistake.

Now they each stood on corners opposite those from which they had started.

"Get back into position," I yelled.

This time, it was the Zealot who charged forward, though Markowitz managed to deflect the blow.

They swung at each other again and again, harder each time. The swords clanged, and the Romans cheered at this new level of intensity.

I didn't, though.

"Ray, damn it; this isn't Hollywood!"

The kid took a powerful swing, but missed, which threw him off balance.

"Now is your chance!" I shouted. "Get him!"

Markowitz saw it too. He thrust his *gladius* forward, just as the legionnaire had demonstrated. To my immense relief, the blow found its mark.

"Now pull back," I yelled.

My caution was unnecessary. The kid let go of his sword and fell to his knees, holding his free hand over his stomach. Moments later, his shield also dropped to the ground. He stared up to his opponent with imploring eyes.

Markowitz just stood there, in shock at what he had done.

"You have to finish this," I said. "Hit him at the base of the neck and he'll die quick. If not ..."

He continued to hesitate.

"Keep your eyes open. Do it right," I admonished.

Still nothing.

"*Now!*"

Finally, he stepped forward and screamed as he thrust his sword through the kid's throat. Then, he yanked the weapon away and took a step back, where he stood transfixed in horror as the young man gurgled one last time before collapsing face first onto the ground.

A few of the Romans groaned while their buddies laughed. Money changed hands, and two slaves came forward to drag the body away while two others mopped up the blood.

Markowitz knelt down, leaning on his sword with his eyes closed as he took several deep breaths.

Pilate shook his head. "A pitiful display of swordsmanship," he said to Lavon. "You are correct that this man is no fighter. You may take him back – this time."

Lavon acknowledged the governor but did not speak. The message was clear: a second offense would prove lethal to us all.

Markowitz finally looked up. His eyes smoldered with rage toward the Roman prefect, so I quickly eased the sword from his grasp and handed it, hilt first, to a nearby soldier.

Then, Lavon and I helped him to his feet and led him toward the stairs and up to our room. Publius passed by and the archaeologist asked him to have some wine sent up. Markowitz would surely need it.

We all would.

Chapter 44

A different servant was waiting for us as we trudged up the last set of steps. He opened the door and guided us in. After filling our goblets, he returned to his post outside.

We all chugged our wine fast, and Lavon and I watched cautiously as Markowitz took a few halting steps toward the window. Though he didn't seem like the type to throw himself out, I eased myself closer just in case.

I needn't have worried. He simply leaned on the windowsill for several minutes, watching the priests go about their business in the Temple compound below.

Suddenly, though, he turned around and hurled his empty goblet across the room.

"I'm going to kill every one of those Roman sons of bitches!" he shouted.

Lavon and I glanced at each other but decided to let him vent.

When he finally ran out of steam, I retrieved his goblet and poured him another cup.

"I know you're upset," I said. "But for the moment, we need to focus on getting Sharon back, and then making our way home."

Markowitz didn't give her a second thought. "I mean it," he exclaimed. "I'm coming back. Those people are animals!"

He stood up, walked back to the window, and once again gazed at the crush of worshippers flowing into the Temple courtyard.

"I never paid much attention, growing up," he muttered.

"Paid attention to what?" asked Bryson.

He gestured toward the Temple. "To *this*; to my heritage. I heard all the stories of course, but why should a kid growing up in the late twentieth century care? My family has lived in America since the time of George Washington. We had gotten rich. This stuff was ancient history."

None of us replied.

"I was wrong. I should have paid more attention."

He lowered his head and stared at the floor, mumbling something about being the only Jew in New York who hadn't lost any known relatives to the Holocaust.

This triggered another unpleasant thought.

"Robert," he asked, "When the Romans destroyed this city, how many people died?"

Lavon's first response was evasive. He could sense where this was heading.

Markowitz, though, wouldn't let up. "I'm not asking for an exact count. Roughly speaking, how many died in the siege?"

"The most plausible figures hover around a million," Lavon said.

"One million dead Jews?"

"Yes – for the whole war, not just here in Jerusalem."

"You're saying these Roman swine killed one million of my ancestors?"

"It's a bit more complicated than that," he replied.

Lavon explained that as the siege progressed, three bands of Jewish fanatics took control of separate areas of the city. One occupied the Temple Mount; another controlled the Upper City around Herod's palace, while a third held the district to the south.

As is often the case in such circumstances, each of the factions first slaughtered anyone they considered a moderate, before they turned against each other with as much gusto as they fought the Romans.

In the process, most of the Jerusalem's food supply went up in smoke; and a city that might have held out for several years fell in six months.

This information, however, did not faze Markowitz.

"You said earlier that the Romans allowed refugees from other parts of Judea to stream into the city in the hopes they would eat through the grain stores even faster."

"They did," admitted Lavon.

Markowitz just shook his head. "Bastards!"

When he turned back to face the Temple, I refilled his goblet once more. With luck, he wouldn't pay attention to how much he was drinking.

"The Ninth of Av," he muttered. "I thought all that stuff was just something old people worried about."

Markowitz continued to rant; none of us attempted to stop him.

"The Ninth of Av?" asked Bryson.

"The saddest day in Judaism," said Lavon, "the day in their calendar when both the first and second Temples were destroyed."

"The same day?" asked Bryson.

Lavon shrugged. "Close enough; probably."

Markowitz turned back to our table. "The destruction of the Temple wasn't the end of the fighting, was it? Weren't there other revolts?"

Lavon nodded. Historians had recorded two: an uprising in 115 called the Kitos War after the Roman general sent to suppress it, and a final explosion of fury in 132, known as the Bar Kochba revolt.

"How many Jews died in each one?" Markowitz asked.

"Nobody's really sure," Lavon said. "We know even less about those conflicts than we do about the AD 70 siege. If either of the latter rebellions had the equivalent of a Josephus to chronicle the event, his writings haven't survived."

"What are the best estimates?"

"Accounts of the Kitos War only describe 'a great slaughter.'"

Lavon didn't elaborate, though after what we had seen so far, a mental picture of what that entailed required no huge imaginative leap.

"What about Bar Kochba?" Bryson asked.

Like most people outside Judaism and the Biblical scholar community, I had never heard of the man. I had no idea that this warrior – a messianic figure whose name translated as "Son of the Star" – had led the greatest rebellion of all.

Lavon explained that around AD 130, the emperor Hadrian – the same man who leveled the early Christians' shrine – visited Jerusalem and decided to rebuild it as a pagan city along Roman lines.

For starters, he issued decrees outlawing Jewish customs like circumcision, which the Romans considered mutilation. But his crowning insult was his plan to build a shrine to Jupiter on what remained of the Temple Mount.

"What happened?" asked Bryson.

"As any fool could have predicted, the Jews rebelled," Lavon said. "And in contrast to the situation sixty years earlier, this time Jewish resistance was unified.

"Ultimately, the Romans had to bring in twelve legions to put down the revolt – almost half their entire army at the time. The fighting dragged on for three years. Roman historians described their own casualties as enormous."

"How many *Jews* died?" asked Markowitz.

"That's even more of a guess than Josephus's war, and I'm not trying to evade the question. Unlike the Great Revolt, the Bar Kochba rebellion didn't end with the siege and fall of a major city. Instead, the last surviving rebels fled with their families to hideouts in caves.

"Rather than suffer even more casualties rooting them out, the Romans simply sealed up the cave entrances as they discovered them. The people inside eventually starved. Some of my colleagues have unearthed whole clusters of their skeletons."

"So how many died?" asked Markowitz.

"Cassius Dio said about 500,000. Others cite figures in the millions."

"Take an average; about a million, then?"

Lavon shrugged. "I suppose."

"A million here, a million there," said Markowitz. "It was as if the Nazis had risen up and had another go at us – twice!"

"Come on now," said Bryson. "The Romans weren't Nazis. There's no record of their going for all that racial purity crap or trying to exterminate the entire population."

Markowitz didn't answer. Instead, he just stared out the window for a few minutes before turning back to face us.

He spoke with a subdued voice. "All we wanted was our small piece of land. We had our place, our Temple. They destroyed it and cast us out of our ancestral home forever – people who had done them no harm."

"Don't tell me you'd want to go back to sacrificing lambs and doves, literally?" said the Professor.

Markowitz stared down at the floor, lost in thought.

"We wouldn't have to do that," he finally said. "We'd figure something out. We always have."

The two of them continued to wrangle back and forth, but I noticed Lavon had gone quiet. Given our current circumstances, he didn't want to acknowledge that Markowitz's last point was essentially true.

After crushing the revolt, Hadrian set out to eliminate the last vestiges of what he considered a stubborn and rebellious people. He banned surviving Jews from entering Jerusalem and renamed the area 'Palestine' after their traditional enemies.

The Diaspora had really begun only after Bar Kochba.

"I'll buy a gun," said Markowitz. "I'll learn how to shoot. I'll come back, and the first thing I do, I'll kill Pilate. He'll never know what hit him. None of them will."

He turned back to watch the Temple ceremonies. "We'll protect this place," he said. "By God we will."

Bryson started to reply when I held up my hand. I refilled Markowitz's goblet again and handed it to him.

"I'll show you how to handle firearms," I said, "but in the meantime, drink up. For you to achieve what you've planned, we have to make it home first ourselves, and we're not going anywhere else today."

I watched with some relief as the combination of the alcohol and the waning of his adrenalin rush began to take effect. After a few more minutes, he yawned and rubbed his eyes. Lavon and I guided him toward the bed and covered him with a blanket.

***

While Markowitz dozed, the rest of us just stood at the window's edge, lost in thought.

"You know he's serious," I finally said.

"He's gone crazy," said Bryson.

"I don't think so," I said. "All that stuff about tossing the Romans out of Judea – he meant every word of it."

"He's obviously suffering from the stress," Bryson replied. "Anyone would be after spending a night in that hellhole, not to mention having to fight like he did."

"That's true enough," I replied, "but that kind of pressure can drive a man to actions he otherwise never would have considered."

Bryson grudgingly conceded the point.

"That's why you *must* destroy that transport machine just as soon as we all get back safe," said Lavon.

Bryson glared at him in shock, as if the archaeologist had asked him to butcher his first born child.

But Lavon had spoken my sentiments exactly.

"He's right, Professor. You've admitted yourself that his father has legal rights to the fruits of your research. He'll get in somehow, with or without your permission."

"He has no idea how to operate it," Bryson argued.

"Do you have documentation?" asked Lavon.

Bryson nodded.

"There you have it," I said. "You've done the hard work of inventing the thing. The rest is simply a matter of following the protocols you've developed. Even if he can't figure out how to work the device himself, he has the resources to hire someone who can."

Bryson shook his head. "No. It won't be a problem to keep him away. We have other safeguards."

"I don't think you understand what we're dealing with here," I said. "As for me, just buy some Wal-Mart and Cisco for my account and I'd go away a happy billionaire. But *he's* not going to do that; not now."

"Even if he returned, a single man acting alone wouldn't be able to accomplish much," Bryson argued.

Lavon started to point out the contradiction between that statement and the Brysons' earlier position on changing history, but he decided to back off. The device, and what it could prove, was not something the Professor would give up easily.

Nevertheless, our problem remained.

"He's probably aware of that already," I replied. "If not, he certainly will be after he thinks this through. So let's say he recruits some like-minded travelers – a unit of the Israeli army, perhaps – men with access to modern weapons and combat experience to boot. 'Free Judea!' he might say. What then?"

"We don't know."

"That's the point," said Lavon. "No one does. Fast forward two thousand years: would he return to our present world, or to a futuristic planet of *Star Trek* and the orgasmatron, or to a post-apocalyptic nuclear wasteland? Do you want to take that chance?"

***

Before Bryson could argue further, a piercing scream nearly shattered my eardrum.

I leapt to my feet, looking for a weapon, when I realized that the voice had emerged from my earpiece.

"Sharon!" I yelled. "Sharon, are you OK?"

I heard a loud pop, followed by shouting in Aramaic.

I swore. "Sharon!"

"What's happening?" said Bryson.

I held my hand up for them to stay silent; then closed my eyes to focus on the background noise. For several minutes, I heard nothing but the shuffling of feet. Then, I could barely make out a frail, quavering voice.

"If you can hear me, they're taking me back to the palace."

And that was all.

I started toward the door as I explained what I had heard, but Lavon held me back, reminding me that the Antonia's officials were unlikely to lift a finger to assist a woman who was not a Roman citizen.

He gestured to Markowitz. "Besides, I'm guessing we've played all of our high cards."

I had to concede the point. Nevertheless, I insisted we find Publius, if for no other reason than to find out what Herod was likely to do with her.

***

Unfortunately, Publius had gone out on patrol and would not return for several hours. Decius was nowhere to be found, either, so we had no choice but to return to our room.

I took a seat and poured some wine, then thought better of it and asked Lavon to have the slave bring up some water. The kid also brought up some half-decent chow, so Lavon tossed him a *denarius* before directing him back outside.

"OK, worst case," I said; "her transmitter no longer works and we get no help from anyone here. How do we spring her from that place?"

Bryson fingered his chip. "This should work by Sunday afternoon. Even if we can't get her out, she'll be able to return to the lab independently of us."

"Totally unacceptable," I said. "Plus, they may have already taken it away. I'm not leaving without her."

Neither of the others spoke.

"We also have to assume that they'll move Sharon to a more secure location than the dormitory," I said. "What do we know about the palace complex? How is the interior laid out?"

"Quite frankly," said Lavon, "we don't know any more than what she described to you earlier. It was only a few years ago that an Israeli archaeologist uncovered the first definitive remains of the palace wall, and that was just part of the foundation.

"I keep trying to tell you: Jerusalem has been destroyed and rebuilt so many times that what's over there now would only be a wild guess."

"Josephus wrote about it, didn't he, in *The Jewish War*?" said Bryson.

"Yes, but not to the level of detail we need."

"Right now, I'd say any detail is better than none," I replied.

Lavon sighed. "Josephus's book was an account of the revolt against the Romans, not a tourist brochure. He describes the lavishness of the palace mainly as a lament to its passing. His book had the usual blandishments about the extravagance of the place – rooms without number, luxurious furnishings, gold and silver and such."

"But no real useful information," I said.

"No."

I was certain we could find a way in – a forgotten sewer line with a rusted grate, or a secret escape tunnel that any king with the reputation of the first Herod would have dug, just in case. But bumbling around without intelligence would do more harm than good. I had been there, and had the scars to show for it.

"Look, I don't like it either," said Lavon.

For now, all we could do was wait.

Chapter 45

Markowitz stirred for a moment and then sat up. I poured another cup of wine and insisted he drink it, though in hindsight that might have been a mistake. His face turned green and he rushed over to the chamber pot.

He didn't even try to return to the bed, so Lavon took a blanket and spread it out on the floor. Then, he helped Markowitz turn over on his side and then draped another one over his chest and legs.

"We'll just let him sleep it off," he said.

Markowitz's well being, though, wasn't Lavon's main worry. He turned to Bryson with a question.

"I have to ask you again, Dr. Bryson: what, *exactly*, did you intend to accomplish here?"

The Professor eyed him as if he were an exceptionally slow student.

"I've already told you: I intend to clear up a controversy; in light of Christianity's impact over the past two thousand years, perhaps the most important issue of all time."

"Yes, but once you have the evidence, the video, what are you planning to do with it?"

That seemed obvious. I sat back, wondering where this was heading.

I suppose the Professor thought the same way. He grew irritated.

"For most of its existence, mankind has wallowed in ignorance and superstition. Now that technology has given us the ability to replace blind faith with objective knowledge, I would be remiss in my *obligation*, both as a scientist and a member of the human race, not to share my findings with the world."

He paused for a moment. "Whichever way it turns out, though I admit I have my own hypothesis. You can't fault me for that."

"No; no I don't," Lavon replied. "Your objectivity as a scientist is commendable; but that's not what's troubling me. In terms of its ultimate persuasive value to the world, it's not a question of what the video will *show*; it's a matter of *authenticating* that video."

Bryson shifted uncomfortably.

"Take your Kennedy tape, for example."

"What about it?"

Lavon stood up, walked toward the window, and patted the *meleke* limestone blocks.

"Given the incontrovertible evidence that we are in fact *here*, in first century Jerusalem, I have no trouble accepting the fact that you went back to Dallas as your wife described.

"The problem is, to a viewer without our level of background knowledge, your Kennedy footage could just as easily be something that an eighth grader cobbled together with a cheap laptop and some off-the-shelf editing software. How do you expect that to prove anything?"

Bryson hemmed and hawed but didn't really answer.

Lavon pressed on. "Let's say you took that video to one of those conspiracy conventions. There, in the middle of all the exhibitors with their 'secret evidence' about Lyndon Johnson, Fidel Castro, the New Orleans mafia, and little green men from outer space, you present what you describe as iron clad proof that the Warren Commission got it right, that Lee Harvey Oswald did, in fact, act alone."

"You'd be laughed out of the building," I said. "And those who didn't laugh would assume that you're an infiltrator, a part of the conspiracy, another cog in the vast machine the US government has created to hide the truth from the unwashed multitudes."

"Exactly," said Lavon. "Now multiply this phenomenon a thousand fold. Whatever your camera ends up recording, it won't change anyone's mind, one way or the other. You're smart enough to know that."

Now, my curiosity was piqued. I had not thought about it in this way before.

Bryson didn't say anything, which got my mind turning.

"You have another plan," I said.

He didn't respond immediately, so I repeated my question.

"Yes," he finally admitted. "Juliet and I recognized your point early on. Once I make the initial recording and get the lay of the land, the next step will be to set up a viewing platform, so that others may witness the truth for themselves."

I sat back in my chair and took another slug of wine. This was insane.

Lavon was even more blunt.

"Have you completely lost your mind?" he said.

He gestured toward Markowitz.

"Just look at *us*! One man in our party barely escaped being flogged to death a few hours ago. Our female colleague is facing God knows what sort of degradation at the hands of Herod and we can't do a thing about it. And the three of us, though safe for the moment, have no idea when, or if, we'll ever be able to go home."

"I understand your concerns," said Bryson, "but it was never our intention to open this world to the masses. We planned to invite only professional historians and other subject-matter experts, under carefully supervised and controlled circumstances."

Lavon rolled his eyes. "How on earth are you ever going to ensure control? Forget about us and just look at *yourself*. This was going to be easy. You planned to come here and record a few hours of video – what could be simpler? But then you plunked yourself directly into the middle of a skirmish you could not possibly have known about ahead of time."

"That was bad luck, to be sure."

"That's the point," I said. "You're always going to overlook something that turns out to be important. It's the same thing your wife said about that trading algorithm Jonah Markowitz paid you to develop: there are too many variables. You're *guaranteed* to get blindsided somewhere."

"No, I'm not," said Bryson. "Once we've scouted the area, we'll know who will be where, and when. After that, we'll be like that guy in *Groundhog Day* who knew precisely when the waitress would drop the plates. We'll be able to steer clear of any danger."

I wasn't sure about the *we* part, but chose not to comment.

And that wasn't the half of it. Even if his historians came back to the first century, saw what Bryson expected them to see, and published their findings in the most prestigious academic journals, Aunt Mildred in Kansas was never going to take the word of some liberal Commie Harvard egghead. The whole thing would reek of yet another left-wing plot to destroy America from within.

On the other hand, if the good professor's guests saw what they did *not* expect to see, would they publish their findings, or would they dismiss their observations as an optical illusion, or a mind trick of some sort driven by the subtle shifting of the brain's neural connections as a result of quantum transformation?

For the moment, though, I decided it was best to keep such thoughts to myself. Lavon wasn't finished.

"And when one of your experts decides to run off and have a closer look, like our friend here did in the Temple?" he asked. "What then? Or are you going to keep them chained to their observation posts the entire time they're here?"

Bryson shook his head, flummoxed with his inability to make lesser mortals comprehend a seemingly straightforward concept.

Lavon, though, didn't let up. "There's one more thing that I can't figure out, Professor: how did you know *when* to come back?"

Bryson acted surprised. "All four Gospels record that Jesus died on the Friday before Passover, do they not?"

"Nice try."

We both laughed, though I wasn't entirely sure why.

"You are correct in that Jesus died on a Friday," Lavon continued. "But the question remains: *which* Friday, and *which* Passover?"

Bryson cast the archaeologist an exasperated glance, but didn't otherwise respond.

"You see," said Lavon, "this is the odd thing: we're talking about the most significant event in recorded human history; but no one knows for sure, within a decade, as to when it actually occurred."

This was news to me.

"A decade?" I said.

Lavon explained. "Pilate governed Judea from 26 to 36 AD, which gives us a ten or eleven year window. That's really all modern scholars can be certain about."

"There are no other clues in the Gospels?" I asked.

"None that are very helpful," replied Lavon. "Luke says that Jesus was *about* thirty years old when he started his ministry, but that was just the author's way of saying he was a mature adult and thus worthy of being taken seriously, not that he was 30 x 365 1/4 days old."

"Not some young hothead, then," I said.

"Right. Luke also ties the beginning of Jesus's ministry to the 'fifteenth year of the emperor Tiberius,' but historians continue to debate whether that count should start when Augustus died, or when Tiberius became co-emperor with his elderly stepfather a few years earlier. No one really knows for sure."

This not knowing was becoming a common theme. We both turned our attention to the Professor, waiting for him to explain.

"As you're surely aware," said Bryson, "Passover always occurs on the same day of the year in the Jewish calendar, the 15th of Nisan. That date, though, varies from year to year in our Gregorian calendar due to the differences between a lunar and a solar reference point."

"Yes, just like Easter," said Lavon. "Go on."

"During Pilate's term as governor, the 15th of Nisan never occurred on a Monday, Wednesday or Friday. I also concluded that Tuesday was too far removed to match the Gospel accounts."

Lavon nodded. "I would agree."

"Fortunately, that allowed me to eliminate five of the eleven possible candidates: the years 28, 31, 32, 34 and 35. Also, since the Gospels specifically state that Jesus died *before* the Passover, I could scratch the two years it fell on a Thursday as well – 27 and 30."

"That still leaves four possibilities," I said. "How did you narrow them down?"

"From my reading of the Gospels, the most plausible day was a Saturday, which coincided with the Sabbath."

"That would still give you multiple options," said Lavon. "I've read decent arguments for all three."

"Yes: 26, 33 and 36," said Bryson. "From a probability standpoint, though, I ruled out 26 as too early, and 36 as too late. That left 33 …"

"Which is obviously wrong," I said. "I thought you said this was the year 29."

"It is."

"So when is the Passover this year?" I asked.

Lavon began laughing. "Sunday."

"What's so funny about that?" I asked.

"It means their days are mixed up this month," he replied.

"You see; if this is the correct year – and everything we've seen so far tells us it is – then something is out of kilter. Under Jewish law, the Passover carried restrictions similar to those of the Sabbath. No one could do any work, which means that if the Passover were truly on Sunday, the women could not have gone to the tomb with the spices to anoint Jesus's body that morning."

Now, I was really confused, and a glance at Bryson told me I wasn't the only one.

Lavon continued. "A Jewish month begins when the first sliver of the moon appears following a new moon. In modern times, this is calculated mathematically so there is no question when a month starts. But Jewish astronomers didn't do that until the fourth century. Before then, they did it the old-fashioned way: somebody – actually two somebodies – climbed up on the roof and had a look. If they agreed, the new month began."

"What if it was cloudy?" I asked.

"You're getting the picture. A particular month could be off by a day, as this one obviously is."

Bryson stared ahead blankly.

"You didn't know that, Professor?" said Lavon. "All the more reason I asked my original question: how did you pick *this* year? Or did you just flip a coin?"

"No, I didn't flip a coin. The year 29 was the most plausible candidate left once I ruled out 33."

"How did you manage to do that?" I asked.

He just looked down at the floor and didn't reply.

"You've been here before," Lavon said.

"No, not *here*. Despite what you think, I was not completely unaware of the dangers I could encounter in this world."

"Then what did you do? Where did you go?" I asked.

"Nazareth," he finally admitted. "I thought it would be safer. The Bible implies that it was a dusty, insignificant little village, which is what it turned out to be. I only needed to be on the ground a few minutes – just long enough to find out whether anyone knew of Jesus' whereabouts. I didn't think it would be as hazardous as Jerusalem."

I couldn't argue with the logic, though I was struggling to believe his story, in spite of our current situation.

"How did you communicate?" I asked.

"I found a Biblical scholar in Washington. I paid him to write for me that 'I seek Jesus, son of Mary and Joseph, the carpenter' in both ancient Greek and Aramaic. I went back before the Passover in the year 33 and showed my note to an old man."

"And?"

"He just shrugged. He pointed up to the sky, and then to the east, toward the desert, as if he had heard so many crazy stories that he had no idea which ones could be true. That told me what I needed to know: whatever happened, it had occurred before the year 33."

"Makes sense," said Lavon.

"Here's something even you can appreciate," said Bryson. "The man must have been a carpenter by trade. After he took my note, he led me to his shop and gestured like he wanted to sell me a table. I don't think he cared anything about religion at all. What seemed to excite him the most was that one of his competitors was no longer in business."

Chapter 46

That thought led to a whole new set of questions I didn't have a chance to ask. We heard footsteps tromping up the stairs, followed by a loud thump as the servant stationed in the corridor opened the heavy door. To our relief, our visitor was the centurion Publius, alone.

He wasted no time with ceremony.

"Your woman has been caught," he said.

We all feigned surprise, since technically speaking, none of us were even aware that she had fled the palace.

Publius explained the details he knew, beginning with her slipping the blanket rope past the sleeping guard and ending with her discovery by a desert Bedouin whom Herod employed to track down the occasional escaped slave.

"Is she OK?" I asked.

Publius nodded. "I think so. The guards roughed her up a bit, but from what I heard, Herod is all the more eager to have her. Tell me: are the women of your country as resourceful in bed as they are outside of it?"

"Resourceful enough," Lavon said. "Do you know where they caught her?"

Publius laughed as he poured himself a cup of wine.

"This is the best part: after dropping from the wall, she headed to the quarry northwest of the palace, looking for a place to hide, I suppose. But the cave she found turned out to be a tomb that the stonemasons had carved for one of the high priests."

"A tomb?" said Lavon.

"Yes; for a member of their Sanhedrin – Joseph something, I believe."

Lavon's eyes lit up, despite his best efforts to hide them. Bryson's did too, after Lavon had translated.

"Where is this tomb?" said the Professor. "Can you show us?"

Publius didn't say anything at first. Instead he stared into each of our faces in turn.

"First I must ask you a question," he finally said. "Who are you? And where are you really from?"

Lavon acted as if he were taken aback, though deep inside his bowels must have been dissolving. I know mine were.

"You know our names, and that we are from Norvia, a land far to north, beyond Germania," he said.

Publius slammed his hand down on the table. "Do not lie to me!" he shouted. "You know this name, this Joseph of Arimathea."

Bryson turned white after Lavon had translated, though the archaeologist himself managed to keep his composure.

"You recognized other names, too, that you would have no reason to know if you were truly from the other side of the world – like that squalid little village we passed through on our way to the city – or, as our informants told us, the old priest Nicodemus, there in the Temple.

"You even knew of that prophet who drove out the merchants the other day. I could see it in your eyes that you did, as much as you tried to conceal it. How is this so?"

"We have not lied to you, Publius," said Lavon. "We have indeed traveled from a far country, beyond Germania. Look at our white skins. Do we resemble anyone native to this part of the world?"

"No, but that does not answer my question."

"We have told you nothing untrue," said Lavon.

"Then you have left part of your story out. What have you omitted?"

Lavon, to his credit, kept his cool and looked the centurion straight in the eye. "The part you would not believe, even if we explained it to you."

"Try," he ordered.

Lavon gestured toward me.

"All right," he said. "Do you recall that bandage that he used to save your soldier after the ambush on the road?"

"Yes; his recovery has been remarkable. It worked almost like magic."

"That's right – magic; and in seven days, it will begin to melt away. In fourteen, it will disappear of its own accord. Within a month, your man will be fit to return to full active duty. By then, his wound will have healed so completely that aside from a small scar, no one who wasn't already aware of his injury will be able to tell that it had ever occurred."

Publius stepped back; his face reflecting an uncharacteristic alarm.

"Are you gods?"

Lavon laughed and pointed to Markowitz, who now lay curled up in the fetal position around a bucket reeking of vomit.

"Gods. Yes, I can see how some would conclude that we are gods."

At this, the Roman smiled and the tension started to melt away. However, his wariness did not completely vanish.

"What is it you want?" he finally asked.

"The same thing you do: to leave this place and return to our homes – after we get our woman back, of course."

The centurion's expression darkened. "How do you know I want to leave?"

I answered after Lavon translated.

"When I commanded soldiers, I spent a year in a country much like this one – a morass of warring tribes and religious fanatics trying to kill me and my men. All I wanted to do was finish my job and go home."

"You did complete your duties?" asked Publius. "You followed your orders?"

"Certainly. If there is anything we soldiers know how to do, it's to follow orders, whether they make any sense or not."

The centurion glanced once more toward Markowitz. "Is that why you tolerated this young man?"

I nodded. "It is as we told you before: his father is rich; we serve him. He ordered us to look after him."

"And the woman: surely she is no princess."

"I apologize for not telling you the whole story," said Lavon. "In truth we have no princesses. We live in a republic, but the people in the lands we passed through do not understand what that is. It is a difficult concept to explain."

"Rome was a republic once," said Publius.

"We did not know that at the time," said Lavon. "Otherwise we would have told you the complete truth."

Publius considered this for a moment.

"If you do not bring her back, your consul will be angry with you, no?"

"In such an event, our disgrace would be so complete that we could not return home at all," said Lavon.

"Can you help us?" he added.

Publius frowned. "I am three years from retirement. I will find a wife and have my own farm. I will not stand for anyone to put this at risk."

"We do not wish to put you in any danger," said Lavon. "We are only seeking to reunite our party once more, so we can leave and return to our homes."

"What about the Pyramids?"

"We can come back later, as the gods permit. If they are as big as we've been told, they are not going anywhere."

Publius chuckled, which was a good sign. Then he signaled to me.

"I am invited to Herod's palace as the prefect's representative tonight. I will take this man as my servant."

"He cannot talk to anyone," said Lavon.

"This is no obstacle. Servants are not permitted to speak."

"What will he do?"

"Stand and watch. He may learn something useful."

"How?"

"He appears to be a resourceful man. He will think of something, and if he cannot speak, he cannot say anything dangerous, on impulse, as you could."

Lavon nodded. "When?"

"After sunset. I will send a slave for him when I am ready to go. The rest of you must remain here."

***

"Do you really think he'll help us?" Bryson asked after the Roman had departed.

Lavon thought so, though he warned us to take Publius's retirement plans seriously.

"As a centurion with a distinguished service record, he's in line for a land grant, at the very least. Depending on where he settles, he might even wind up with a cushy posting at one of the Roman training facilities. By first century standards, he'll have a very nice life. He can't afford to take any chances."

"I'll do my best to see that he doesn't," I said.

"What do you expect to accomplish?" asked Bryson.

I shrugged. "A little knowledge is better than none, I suppose."

Chapter 47

For the next few hours, we had nothing to do but wait. We watched the priests perform the evening sacrifices as our servant brought in an oil lamp, along with more bread and wine, a plate of boiled vegetables, and a chunk of meat that looked like the breast of a duck.

The air had grown chilly, so Lavon draped another blanket over a sleeping Markowitz. Then he returned to his window and stared out toward the southwest, lost in thought.

As the twilight began to fade, he turned to us and directed our attention the same way.

"At this moment, right over there, Jesus and the disciples are getting ready for the Last Supper."

Before Bryson or I could react, Lavon walked back to the table, took a piece of bread, tore it into three pieces, and handed one to each of us. Though he knew Bryson wasn't a believer and probably had his doubts about me, it just seemed like the thing to do.

"On the night in which he was betrayed, he took the bread and broke it, saying 'this is my body, given for you. Do this in remembrance of me.'"

After we ate, Lavon took the wine jug and refilled our goblets.

"In the same way, he took the cup, saying 'this cup is the new covenant, in my blood, which is poured out for you.'"

We each took a sip of our wine and stared once more to the southwest, in silence.

"I can scarcely believe this is happening," Bryson said after a few minutes had passed. "I wish we had some way to follow him around."

"Knowing the exact location wouldn't help us much," Lavon replied. "It's not like any of the parties involved would let us stand to one side and observe."

The archaeologist shook his head. "It's just as well, anyway. I'm not exactly sure how I would react."

To be honest, I wasn't sure how I would, either.

A few minutes later, Markowitz rolled over and belched. I heard him mutter an obscenity, though he made no move to stand up. I went over to check on him, but by then he had gone back to sleep.

"Nothing to worry about," I said.

"What are we going to do about him?" asked Bryson.

Lavon shrugged. "The two of us aren't going anywhere tonight, so we can be sure to keep him on his side. As long as we don't give him any more wine, he should sober up by morning."

"No, I meant after we get back. Given what he's been through, he's going to need counseling."

I didn't think so. As it turned out, neither did Lavon.

"Whatever issues he has, he's going to have to work them out himself, or with us," he said.

"We have no professional qualifications in that field," said Bryson.

"That doesn't matter. How is he going to explain to some shrink that Pontius Pilate forced him to kill a man in an impromptu gladiatorial contest? If that doesn't get him locked up in a padded room with a box of crayons, I don't know what will."

Chapter 48

I couldn't argue with that logic; though the way things were going, we'd all be lucky if a cell in the nut-house was the worst thing that happened to us.

Not long thereafter, a slave appeared at our door to lead me to the Antonia's northern gate, where Publius and a small contingent of soldiers waited with horses. The Romans weren't exactly patient, either. As soon as I climbed onto my mount, they took off at a rapid clip.

I hadn't been on a horse since I stumbled off a worn-out old nag at summer camp in the eighth grade, so I don't recall much about the journey other than struggling to hang on for dear life, to the great amusement of my companions.

Fortunately, the distance to Herod's palace was not great, and we could travel by the light of the full moon. By some miracle, I managed to arrive in one piece.

I handed the reins to a groom and followed Publius into the palace, careful to maintain the requisite two paces behind the Roman officer. Herod greeted him profusely and beckoned the centurion to accompany him into the great hall.

As for me, I might as well have been furniture. I followed behind my "master" without saying a word.

I'll say this for Herod: the man enjoyed grand style, and it took some effort not to gawk. Even I could see that the king had employed some extraordinarily skilled craftsmen.

In contrast to the bare *meleke* blocks of the Antonia, polished marble or elegant cedar paneling covered every palace wall.

Even the supporting columns were works of art. Sculptors had carved elaborate designs into each one, though in keeping with the traditional Jewish prohibition against the rendering of living creatures, they had confined their patterns to intricate geometrical arrangements.

To top it all off, gold candelabras and oil lamps illuminated the exquisite silk draperies, cushions and pillow cases.

The king himself stood at the center of attention, and his appearance matched roughly what I had expected. He was a couple of inches taller than his subjects – about five foot seven, I guessed. His black, somewhat curly hair was trimmed short, as was his beard, in the custom of the day. He wore a purple silk robe and a jeweled gold crown, topped off with enough bling to do an LA gang leader proud.

***

We stayed in the reception area only long enough for slaves to wash the Romans' feet. When they had finished, Herod gestured for Publius to lead the way into the great hall. There, servants directed our party to the head table, which turned out not to be a table at all.

Rather than sit in chairs, Herod's guests reclined around what Lavon called a *triclinium*, a low three sided platform surrounded on the outside by piles of cushions. Aside from its obvious comfort, the arrangement conveyed one further advantage I was to see later, once the dancing girls had made their appearance.

Surprisingly, the head of the table was not the center position. From my vantage point, the king's *triclinium* resembled an upside down U. Herod plunked himself down on a cushion near the middle of the left-hand wing, while a servant directed Publius to the guest of honor's spot at the monarch's right.

Once Herod had been seated, his favored guests joined him, while the B and C list made do with the twenty or so similar "tables" scattered throughout the banquet hall.

Publius pointed to a station along the wall, about twenty feet away, and gestured that I should remain there. Then, he turned his attention back to the king.

A few minutes later, scantily clad servants brought in wine and the first course, and not long after that, the festivities moved into high gear.

It was strange, as I thought about it: despite the two-thousand year interval, Herod's banquet struck me as little more than an over-the-top version of a Las Vegas strip club.

A poorly compensated work force dispensed copious amounts of alcohol to the same drunken, obnoxious patrons, who spent their evening ogling naked women gyrating to tunes of bad musicians. In truth, the only things lacking were televisions tuned to sports channels along every wall.

Once I could see that no one paid me any mind, I turned my attention away from the festivities and forced myself to concentrate on my real objective.

Unfortunately, I saw no obvious answers.

The hall itself was an open space about a hundred feet long and half as wide. Massive cedar beams spanned the ceiling, supported by the occasional stone pillar. Aside from the main entrance, though, I saw only two other exits: a set of double doors at the end opposite from my position and a narrow opening not far from the king's table.

I was certain that the latter passage led either to Herod's bedchamber or to a place of refuge outside, but I had no way to know for sure. The two surly guards stationed on either side didn't look like they'd allow me to take a quick peek.

Meanwhile, the banquet picked up steam: more dancing girls, more wine; and I'll just say that whatever inhibitions the diners might have had coming in disappeared in short order.

***

After an hour or so, a man pushed through and made his way to the head table. He whispered into Herod's ear, and the king visibly brightened.

"Publius, you are a fortunate man," he said. "They are bringing me my Amazon."

Herod waved his hand and the raucous crowd grew quiet.

Two eunuchs escorted Sharon into the banquet hall from the doors at the far end, leading her with thin golden chains they had fastened to a gold collar clasped around her neck. That, and the first-century equivalent of a G-string, was the full extent of her attire.

I could see that her captors earlier in the day had not been gentle. Though she had been bathed and perfumed and whatever else the palace attendants could manage on short notice, no makeup could conceal the purple welt on her cheek, nor hide the fact that her left eye had swollen almost completely shut.

Herod must have already known of her injuries, for he made no comment about them. Instead, he seemed transfixed by her presence.

That wasn't hard to understand. Her lithe, athletic figure could still stop traffic, and I'll give credit where it's due: she stood tall, and walked forward with a dignity that I could never have mustered under similar circumstances.

Their procession continued until the eunuchs had brought her within an arm's reach of the king. Then, they unwound about six more feet of chain and took two steps back.

Herod just looked her up and down for a couple of minutes. Then, he held up a golden goblet.

"A toast to my Amazon," he said. "At last, a woman with spirit."

The guests raised their goblets.

"In fact, she is such glorious sight that I'm tempted to enjoy her right now."

I struggled not to react. Before Sharon's arrival, a number of Herod's guests had been doing exactly that with other women.

To my great relief, Publius quickly stepped in.

"Your highness, you surprise me," he said.

"In what way?"

"I agree she is a glorious specimen, but I was led to believe that your Amazon was truly without blemish. This one looks like she has been whipped into the hall. Look at her face: I doubt she can even see out of that eye."

"I did no such thing."

"I am certain that you did not, but perhaps those in your service were not as discerning."

The king didn't reply, though I did see the first hints of doubt cross his mind.

"I could understand why a degenerate Parthian might have to resort to such means to obtain female companionship," said the Roman, "but it is ill suited to a great king such as yourself."

Herod stared forward, unsure of his next action. Meanwhile, Publius laid it on thick.

"Your majesty, we all know that when women encounter a real man, you cannot keep them away. For instance, I am told that last night, the girls literally fought among themselves for the chance to leap upon your royal, um, presence."

A satisfied grin crossed Herod's face. "Indeed they did."

"When this one is able to see your manhood with both eyes open, she, too, will be unable to resist, but until then, she is a forced captive who does your reputation no credit."

Herod considered this as a reveler a few tables away cried out. "I just get them drunk."

His retinue broke into riotous laughter.

The king stared at her for a few moments, and then waved a hand at the eunuchs.

"Take her back and salve her wounds. I will enjoy her tomorrow night. Her eye should heal sufficiently by then."

But before they could do so, something caught the king's eye.

"Wait," he said. "Bring her back. Let me see her up close."

I saw a look of confusion cross the Roman's face. Publius wasn't sure what was coming next, either.

Herod reached up and ran his fingers across Sharon's breast and then up toward her neck. It was only then that I saw the pendant dangling, half caught in the golden collar.

"What is this?"

She glanced over in my direction, but there was nothing I could do. I just stared ahead as Herod grasped the listening device in his fingers, trying without success to figure out what it was.

At that moment, a man slid into the room from the nearby tunnel – Azariah, probably, if I had understood Sharon's description correctly.

"She values it for some reason, your majesty, though I cannot understand why," he said. "It is not made of a precious gem, nor of gold, yet she became very upset when we tried to take it away."

Herod smiled and reached to lift the pendant over her head. Sharon had no choice but to let him have it, though her struggle to keep an even expression did not pass unnoticed.

"Look at her now," said the king. "Parting with it is causing her great distress."

Herod then draped it around his own neck.

"She must not worry: I am only keeping it a reminder of the pleasure we will enjoy tomorrow. Afterwards, I will give it back, along with another one of pure gold."

This was unwelcome, to be sure. Without her ability to guide us with the transmitter, our task of extracting her from the palace complex had become considerably more difficult.

She glanced in my direction.

I nodded as imperceptibly as I could, to acknowledge that I had observed what happened. But I could do nothing else.

Herod waved his hand as a signal for the eunuchs to lead her away. Sharon, though, had taken only five steps when she suddenly stopped and turned around. She made a deep, slow bow to the king, going all the way to the floor while extending her arms out to each side

Then she stood, raised her arms and sang – not shouted, mind you – *sang* – "top floor, middle tower; top floor, middle tower" before bowing again and turning away for good.

***

Shortly thereafter, another naked girl bounced onto the king's lap, and I could tell from their exertions that Herod wouldn't spend another moment of this night pining after unrequited love; nor would anyone else at the head table, for that matter.

Given the circumstances, the king's jovial conviviality was easy to understand. What followed, though, took me by surprise.

As the evening's festivities began to wind down, Herod leaned toward the centurion and glanced over to me.

"Publius," he said. "Is this man a slave?"

"No, your majesty; he is a free man, who now serves us as a physician."

"A physician? Is he good?"

"We have found him quite skilled."

"He looks like a soldier."

"He was, but he is now retired, as I hope to be in three years," said Publius.

The king called for a more wine, though he took only a half goblet this time. After drinking it, he glanced in my direction again.

"Since this man serves you well, I will give him a girl."

He pointed to the closest nearby woman. "You there, see to this man's, um, requirements."

Before the girl could comply, Publius shook his head.

"I am afraid he is on duty, your majesty."

"Ah, duty. You Romans all talk of duty. You should learn to enjoy life more."

"Unfortunately, that is our law."

"Well, then, here's what I'll do. Tell him to take her to the fort when you go back tomorrow morning. You can send her back here the following day."

Publius considered this to be an altogether satisfactory arrangement and managed to pantomime the gist of what the king had in mind.

I forced a grin – any servant who had been awarded such an unexpected boon would have done so – but at the same time, I realized that the king's choice, a timid creature not much older than sixteen, just wouldn't do.

I gestured toward another woman dancing at the end of the adjacent *triclinium* – a dark-haired beauty in her mid-twenties.

I'm not always the best judge of human character, especially at first sight, but she had alert, intelligent eyes. More importantly, her spirit did not appear to have been crushed by her "responsibilities" in Herod's service. If anyone knew the ins and outs of the palace, she would.

Publius saw whom I had in mind.

"I believe he would rather have that one, if it is not too much trouble," he said.

"An excellent choice," said Herod. "You may take her when you go."

Chapter 49

Servants directed our party to our quarters through a series of narrow tunnels, which only compounded my belief that without inside knowledge, we'd never find our way through the palace's tangled web of passageways.

Publius sent the woman to a side chamber and then scribbled something in Greek on a wax tablet. He gestured that I should take advantage of my free time to have a look around, which I did – though after half an hour of stumbling about in the dim light, I decided that I could accomplish more by getting a good night's sleep.

A slave woke us just before dawn and led us down to the stables, where I could see that my reputation for horsemanship had preceded me. The Romans all laughed as one of the hands brought up an elderly mare only a step or two away from the glue factory.

At least it wouldn't throw me. I hoped.

We made our way around the northern perimeter of the city at a leisurely pace, though we sped up toward the end as the Romans sensed trouble brewing.

They weren't wrong in their assessment, either. A crowd had begun to gather at the northern end of the plaza fronting the Antonia. Though I couldn't understand what they were saying, there was no mistaking the angry murmuring. This was not a happy bunch.

The interior of the fortress had turned into an anthill of activity as well. As soon as we charged through the gates, grooms took our horses – mine to cut up for breakfast, in all likelihood – as a Roman messenger called out to Publius.

The centurion directed me to follow him and shortly thereafter, I found myself once again in Pilate's office.

The governor was pacing back and forth, mumbling to himself. Publius saluted and inquired about his foot, but Pilate just waved his hand as if he couldn't be bothered.

Seeing that no one paid any attention to me, I backed up to the wall and did my best to blend into the stone. I tapped the earpiece's transmitter so Lavon also could listen to the most amazing conversation I have ever heard. To this day, I can recall every single word.

***

Pilate finally stopped pacing and beckoned Volusus and the centurion to sit.

"You might wish you had stayed with Herod," said the governor, who was no doubt well aware of the standard operating procedure at the king's feasts. "We have a situation on our hands."

"What's happening," said Publius.

"It's that prophet," said Volusus. "The Temple police picked him up last night."

"They're questioning him as we speak," said Pilate. "In order to overcome the objections of his sympathizers in their council, Caiaphas will provide him a final opportunity to renounce this kingdom nonsense, publicly and unequivocally. If he does, I've agreed they can let him go. If he does not … well …"

"This is good, isn't it?" said Publius. "I thought you wanted to get rid of him."

"I do indeed," Pilate replied.

But the governor did not appear to display any real enthusiasm for the task – something Publius found confusing.

"The problem," said Volusus, "is his followers."

"How many do we have in custody?" asked Publius.

"None," said Pilate. "We weren't involved in the arrest at all. I thought it best that their Temple police handle the business. I only sent an agent to observe."

"Well then, how many did *they* take into custody?"

"Again, none," said Volusus.

Now the centurion looked really perplexed. "Their soldiers couldn't catch them? Didn't any of his followers try to resist?"

"One of them took a half-hearted swing with a sword," Volusus replied. "He sliced off a guard's ear or something like that; so I'm told."

"Only one?"

Volusus chuckled and held up a finger. "Yes; *one*. A single, solitary man fought back for a brief moment. The rest of them ran like rabbits."

"Where did they go?" asked Publius.

"We don't know," replied Pilate. "Like I said, we had no direct role in picking him up. Our friends in the Temple have never demonstrated our customary *thoroughness* when handling this type of affair. You know that."

Publius stared down at his feet. Finally he looked up. "You're worried that this is a trick; a deception of some sort?"

Pilate nodded. "The whole thing was too easy. Only a few days ago, at least two thousand people lined the road waving palm branches as he rode into the city. They're still out there. Some of them may be inside the walls as we speak, waiting for a signal."

"Our intelligence networks are pretty good," said Publius. "Surely we would have picked up at least some hint of that?"

"I would caution us all against overconfidence," said Pilate. "An assumption like that is a time-honored path to disaster."

"Herod, too, would have warned us if he had knowledge of trouble," said the centurion. "I heard nothing to that effect last night."

"That's because your head was between – "

Pilate cut himself off. "Never mind," he snapped.

The governor stood up and got something to drink; then he started pacing back and forth once more. As he did so, the two senior Romans talked quietly amongst themselves.

I couldn't understand what they were saying, but their faces visibly brightened. Whatever they were cooking up, they seemed well pleased with it.

"Perhaps, excellency, there is another solution," said Volusus. "As you know, a crowd is beginning to form to the north of the fort."

This got Pilate's attention. He stopped pacing and returned to his seat.

"Did you find out what they want?" he asked.

"We heard grumbles about Barabbas," said the centurion.

Pilate sighed. "With this prophet business, I had forgotten about him. What do you have in mind?"

"We let him go," replied the commander.

"Let him *go*?" said Pilate.

"Yes, excellency."

Pilate shook his head, vigorously. "No. Not a chance. This man is directly responsible for the deaths of Roman soldiers. *Your men*," he added. "He must die."

"And die he will," replied Volusus. "Please hear us out."

The governor signaled for them to proceed.

Volusus spoke carefully. "As I understand it, your intention is to make a public example of this prophet, but only in circumstances that will minimize the danger of a riot slipping out of control."

Pilate nodded. "That is the heart of the matter. Go on."

"And our primary hesitation in carrying out this objective is that we have too little in the way of reliable information about his followers – how many of them are in the city, where they are hiding, or their propensity for violence."

"Hundreds of them may be planning to launch a revolt this very day," said Publius, "or a few dozen may be cowering in fear inside tiny closets. We simply don't know."

"Yes," said Pilate, "but what does this have to do with releasing Barabbas?"

"Our thought was that you could, perhaps, offer a choice between this prophet and the type of prisoner that certain, um, *sectors* of the society here are likely to support," said Volusus. "Let *them* decide who lives and who dies. By doing so, they would give a stamp of popular approval to your decision."

"And in the event a disturbance does break out as they choose," said Publius, "two factions of the crowd would be set against each other. Eliminating the surviving troublemakers will be much less hazardous for us once they have exhausted themselves."

I could see Pilate wasn't entirely convinced, though he was obviously intrigued by the concept.

"Tell them that you've decided to release a prisoner as a goodwill gesture for the Passover, or something like that," said Publius. "You've done it before."

"Once," grumbled Pilate. "And I swore I wouldn't make that mistake again. The ungrateful bastard went out and murdered your predecessor straightaway."

"That will not happen this time," said Volusus. "Barabbas may leave this fortress today, but I can assure you that he will not die at peace in his bed, nor will any of his spawn. Within a month, after these crowds have gone home, he will begin his journey to the underworld."

Pilate considered this in silence for a couple of minutes.

"All right," he finally said, "The idea has promise. But how can we be sure the crowd will select the right man? What if too many of this prophet's followers show up?"

"Barabbas's supporters are already starting to assemble," said Volusus. "Once enough of them are present, it won't be hard to block a few streets, if the need arises."

"We can also sprinkle agents in with the crowd to make helpful suggestions, just in case," said Publius.

"Yes, do that," said Pilate.

"Actually," said Volusus, "if you stage-manage this properly, by the time you're finished, you could even have the crowd cheering for the prophet's death. Any repercussions will be their fault, not yours."

"Take the theatrical approach," said Publius. "Get a big bowl; wash your hands of the entire matter in front of them while they decide. Once it's clear they're going to vote the right way, you can act perplexed – like what you are supposed to do with their king? If you use the right tone of voice …"

Pilate considered this for a moment and then broke out into a smile.

"I like it," he said, "although one thing still troubles me: freeing Barabbas could send his sort of vermin the wrong message. Even if you do plan to dispose of him later, the crowds will not be around to witness his death. Some of them may take away a mistaken impression of our resolve."

The three Romans thought for a few moments. Then Volusus turned his head downward, as if toward the dungeon.

"A handful of the bandits we caught with Barabbas are still alive. Once the crowd has made its decision, wait an hour or so to let them disperse; then pick a couple of the prisoners and crucify them along with this prophet. That should send a clear enough signal."

Chapter 50

A few minutes later, a courier rushed into the office and handed Pilate a note. The governor read it and then immediately strode out with Publius and Volusus in tow. Since no one had spoken to me, I took the opportunity to slip back up to our room and rejoin the others.

The palace woman was waiting for me at the base of the stairs. I had become so engrossed in the conversation I had just overheard that I had completely forgotten about her.

We jogged up the steps, and as the servant opened the door, I saw that Markowitz was awake, though a bit groggy and suffering from the effects of a hangover.

"Can you get that servant to bring us some coffee?" he grumbled.

"Sure," Lavon laughed, "you'll only need to wait eight hundred years."

Coffee, as it turns out, didn't appear in the historical record until the ninth century.

Markowitz made a barely audible grunt while I introduced the woman to the others. Naomi examined us with the trained eye of a practiced courtesan. Then she stepped over to the bed and began to remove her clothes.

I hadn't expected this – at least not yet.

"Tell her to stop," I said to Lavon.

He did so, and we were all surprised by her puzzled reaction.

"You don't like women?" she asked.

We all laughed after Lavon translated.

"Of course we like women," I said. "*Only* women, we must emphasize."

I, for one, wanted no confusion on that point.

Lavon told her what I had said, but she only grew more perplexed.

"Very well; I am yours all day," she said.

I considered this for a moment.

"Tell her the day is early," I instructed Lavon. "We have some things we'd like to discuss with her first."

That seemed to satisfy her that we were ordinary, red-blooded men. She jostled with her clothes for a minute and then sat down on the bed.

Lavon sent our servant to fetch some breakfast, both because we were hungry and because we needed to be certain that we weren't overheard. Once the kid had gone, he asked her what she knew about the Amazon.

"You know her?" she asked.

"We serve her father," said Lavon. "She was taken to the king against our will."

I couldn't help but chime in. As goofy as it sounds now, it seemed like the thing to say.

"And *I* have sworn an oath to my God not to enjoy the company of women until we get her back. Surely you understand why this makes our task all the more urgent."

At that, she smiled, though her face also reflected concern.

"I have heard the soldiers talk: the king is smitten. He will never release her."

"We know. That's why we need your help," said Lavon.

"We have reason to believe she is being held in the Phasael Tower," I said.

"Yes, she is being kept in a chamber at the very top. After her escape, the guards are taking no chances."

"How did her face get bruised?" I asked.

"The tracker caught her sleeping. When he moved to seize her, she screamed and jabbed him in the eye. From what I heard, he punched her and threw her to the ground."

So that's what had happened.

"Was he punished for this?" I asked.

"I don't think so. Herod requires the Bedouin's services to track down fugitives. The man has never once failed to locate his quarry."

"What about the guard she slipped by; the one atop the wall?"

Her face turned grim. "Herod had him flogged, for dereliction of duty. I think he survived, but I am not certain of this."

This was unwelcome news.

"He has also forbidden wine on the walls."

This was even more unwelcome. I explained to the others that Sharon would remain alive as long as she retained the king's favor. The instant she lost it, she could expect nothing but the worst sort of abuse.

I suppose one had to be an old soldier to know.

Sharon's escape had turned what had been a cushy posting into a tedious chore. The men would now have to endure inspections and drills for months on end, even though everyone, from the king on down, knew that nothing of consequence would happen on those walls for the next decade.

Lavon frowned; then he turned back to Naomi with a look of newfound urgency. "Will you help us?" he asked.

"What can I do?"

"You are aware of secret passageways through the palace, are you not? Tunnels, drains, water conduits – places a person could slip in and out undetected?"

"Yes, I have been through many passageways that few others know about."

"Then you can lead us to her, and show us how to get away once we have rescued her."

Her head drooped and she quit smiling. She didn't say anything for a minute or two; then she glanced up at Lavon, with a sad expression on her face.

"I cannot," she said. "I told you: the king is smitten with her. If he discovers my role in her escape, as he surely will, he will have me beaten."

She shook her head and shuddered. A woman being thrashed was something she had undoubtedly witnessed, more than once.

"And if I survived that, Herod would order me sold – to a filthy shepherd's brothel, or to a squad of soldiers, or worse. I cannot take that chance."

No one could argue with her logic, so we spent the next few moments brooding in silence.

"We understand," Lavon finally said, "but we can offer you another option. Once Sharon is free, we will go back to our country. You may come with us and live as a free woman, obligated to no one."

She sat up straighter, clearly interested.

"How does your country differ from this one? What can I expect to see in your lands?"

"Wonders beyond your wildest imagination," replied Lavon. "If you'd like, you can even fly through the heavens, like a bird."

I shot Lavon a dirty look. We'd gain no advantage by pushing things too far.

"Fly like a bird?" she said.

Then she began laughing. "You are amusing, Lavonius. What will you say next? That men from your land have walked on the moon?"

Lavon glanced in my direction and smiled before turning his attention back to Naomi.

"I am serious," he said. "If you choose to help our woman escape and return to our country with us, you will not have to worry about earning a living. Her father will reward you, in gold. He is very rich."

"How much gold?" she asked.

Lavon looked around the room and finally pointed to the water jug, which looked like it held a couple of gallons.

"Do you see that jug?" he asked.

"Yes."

"Fill it with gold; it will all be yours."

Her eyes lit up for a moment, but then I could see her grow skeptical. Whatever that amounted to in modern US dollars – roughly $5 million, I learned later – I knew Sharon's old man had it. But once again, Lavon seemed to be overselling our case.

Naomi sat quietly on the bed, considering her options.

"I can't believe she doesn't jump at the chance," said Bryson.

From the modern perspective, the Professor might have been right, but as I thought about it, her hesitation was understandable.

Despite her duties, Naomi lived in the palace, while most women of Jerusalem spent their days emptying chamber pots, or standing in line for water and carrying it half a mile, several times a day.

"You may find it hard to comprehend, but by their standards, she has something to lose," I said.

That gave Lavon an idea.

"Naomi, how long have you lived in the palace?"

She considered this for a moment. "Fourteen years. Azariah bought me when I was eleven."

"So you are twenty-five years old?"

"Yes."

"What will you do when you get older?" he asked.

She paused to think. "I will oversee the palace women, when I am too old to serve men directly."

"How can you be sure of this?"

"The king and his officers all favor me."

"Yes; for now," said Lavon, "but the king can change his mind, can't he? Besides, kings die; and kings are overthrown, all over the world, all the time. If Herod were no longer king, you could just as easily spend the rest of your days scrubbing latrines."

She frowned. I was certain that this had crossed her mind before; but as with other unpleasant truths, she had pushed it to the back of her consciousness. It was something I did often enough.

"Help us," said Lavon. "We can spare you that fate."

She sat there for maybe five minutes, weighing her decision, with her mind going back and forth.

I began to grow concerned: we had only a limited time window, and without someone who knew the ins and outs of the palace, our mission was almost certainly doomed.

As it turned out, it wasn't the prospect of buckets of gold or flights through the heavens that saved us; nor was it her dread of an old age spent in degrading servitude.

It was a tooth.

She suddenly gave a sharp cry and reached up to her jaw with her hand.

Now I'm even less of a real dentist than I am a doctor – I don't even play one of those on TV – but I made a great show of examining her, even if all I had to offer was a small tube of oral analgesic.

Luckily, it worked.

Lavon explained to her that if she came back with us, we could fix her teeth permanently and she would experience no more pain. As strange as it may sound, that did the trick.

Chapter 51

After the servant had brought our breakfast, I asked Lavon to have him run back down and fetch a pen and paper, intending to use Naomi's assistance to scribble out a basic diagram of the palace, so that we could have at least a semblance of a plan before we set off.

The archaeologist just laughed.

What we called paper in the modern world didn't exist, and papyrus was far too expensive to hand out on a casual basis. Complicating matters still further, ancient scribes made their inks on the spot, just before use.

"The inks are organic," he explained. "They'll spoil if they are not used quickly."

I sighed and began rummaging through my kit for a substitute, though I hadn't made much progress when Lavon called out.

"I hear something," he said.

I reinserted my ear bud and heard a male voice, but the translation was only gibberish. The speaker, whoever he was, wasn't conversing in Greek.

It was only then that I recalled who the speaker probably was.

I gestured toward Naomi. "Knowing what they are talking about could make or break our enterprise," I said.

The archaeologist cast me a dubious glance, but after considering our limited options, he shrugged, as if to say "why not?"

"Let's just hope she doesn't scream," he said.

Lavon walked over to the bed and sat down beside her. He removed his ear bud so that she could see it. Then, he went through a charade of putting it in his own ear and taking it out again, several times.

Afterward, he held it up to the side of Naomi's head. A few seconds later, the same voice I had heard earlier came through loud and clear.

She leapt from the bed.

"It is Azariah!" she gasped.

Lavon just smiled. "We know."

I popped my earpiece out and smiled also as I showed it to her. Lavon and I both chuckled softly as she gaped at us, wide-eyed, in open astonishment.

She stood as if frozen in place for a few more seconds; then, suddenly, she dropped to her knees and pressed her face to the ground.

"Who wants to be Zeus?" I said.

Lavon didn't reply. Instead, he reached down, gently grasped her hands and lifted her to her feet.

"We are men," he said, "not gods. Do not be afraid."

Naomi cast nervously about the room; her face a ghostly pale. When she appeared to have recovered a small fraction of her composure, he guided her back to the bed and once more sat down at her side.

She turned toward me. I tapped my ear and spoke.

"Tell her it's OK," I said to Lavon.

He did so, and then had an even better idea. He instructed me to disable the translation feature and to hold my device up to her ear. He walked over to the opposite side of the room, turned his back, and whispered in Greek.

She couldn't hear his normal voice from that distance, but she understood his words perfectly. Whatever he said had a soothing effect.

Lavon came back, cupped her face gently between his hands, and lifted it up until their eyes met. Then he repeated what he had whispered into the transmitter.

"Did I not tell you that if you helped us, you would see wonders beyond your wildest imagination?" he said.

"Tell her if she doesn't help us, she'll be consumed in a giant fireball," said Bryson.

I wasn't sure whether the Professor was joking, and to his credit, Lavon knew a stupid idea when he heard it.

I glared at Bryson to remain silent, and after a little more time had elapsed, Naomi's breathing dropped back close to its normal rate. Whatever this strange object was, she appeared to have concluded that it was unlikely to cause her immediate demise.

Lavon spoke again, even more softly this time, and asked her to translate the Aramaic into Greek. He helped seat the device properly in her ear, then instructed me to listen in as an additional safeguard.

Naomi listened with her eyes closed. At the first lull in the conversation, she turned to Lavon and explained.

"It is Azariah," she repeated. "I would recognize his voice anywhere."

"Can you tell where he is?" asked Lavon.

She listened for a few more seconds. "He is with the king."

So Herod had kept his "gift" after all.

Naomi rattled off other names that were unimportant, all something-*iah,* who had gathered together with a flock of her fellow palace courtesans. From the way she described it, the denizens of Herod's playpen were only now waking up.

"Do you know *where* they are?" I asked. "Where is the king right now?"

She considered this for a moment. "The king's personal bed chamber is on the third floor, at the southern end of the palace complex. When he is in Jerusalem, he is always there at this time of day."

This surprised me – pleasantly, for a change. I had always thought that ancient monarchs spent their entire lives in mortal fear of assassination. Such people tended to move around a lot, rarely sleeping in the same place two nights in a row.

"No," she said. "This is the most luxurious room in the palace. Herod would have no other."

"Can you take us there?" asked Lavon.

She didn't say anything as she thought through the options.

"Yes," she said. "I know a passage."

But then she paused. I suppose she had too much tact to say so directly, but the question was obvious: what, exactly, did we plan to do once we arrived?

I had been thinking about the same thing.

I drew the outline of a rectangle on the floor with my finger. Herod's bedroom was located on the southern end of the palace complex. The tower in which Sharon was being held was on the opposite side.

Both, I suspected, would be heavily guarded and equally impenetrable. The weak link, if one existed, would be the transit between the two.

As Lavon explained, Naomi's eyes brightened. "I know just the place," she said.

"That seems easy enough," said Bryson, after Lavon had explained.

I nodded – and kept my thoughts to myself. However straightforward this scheme might have sounded, if any of us were still alive 48 hours from now, I'd concede that miracles truly did happen.

***

"We'd best get going," said Lavon. "All the activity to the north of the fort will give us a limited window of opportunity to slip out the other way."

As to what that activity would be; well, that was something I really didn't want to think about. Lavon must have had a similar notion, for he directed our attention to our unfinished breakfast.

"Eat up," he ordered. "This is all we're going to get for a while."

"Grab all your stuff, too," I added. "Whatever happens, this is a one way trip."

That seemed to jolt Markowitz into a higher level of awareness. He wolfed down his chow and walked back over to the window, where he just stared in silence into the Temple courtyard, watching the morning sacrifices, one last time.

I noticed also that the look on his face had changed, and I didn't think it was just the effects of the wine wearing off. I sensed a newfound firmness, even a resolve, that I had not seen before.

"Next year in Jerusalem," he said.

Bryson looked at him with a puzzled expression, though neither Lavon nor I cared to explain. Markowitz's statement had been the Jews' Passover rallying cry for nearly two thousand years, until the Israeli army seized the city in 1967.

Lavon and I exchanged a quick glance. Unless we found a way to stop him, he was definitely coming back.

But we had no time to worry about that now.

"Do we have anything resembling a weapon?" Lavon asked. "Just in case."

I lifted my tunic to expose a *gladius* I had strapped to my right leg.

"I picked up a souvenir last night." I said.

But this was more for show than anything. I had no illusions regarding my swordsmanship skills. In a fair fight, a trained soldier would kill me with ease.

Lavon had the good sense to recognize this. I only hoped the others did.

"Need I remind you that our success depends on *stealth*," I said. "We can't exactly call for reinforcements."

Chapter 52

As we made our last-minute preparations, I showed Lavon the wax tablet Publius had given me the night before. He read the Greek and laughed. As I had suspected, it was my get-out-of-jail-free card, in case Herod's soldiers caught me snooping.

The writing described my poor sense of direction and instructed whoever found me to "return an obstinate, dim-witted servant to the centurion Publius so that the appropriate disciplinary measures may be taken."

"Those 'appropriate measures' won't be such a joke today," said Lavon.

I had no doubts on that score. I closed the tablet's cover and slid it back into my bag.

"What are you talking about?" asked Bryson.

Lavon started to explain, but thought better of it. He just turned and gave our room a final inspection as he headed for the door.

"Let's go," he said.

While I had been out, the archaeologist had done some exploring of his own and had located a little-used passageway that led directly into the northwest corner of the Temple compound. We followed it and soon found ourselves on the second level of a colonnaded walkway that ran along the edge of the complex's massive western wall.

About halfway across, we veered off to the right and down some stairs, where we joined a stream of pilgrims heading west across the stone bridge that connected the Temple Mount to the wealthy enclave of the Upper City.

"Wilson's Arch," Lavon reminded us.

"Do you have any idea what they call it now?" I asked.

He didn't. I could see him struggle with the temptation to inquire of our fellow pilgrims before he decided not to risk highlighting our foreignness any further. Neither of us thought to have Naomi ask for us until the opportunity had passed, and oddly, she did not know herself.

About fifty yards ahead of us, a donkey stumbled under its load, and our procession ground to a brief halt while its harried owner struggled to right the overburdened creature and prod it forward once more.

Since we had a free moment, I couldn't resist asking Lavon a question that had nagged at me all morning, though I pulled him forward a few feet so the others could not hear.

"Were you able to listen in on that conversation in Pilate's office?" I asked.

Lavon nodded. "Amazing, wasn't it?"

"You don't sound surprised."

"Not really. Are you?"

"A little bit," I admitted. "I always had the impression that the high priests manipulated a reluctant Pilate into killing Jesus."

Lavon didn't respond immediately. Instead, he turned around to face the Temple and spent a few moments staring at it, lost in thought.

When he spoke, he did so in a low voice. "People have argued about this for centuries," he said, "and with more than words."

Sadly, that was all too true.

He hesitated once more. I suppose he was wary of provoking an unnecessary quarrel, or perhaps he had been drawn into so many debates over the subject that he was sick of the question altogether.

"I think we can agree that *everyone* in authority around here wanted to get rid of him," he said. "Put it to a vote and you'd get thumbs down from them all – the high priests, Pilate, Herod, the lot."

I agreed. "That seems pretty clear."

He paused again, as if he were trying to phrase his thoughts exactly the right way.

"Each party had its own reasons to fear the crowds; and for trying to shift the responsibility for the deed to someone else; or at least the *appearance* of responsibility. We heard Pilate's thoughts on the matter earlier this morning."

"What about the high priests?" I asked.

"I had always wondered why they didn't just stone him in a mob frenzy, like they did with Stephen a few years later. Whatever the actual rules were, had they done so, do you think Pilate would have cared?"

"No," I replied; "but with so many people in the city, they probably didn't want to risk a mob getting out of hand."

"Exactly; so they had to find another option," he said. "It served their interests for the Romans to carry out the actual killing. The high priests' dilemma was that no matter how much they wanted to eliminate him, neither Jesus's sympathizers in the Sanhedrin nor the crowds outside would take kindly to their handing over a brother Jew to the pagan occupiers for torture and death."

"Hence the blasphemy charge?" I asked.

"That's the way I see it. Once he answered Caiaphas's question the way he did, not even his highest-ranking supporters could save him. And the pious masses wouldn't rise up on behalf of anyone guilty of such an offense."

"So the priests thought they were home free, then?"

"Probably," he replied. "But it looks like they underestimated both the Roman craftiness and the divisions in their own ranks."

Neither of us had to mention the fatal consequences this oversight would have for their descendants.

"Why do the Gospels present their accounts the way they do, then?" I asked.

"The first one wasn't written until the 50s," said Lavon. "By then, the early Christians were beginning to have serious trouble with the Roman authorities. The writers were well aware of this, and wouldn't have wanted to compound their difficulties by placing *direct* blame for the death of their Lord on a Roman governor."

He paused again.

"At least that's my take on it. It's a reasonable interpretation, if you read between the lines and pay attention to what was happening here, on the ground, at the time."

I had more questions, but Markowitz interrupted us. He pointed to a lower level door about a hundred meters to our north, where another long stream of pilgrims poured out from the Temple Mount.

"That's where I got caught," he said.

A squad of two dozen Romans observed the procession, but the legionnaires made no move to interfere with the worshippers. Markowitz stood still for a moment, watching the soldiers. Then he muttered an obscenity and spat in their direction.

Lavon and I both glanced at each other, but we chose not to comment.

***

By then, the crowd ahead of us had grown impatient with both the recalcitrant donkey and its owner's futile efforts to prod it along.

Tired of wasting time, four burly ruffians stepped forward and shoved the man out of the way. One of them promptly slit the animal's throat, and after its quivering kicks had weakened sufficiently, they wrestled the unfortunate beast up to the bridge railing and heaved both it and its load over the side.

The multitude behind us cheered and we started forward once more. As we reached the edge of the Upper City, the crowd's momentum pressed us deep into another rat's maze of narrow alleys. I, for one, quickly became disoriented, though we all took comfort in the fact that Naomi seemed to know where she was going.

We passed through a series of twists and turns before she stopped in front of a collection of baskets, each about the size of common rolling household trash bins. These appeared to be scattered haphazardly among piles of miscellaneous debris.

"Where are the houses?" asked Bryson. "I thought this was the wealthy part of town."

As it turned out, we were at the back of one. Jerusalem's elites, like their counterparts in the modern developing world, took pains to conceal their opulence behind high walls.

Although we seemed to have reached the place Naomi intended to lead us, I noticed that she was becoming quite nervous.

She spoke quickly to Lavon and motioned for the rest of us to pick a container and hustle inside; one person per basket. Once we had done so, she arranged the lids at haphazard angles and then covered them with a handful of filthy rags.

She stepped back to observe, and after giving us a quasi-satisfied nod, she snuggled up to Lavon. They spoke briefly; then she took his right hand and cupped it under her rump. Afterward, she squeezed him tight and led him around the corner.

I had spent enough of my early Army career hunkered down in squalid holes, and I could see that my bad luck in drawing duty assignments hadn't yet deserted me.

The previous evening, I could only stand in place and observe the celebrations. Now, I found myself packed into a fetid receptacle while my colleague had the privilege of scouting the territory with Rahab the harlot leading the way.

Some guys get all the breaks.

But I shouldn't complain. We only had to remain still for a quarter hour before the two love-birds returned.

Lavon lifted the foul-smelling refuse off the top of my basket and whispered the all-clear, while Naomi did the same with the Professor and Markowitz.

"Follow me," said Lavon, "and keep your mouths shut."

We scrambled around the corner and slid through an open doorway, pausing to let our eyes adjust to the low light. After a few seconds, Naomi stepped into the lead, and Lavon drifted back to ensure that no stragglers remained behind.

We hadn't gone far when we passed into a narrow tunnel. As soon as all of us were inside, Lavon reached back and pulled a recessed handle, closing the door and plunging us into darkness.

We stood still for a brief moment, waiting – in vain this time – for our eyes to adjust. Then we crept forward.

We had gone about a hundred paces when Naomi stopped to explain.

"I have worked here," she said.

As it happened, the madam who supervised the palace entertainers ran a thriving sideline supplying women to the Upper City's most exclusive brothel, conveniently located at the terminus of a neglected escape tunnel the first Herod had dug over half a century before.

Naomi sounded surprisingly positive about it, too. In contrast to their labors in the palace, these extracurricular duties were voluntary, and the women were permitted to keep a quarter of what they were paid. One had even managed to save enough to buy her own freedom, though what she had done afterward, Naomi didn't know.

Now the charade by the baskets made perfect sense. Had they been caught, Lavon could have passed for yet another satisfied customer.

I was about to ask where this particular tunnel led when I heard voices in my earpiece. Lavon heard them too. He listened for a moment and then handed the device to Naomi.

"What's happening?" said Bryson.

"Shh," I whispered.

Naomi translated the Aramaic into Greek when the conversation paused. Like the discussion in Pilate's office, I will never forget the exact words she related to us.

Chapter 53

Herod spoke first. "Azariah, I commend you. Her eye is healing nicely. By tomorrow evening, no Roman will be able to say that I have to flog my women into submission."

"She is truly a unique specimen, my lord. It is a shame she cannot speak a word of our language."

"She knows no Aramaic?" asked the king.

"Nor Greek, I'm afraid."

"Latin?"

"A word or two at most."

Herod shrugged off this complication.

"Well, it is of no importance. To carry out her responsibilities, she will not need to talk. The others chatter too much anyway."

The courtiers in the room laughed, and one of them cracked a joke Naomi didn't bother to translate.

For the next few minutes, we heard nothing but idle gossip. But then I could hear the approaching sound of marching feet.

"About half a dozen, I'd guess," I whispered to Lavon.

The soldiers halted some distance away. One of their number broke off and came closer. He came to attention and saluted – I'd recognize that sound anywhere – and then I heard some brief shuffling before the man saluted once more and backed away.

Nothing happened for a minute or two. Then we heard a voice.

"It appears that Pilate is sending us a prisoner, my lord," said Azariah.

I heard a brief grunt. Whatever was happening, the monarch didn't like it.

"Despite holding the title of prefect, Pilate is only of the Roman equestrian order," said Herod. "Yet he, a mere knight, presumes to tell a crowned *king* how to handle our affairs."

From what Naomi said, this was a familiar complaint.

"A most lamentable circumstance," said Azariah.

A brief period of silence followed.

Finally, Herod spoke again. "Well, who is this prisoner?"

"The message says that it is the Nazarene."

"The Nazarene?"

"The same, my lord. He is a Galilean, so Pilate is sending him to us."

We heard another grunt. Herod did not welcome this news.

"Just what I would expect. He fears a riot, and if one does occur, he wants someone else to bear the responsibility."

"Yes, my lord. That is how I see it, too."

As did I, though I regretted that we would never have the chance to find out whether Publius or Volusus had planted this idea in the governor's head or if Pilate had thought of it himself. Both struck me as plausible.

"How was he caught?" asked Herod.

"Apparently, one of his followers saw the light."

"No doubt reflected off some silver," grumbled Herod. "Who arrested him: the Romans or the Temple police?"

"I don't know. Whatever happened, though, he ended up in the hands of Pilate, who will crucify him; of that we can be certain."

"Yes, but Pilate is afraid that his followers will cause a disturbance, like, um, what's his name –"

"Barabbas," said Azariah.

"Yes, Barabbas. Pilate will not want to write a dispatch to the Emperor explaining why he could not keep order, so he seeks a way to blame any problems that might arise on me. Perhaps the Romans will use this as an excuse to remove a portion of Galilee from my jurisdiction as well, and keep its revenues for themselves."

"That may be their intention."

After last night's shindig, I could feel Herod's concern. From my limited observations, the king didn't seem like the type who troubled himself much with budgets.

"What do you suggest?" Herod finally asked.

Azariah didn't have a ready answer. Like all courtiers caught in such circumstances, he seemed to be stalling for time.

"You wanted to see him, my lord, did you not?" he finally said. "Perhaps he can work some sign."

"You're certain this is not the Baptist?"

"Positive, my lord. He and the Baptist are distinct individuals, though they are cousins, which would explain the resemblance."

"That man tormented me to no end. I could not have let him live and kept my dignity."

"No, my lord. You only did what had to be done."

Another pause.

"Well, bring him in."

I heard the sound of shuffling feet and metal dragging across the floor, as if soldiers were leading a prisoner bound by a heavy chain.

No one said anything at first. I suppose the king was examining whether the prisoner's physical appearance matched what he had expected to see.

Finally, Herod spoke. "I hear you are a miracle worker."

The man did not respond.

"The Romans have sent you to me. Show me a sign, and I can set you free."

Again, silence; and sign or no sign, this was almost certainly a lie; unless Pilate had some new scheme up his sleeve that he hadn't mentioned before.

Herod made the request again, and I could tell that he was becoming irritated. The prisoner, though, never uttered a word.

A little later, one of the retainers made a crack, but neither the king nor Azariah said anything in response. Then, finally, we heard a loud cry.

In English.

"Oh my God!"

Sharon's breaths came rapidly. "Oh my God! My Lord!"

"What's this?" I heard Herod say.

"Oh my Lord! My God!" she repeated.

Whatever Sharon was doing, the king didn't care for it much.

"How does this one know the prisoner?" he barked. "I thought you said she cannot speak our language."

"She cannot," said Azariah. "I am absolutely certain of this."

"Yet she grovels before him as if *he* were a king, and not me. Look at her! She is afraid even to look into his eyes."

"I cannot explain it, my lord."

I could feel the tension from our hiding place in the tunnel, though I suppose that was because my own stomach was turning in knots.

Nothing happened for a few moments. Then we heard Azariah bark an order and several pairs of feet trotted off.

They returned shortly, and after the next few words, we needed little imagination to visualize what was beginning to happen.

"As you know, some call him King of the Jews," said Azariah.

"So," Herod groused.

"Well, then," said Azariah, "if he is a king, we also must honor him."

I heard a loud guffaw from a distant courtier, but for the moment, the others kept silent. Like parasitic sycophants everywhere, Herod's entourage waited to see which was the safe side.

The king himself said nothing for a brief instant, but then he, too, burst into laughter. "Yes, yes; you are correct. We must all bow before our new master."

At this, the floodgates opened.

"A monarch must have a scepter, and a crown," said one of the retainers.

I heard footsteps recede into the distance and return shortly thereafter. After a short interval, whoever it was must have been satisfied with his handiwork.

"All hail, King of the Jews," I heard him declare.

"All hail," shouted other retainers.

One even came forward with a bucket of water, with the excess sloshing over the side.

"We have run out of wine," he said. "If it's not too much trouble, we'd like you to make us some."

"Hear, hear," said another.

Then a woman's voice burst out. "I will prostrate myself before my lord, just like the Amazon here."

We could hear her throw herself to the ground.

"All hail, my lord and master" she said. "We celebrate your visit."

Two other women joined her, and the mockery continued until the courtiers finally began to grow bored.

"What do you recommend that we do with him now?" Herod asked as the chamber fell quiet.

"Send him back to Pilate," said Azariah. "Tell him we have paid homage to our king. He must now do the same."

Laughter echoed through the room as guards led the prisoner away. We learned later that Herod then walked over to a prostrate Sharon and gave her a vicious kick in the side before launching into a couple of obscene hip thrusts.

"She wants a lord," we heard him say. "Now, I will go to the baths. When I return, we will have a small festival, and I will show her who is lord around here."

Chapter 54

I felt that old familiar sense of dread. In the parlance of my instructors at the Army War College, our plan, such as it was, had been "overtaken by events." I could only be thankful that the king had not assaulted her on the spot.

Lavon and Naomi whispered briefly amongst themselves as they considered our new situation.

"They must bathe her also," she finally announced.

Apparently, Herod had a fetish for cleanliness.

"Where?" I asked. "Will they take her back to the tower?"

She considered this briefly and then said no.

Sharon's preparation would require two to three hours. Given the king's newfound impatience, the attendants would not want to delay matters further by escorting her all the way back to the opposite end of the palace. Instead, they'd prepare her in the baths under the women's dormitory, under heavy guard.

I started to ask whether we'd be able to intercept her party, but Naomi was already thinking several steps ahead.

"Follow me," she ordered.

Since it was still almost pitch-black, we crept slowly down the tunnel until I could make out a dim light about thirty yards away. We paused. She and Lavon whispered again, and then she motioned us forward once more.

At that point, the tunnel broadened out and intersected what appeared to be a regularly used corridor, complete with ventilation shafts leading to the lawn above. These admitted a faint hint of the morning sunlight, so we could finally see exactly where we were going.

Naomi stepped into the corridor and looked both ways. Seeing and hearing no one, she directed Lavon to cross over to the other side and to back himself into a small indentation, a relic from a section of tunnel that had been bricked up years before.

After he was securely ensconced in his hiding place, she stripped completely and tossed me her undergarments, which I then passed back to Bryson. Then, she draped her robe back over her olive skin in a loose and provocative manner.

I glanced across the corridor to Lavon and quickly got the picture. He held a leather sap – an item he picked up at the bordello while I squatted in that basket – and pointed to my leg. I nodded and unstrapped the *gladius*, motioning for Bryson and Markowitz to take a few steps farther back.

We waited quietly until we heard footsteps approaching. When they had come within about twenty feet of our position, Naomi tugged on her robe to reveal more of her ample cleavage. Then she staggered into the corridor.

The girl could have won an Oscar.

She gasped as she saw the soldiers and immediately yanked up her robe to cover her breasts. She blinked both eyes twice, signaling to us how many opponents we faced. Then, she began to ease herself backwards, as if she wanted to make a run for the baths but didn't dare to turn her back on these strange men.

The first of the guards took three quick steps forward. Apparently, he was unable to resist an opportunity to ravish a stray lamb before returning her to the fold. The other man, a bit more senior, rushed up and barked an order – no doubt telling the kid that they had a job to do and had better be getting on with it.

Those were the last words he spoke. Lavon swung the leather sap and caught him squarely on the back of the head. The soldier, who wore no helmet, crumpled without a word.

Before his young comrade could react, I held the point of my sword to his throat, while Bryson, per my instructions, managed to jam my last ampoule of Sufentanil into a vein in his foot.

He collapsed without a peep. More importantly, neither man left a drop of blood.

I lowered my *gladius* and turned to face Sharon, who stood, frozen, as if her mind had not yet comprehended what her eyes were telling her.

When it did, she rushed forward, threw her arms around me, and squeezed as if she were holding on for dear life.

I held her as long as I thought prudent, though we really did need to move on.

And I wasn't the only one to share that thought.

"We're not yet out of danger," Lavon insisted.

I gently pulled away. I continued to clasp Sharon's shoulders with my hands, although by then, she scarcely seemed to notice.

Instead, her initial shock at encountering us in such an unexpected spot had been replaced with an odd, almost beatific, radiance that made me wonder whether she had been drugged.

"I have seen him," she said.

"Seen wh –"

I cut myself short as I realized the obvious.

"*I have seen him*," she repeated, more insistently this time.

I glanced over to Lavon, hoping he'd have an answer to this unexpected complication.

I took a half-step sideways as he shook her gently and spoke.

"Sharon, we're not home yet. Until we get there, we are all in great peril. Do you want to go back to Herod?"

She didn't respond for a few seconds, but the mention of the king's name snapped her out of her reverie.

"I'll never go back to that monster," she said.

I took her hand and led her forward. "Then let's do what we must to ensure that doesn't happen."

She didn't say anything, so after a brief moment, I halted and repeated Lavon's question.

"Are you with us, Sharon?" I asked.

Finally, to our great relief, she answered as though she meant it.

***

"Keep 'em busy," is a proven technique I learned in the Army to divert upset soldiers from troublesome thoughts, but as I turned around to look for a task I could assign Sharon, I only saw a visibly agitated Naomi.

By now, she had put her clothes back on. She whispered, insistently, to Lavon while she gestured for Markowitz and Bryson to pull the two unconscious guards back out of the tunnel through which we had come and to lay them in the corridor.

They looked at me in confusion, but I directed them to comply with her wishes.

Once they had done so, Lavon instructed Bryson to help him carry one of guards while Markowitz and I toted the other.

"Don't let their clothing drag the ground," he ordered.

We carried both men about a hundred feet until we arrived at a storage closet. From the dust patterns around the door, I could see that it received regular, but infrequent, use.

I glanced over to Naomi and smiled, nodding my approval at both her choice of disposal site and the remarkable stroke of good fortune that had brought us together. She smiled back, though her worried expression didn't entirely go away.

The others stood out of our way as Lavon and I carried the first man inside and laid him on a stack of what appeared to be scrap lumber. We came back out and repeated the drill with the second man.

This time, though, Naomi blocked our exit.

I knew immediately what she wanted. Without saying a word, I unwrapped the cloth belt around my outer robe and signaled for Lavon to do the same.

The archaeologist wasn't slow on the uptake. He started to protest, but he could see that her eyes had hardened.

"No blood," was her only comment.

"I don't like it either," I said.

And I truly didn't; but we couldn't take the chance that one of these people would wake up unexpectedly. Some things just had to be done.

We each wound a cloth strip around our man's neck in the manner of a tourniquet. I counted off several minutes and then checked each soldier for pulse or breathing. Sensing none, I signaled for Lavon to move on.

Once we had rejoined the others, Naomi explained that leaving evidence that Herod could trace to the tunnel could have devastating consequences for the girls left behind, though personally, I think her motivations ran deeper.

After a lifetime of degradation and servitude, she had her first chance to strike back. I only hoped she wouldn't learn to enjoy it too much.

Chapter 55

We scurried behind Naomi through a confusing labyrinth of passageways and had gone about two hundred paces when she stopped suddenly and raised her hand.

By instinct, I pressed myself flat against the wall and listened. I held a finger up to my lips to warn the others, but my caution proved unnecessary. The others understood, and were doing their best imitation of wallpaper as well.

We heard voices and the noise of large objects being thrown, but at that moment, I couldn't place the sound. The conversation's tone seemed casual, though, and after a few minutes, whoever these people were headed the other way.

Naomi's face didn't reflect any real anxiety, so whatever had just happened must have been normal. She listened for another brief moment and then finally gave the all-clear signal, directing us forward once more.

We rounded a corner about thirty feet away and entered an open chamber about the size of the transit room back in Boston. Stacked against one wall were piles of split logs, which proved to be our exit ticket from the palace.

I hadn't given the matter any thought when I had taken my bath in the Antonia, but it finally dawned on me that a furnace capable of heating the equivalent of my hometown Y's swimming pool consumed enormous quantities of fuel.

In the first century, this fuel was wood, which meant that a facility the size of Herod's employed an army of timber cutters to keep it supplied.

Naomi knew their routines. At dawn each morning, the lumbermen fanned out across the hills to the west. Typically, these men spent their entire day in the field, and though they occasionally dispatched a heavily laden wagon back to the palace in the early afternoon, she had never seen one return before noon.

"What did we just hear, then?" I whispered

"She says that a few workers stay behind to stoke the furnace," Lavon replied.

This gave us a window of opportunity. We reached another tunnel, this one a broad sloping incline, and we scrambled up until we came to another stack of freshly split logs.

"They dry here," Naomi explained.

I looked beyond the pile and could see daylight for the first time. As it turned out, we had already passed through an opening in the main wall.

Except for Lavon, this surprised the others, who had always imagined a city's fortifications as being a single monolithic block.

"They could seal these small gaps very quickly if they needed to," he explained," just like the sewer drains. But in the meantime, servants and craftsmen who needed to go inside could pass through without interfering with the regular palace business at the main gates."

This wasn't as odd as we had first thought.

In the twenty-first century, few realized that even as recently as a hundred years before, one of the most common US occupations had been that of household servant. These workers used one entrance; the family used another. Their paths only occasionally crossed.

"Herod wants his creature comforts," Lavon said, "but he doesn't have the slightest interest in the mundane details of how those comforts are provided."

***

The structure in which we found ourselves had begun its existence as a temporary storage shed leaning against the city's main wall. Over time, the workers had expanded it into the present facility. Aside from the piles of cut timber, a motley collection of axes and saws leaned against the opposite wall.

Naomi crept around the firewood toward the outside entrance. Once there, she watched carefully for a few minutes and then signaled for us to follow.

After we had caught up, she first wrapped her scarf around Sharon's hair. Once she was satisfied that the blonde tresses were properly concealed, Naomi whispered to Lavon, who in turn signaled Markowitz.

The two of them each grabbed one end of a long cross-cut saw and sauntered outside. I watched them go about fifty yards before they disappeared into a brushy ravine.

The rest of us understood what to do next. We each grabbed a tool and followed the others into the scrub.

Once we had reunited, we continued south for another quarter mile until we found a collapsed limestone overhang partially concealed in a tangle of dense brush.

Out of force of habit acquired during many years of service, I did a quick head count and set up an observation post. From there, I stared back at the city, half expecting to see Herod's thugs charging down the slope after us.

But no one followed, to my great relief.

"I can't believe we got out that easily," said Markowitz.

Quite frankly, I couldn't either, though after Naomi explained, it made perfect sense.

The city confronted no significant external threats, and the common peasants knew that nothing good could come from sneaking inside the palace; so they didn't try. During daylight hours, at least, sentries weren't really necessary.

I also suspected that those who were stationed near the wood shop would be as bored, and as drunk, as the ones Sharon had slipped past on the wall.

***

As I assessed our situation, my instinct was to strike out to the west and put as much distance between ourselves and the city, as fast as we could. With the full moon, we could even push on through the night.

"They have no way to call ahead," I argued.

Lavon initially was inclined to agree.

Once we reached the more cosmopolitan coast, our appearances would be less likely to stand out. Plus, he admitted later that he was grasping for an excuse to see Caesarea. Some of that city's ruins had survived into modern times and the original was supposedly an architectural gem.

On the other hand, when pressed, he couldn't guarantee that we wouldn't encounter robbers, or worse, the Zealots – some of whom might even recognize us from the ambush a few days earlier.

Bryson started to join the debate, but he soon fell silent. Rather than argue, he got up and began to hobble, as if he had a sprained ankle.

"I can't make it that far anyway," he said. "We don't even have water."

I suspected he was faking the injury, but decided not to challenge him. We couldn't afford to waste our energy squabbling amongst ourselves. Besides, his second point was correct.

"All right, then," I said, "we'll stay in the area. How long do we have before all hell breaks loose?"

Lavon glanced up to the sun and guessed that it was about 9:00. Since we had rescued Sharon an hour earlier, he estimated that we had another hour, perhaps two, before the king finished with his bath.

"The servants already know I'm missing, though," said Sharon.

That they did, and the bath attendants were undoubtedly scrambling to find her that very instant. But from what Naomi told us, they would do so as quietly as possible. Word of Herod's dark mood had surely spread.

Naomi also reminded us that Azariah had assembled every slave in the palace to witness Sharon's guard being flogged.

"No one will dare admit to losing the king's woman a second time," she said. "Until the servants can be certain that they themselves can escape blame, they will obfuscate and delay as long as they can."

"Eventually, they'll have to fess up, though," I said.

"Yes. When the king returns from his bath, he will call for her."

"What then?" I asked.

"They'll keep stalling as long as possible," said Naomi. "They'll ask the king to be patient, say she is not quite ready …"

"If Herod is as angry as he sounded, that won't last long."

"No; half an hour at most. Then the steward will be forced to confess to Azariah that they cannot locate her. Azariah will conduct a brief inquiry, but once he realizes no one has answers, he will have no choice but to inform the king."

"And then?"

"They will turn the palace inside out."

Chapter 56

Whatever the actual timetable proved to be, we needed to get moving, though Naomi insisted that we leave our tools behind where they would be discovered by the lumberjacks at the end of the day.

I started to object – at the very least, an axe might come in handy – but she explained that the slaves responsible for their maintenance would be held accountable for their loss.

"A guard being flogged is one thing," said Lavon, "but she doesn't want an ordinary servant to suffer that fate."

This was understandable, though for a brief moment I began to wonder whether she might also be hedging her bets. If we got caught, she could go back to being a demure slave girl who had no choice but to accompany the savage beasts whom the king had assigned her to serve.

Once again, I needn't have worried.

"Slaves like her can be tortured at will," Lavon explained. "The truth would eventually come out, and she knows it. Whatever happens, she's not going back."

This was comforting, in its own twisted way.

Even more reassuring, Naomi told us that if Herod kept dogs, she had never seen them. This would buy us at least a few additional hours, though probably not the two whole days we needed.

We crept through the increasingly thick brush, heading south through what was known as the Hinnom Valley, on a course parallel to the city's western wall.

About half an hour later, we reached the corner where Jerusalem's fortifications turned to the east. There, we paused for a brief rest at the base of an enormous bridge leading into the city from the southwest.

"This looks like an aqueduct I saw in Spain, years ago," I said.

"That's what it is," replied Lavon. "Pilate's aqueduct."

Lavon stared up at the structure for several minutes, carefully noting its features.

"This is magnificent," said Bryson.

"Yes," said Lavon. "It's unfortunate that barely a trace has survived into modern times. Archaeologists have always wondered what it looked like."

"Where does it start?" asked Sharon.

"Somewhere south of Bethlehem, we think," he said absently. "About ten miles away."

"Why don't we go there?" asked Markowitz.

This jolted Lavon's mind back to our present situation, but before he could answer, Bryson brought up the same objections he had raised to prevent us from fleeing to the coast. He even started hobbling again.

I started to argue – by following an aqueduct, we'd at least have no trouble finding water – but by then I also noticed that Naomi had begun to lose her reassuring sense of confidence.

She explained that she had traveled many times with the king to Tiberias, his capital to the north on the shore of the Sea of Galilee. Once, she had even journeyed as far as Caesarea, on the Mediterranean coast to the west.

But the territory to the south of Jerusalem was as unfamiliar to her as it was to us.

***

We concealed ourselves behind a support column as we considered our alternatives.

We quickly ruled out Bryson's suggestion to return to the Antonia, and not just because of the obvious danger to Naomi. Markowitz had his own good reasons to avoid the governor, and Sharon categorically refused to go anywhere near the place.

"Pilate would send me back to the king," she insisted.

Bryson turned to Lavon. "You told us those two hated each other," he said, explaining the logic behind his brainstorm.

"They *did*," replied the archaeologist, "but Herod and Pilate became good friends after Jesus's death."

The Professor now looked thoroughly confused. "Why?"

"Luke's gospel doesn't say," answered Lavon. "My guess is that Pilate could appreciate the skillful way the king ducked the issue. Herod could have sent Jesus back to the Romans with a blunt note saying the prisoner had committed his offense in Jerusalem – and thus was the governor's problem.

"But he didn't do that. By mocking Jesus, Herod signaled his approval of what Pilate was about to do, in a manner that acknowledged the quandary the governor faced."

That struck me as a reasonable interpretation, though from the conversation we had heard a few hours ago, the skill involved was Azariah's.

"So you're saying the *Romans* are our enemies, too?" said Bryson.

"Oh, I think we've done better than that," I said. "Accounts of Ray's swordsmanship undoubtedly filtered down to the dungeons. We know that at least one prisoner, Barabbas, got away. Any Zealots we encounter will be highly motivated to kill us."

I couldn't resist needling him, though given the horror to which two of their compatriots were being subjected at that very moment, any of Barabbas's ill-fated crew who had managed to get away would undoubtedly be laying low.

***

Lavon and Naomi conversed in Greek for a few minutes and then explained their plan. In light of our circumstances, they concluded that our best bet would be to head for the Mount of Olives. Lavon and the others had at least a passing familiarity with the surroundings, which covered a broad area of broken, rocky terrain.

"We should find a number of places to conceal ourselves, at least temporarily," said the archaeologist. "The Mount's difficult topography was the reason the authorities needed an insider's knowledge of Jesus's whereabouts to arrest him. They knew they would never find him stumbling around by themselves."

This made sense to us all, so we started in that direction. For the most part, we were able to remain hidden in the deep ravine to Jerusalem's south as we worked our way toward our destination.

We had only one brief uncomfortable moment; a short interval in which we had to climb out into the open to cross the main thoroughfare leading to the Tekoa Gate – the same portal we had passed through two days earlier, in what now seemed like a different age.

Naomi, however, assured us that the line of travelers waiting to go inside were far more concerned with getting past the Roman soldiers who now monitored the entrance than they would be with a handful of individuals going the other way.

This proved to be the case, and we slipped back down into the Kidron Ravine without incident. Shortly thereafter, we wound our way through a narrow trail until we reached the southern end of the Mount of Olives, where we halted at the edge of a copse of trees.

Lavon studied the terrain carefully, as did I. He and Naomi exchanged a few words; then he turned back to the others.

"We can rest here, under the cover of the trees, for an hour or two," he said.

***

Sharon had had virtually no sleep for two nights in a row, so I cleared out a hollow space between two boulders and folded my robe to provide her a thin layer of padding.

"Not much of a mattress, I'm afraid."

She smiled, though she was so tired that it didn't matter. She curled up into a ball and within less than a minute, she had fallen into a deep slumber.

Citing ancient Army wisdom about sleeping whenever the opportunity presented itself, I instructed Bryson and Markowitz to rest also – though in truth, I just wanted them out of the way while Lavon, Naomi and I worked up a new a plan.

By now, we had to assume that knowledge of Sharon's disappearance had reached the king's ears, and that a search for her whereabouts had begun.

"How long before they discover the dead guards?" I asked.

Naomi admitted that she could not answer that question with certainty. The palace grounds covered more than twenty acres, which could take days to search, though Herod's investigators would concentrate their initial efforts on the known routes from the king's bedchamber to the central baths.

"Sooner, rather than later, then?" I asked.

"Probably," she said.

"Perhaps we shouldn't have strangled them," Lavon added.

"If we're caught, we're dead either way," I replied. "Besides, if those two had lived, they could tell Herod exactly where they were attacked, and how we got in. Naomi had to protect her friends."

Lavon was aware of this, though his conscience resisted admitting it.

He pointed out that once Herod's men found the guards' bodies, they would be certain that she had outside help. Despite Sharon's proven resourcefulness, none of them would believe that a lone woman could disarm and kill two soldiers by herself.

This was true; but on the positive side, even if the king's guards knew she had external assistance, they wouldn't necessarily know who had provided it, unless –

"If someone saw us exit the palace, would they report it?" I asked.

As before, Naomi couldn't be sure. Given the harsh punishment administered to wayward slaves, she acknowledged that if questioned, they would quickly admit the truth.

On the other hand, the free common people did their best to avoid contact with officialdom, so in the absence of an incentive, they would hesitate to come forward.

This sounded vaguely promising, and for a moment, I began to believe that we might survive until sundown.

And if we stayed alive until then …

"What about the Sabbath?" I asked. "Do Herod's people observe it?"

The question amused her.

"Inside the palace, he ignores it, but the king is aware of the importance of demonstrating outward piety to his subjects."

Her answer was the one I had expected.

"Too bad he can't run for Congress," I muttered. "He'd fit right in."

"I think Christ himself answered your real question," said Lavon. "When the priests complained about his healing a man on the Sabbath, he noted that they didn't have a problem with rescuing their own livestock on that day."

"In other words," I said, "the emergency justified what would otherwise be forbidden work."

"Yes. Besides, that tracker who found Sharon is probably not even Jewish."

Chapter 57

As the others rested, Lavon and I each checked our earpieces, but we both recognized that we'd probably gain no more useful information from the palace. We no longer even heard background noise.

"Do you think we've traveled out of range?" he asked.

That had been my first thought, too, but then a more likely explanation came to mind.

"I'll bet Herod smashed it," I said.

I explained the precise manner by which the king had wound up with Sharon's device the previous evening. With everything that had followed my return to the Antonia, the opportunity to do so never presented itself until then.

Lavon burst out laughing. He could picture, as I could, the irate monarch grinding Sharon's transmitter into the stone floor with his heel; but that was not the only reason for his mirth regarding the subject of Herod and anger management.

"Less than a month ago," he said, "two of my colleagues nearly came to blows at a conference over the issue of whether Jesus appeared before the king at all."

I cast him a curious glance. "That's disputed?"

He nodded.

"Those who argue it never happened maintain that the Romans would not have had enough time to send Jesus from the Antonia to the palace and still squeeze in all the other events of the Good Friday sequence. Walking through the streets would have taken at least an hour, each direction."

"They wouldn't risk going through the streets at all," I said; "not with that crowd. Publius and Volusus both have far better sense than to try something like that."

"I know," said Lavon. "What do you think they did?"

I considered this for a moment.

"I'll bet they just threw him on the back of a horse and went around the city walls, like I did the other night. That couldn't have taken more than fifteen minutes."

He nodded; then stared back in the direction of the city, lost in thought.

"I suppose you're right," he said.

***

I noticed that dark clouds were beginning to roll in from the west.

"We have more pressing concerns at the moment, anyway" I said; "although the rain should work to our advantage, by making our tracks harder to follow."

"*If* it rains," Lavon corrected. "The movies all show a downpour, but the Gospel texts only mention 'a great darkness' covering the land after the sixth hour."

"Oh."

"But it might rain," he continued. "Since we're not wearing waterproof clothing, we should try to find a better shelter. Six drowned rats will stand out even more than we do already."

This made perfect sense. I remained in our makeshift observation post while Lavon crept about fifty yards to the north, where he located an overhang that sheltered a gap in the rock large enough for us all to squeeze in.

We waited another half hour after he returned to give the others some extra nap time, but finally, the wind picked up, impelling us to move along.

Lavon and I established a new observation post; then we woke the others. As we did so, I tried without success to stifle a yawn and I couldn't help but chuckle as I watched Lavon do the same.

He had to be mentally exhausted as well, having to converse in a foreign language for several days under difficult circumstances with no room for mistranslation.

I had enough field experience to know that tired men make stupid mistakes, but since the archaeologist and I had both concluded that we'd be safe for a few hours, we decided take a chance and get a little sleep while the others stood guard.

Like I said, tired men make stupid mistakes.

***

The next thing I remember, Sharon was shaking me awake. I grumbled for a moment, but then I came to my senses enough to detect the raw urgency in her voice.

"They're coming," she said.

"Wh – "

I swore, then sprang up and woke Lavon. After I explained our situation, I followed Sharon back to our first sentry post – a small gap in the limestone ridge shielded by an uprooted olive tree.

Not more than a quarter mile away, and slightly downhill from our position, four soldiers stood behind a man who had bent down to inspect an object I could not see.

Though only one of the four sported the black uniform of the palace guards, we could not mistake their identities.

Sharon focused her attention on the apparent leader, a dark-skinned man wrapped in a headdress and a flowing white robe.

"That's the tracker who found me," she whispered. "I'm certain of it."

This was bad news indeed.

Every few steps, the Bedouin crouched down to examine the ground. Had I been on the other side, I would have admired the man's remarkable expertise.

Now, though, I could only sense our impending doom. At the rate they were moving, the soldiers would be on us within minutes.

I turned around to see Lavon heading our way. I signaled for him to fetch Naomi and to stay low and keep quiet. Markowitz caught my gesture as well, and flattened himself to the ground.

As I assessed our situation realistically, I struggled not to lose hope. We had only one sword between the six of us, and the only member of our party who had ever wielded one in anger had no military training other than the hour on Pilate's parade ground.

Lavon, fortunately, retained a clear mind. He crept up to my side, holding a stout branch the size of a baseball bat.

"We have to split them up and ambush them," he whispered. "Otherwise, they'll eventually corner us and kill us."

After a moment's reflection, that was the way I saw it, too. We had only a slim chance; but once again, I'll pick slim over none any day.

Lavon and Naomi whispered for a few moments before he explained the plan to Markowitz. The young man looked toward me with a growing sense of unease, but I just smiled and nodded, hoping that I projected more confidence than I felt.

I remained at our post with Sharon until the others had eased down the hill and begun creeping slowly toward the north. When they disappeared, I tugged on Sharon's arm and motioned for her to turn around, too.

***

We had gone about fifty yards when we crawled behind a ridge to the rear of our erstwhile shelter – and to show where my mind had gone, I noticed the wet ground for the first time. It had rained, after all.

By then, the tracker had reached the spot where we had split up. He crouched down to study the new trails and then raised three fingers and pointed to his right. Two of the soldiers pressed forward along the path Lavon had taken with the others, while the other two remained with the Bedouin.

I held my breath. Moments later, we heard a woman's piercing scream. Our two most distant adversaries then charged down the hill and disappeared from view.

We heard Naomi cry out once again, followed by the shuffling of feet and some thrashing of the underbrush. A few seconds later, I counted two muffled blows, followed by one more forceful thump. After that, we heard nothing, except for Naomi's pleading sobs.

"She's begging for her life!" whispered Sharon.

We had no idea what had just happened, or whether either of the others had managed to survive.

Not that we had time to reflect.

The Bedouin crouched down to study the ground again, and as far as he was concerned, we might as well have painted our trail with a bright yellow line.

Sharon gasped in horror as a broad smile crossed his face.

The tracker glanced up to one of the soldiers, who reached into a pouch and tossed him a coin – a payoff against an earlier wager, I guessed.

I told myself that at least I wasn't the only person who had underestimated the man's ability; not that it was any great comfort at the time.

The Bedouin pointed in our direction and signaled to the other soldier, who immediately began trekking toward our position.

I whispered and pantomimed my hastily improvised plan. After Sharon nodded, I eased off to our left and crouched behind a boulder, sword in hand.

Sharon slowly raised her head above the olive trunk that had concealed us, and at the sight of her blonde hair, the man's eyes lit up as he charged ahead.

It was his last move. Sharon had started to run backwards, and as the guard chased past me, I wheeled out from behind the rock and rammed my blade through the base of his throat. He gurgled as I kicked his chest to free my *gladius* and then collapsed, wide-eyed with shock.

One down.

The others, however, had watched the man fall, and both of them came running up the hill in rapid pursuit. I had scarcely enough time to ready my weapon before they were upon me.

The Bedouin held back as the more experienced fighter came at me with his sword low, preparing to run me through the gut, Roman-style. I spun around to face my new adversary and barely managed to deflect his attack.

Our swords clashed several more times before I perceived an opening and lunged for his arm. If I could cut that, I could at least slow him down.

Regrettably, I missed.

Not only did I fail to inflict the slightest damage, but my clumsy attempt to do so threw me off balance.

I jumped back as fast as I could, and in desperation, I grabbed a handful of dirt and tossed it toward his face, which forced him to swing his free hand to swat it away.

I used this brief respite to square myself into a proper fighting stance, but the ill-mannered brute merely laughed.

It was only then that it dawned on me, to my manifest horror, that a lack of skill had not prevented him from killing me immediately. Instead, the warrior was enjoying this, like a cat playing with a doomed mouse.

Finally, I suppose he had enough. He swung his blade in a practiced rhythm, and I had to strain harder and harder to dodge each blow.

Moments later, my luck ran out. He pressed his sword forward with a well-timed thrust. I managed to swing my own *gladius* hard enough to the left to parry the blow, but in doing so, I slipped on a wet stone and fell backwards, which left me sprawled on the rocks with my weapon lying uselessly about five feet to my right.

I can't say that my life flashed before me – though I suspect this was only because my mind had not yet come to grips with the absurd way in which I was to meet my end.

My opponent edged slowly forward, savoring every moment. The Bedouin, too, had come up to watch the fun.

I took a deep breath and tried put the thought of pain out of my mind as the black-helmeted executioner moved in for the final strike.

It never came.

I just laid there for a moment, frozen in place, as my brain slowly registered the sight of a steel point, dripping with blood, protruding from the base of the man's neck.

Fortunately, I wasn't the only one shocked by this image.

I realized what had happened a mere fraction of a second before the Bedouin did, but that was enough.

Before he could react, I wheeled my body around and caught the side of his knee with my shin. I heard a sickening crack – or what would have been sickening under different circumstances – as he gave out a sharp cry of pain and spun to the ground.

Sharon yanked her weapon free and fell on him in an instant.

I hadn't noticed, but while our tormentors focused on me, she had slipped quietly through the underbrush to retrieve the sword belonging to the first man I had killed.

She drove her weapon into the tracker's chest with all her might, stabbing him blindly, again and again. Finally, after about the tenth blow, she ran out of steam. With the blade still sunk in the Bedouin's heart, she leaned forward on it and sobbed.

For a moment, I didn't move – mostly because I was still bewildered at how I had managed to stay alive.

Then, Naomi came scampering through the scrub, followed by Lavon and Markowitz. Each man held the *gladius* he had taken from their attackers.

"Damn," said Markowitz as he surveyed the scene. "I didn't realize you were so handy with a sword."

I wasn't. I had just proven that.

"I didn't do it," I said.

"*She* killed him?" he said incredulously.

"Them," I corrected. "She killed *them*. Plural."

Chapter 58

We left Sharon alone for a moment; but when the time seemed right, I reached down and helped her to her feet.

"*You saved my life*," I said. "I don't know how to thank you."

And I *was* truly grateful; though at that instant, I was more concerned about diverting her attention from the full realization of what she had done.

I needn't have worried. Sharon proved resilient, and none of the others displayed the slightest unease over the fate of our adversaries.

For her part, Naomi viewed the spectacle with wholesale approval; and to my surprise, Markowitz appeared almost giddy – a complete reversal of his reaction after the contest in the Antonia.

Lavon reminded us that we still had a few loose ends to tidy up as well.

"We need to get these bodies hidden," he said. "If we don't, the vultures will start circling and somebody will wander over to check out why."

After a brief search, I located a crevice where we could stuff the corpses before we sealed the entrance with rocks. With luck, the wild dogs wouldn't dig them out for a couple of days, although passers-by would most likely notice the smell before then.

Naomi helped me manhandle the first three into the gap while Lavon and Markowitz ambled back down the hill, returning a few minutes later with their respective victims in tow.

As we wedged them into the fissure, Lavon explained that Naomi's plan had worked to perfection. Just as she had done with the guards in the palace, this ostensibly demure, timid creature had led these men to their doom.

This time, she had "panicked" and set off on a dead run. Lavon and Markowitz had hidden to one side and bludgeoned their targets with stout olive branches as they rushed by in hot pursuit. Ray then crushed what was left of his opponent's skull to ensure he would remain silent, which accounted for the third thump I had heard.

Topping off her Academy Award-winning performance, Naomi had then fallen to her knees, begging and whimpering for her life so that the soldiers chasing Sharon and me would not become alarmed.

"Remind me to stay on her good side," I said to Lavon.

He laughed. "Yeah, I think we all should."

It was only as we completed our macabre task that I realized we had one additional problem.

"Where's Bryson?" I asked.

Lavon hadn't noticed until then, either.

He shot Naomi a dirty look. She and the Professor were supposed to stand watch together, while the archaeologist and I rested.

"I couldn't stop him," she said. "I couldn't understand him. You know that. He started going north."

Lavon rolled his eyes, as did I. The damned fool.

She began to babble more urgently, "You told me to stay in one spot. You told me – "

Lavon sighed and held his finger up to her lips. "Don't worry about it. *You* did the right thing."

Naomi, though, wasn't yet convinced of that.

"I should have woken you," she repeated, "but you said to stand and watch. You said not to disturb you unless we saw soldiers. You said …"

We both realized that the poor girl had probably been beaten for less.

Lavon let her ramble on for a moment; then reiterated what he had said before. He emphasized once again that we did not blame her for Bryson's disappearance, and finally the message began to sink in.

As she recovered her composure, she also recognized that we didn't consider the event a complete surprise.

"Do you know where he's going?" she asked.

Lavon sighed. "Yes."

"Where *is* he going?" asked Markowitz, after Lavon had translated.

"Where do you think?" I said.

"The tomb?" said Sharon.

Lavon nodded.

"I didn't think he knew where it was," she replied.

"He might not know the absolute exact spot, but we now have a pretty good picture of its general location."

"How?" she asked. "Who figured that out?"

Given Sharon's fragile mental state, I had hoped to avoid this distraction; but there was no getting around it now.

Lavon laughed. "You did."

The implications took a moment to sink in.

"Oh my God!" she finally said.

"As it turned out, you kicked off a bit of a fuss among the Temple authorities. From what Publius told us, Joseph was not pleased."

She didn't answer. She just kept repeating to herself, "Oh my God."

I let her go on until her breathing came back close to normal. Then I reached over and took both of her hands.

"Sharon, we're not home yet."

"I *saw* him," she exclaimed. "I can't believe I *slept* in his tomb."

I didn't think that could be any more sacrilegious than what modern gawkers did every day, but in her current frame of mind, she didn't seem like she'd be open to that particular point of view.

Still …

"Listen to me, Sharon," I said. "We need you with us, in the present, right now. Whatever you saw; whatever you want to do as a result; you have to *live* to make that happen. You can do nothing for him as a corpse; certainly not here."

She nodded weakly.

"Sharon, do you understand? We *need* you."

After a moment, she nodded again, and this time I could see that she meant it.

"Can you find it again?" asked Lavon. "Can you locate the tomb if we go back?"

Sharon briefly hesitated and looked up toward the rapidly clearing late-afternoon sky.

"I think so," she finally said.

Then she closed her eyes and took a deep breath. When she opened them again, her voice carried the ring of authority.

"Yes, I will find it."

Chapter 59

We headed north as fast as we could travel without giving the appearance of undue haste to passers-by. Everyone wanted to put as much distance as we could between ourselves and the site of our skirmish, just in case, though otherwise we were in no hurry.

I calculated that if Bryson had made his departure just after Lavon and I had fallen asleep, he had about a three hour head start on his journey to the tomb. We'd catch up to him soon enough, unless …

"Do you think he'll get lost?" I asked Lavon.

The archaeologist laughed. Over the past few years, both of us had watched otherwise brilliant and capable technologists become hopelessly disoriented whenever their GPS gadgets had failed. Old-fashioned orienteering remained a useful skill, despite the ridicule of the "dead tree" crowd.

However, as we considered the matter, neither of us believed this would be a problem today. To reach the quarry complex, all the Professor had to do was trace a circle around the city's main walls. He knew generally where it was, and as long as he avoided conflict with other travelers, he'd stumble onto it eventually.

***

As we came closer to the Antonia, I felt brief pangs of worry that we might encounter Roman pursuers as well, but the more I thought about it, the more my concerns diminished.

In the broad scheme of things, we were small fry – at least today. Given everything that had happened over the past week, Pilate and the senior officials were undoubtedly breathing deep sighs of relief that they had made it to the Passover without an explosive cataclysm of violence.

As for the ordinary soldiers, I had been in their shoes long enough to know that they were probably just beginning to knock back their first goblets of wine, thankful to be alive, like their counterparts throughout the ages.

The others, though, didn't completely share my assessment. Sharon, in particular, grew more worried the closer we came to the western side of the city, so we finally decided to conceal ourselves behind a small ridge and take a brief rest.

"I'm not wild on the idea of going *anywhere* near the palace again," she said. "Do you think Herod will send more men after us?"

I was certain he would – though not of the timing.

"It depends on when their commanders realize the first batch has gone AWOL," I said.

Lavon put the question to Naomi, who explained that the city's gates would be sealed tight at sunset for the Sabbath and the Passover. If the soldiers couldn't make it back by then, they'd just camp out for the night.

"They'd probably prefer that, anyway," she added.

"Wouldn't it be difficult to guard five prisoners?" asked Sharon.

Lavon couldn't help but laugh. He knew, as I did, that no guarding would be necessary. If we got caught, the soldiers would pass the time taking turns with the two women, while the remainder of our heads greeted the dawn from the bottom of a sack.

But these thoughts, ironically, made me feel better about our chances.

Lavon agreed. "In all likelihood," he said, "no one will begin asking questions about the guards until mid-morning, at least."

Sharon glanced over to me. "If that's the case, why don't we do what you suggested earlier and put as much distance between ourselves and the city as we can. We can travel through the night if we have to; the moon is full."

This was eminently sensible. I felt sure that we could find water somewhere. Moreover, according to Lavon, the most fanatical Zealots refused to fight on the Sabbath, so our odds were at least reasonable that we could avoid any conflicts with the crew who had ambushed us coming in.

The others rose up and started off to the west, but as they did, a darker thought entered my mind.

I reached up to touch the comforting Kevlar thread around my neck, which suddenly felt much less reassuring.

"We may have another problem," I said. "Do you all still have your chips?"

They did not. Sharon had lost hers when Herod had taken her transmitter, and Markowitz's had disappeared in the dungeon. Only Lavon and I had managed to hang on to our precious composites.

"As long as we stay together, we don't all need one," the archaeologist said.

"OK," I replied. "But …"

Sharon interrupted. "Then we don't have to risk it. Let the Professor take his chances, if he's so inclined."

"Quite frankly, I'd like nothing more than to do just that," I said. "But I'm not certain we can any longer; not now."

I held out my chip and displayed it to the others.

"Do you remember when we first got to the fortress, when Bryson showed us his, with the LED warning light?"

"We didn't have them," said Markowitz. "He said ours were earlier prototypes."

"That's right."

The others weren't slow to catch on.

"Are you saying they might not work?" asked Sharon.

"We have to consider the possibility," I replied.

"But that doesn't make sense," said Sharon. "When we departed the lab, our whole objective was to conduct a rescue operation and bring Dr. Bryson back home. Juliet had no incentive to block our return."

"That's also correct," I said. "She had no incentive *then*. But what if they can communicate – for instance, with light signals, like Morse Code?"

"Why?" gasped Sharon. "Why would he strand us here now?"

"It would eliminate an inconvenient obstacle to his plans," said Lavon.

The archaeologist explained to Sharon the nature of the arguments we had undertaken while she endured her captivity in Herod's palace. To her credit, she found Bryson's schemes as barmy as we had.

"Recall also that Juliet had us sneak in the back door at five in the morning," Lavon added. "Our cars are still at the hotel. Sure, someone will eventually ask questions when we never come back, but what's that phrase the politicians use?"

"Plausible deniability," I said. "When the police show up, as they will at some point, she can give them the run of the place. Sure, we *were* there, but …"

"This is still completely illogical," said Sharon. "Jesus's tomb isn't the only one in the area. It's not obvious which one is correct."

"I wonder if *he* knows that?" I asked.

That was a question we couldn't answer. We wrestled with our options a little longer, but ultimately we made the practical choice. None of us had the confidence to do otherwise.

***

By this point, we observed only scattered clusters of travelers making haste to enter Jerusalem before the gates closed at sundown. This proved to be a reassuring spectacle.

"We have a perfect window of opportunity," said Lavon. "By now, the burial party has returned to the city. We'll have nearly an hour to see the tomb before it gets completely pitch-dark."

"What about the guards?" I asked.

"There shouldn't be any tonight. According to Matthew's account, the Jewish authorities didn't go to Pilate and request a guard until the following day."

That was comforting, though we'd still have to face them on Sunday.

"Do you think the legionnaires took their assignment seriously?" I asked.

Despite their rigorous discipline, I felt sure that the Romans would consider their mission a pointless waste of time.

Lavon considered my question but didn't immediately reply.

"It could lessen their vigilance," I added.

"Maybe," he finally answered. "Most people assume the sentries were Romans, but Matthew's wording is enigmatic. Pilate said 'you have a guard' or something to that effect. Did that mean, 'I'm giving you a *Roman* guard,' or 'you have your own Temple police, use them.' I've heard good arguments both ways."

"What do you think?"

"Temple police," he said without hesitation. "Do you really believe that the legionnaires we've encountered would take a bribe to confess to what amounted to a capital offense?"

"Not a chance," I replied. "I'm sure they'd take bribes, but not for that. The risk versus reward wouldn't stack up."

"That's how I see it," Lavon added. "Besides, the Gospels say that the guards gave their initial statements to the high priests. Roman soldiers would have reported through their own command structure. In that case, Pilate, or at least Volusus, would have heard about it before the Jewish authorities did."

"Then why ask for Pilate's permission at all? Since they had the Temple police at their disposal, why not just send them out?"

"I'm sure that was forbidden. I'd imagine the Romans were pretty touchy about letting any sort of organized armed force roam about outside. That may have been why only one of the goons chasing us today wore a uniform."

This made perfect sense, although one thing still bothered me: "Don't the Gospels also say that the priests promised to take care of soldiers in case they got into trouble with the governor?"

"Yes, they do."

"In that case, if they were just Temple police, why would Pilate care?"

He smiled. "Now you know why we have so many arguments about it."

Chapter 60

We continued onward, though we gave the Damascus Gate a wide berth. While we assumed that the bodies of the two prisoners executed with Jesus had been removed, none of us wanted to take the chance that we could accidentally witness that horrific spectacle again, in the event they had not.

After we had traveled another half mile, Sharon directed us down a rocky knoll and into a warren of narrow trails. The topography matched her previous description: the surrounding hills were pockmarked with small caverns, a number of which had been crafted into burial sites.

Behind what appeared to be the tallest ridge, we discovered Bryson studying one particular chamber, whose entrance was covered by a thick 4x8 foot slab of brilliant white polished marble.

"You decided to come after all," he said cheerfully, as if we had all simply gone for a walk in the park.

"Wouldn't miss it for the world," said Lavon.

I tried to read the Professor's expression, but for once my instincts failed me. Did he know he had us by the short and curlies, or had he simply assumed that our curiosity would get the better of us?

With no way to tell for sure, I turned my attention back to the marble block, which fit snugly into an elaborate framework that skilled masons had carved out of the surrounding limestone. An inscription, in what I guessed to be Aramaic, ran across the top.

Lavon questioned Naomi, but she just stared at the ground, embarrassed and disappointed that she could provide no further assistance.

Her duties at the palace had not required that she know how to read.

"We'll fix that," Lavon muttered, to no one in particular.

He spoke to her in a soothing tone, in Greek. As he did, Bryson turned to Sharon and asked if she could confirm that he had picked the correct site.

To no one else's surprise, he had not.

Sharon led us back and forth along the trails as she studied each tomb. Finally, she stopped, glanced around in all directions once more, and motioned with her right hand.

"It's this one," she announced.

Bryson observed her skeptically. Her chosen location was both smaller and considerably less elaborate than other tombs in the area, though the surrounding ground did display signs of recent foot traffic.

"Are you sure?" he asked. "Wasn't it nearly dark when you went inside?"

She didn't reply. Instead, she scrambled up the hill behind us to get her bearings on the palace towers. Then she veered off to her left and disappeared behind a ridge.

A few minutes later, she emerged along another trail, slowly moving forward and concentrating on her surroundings with each step.

"I'm certain: this is the way I came. Besides, it was bright enough when they dragged me out."

"Absolutely, *positively* sure? We only have one chance to get this right."

I detected a faint whiff of condescension in the Professor's voice. Had he realized that in the body count standings, he remained the only member of our enterprise without a notch in the win column, he might have treated her with a little more respect.

She brushed aside the provocation, giving him instead the classic "I'm positive you idiot" look that women express so well. I should know; I've seen it often enough.

Bryson had the good sense not to press further. He studied the terrain for another brief moment, then walked over to a spot about fifteen yards away and laid the camera on a flat chunk of limestone.

He shoveled a handful of dirt underneath to correct the elevation and patted it down to ensure that the gadget would not slip.

"What is he doing?" asked Naomi. "What is that thing in his hand?"

Lavon glanced at me and I shook my head. Neither of us wanted to have that particular discussion at the moment.

"I'll tell you later," he said.

Naomi didn't like this, but she chose not to argue.

Meanwhile, Bryson had nearly completed his preparations. He set the timer and pressed 'record.' Then, he folded the screen back onto the main body of the camera and proceeded to conceal his handiwork with stones.

"Did you remove the lens cap?" I asked when he ambled back over to us.

Bryson scowled at my feeble attempt at humor but did not comment otherwise. We both knew that the latest models had automated this process.

***

Had I kept my wits about me, I would have gone back to the camera and smashed it to pieces with a rock, then and there. Now that we were all together, nothing prevented us from making a beeline for the coast, dragging the Professor with us if he wouldn't go voluntarily.

But except for a bag of raisins we had found on one of Herod's dead guards, none of us had eaten since early that morning, and years had passed since I had to think clearly under such conditions in the field.

By this time, only a brief interval of daylight remained; so we all just stood back and soaked in the panorama until it became too dark to see clearly.

All but Naomi, that is. Try as she might, she could not comprehend why foreigners from a distant land would find a collection of Jewish tombs so fascinating, especially given our ongoing peril.

She tugged at Lavon. "Why are we *here*?" she asked.

"It's not important," he mumbled.

Naomi, though, proved unwilling to be put off a second time. She gestured in Bryson's direction.

"*He* thinks this place is important; so do the others. *You* think it's important. I can see it in your eyes. Tell me what is happening. Who is buried here?"

"I'll show you in two days," he replied.

"Please," she insisted, "tell me now."

She paused.

"Haven't I *earned* the right to know?"

Since she most assuredly had done that, Lavon felt he had no choice but to explain.

"It's the prisoner we heard Herod questioning this morning," he said. "The Romans crucified him, and now he is buried here."

She eyed him suspiciously. "How do you know this?"

Lavon and I both popped out our ear buds and displayed them to her.

She seemed to find this plausible, although I could tell that her doubts had not completely vanished. On the rare occasions when they were buried at all, the Romans tossed the corpses of such victims into a refuse pit. These tombs belonged to the nobility.

"It's something scholars continue to debate today," said Lavon as he explained her misgivings to the rest of us. "Some even argue that the Gospel accounts are fictional, given the standard Roman practice."

"Obviously they're not," said Sharon.

"No."

"Then why?" asked Bryson.

"My guess is that Pilate decided that he could afford to be magnanimous," said Lavon.

"Despite his fears of a violent uprising, he had managed to eliminate a person the Romans considered a threat to their rule without triggering a riot. Allowing Joseph to take the body served as a goodwill gesture to Jesus's sympathizers in the Sanhedrin – a small, practical token that cost him nothing."

This squared with my impressions of the governor, though unfortunately, we'd never be able to find out for sure.

"You speak as if you knew this man." Naomi said after Lavon had explained our discussion.

Lavon started to answer; then his voice trailed off in an odd manner. I started to feel a bit unsettled myself, which I found strange.

On the one occasion in which I had visited the Holy Sepulcher, I had felt no inkling of the transcendent.

Whether that was because of my own innate skepticism, a consideration of the many thousands who had died fighting over the purported resting place of the Prince of Peace, or just the sight of obese, elderly tourists being herded through like cattle, I couldn't tell. Probably all of the above.

But now, seeing the actual site, and realizing whose body was inside –

"We need to leave," said Sharon.

Lavon nodded without saying a word, and Naomi, ever perceptive, could sense our growing unease. Only Bryson and Markowitz remained unaffected.

Lavon took Naomi's hand and signaled for the rest of us to follow.

Chapter 61

Though the moon had not yet risen, we managed to pick our way through the scrub via the light of a glittering celestial canopy – an inspiring sight, and one sadly invisible to modern city dwellers.

After a few iterations of trial and error, we reached the main road. Although Polaris, our familiar north star, had shifted considerably in the intervening two thousand years, it was still, in the words of one of my old commanders, "directionally correct."

Thus guided, we continued on to the northwest until we arrived at a crest of low hills that I recalled from our trip in. Following some brief stumbling around, we managed to locate a rock overhang that would serve as sufficient shelter for the night.

Lavon and I decided to divide our party into three shifts. He and Naomi would take the second watch, followed by Markowitz and Bryson toward the dawn. Sharon and I agreed stand guard first.

We climbed up and situated ourselves just below the peak, so our silhouettes could not be spotted from a distance. Being proper sentries, we sat with our backs to each other in complete silence. For a couple of hours, we heard nothing but the soft murmur of insects.

I didn't really expect trouble, and as the night wore on, I grew more confident that the combination of the Sabbath and the Passover would keep people from moving about.

So I finally whispered to Sharon the question I had pondered throughout the day.

"Last night, in Herod's palace, how did you hold yourself together?"

She didn't immediately respond, and for a moment I thought I might have trodden on overly sensitive ground.

"I'll just say that I found your quick thinking extremely impressive – especially how you managed to let me know where they were holding you in a way that wouldn't raise the king's suspicions."

"Thank you," she finally replied. "But to tell you the truth, I didn't have any grand design. It just came to me, there on the spot. I had to do *something*."

That, I knew, was the way most heroes were made, despite what the storybooks said.

"Well, however you concocted your scheme, that bow was a piece of work. Where on earth did you learn to do that?"

She chuckled softly. "It's called the Texas Dip. You were never a debutante, were you?"

I admitted that the honor had eluded me.

"But only because my gown wouldn't fit properly on my big day." I said.

She laughed again. "Of course."

"Seriously, if you don't mind me asking, how did you deal with the shame of being paraded through the palace naked like that? You had to have been scared."

She considered this for a moment.

"I was terrified," she finally said. "I thought I was done for; that I really was going to have to sleep with that pig."

"If it's any comfort, he wasn't the one with the worms," I said.

"I know; I finally remembered that was his nephew Agrippa. But I wasn't thinking about worms. I was more concerned about the disappointment – that in my first real test, I would fail to stand up for my principles."

"Defying the king would have been suicide. Anything you would have done would have been under extreme duress."

"The other women didn't see it that way. From what I could tell, they viewed their situation as a great opportunity."

"The first century's version of the 'casting couch,' I suppose."

"Yes. I'll never forget this one girl – she couldn't have been older than seventeen – who spotted me as her primary rival from the first minute I arrived at the palace baths. In other circumstances, the situation would have been almost comical."

"So what kept you going? How did you manage to hold your head up so high?"

"I wanted to live," she replied. "I wanted to see my home again. I decided I'd do whatever I had to do to accomplish that."

But she sounded ashamed of herself for doing so.

"Do you know how I justified it?" she asked.

"In the Book of Esther, a young woman had to take part in a contest: whoever could screw the king's brains out better than the others won the prize. Hers was the safety of her people. Mine – well, like I said, my goal was to stay alive one more day."

That wasn't quite how I remembered the nuns telling the story, but that was the gist of it.

"There's no fault in that," I said.

"You didn't *see* him this morning," she replied. "The whole time they were mocking him, I cried. *He* wouldn't have compromised."

"You did nothing wrong," I repeated.

"It wasn't what I *did*, it's what I had already made up my mind to do. I can thank you that in the end, I didn't actually have to go through with it, but that doesn't negate the choice I had already made inside."

"Well, if you're going to thank anyone for getting you out of there, thank Naomi. And if anybody has cause for shame regarding his conduct last night, it's me. In spite of all that duty, honor, and country stuff we talk about so much, I didn't exactly sacrifice my life to save a damsel in distress."

"You wouldn't have accomplished anything if you had."

"No, nor would you, had you refused the king."

She thought about this for a moment.

"If you want to dwell on what you *did*, focus on your escape," I reminded her. "Even some of my old Ranger colleagues would have struggled to pull that off. You should have seen the way Publius described how you got away; the look of admiration in his eyes. If it makes you feel any better, even Herod was impressed."

She smiled, though her pensive mood remained.

"What's going to become of us?" she finally asked.

I knew what she meant; though I wanted to focus her mind on less troublesome topics for the moment.

"I sincerely hope that within forty-eight hours, we will find ourselves seated comfortably behind the first-base dugout at Fenway Park," I replied.

This was true enough.

She chuckled quietly, though I could tell that she wouldn't let me dodge the question indefinitely. The trouble was; I had no answer, even if we survived – an outcome I still considered problematic at best.

"I'm still working on that," I said. "I think we all are."

"Whatever happens, it's going to be hard to listen to those preachers," she said. "From what I've seen, the ones who jabber the loudest about remaining steadfast in the face of great peril have never been in the remotest danger of encountering it themselves."

Except for those clowns on TV, that seemed a bit unfair, though I could sense where she was coming from.

I told her that for six months, I had the 'privilege' of serving as a US Army liaison to Mobutu's forces in Zaire. The missionaries I had encountered in that country easily surpassed me both in raw courage and in their ability to navigate through exceptionally challenging circumstances.

"Did they bluster and pontificate?" she asked.

They had not, which I took to be her point.

"As they led me to Herod this morning, I thought back to a trip I had taken a few years ago," she continued. "I had gone to Rome with my mother, in February, so we could see the sights before the hordes of summer tourists invaded the place.

"One beautiful morning, we took our coffee into the Colosseum, and just sat there on the stone benches, reflecting on the early Christians and what they had to have been thinking as they were herded into that very arena, to be torn apart by wild animals."

I had done the same, years ago, and told her so.

"I'm sure they had all heard the story of Daniel," she said. "Yet he was saved and they were not. Why?"

I had no answer.

"And what about the ones who were burned alive? They had to have known of the men who were rescued from Nebuchadnezzar's fiery furnace. Yet out of all the thousands, over the centuries, only three were saved. *Three!* The rest died screaming in agony, on the orders of the king, or the emperor."

Or the Pope, I didn't add. That last part was an inconvenient fact I had been brought up to ignore.

"These people had been just as faithful," she exclaimed. "They had to be asking why; why God didn't save them?"

She started to cry softly. I turned and slid my arm around her, and felt her warmth.

"It's OK," I said.

She rested her head on my chest and squeezed tight.

"I shouldn't ask these questions, but I can't make them go away. Can you believe it? There in the palace, I didn't believe God would save me from Herod, even after I *saw* him."

My first thought was to ask what he looked like, just to divert her mind to another subject, but the time didn't seem right.

I also considered telling her that the Lord *had* sent his angels of mercy, in the unlikely form of a sympathetic Roman official and a clever, imaginative palace courtesan.

But as I looked around, I couldn't be sure of that, either. We weren't yet out of the woods, and that same official, over the next couple of days, might be the very man charged with hunting us down.

So I just wrapped her in my arms and spoke softly.

"It will be OK," I repeated. "God is complicated. I'm not sure we're meant to understand everything."

Aside from an occasional glance around – after all we were still on guard duty – we just held onto each other and barely moved.

Some time later, I heard rustling coming up the hill. By instinct, I reached for my *gladius*, though I needn't have bothered. Our interlopers were only Lavon and Naomi, arriving to give us a break.

"Relief shift," he whispered.

I told Sharon to pick a spot down with the others and that I'd join her in a few minutes. After she had disappeared around a tree, Lavon gestured in her direction.

"I don't think she'll strive to chair the Emerald Charity Ball anymore," he said.

Apparently that was the pinnacle of Dallas high society, though from the way he described it, the event sounded more like a tax deductible fashion show than a boon to the poor and downtrodden.

"No," I replied. "I think her social-climbing days are over."

"Assuming we make it back in one piece, I don't see D. Percival Throckmorton, III as long for her world either," he said.

I felt a knot tighten in my stomach. I had forgotten about D. Percival.

On our trip to the lab in Tel Aviv, Lavon had described him as a scion of Old Money Dallas, whose "job," from what he could tell, consisted of being wined and dined by his pals at the toxic, crony-ridden cesspools we otherwise recognize as the big Wall Street banks.

The archaeologist must have noticed my strain, though I hoped he couldn't read my true thoughts.

"What about you?" I asked, more to change the subject than to gather information.

"I'm struggling through some things myself," he said. "Assuming we make it back, the world's going to be different for us all."

Of that, I was certain. I simply had no idea how.

Chapter 62

The rest of the night passed uneventfully. Markowitz returned to our shelter at dawn to wake the rest of us, after which he trudged back up the hill to resume his duties alongside the Professor at our makeshift observation post.

Once we had light enough to see, we discovered a small pool of water tucked away in an isolated corner of our rocky lair – a remnant from yesterday's showers – though food remained an issue.

Lavon gave us a brief moment of hope in that regard.

As we had observed at the village coming in, ancient harvesting practices were remarkably inefficient. Furthermore, Mosaic Law allowed the reapers only one pass at each field. After that, the poor had the right to come in and glean anything that remained.

Since the barley harvest had just concluded, this sounded promising, although Naomi quickly discovered that any fields within striking distance of the main road had already been picked clean.

"Worth a try, anyway," Lavon said as she returned.

She offered to venture farther out, but none of us wanted to take the chance that we could become separated.

I briefly considered slipping out and trying to nab a stray goat, but Lavon vetoed this as well. We had enough trouble as it was without bringing a posse of angry shepherds down upon our heads.

"We'll just have to put aside thoughts of food," he said.

In an effort to divert our minds, the four of us crept up to the crest of the ridge overlooking our shelter. In the distance, we could see a couple of boys driving a small flock of lambs, but otherwise all remained quiet. The denizens of Jerusalem took the Sabbath very seriously indeed.

"I wonder how voluntary this is?" I asked.

Lavon didn't know, nor could he ascertain from Naomi the degree to which compliance was underpinned by an organized body of religious enforcers, like the Saudi *mutaween* or the Iranian *basij*.

"Given her situation, she has no interest in the topic, one way or the other," he explained.

***

In truth, the enforcement of the Sabbath wasn't *our* most pressing issue, either.

I glanced back to the opposite side of the ravine to verify that Bryson and Markowitz remained at their posts and then directed the others to return to our shelter.

"What's our plan now?" I asked after we had found a comfortable spot in the shade.

They agreed that we had a choice to make.

At that moment, we still had an opportunity to flee to the coast. But the window would close quickly, and when it did – and if the transport apparatus remained inoperative past Sunday – our odds of survival would dwindle to zero.

"It's that simple," said Lavon.

None of us argued; but none of us got up to make a run for it, either. The truth was: we all wanted to know, and I had become as fixated on the topic as the others. We had come too close to do anything else.

Working in our favor, Naomi still believed that the palace commanders would wait until mid-morning before sending out other guards to make inquiry.

Furthermore, these men would sally forth with the expectation of finding their comrades resting under a shade tree, sated and drunk, using the Sabbath as an excuse for their inactivity. At least initially, they would be in no hurry.

I did some mental arithmetic and felt even better.

Even if Herod's relief party found their comrades' bodies quickly, they would need time to get back to the palace on foot. If Lavon's hypothesis was correct, Herod, like the Temple authorities, would then have to obtain clearance from Pilate to assemble a larger armed force.

None of this would happen immediately, and with luck, an intensive search for our whereabouts wouldn't begin in earnest until the following day.

"Of course," Lavon explained, "the downside is that the Romans might feel compelled to join in the hunt, if for no other reason than to save face. That will change everything."

I had to concur. While Naomi's tricks had worked on Herod's men, I had no doubt that once Roman professionals set out to track us down, we'd never stand a chance.

But the question still remained: when?

"What is our window to retrieve the camera?" I asked. "I read somewhere that the Resurrection accounts all differ in their chronology."

Lavon conceded that the Gospels varied in their particulars, such as the number of women who first ventured out to the tomb, whether they saw one angel or two, or the names of the disciples who ran back to the grave site to investigate the women's tale.

"But the timing is consistent," he explained. "The women showed up at the tomb with their spices at the crack of dawn, more or less. Once there, they saw that someone had rolled the stone away and that the body was missing.

"Although the Gospels differed as to the exact sequence of what happened next, they all agreed that shortly thereafter, the women hurried back into the city to inform the others."

"How long would this take?" I asked.

Lavon glanced up at the sky and conversed briefly with Naomi.

"We don't know exactly where in Jerusalem they were coming from," he said, "but I'd guess it took at least half an hour to get back to their hiding place; maybe more. They would have wanted to make sure they weren't followed, so they probably didn't take the shortest route."

"Once they returned, the disciples didn't believe the story," Sharon added.

"That's right," said Lavon. "Luke says they 'considered it nonsense,' and we all know about Thomas. I'm sure they argued a while before a few of them finally decided to check things out for themselves."

"So we have at least another half hour, then, to retrieve the camera and make ourselves scarce before anyone comes back?" I said.

Lavon nodded. "Probably an hour; perhaps even two. Remember, the disciples feared they were still being hunted. Pilate may have decided to take the 'strike the shepherd and the sheep will scatter' approach, but the remaining eleven didn't know this at the time."

"Didn't they run; run to the tomb, I mean?" asked Sharon.

"Yes, but the Gospels don't say exactly when they started. Running men would have drawn attention, so my own thought is that they tried to keep a low profile until they got safely outside the city walls."

"What about the guards?" I asked.

"Matthew is the only one of the four Gospels to mention them, and he only says that they went back into the city along with the women. Unfortunately, we don't have any more details."

"Any idea how many there will be?"

"More than one. That's all I can say."

***

Now that we had a plan, we spent the rest of the day watching and waiting – which in many respects is the hardest task of all.

For his part, Bryson paced back and forth all afternoon as he rehashed a litany of potential technical disasters.

"What if the recording fails?" he muttered.

"What if the battery runs out?"

"What if I've set the timer wrong?"

"What if the low light compensator doesn't work?"

"What if – "

Though I could understand his concerns, after a little while, I had had enough.

"Calm down, Professor," I said. "Please."

Then I laughed. "You're scaring the others."

In truth, though, even I felt the butterflies; and in my famished, sleep-deprived state, I failed to grasp the implications of what Bryson had been saying.

Chapter 63

As we had the previous night, we agreed to divide guard duty into shifts; only this time, Bryson insisted on taking the last watch.

Since I wasn't entirely convinced that he wouldn't retrieve the camera and abandon the rest of us to our fates, I told the others I'd join the Professor on the late shift. Except for one small oversight, this would have been a fine plan.

Some time past midnight, Lavon shook me awake and announced that my turn to stand watch had arrived. Bryson and I gathered our things and then climbed up to our observation post, where we settled into reasonably comfortable spots, facing opposite directions.

After an hour had passed, the Professor volunteered to go back down to the shelter and bring up some water. At the time, I thought nothing of it, and when he handed over one of our makeshift cups, I quaffed the whole serving in one gulp.

The next thing I remember, Sharon and Lavon were shaking me awake. It took me a couple of seconds to get my bearings. Once I did, I saw the orange glow to the east and realized to my horror that I had slept though my watch. Worse, Bryson was nowhere to be found.

"I screwed up," was all I could say.

The others were gracious, or realistic, enough not to press. Naomi and Markowitz climbed up to join us, so we gathered in a small circle to work out what to do next as the first faint sliver of the sun peeked over the horizon.

"According to the Gospels, the women are at the tomb, right now," said Lavon.

The question was: was Bryson?

Making our situation more complicated, a long line of people and livestock had already begun to fill the road leading to the Damascus Gate.

"We don't really need company," I muttered.

Naomi, though, told us not to worry.

"They're merchants," she explained. "The first ones into the city after the Sabbath receive much higher prices for their goods. I am certain of this, because afterward, they often visited the house where I worked, and boasted of their earnings."

That made perfect sense. More importantly, these traders would be inclined to ignore us unless we appeared to be competitors.

We paused to ensure that Sharon's scarf completely covered her blonde hair; then we hustled to the main road and joined the growing file of travelers.

After we had proceeded nearly a mile, we veered off toward the edge and into a labyrinth of pathways that wound through the twenty-acre complex of quarries and tombs.

"Now what?" asked Markowitz.

***

I thought back to the previous day and it all started to make sense, beginning with Bryson's worries about technical malfunctions.

"The damned fool," I said, now certain that he had spiked my drink with sedatives from my medical kit so he could slip away and witness the events in person.

Lavon had reached a similar conclusion.

"I'll bet he got caught," he added. "Since the moon was full, I'm sure he could find his way down the road. But once he got into the quarries, odds are that he got lost and stumbled onto the guards."

If indeed he had – and this *was* the most likely scenario – we didn't have a second to lose. Once the soldiers hauled the Professor out of the quarries and onto the open ground leading to the city gates, we'd have no chance to get him back.

"Can you take us to the tomb from this direction?" I asked Sharon.

She nodded and led us forward without saying a word. After we had gone a hundred yards or so, she held up her hand and peered around the same rocky incline I remembered from the day before.

"Do you see anyone?" Lavon whispered.

She didn't, but she didn't dare expose herself by venturing out farther.

Since nothing in the Gospel accounts suggested that a woman native to the area would encounter trouble, Lavon pulled Naomi close and whispered into her ear. I watched a puzzled look cross her face, but after a brief moment's hesitation, she strode toward the tomb.

Naomi peeked inside, then turned back to us and shook her head: nothing.

Lavon then signaled for her to check out the surrounding area. She disappeared, though a minute or two later, she came back and motioned for us to come forward.

I'm no expert, but I could count at least a dozen sets of fresh prints in front of the grave site, all pointing toward the city to the east.

"Do you see the camera anywhere?" Markowitz asked.

Lavon pointed to the spot where Bryson had left it the previous evening.

"There it is," he said.

The pyramid of stones appeared to have remained untouched, so Markowitz started heading in that direction to retrieve it.

I reached out and pulled him back. "No time," I said.

Instead, I unsheathed my *gladius* and directed Lavon to do the same. The archaeologist agreed that since the guards would take the most direct route back to the city, we could probably swing around them undetected – if we got there fast enough.

"When we get into position, wait for my signal," I ordered.

Lavon nodded.

"What if I'm wrong about the guards?" he asked, almost as an afterthought. "What if they *do* turn out to be Romans?"

I shook my head. In that case, our only chance of survival would be to abandon the Professor and run.

I tried to make a joke of it, but after the others had turned away, I lifted my sword and held the point to my own throat.

I stared straight into Lavon's eyes.

"Can you do it?" I asked, "if it comes to that."

His grim expression showed that he knew what I had in mind.

"I won't let them be taken," he replied.

Then he scurried off quickly behind the hill to our left, with Sharon and Naomi in tow.

***

I led Markowitz off to the right to form the other arm of our pincer movement. In a few minutes, we reached the edge of the quarry and circled back toward the center, where we crouched behind an oversized boulder lying only a few feet from a heavily traveled path.

Not long thereafter, I saw Lavon slip out from behind a ridge on the opposite side, along with the two women.

We listened carefully and to our great relief, neither of us heard the distinctive clanging of metal plates. The Temple police protected themselves with thick leather armor. Bryson's captors were not Romans.

As the marching footsteps came closer, we eased back to avoid being spotted.

Moments later, a dozen black helmeted soldiers strode past us and up the incline that led up to the level ground surrounding Jerusalem's main walls.

Though I couldn't understand what they were saying, the men appeared to be engaged in an animated discussion – no doubt concerning how they would explain the events of the previous night to their superiors.

We breathed a quick a sigh of relief as they passed. For a brief moment, I worried that they might have first disposed of the Professor, before I realized that a prisoner would serve as a handy prop for whatever story they managed to invent.

The fact that their captive would be unable to contradict their tale would serve as an added bonus, assuming it came to that.

A few minutes after the first bunch had passed, we heard another set of footsteps. Lavon gestured toward Naomi, as if encouraging her to try an encore performance, but this time I shook my head.

Naomi, God bless her, ignored my instructions.

Rather than exude her natural charms, this time she took pains to disguise them. She pulled her hair back and her shawl up to cover her entire head. Then she hunched forward with her back bent at a painfully awkward angle.

If I hadn't known better, I would have guessed that she had aged thirty years, which was the whole idea.

She shuffled her steps, favoring her left leg, as she trudged slowly up the ramp, with her downcast eyes glued to the ground only a step or two in front of her feet.

As she had intended, the two men escorting Bryson stopped, just behind where we had been hiding.

Once again, we achieved total surprise.

Before they could cry out, Lavon and I held our sword points to their throats. The two guards stared ahead in silence; their eyes reflecting silent terror.

"Don't kill them," said Markowitz.

I hadn't planned to unless it proved absolutely necessary, but this intrusion irritated me.

"Be quiet, Ray," I whispered.

"They're Temple police, not Herod's men. They're Jews; my brothers. Don't kill them."

I sighed, though in hindsight, we couldn't have playacted the scene any better.

The two guards had been careless, but they weren't stupid. From the tone of our discussion, they developed a clear picture of how to save themselves and meekly submitted to our instructions.

Sharon handed over strips of cloth she had cut from her robe, and within less than a minute, we had bound and gagged each one.

We left our prisoners leaning against the side of a hill a few yards apart from each other.

I was angry enough to leave Bryson in the same condition as well, though I knew that would impede our progress. Reluctantly, I cut his bindings loose.

He immediately started to babble an explanation for his conduct, but I was in no mood to hear it; nor was anyone else.

"Shut up, Professor. Let's get out of here."

***

As we threaded our way back through the labyrinth heading the other direction, Lavon had the presence of mind to examine Bryson's chip.

"Yellow," he announced.

"Thirty minutes," said Sharon. "Maybe even less."

How much less, we had no way to know.

"Keep going," I said. "It won't be long before the main body realizes their comrades aren't following behind."

We had advanced to within striking distance of the western end of the quarry when Bryson suddenly jerked away.

"My camera!" he shouted.

Before any of us could react, he had already started to rush back to the tomb.

Had I been thinking clearly, I would have tackled the jackass and sent Naomi, by herself, to retrieve the infernal device. She had shed her old-woman act as quickly as she put it on, and I didn't think the two we had trussed up would recognize her.

But I had been out of action too long to fight tunnel vision, and by the time the idea occurred to me, it was already too late.

Bryson had such a head start that we could do nothing but crouch behind the familiar hill and watch as he strode across the narrow bit of open ground to retrieve his precious camcorder.

He cautiously moved the rock pile aside, stone by stone, as if the device would crumble under the slightest impact. Once he had uncovered it, he lifted it up and brushed off the dust.

Then, to our utter dismay, he opened the viewfinder.

"He's going to watch it right now!" Sharon whispered. "I can't believe this!"

"Get back here, you idiot," I said, trying my dead level best not to shout.

He ignored me for a moment, but the sound of approaching footsteps became unmistakable, even to him.

"Run!" I yelled.

Chapter 64

The Professor finally grasped the seriousness of his predicament. He snapped the viewfinder shut and headed toward me at full speed, while I waved to the others, imploring them to go ahead.

Just as Bryson approached me, two men – neither in uniform and both clearly winded – emerged from behind the rocks and paused in front of the tomb. One started to give chase, but his companion held him back. Neither seemed quite sure what to make of us.

I could guess who they were, but didn't dare stick around.

I grabbed the Professor's arm and rushed him along for a couple hundred yards before we caught up with the others.

"Keep moving," I said.

By then, though, Bryson was gasping for air, so we finally had to stop.

As we paused for him to regain his wind, we couldn't help but reflect on the irony of it all: the confused, angry men from whom we had just fled would lend their names to the largest cathedrals on two continents, one of which they would never know even existed.

"Who could have thought it?" said Lavon.

None of us really could, but as much as we wanted to go back and speak to them, we had to keep going.

We proceeded at the pace of a brisk walk and had nearly made it out of the quarry when we stumbled onto our next surprise: a cluster of rough-looking characters unpacking sacks filled with hammers, picks and chisels.

Sharon's scarf had fallen back, exposing her hair, and this crew had noticed its unusual hue. One of them pointed at her and yelled out something in Aramaic.

Naomi answered straight away. Though her tone sounded abusive, the men laughed heartily, and when one of their party shouted back, they laughed even harder.

Lavon grinned as Naomi gave him a brief, G-rated translation.

"Stonemasons," he said. "We tend to forget that Easter Sunday was the first day of their work week. These guys are just getting started."

Sharon rolled her eyes. "I see some things never change."

Naomi and the construction workers continued to trade good-natured barbs until we passed behind a final hill and scrambled up toward the main road. From there, we made our way to the northwest, keeping a parallel track to avoid the crowds heading into the city.

***

It wasn't long before angry shouting from the edge of the quarry told us that the men on our tails weren't all that far behind, although we did encounter one unexpected bit of good fortune.

Naomi explained that from the perspective of the masses, the Temple police ranked only slightly above the Romans at the bottom end of the popularity scale. Her new friends – the stonemasons – would do what they could to slow our pursuers down, if only out of spite.

But she admitted that we'd gain only a momentary delay. We could hold no illusions that the laborers would risk their own necks to save ours.

"That may be all we need," I said.

We all took another look at the Professor's LED. This time Naomi saw us do it, and asked why.

As we pressed on, Lavon tried to explain our situation to a now very confused woman, who once again had to be wondering if she had made the right call, and whether instead of producing freedom and wealth, her alliance with us would leave her broken body trampled in the dust.

The rest of us, though, had no time for such considerations. A couple of minutes later, we glanced back to see the first black helmets rise up to ground level, less than half a mile to our rear.

"What *color*, Professor?" asked Lavon, trying without success to conceal his worry.

"Still yellow," he replied.

The others heard this exchange, along with the nervous tones that accompanied it.

As if by instinct, and without any prompting, we each shed our outer robes and took off at a dead run toward a clump of scrub trees nestled into the top of a narrow ridge about two hundred yards to our west.

Just beyond the trees, we leapt over a pile of rocks – the remains of a long-decayed stone wall, as it turned out – and fell panting to the ground. Even Sharon seemed a bit winded, while Bryson gasped for his next breath.

I reached for his tunic.

Yellow.

We peered over the rocks without seeing anything, but our respite only lasted a brief moment.

"Here they come," said Lavon.

The black helmets edged slowly toward us once more, although this time, we could see that the guards' demeanor had changed. They no longer appeared to be a hundred percent confident of success.

A moment later, we saw why.

Lavon gestured to our right. "Look over there," he said.

As if to confirm Naomi's description of the gendarmes' unpopularity, a group of shepherd boys began to pelt our persecutors with stones. Though these served more as an irritant than any serious danger, the guards could no longer be certain that they were chasing only a handful of bedraggled foreigners.

We watched the activity for a brief moment before I concluded that we should take advantage of the interlude to buy ourselves a few more precious seconds. I hefted Bryson up by the tunic and turned him toward the next ridge, a hundred yards beyond.

"Let's go."

***

In hindsight, this was a mistake. Our party lost all semblance of order as we dashed up the hill in a mad scramble. Worse, toward the end of our run, Bryson stepped into a hole and twisted his ankle. Lavon and I had to drag him the rest of the way to the top.

Compounding our predicament, the ruckus caused by the stone-throwing boys had drawn the attention of a Roman patrol, which immediately wheeled around and trotted toward us at a brisk double-time pace.

The shepherd kids knew trouble when they saw it, and as the legionnaires drew closer, they scattered in all directions, leaving the soldiers' attention focused squarely upon us.

I glanced around toward the next hill to the west, but by then, Bryson's ankle had become painfully tender. He'd never make it, nor would we, if we tried to carry him.

I reached for the Professor's pendant and saw that the LED still glowed with the same hideous color. This time, I ripped it from his neck and surprised even myself.

I handed the chip to Sharon and pointed to our rear.

"Go. You and Naomi might be able to make it. We'll stay here and hold them off as long as we can."

I knew the time would be short, but every second might count.

"We still have a chip," I added. *"Go!"*

Sharon hesitated long enough for Lavon to translate what I had said to a now thoroughly bewildered Naomi, who categorically refused to leave the archaeologist's side.

By then, Sharon, too, had determined not to budge.

She handed the chip back to Bryson. "We stay together," she said, "to the very end."

Chapter 65

And this was good, for by then, the choice was no longer hers to make.

While we had debated, the Roman commander divided his forty men into three groups. He sent two on a double-time pace to circle around to our left and to our right, to cut off any possibility of escape.

Then he paused to confer with the Temple guards, to ascertain any details he might have missed.

Once again, I found myself admiring the Romans' raw efficiency. This officer knew his business.

I instructed Markowitz and Bryson to keep their eyes on the soldiers to our rear, to warn us if they started to advance. Meanwhile, the rest of us could do nothing but observe the gathering storm to our front, as we racked our brains in search of options.

Suddenly, Lavon cried out. "That's Decius! He's the one in command."

Without further discussion, the archaeologist stood up and shouted something my translation software didn't catch.

"There's no use trying to hide our identities," he said as he turned back to us. "Perhaps we can stall them by negotiating long enough for our return ticket to be validated."

This was true enough, and very smart thinking.

By now, the Romans had advanced to within a hundred feet of our position. There, they paused and lowered their shields to the ground.

While his men rested, Decius shouted back.

"Your bravery and skill are worthy of Rome. I heard the governor promise that he will spare your lives."

Lavon translated this for us before turning back to the Roman.

"Will the governor also promise that we will not spend the rest of those lives in slavery?" he replied.

Decius paused to converse with another *optio*. After the second man nodded, the Roman turned his eyes back to us.

"Yes, you will be allowed to go free. We will keep you as prisoners only until the king has gone back to Galilee. Afterwards, you may depart and return to your homes."

"Why that long?" Lavon shouted.

"We must maintain appearances," said Decius. "Surely you understand?"

This made sense, though I didn't relish the thought of spending one second in a Roman dungeon. Governors have been known to change their minds.

"And our women?" said Lavon. "What of them?"

"Herod has insisted upon the return of his property. But do not worry: a brave and resourceful man such as yourself will have no difficulty finding others of equal quality."

Before Lavon could reply, Naomi leapt up and unleashed a torrent of violent abuse.

The Romans laughed, at least at first, but this time, I could detect nothing good-natured in her tone. As her tirade continued, several of the soldiers grew visibly angry.

At last, Naomi ran out of steam and slumped down, dejected, behind the cover of a pile of stones.

Decius waited for a brief moment, and then spoke, one last time.

"In recognition of your service to us, I will offer you a final opportunity to surrender peacefully. If you refuse, then my conscience is clear, and the responsibility for your deaths will rest entirely upon your own heads."

I glanced back to Bryson's pendant: still that nasty puke-yellow.

"Ask him if he'll let us discuss it among ourselves," I said. "Tell him we're all free men, and thus each of us must choose his own individual fate."

Lavon did so, and the Roman granted us a momentary reprieve.

My mind raced as I tried to work out which tactic would provide us with the greatest delay: whether we should demonstrate that we would resist – perhaps causing the soldiers to reconsider their battle plan – or whether we should feign cooperation.

Though we risked being separated after our capture, my inclination was to go for the latter option.

"If we fight," I said to Lavon, "they'll kill us in short order. You know this."

The archaeologist reluctantly agreed, and we both rose slowly, as if to make a grand demonstration of our peaceful intent.

***

Some times in life, we get to make our own choices. On other occasions, despite our most careful calculations, our choices are made for us.

This became such a moment.

As we considered Decius's ultimatum, Lavon and I had focused so single-mindedly on delaying the Romans long enough for the LED to turn green that neither of us recognized that Naomi had reached her final tipping point.

Before we could stand fully upright to surrender, she cut loose with an unrestrained burst of profanity, berating both the Romans and our own party with equal vigor.

Her face reflected a volatile mixture of anger and betrayal, and it was only with great difficulty that Lavon managed to prevent her from grabbing a weapon.

It suddenly dawned on me why.

"She thinks we're selling her out!" I shouted.

She did indeed. Despite Lavon's best efforts to persuade her to the contrary, he could do nothing but hang on for dear life to prevent her from hurting either him or herself.

Sharon ran over to help, but by this point, Decius had lost patience. Somewhat reluctantly, he signaled for the dozen men at his side to proceed ahead.

I took one glance back, where I saw Bryson huddled behind a rock. Then I picked up my sword.

"Might as well go down fighting," I said.

The Romans advanced slowly and methodically, reluctant to take casualties when the result of the engagement seemed so certain.

"*What color, Professor?*" I asked.

"Still yellow," he muttered. "I don't know what could be keeping her."

He mumbled some other excuses, too, but I had lost any desire to listen. By now, the legionnaires had come to within twenty five yards of our position.

I called Sharon to come over to my side.

"Twenty yards!" I cried out.

Lavon understood, though he continued to wrestle with Naomi. If we timed it just right, we'd have time to fall on our own swords afterward.

"Fifteen! *What color, Professor?*"

Still yellow.

"Ten!" I shouted, though this time, I did so more to buck up my own courage than to convey any meaningful information.

I was struggling to keep my eyes open, to look my impending doom square in the face, when a man who had gotten us into so much trouble saved us in the end.

I heard a shout – really more of a primeval scream – coming from just behind where I stood.

"You bastards!"

"Noooo!" yelled Bryson.

But it was too late.

One Roman had gone out ahead of his comrades, but the man slipped on a damp stone and fell hard. Immediately upon seeing this, Markowitz rushed forward to take his revenge – his people's revenge.

His blow caught the legionnaire squarely in the eye as he rammed the point forward with all his might. Then he yanked the sword back out and screamed for his next opponent just as three others tossed their long javelins.

At that range, the soldiers could not miss, and what their spears started, they finished with their swords.

Our party could only stare in shock at the dismal scene. As the Romans resumed their final advance, I reached around to grasp the back of Sharon's neck.

"I'm sorry," I muttered, as I held up my blade.

I kept it pointed toward the Romans, hoping to wait until the absolute last infinitesimal fraction of a microsecond to carry out the awful deed that I knew I had to perform.

***

And that was it. The next thing I recalled, the five of us lay sprawled on a smooth white floor. I rolled over, grabbed my weapon, and quickly jumped to my feet, looking left and right, like a wild man ready to pounce.

It was only then that I realized we had made it home.

Chapter 66

I tossed my sword to one side, completely indifferent to any damage I might have done to the polished ceramic floor.

While I verified that I still possessed the correct number of appendages, all connected in their proper places – a legacy habit from hundreds of low altitude parachute jumps – the sliding panel opened, and Juliet Bryson rushed in to embrace her husband.

The others just sat on the floor in stunned silence, though they gradually relaxed as they, too, realized that we were no longer in mortal peril.

Everyone but Naomi, that is. She huddled against Lavon, and her eyes darted back and forth like a panicked animal.

I couldn't help but laugh.

I reached down to help her up, but she didn't budge. Instead, she squeezed Lavon even tighter and stared into his eyes with an imploring, questioning gaze.

"Where are we?" she asked.

Lavon smiled. "We're back, in our country, as we promised."

To no one's surprise, she remained doubtful, although we had clearly gone *somewhere*.

"How did we get here? Where are the soldiers?"

I didn't wait for his answer. However Lavon chose to explain it, his response couldn't be quick.

Instead, I slid through the open door and continued into the changing room. There, I rummaged through the kit I had left behind and found five bottles of water, a handful of MREs, and a dozen energy bars.

When I returned to the chamber, I could see that despite Naomi's remaining uncertainty, Lavon had at least managed to reassure her that we had no intention of abandoning her to the Romans or to Herod's goons. Sharon's relaxed attitude also bolstered her confidence that nothing untoward would happen.

I passed around the MREs, and we attacked the food like ravenous wolves; likewise, we drained the water in seconds. Unlike the rest of our group, though, Naomi did not cast her bottle aside after finishing it. Instead, she slowly rotated it, puzzled by the odd transparent material.

Lavon tried to explain, but quickly discovered how much background information we take for granted.

And that wasn't her only worry.

"This writing: these are Roman letters."

Though she couldn't read, she recognized the script, and her tone reflected a concern that perhaps we had not escaped trouble after all.

Lavon took the bottle and examined the label. "Hydro-max Pure Spring Water," he deadpanned. *"Ideally Formulated for Low-Carb Diets."*

Seriously, it said that.

We all laughed, and between our amusement and the wildly varying typefaces on the bottle, Lavon managed to convince her that we had left our pursuers far behind.

To make things even more interesting for her, I reached into my bag and pulled out another surprise.

I handed her a flashlight, and Lavon directed her to press the large yellow on-switch.

She fumbled it in sudden alarm the first time, but after she saw us laugh, she picked it back up and switched it on and off, over and over again. As she did so, her expression shifted from a tentative apprehension to open delight.

"Light, without fire," Lavon explained. "Did I not promise that if you helped us, you would see wonders beyond your imagination?"

She barely acknowledged his reply. Instead, she continued to flip the switch on and off and to dance the beam across the room. The effect was like watching a small child who had just unwrapped the hottest new toy.

This would be fun.

A few seconds later, Naomi focused the light on me, with a huge, playful smile on her face.

"Welcome to our world," I said. "And to America, a magnificent country, where the food is fat free but the people are not."

Lavon flashed his best smile as he translated, though he skipped the last part. Some things just couldn't be explained.

I was certain she would adapt over time. I could only hope that she would have a more peaceful experience in our country than we had had in hers.

***

And that brought us back to our unfinished business.

Juliet had finally overcome the initial shock of seeing her husband, once again alive and well, and she glanced around the room to assess us more carefully.

Her head count came up two short.

"Where are Ray and Scott?" she asked.

"Dead," I replied, without any real emotion in my voice. "It's a long story."

She gasped, although she couldn't have been completely surprised at the news. When we failed to return after a brief interval, she had to have suspected that our endeavor had run into unexpected difficulties, if not outright disaster.

After a moment's silence, her husband whispered something into her ear. Whatever he said was instantly reassuring; for she recovered her composure and gestured toward Naomi for the first time.

"Who are you?" she asked.

"She helped us," said Lavon. "It will take some time to explain how."

***

The Professor spent the next half hour outlining the basics of our excursion. Finally, though, the rest of us grew impatient. The moment of truth had arrived.

Juliet led us into the conference room, and after a brief pause for Naomi to grow comfortable with wall-mounted light switches and overhead projectors, we all settled into the chairs closest to the drop-down screen.

By that point, I wasn't sure who was more nervous. Although Naomi might not have understood the intricacies of how we commanded light to appear on a whim, she also had no conception of the infinitely more transcendent mystery that Bryson's device was about to reveal.

I, for one, felt a veritable swarm of butterflies emerge from their cocoons in my stomach as Juliet booted up the computer. From the others' expressions, I could see that they did as well.

The screen displayed the familiar blue backdrop while the Professor hooked his camera to the machine. When he finished, he glanced around the room and we all took a deep breath.

"Here we go," he said.

Then he pressed 'play.'

As with his earlier venture, the screen first displayed only the date and time: *2029 04 15; 02 30 00.*

Bryson started to explain that the camera's date couldn't be set before the year 1950, but we had already gotten the idea: Sunday, April 15, of the year 29 AD, at two-thirty in the morning.

A few seconds later, we could begin to make out the tomb in the full moonlight. A Temple guardsman, dressed in full uniform with his right hand resting on the hilt of his sword, stood on each side of the entrance.

"That's the tomb?" exclaimed Juliet.

We all mumbled our concurrence without taking our eyes off the screen. The guards weren't moving around much, though it was obvious that neither man was asleep.

"Where did you get caught?" I asked Bryson.

"I tried to sneak up behind the location where I placed the camera," he said, admitting for the first time what we had suspected: that his real goal had been to witness the event in person.

"But I had the bad luck to run into the spot where the relief crew was taking a break," he continued.

Personally, I thought he had become disoriented in the twists and turns of the quarry's many trails, but whatever had really transpired, it was no longer our primary concern.

We all kept our full attention focused on the image on the screen, though for nearly an hour, very little happened.

The guards appeared to chat back and forth – undoubtedly complaining, like soldiers everywhere, about why *they* got stuck standing out in the cold all night while their colleagues dozed comfortably in their beds.

But their voices were too low and the camera too far away for the microphone to pick up enough details for Naomi to translate.

2029 04 15; 03 27 42

A few minutes later, we saw the first real movement. The initial two guards stepped away from their posts as two others took their places.

"Shift change, by the look of it," said Lavon.

The same relative inactivity continued as before, though, and I couldn't help but chuckle as the others grew restless. Ordinary sentry detail remained as boring as it ever was, two millennia later. Some things truly never changed.

2029 04 15; 04 08 17

"When does it start getting light?" asked Sharon.

Juliet had printed out a sunrise/sunset table and read out the numbers.

"Nautical twilight begins at 4:17. Civil twilight, the time when dawn first begins to break, starts at 4:46."

Upon hearing this, my butterflies began to leap around in a renewed burst of activity. For that matter, everyone's did. Whatever was going to happen would do so very soon.

2029 04 15; 04 16 52

Though the guards remained at their posts, they suddenly perked up, and one of them noticed something to his left. He craned his head and called out to his colleagues.

Then suddenly, we saw a brilliant white flash – and then nothing at all.

***

The rest of us stared at the screen in silence as Bryson rewound, then replayed, then rewound, then replayed the last couple of minutes, over and over.

Each time the result was the same, and when he repeated the drill in slow motion, we could see no discernable difference.

To a believer, what we had just witnessed could represent the incredible surge of energy that accompanied the resurrection, or the brilliance of glowing angels, afire with God's power.

To those taking the other side, it could be the result of an unknown quantum effect that altered the device's memory during our return to the present. Or, perhaps, the flash could have derived from the more mundane possibility of an equipment malfunction, or even a guard moving a torch too close to the camera's primary lens.

What *was* clear, was that the recording wouldn't convince anyone either way.

From the very beginning, it had been matter of faith.

It always would be.

Epilogue

Eighteen months later

I glanced down at the directions Lavon had emailed a few days earlier and then back over to my map, curious once more as to the reason he insisted that I drive eight hours without knowing exactly why.

In truth, though, I didn't really mind.

I had some time on my hands, and no more financial concerns, either, courtesy of the Brysons, who had mourned the loss of their brilliant student – and who worked out a plan to get him back.

Their scheme was straightforward enough. It called for me to return to our original cave just a few minutes before we had "landed" on our earlier journey. As long as the Professor remained in Boston, he couldn't simultaneously appear in Judea to bowl over his assistant and knock him silly.

I would therefore have a brief window to pull the kid to safety before the Romans turned him into a pincushion. As an additional bonus, I could pull Markowitz out of the cave, too.

This sounded reasonable enough, with two modifications.

First, I insisted that Juliet accompany me, ostensibly to show her a brief glimpse of the first century world – though in reality we all knew that her real purpose was to serve as a hostage to guarantee the Professor's end of the bargain.

I didn't think Bryson would abandon me with Lavon and Sharon remaining behind as witnesses, but I saw no need to take the chance. As a former President had once said – trust but verify.

Second, I had my own equipment list, which consisted of a bullhorn, a bag full of flash-bang grenades and my trusty Glock, just in case.

***

After a brief interval to confirm that the Brysons had indeed made the necessary *adjustments* to my own investment account, Juliet and I set forth out on our journey.

We returned in less than five minutes, with both Markowitz and the geeky kid safely in tow. Thankfully, I never had to fire the Glock, though I did have some fun with the flash-bangs and the bullhorn, which stopped the combatants in their tracks.

I could only laugh as I considered the report Publius would make when he arrived in Jerusalem later that day.

In any event, I could reassure my conscience that I had not ruined the centurion's retirement plans. Despite the last bit of unpleasantness, I respected the man and the soldiers he commanded, and wished them no harm.

A few weeks later, I read that the Brysons lost their entire facility to a mysterious fire, though fortunately, no one suffered injuries in the blaze. According to the newspaper, the couple had then decided to return to MIT, much to the delight of their former students.

On most occasions, I consider myself an eminently reasonable person – though I can drive a hard bargain when pressed.

As for Markowitz, I saw very little of him after his rescue. Though he had complained vociferously about having his journey cut short, he seemed to calm down after we explained how his first venture had ended.

More importantly, he would recall nothing from the earlier trip, so we no longer had to worry about him devising a hare-brained attempt to free Judea from the Roman yoke, and all of the unintended consequences such a venture would entail.

***

Just as Lavon had foreseen, Sharon dumped D. Percival within days of arriving home.

She and I stayed in touch – after all, we shared a bond like none other on the planet – and not long thereafter, our relationship exploded into a passionate affair that eventually morphed into its current form – a complex *ménage a trios* between Sharon, myself, and the Cause.

Ah, the Cause.

Given her experience at the hands of Herod, I can't claim to be surprised.

Almost as soon as we returned, she began to use her drive and energy – along with a chunk of her old man's fortune – to turn a dispirited collection of volunteers into one of the planet's largest organizations devoted to the elimination of human trafficking and the exploitation of women throughout the world.

In fact, as I drove to meet Lavon, she was in the process of opening her group's fifty-fourth crisis center. Unfortunately, I had to stay behind. In a previous life, I had spent months in that particular garden spot, and I had no inclination to return – at least not without diplomatic immunity.

For a brief moment, I almost felt sorry for the exploiters. I had watched Sharon kill two hardened soldiers, with a sword. Now she stood at the forefront of an institute backed by more than a billion dollars. God help them.

***

As for Naomi, her adjustment did not pass without complications.

For her own safety, we booked a hotel room, where we kept her for a couple of weeks as I hit up my contacts for the requisite paperwork that would permit her to stay in the country permanently.

She spent most of that time with her eyes glued to the television, while Lavon tried to explain her new world in a way she could begin to comprehend.

For my part, I was most concerned about her ability to adapt to the *speed* of modern life – that she could come all this way and then get run over, on her first trip outside, crossing the street.

As it turned out, I needn't have worried.

**

A few minutes later, I spotted the US 60 exit from Interstate 24, just outside Paducah, Kentucky, and headed west. I kept going on Highway 60 for another ten minutes, and then turned left and followed a narrow, winding two-lane road for a couple of miles.

At the sight of a big blue mailbox, I turned right onto a gravel driveway and followed it up to a restored antebellum-style farm house that belonged to one of Lavon's old college roommates – a man who had spent a decade on Wall Street before deciding to get out while he still possessed a vestigial remnant of his soul.

I hadn't even made it up the steps when Naomi rushed out the front door.

"Beeeeel," she shouted as she threw her arms around me.

For someone who had been at it for less than two years, her English was surprisingly good, though she and Lavon occasionally broke into Greek between themselves.

They had gotten married, too – though they didn't say where – and even a spirit as unromantic as mine could tell that she and the archaeologist were madly in love.

She patted her belly, which displayed just the slightest hint of a bump. She and Lavon both smiled.

"Due in April," he said.

"If boy, his name Beeel," she exclaimed.

I didn't know what to say.

"This is great news," I finally mumbled.

We went back into the house, where Lavon poured a steaming mug of coffee and caught me up on what had happened since I had last seen them, a few weeks after we had all left Boston.

"A few months after we got back, I tried to return to our dig, but it only took a couple of days for me to realize that it was hopeless," he said.

That was exactly what I had expected to hear.

"I was invited to a conference several weeks later," he continued. "The leading lights of my profession were all in attendance. They spoke about their projects, about the important things they were learning, about how much they had been able to deduce from the tiniest fragments of their excavations."

"And?" I asked, knowing what was coming next.

"I had to sit there for two days, smiling politely, when so much of what they said was wrong – painfully aware that I'd never be able to prove otherwise. I knew that was the end."

Fortunately, he had some time to consider a second career. He and the Brysons had also reached an accommodation.

"Did you go, too?" I asked Naomi. "Back to Israel?"

She had, though she had initially resisted the idea of returning to Jerusalem.

"Robert finally convince me that Herod dead and palace, uh – "

"Destroyed," he said.

"Yes, palace destroyed."

Unlike Josephus, she didn't seem all that upset about it.

"And Rome ruined, too," she said. "Not destroyed, but Empire … gone away," she corrected.

"We stopped there on our way back from Israel," Lavon explained.

Like many visitors, Naomi had laughed at the faux legionnaires who hung out in front of the Colosseum, smoking cigarettes and hustling tourists for a quick buck. But she had found the Roman cathedrals baffling.

"It all very strange," she said.

I couldn't argue. A single event had spread to a religion that now covered the globe. The leader of a persecuted sect became as powerful as any emperor. The followers of a Jewish rabbi had led attacks on Jews throughout the centuries.

"We're still working through some things," he said.

"Aren't we all," I replied. "Aren't we all."

***

Though this was all very interesting – wonderful news, in fact – I still wasn't sure why they had asked me to drive eight hours to hear it.

"Why did you want me come *here*?" I finally asked.

Naomi's face lit up; she jumped out of her chair and hugged Lavon, her eyes bursting with delight.

"Robert … he keep promise!" she exclaimed.

Then she rushed outside without another peep.

Lavon didn't say anything. Instead, he just gestured for me to follow her out the door.

We walked down a gravel pathway toward a freshly painted red barn. As soon as we approached the entrance, Naomi dashed out with a video camera, grabbed me by the arm, and led me around to the other side.

There, resting at the end of a long grass strip, sat two ultralights, both painted a mottled gray interspersed with brown and white flecks.

She pointed her camera at the sky and beamed. "We fly *bird!*"

I could only laugh at the irony of it all. Lavon had indeed kept his promise.

"We're only a few miles from where the Ohio empties into the Mississippi," he explained. "It's one of the greatest migration pathways in North America."

Moments later, his buddy emerged from the barn with four helmets and sets of goggles. After grabbing one of each, Naomi scampered over to the pilot's seat of the lead craft and motioned for me to follow.

"She can fly that thing?" I asked.

"Better than I can," Lavon replied. "She's learning how to read, too. As soon as her English is good enough to pass the test, she wants to get her regular pilot's license. Once she realized we weren't spinning some wild tale, she became completely enthralled with the concept."

"When did she first see an aircraft for real, and not just on TV?"

The archaeologist laughed. "A medivac chopper flew over as we walked out of the hotel for the first time. She hit the ground and tried to crawl under a trash can."

Obviously, Naomi's aviation knowledge had progressed a long way since then.

"She's fascinated with the big jets," he continued. "The first takeoff on the trip to Israel was a bit unnerving, but now that's her favorite part. Even when she's not flying, she likes to go to the airport and watch the planes come and go, all day long."

Far from being afraid of the speed of modern life, it appeared that Naomi had developed an almost maniacal addiction to it.

"Does she drive?"

"Scares me half to death every time," he replied. "But she's getting the hang of it."

"What about scuba diving?"

He shot me an evil look. "Don't even think about it."

Then he smiled. "One thing at time, Bill; one thing at a time."

I glanced up to see what looked like hundreds of black specks in the distance.

"Here they come!" she shouted.

Lavon directed me to climb into the back seat of Naomi's ultralight while he headed for the other one. A minute later, after a quick run-up, both aircraft lifted off the runway and climbed into the autumn sky.

We leveled off at around a thousand feet, and the geese, accustomed to the presence of these unusual relatives, flew alongside us, with their honking audible even above the noise of the engines.

As we turned to the south on a glorious October day, I felt privileged to be alive – to be a part of this. Did I have more faith in God as a result of our journey, or less? I still wasn't sure; maybe I never would be.

But amidst the wonders of nature that surrounded us, and bathed in the radiance of the afternoon sun, I could see the reflective glow of a bright, vivacious woman, free and full of spirit, living for the first time without fear.

That was enough.

Author's Note

Unlike other world religions, the foundation of Christianity rests not only on one man's teachings, but on a specific *event* involving that man – one that occurred at a fixed time and place and therefore could, at least in theory, be proven definitively one way or the other.

I've always had an interest in Biblical history, and after reading Michael Crichton's *Timeline*, I thought it only natural – given Christianity's impact on the world for the past two thousand years – that a scientist who discovered a way to travel to past ages would attempt to prove or disprove the Resurrection.

This is especially true in light of the centuries of conflict between the scientific community and certain factions of Christianity – ranging from the Inquisition's persecution of Galileo in the 1600s to today's ongoing controversies over stem cell research and the place of evolution in biology textbooks.

That such a venture would prove troublesome seemed equally natural. Through the diligent work of modern archaeologists, we are learning more about ancient societies every day, but we still *know* relatively little. A modern man venturing forth into the first century world would undoubtedly stumble upon *something* unexpected – and dangerous.

As to the events in the book itself, time travel, of course, is fictional. Although physicists have known for nearly a century that time is not linear, scientists continue to have lively debates as to whether travel to past or future ages is even theoretically possible.

The bandages Culloden uses to save the wounded Romans are also fictional, although medical and material science researchers – funded in large part by the US military – are bringing the day in which they are not ever closer.

Similarly, DARPA scientists continue to develop technologies that will allow US forces to communicate in languages unknown to the troops without reliance on local interpreters, who may be unavailable, unreliable, or refuse to assist due to fear of retribution. However, researchers have miniaturized nothing yet to the level of a common ear bud – or if they have, their invention remains classified.

A note, too, about terminology. Readers will notice that I use the term "prefect" as Pilate's official title, rather than the more familiar "procurator" used in the Gospels.

The explanation is that Roman governors of Judea *were* known as "prefects" until the term of Cuspius Fadus, beginning in the year 44. The Gospel writers, who composed their works starting in the 50s, used the term in use at the time of their writing, rather than the one in use during Pilate's actual time in office.

As to the events of Holy Week depicted in the book, I would urge readers to keep in mind that this is a work of fiction, and that the specific circumstances in which my characters find themselves represent only one of the many possible interpretations as to what actually happened during those fateful days.

About the Author

Educated in law and finance, David Epperson served clients across the globe before turning his attention to writing. *The Third Day* is his first novel.

When not writing, David teaches international business classes at a local university, runs the occasional marathon and enjoys flying small aircraft and scuba diving. He lives in Texas.

David welcomes feedback from interested readers and holds to the advertising mantra of "if you don't like it, tell me; *if you do like it, tell your friends!*"

Please contact David at www.davidepperson.com;

Email: david@davidepperson.com